CONTENTS

Chapter I

A squat grey building of only thirty-four stories. Over the main entrance the words, CENTRAL LONDON HATCHERY AND CONDITIONING CENTRE, and, in a shield, the World State's motto, COMMUNITY, IDENTITY, STABILITY.

The enormous room on the ground-floor faced towards the north. Cold for all the summer beyond the panes, for all the tropical heat of the room itself, a harsh thin light glared through the windows, hungrily seeking some draped lay figure, some pallid shape of academic goose-flesh, but finding only the glass and nickel and bleakly shining porcelain of a laboratory. Wintriness responded to wintriness. The overalls of the workers were white, their hands gloved with a pale corpse-coloured rubber. The light was frozen, dead, a ghost. Only from the yellow barrels of the microscopes did it borrow a certain rich and living substance, lying along the polished tubes like butter, streak after luscious streak in long recession down the work-tables.

'And this,' said the Director opening the door, 'is the Fertilizing Room.'

Bent over their instruments, three hundred Fertilizers were plunged, as the Director of Hatcheries and Conditioning entered the room, in the scarcely breathing silence, the absent-minded, soliloquizing hum or whistle, of absorbed concentration. A troop of newly arrived students, very young, pink and callow, followed nervously, rather abjectly, at the Director's heels. Each of them carried a note-book, in which, whenever the great man spoke, he desperately scribbled. Straight from the horse's mouth. It was a rare privilege. The D.H.C. for Central London always made a point of personally conducting his new students round the various departments.

'Just to give you a general idea,' he would explain to them. For of course some sort of general idea they must have, if they were to do their work intelligently--though as little of one, if they were to be good and happy members of society, as possible. For particulars, as every one knows, make for virtue and happiness; generalities are intellectually necessary evils. Not philosophers, but fret-sawyers and stamp collectors compose the backbone of society.

'To-morrow,' he would add, smiling at them with a slightly menacing geniality, 'you'll be settling down to serious work. You won't have time for generalities. Meanwhile...'

Meanwhile, it was a privilege. Straight from the horse's mouth into the note-book. The boys scribbled like mad.

Tall and rather thin but upright, the Director advanced into the room. He had a long chin and big, rather prominent teeth, just covered, when he was not talking, by his full, floridly curved lips. Old, young? Thirty? fifty? fifty-five? It was hard to say. And anyhow the question didn't arise; in this year of stability, A.F. 632, it didn't occur to you to ask it.

'I shall begin at the beginning,' said the D.H.C., and the more zealous students recorded his intention in their note-books: *Begin at the beginning*. 'These,' he waved his hand, 'are the incubators.' And opening an insulated door he showed them racks upon racks of numbered test-tubes. 'The week's supply of ova. Kept,' he explained, 'at blood heat; whereas the male gametes,' and here he opened another door, 'they have to be kept at thirty-five instead of thirty-seven. Full blood heat sterilizes.' Rams wrapped in thermogene beget no lambs.

Still leaning against the incubators he gave them, while the pencils scurried illegibly across the pages, a brief description of the modern fertilizing process; spoke first, of course, of its surgical introduction--'the operation undergone voluntarily for the good of Society, not to mention the fact that it carries a bonus amounting to six months' salary'; continued with some account of the technique for preserving the excised ovary alive and actively developing; passed on to a consideration of optimum temperature, salinity, viscosity; referred to the liquor in which the detached and ripened eggs were kept; and, leading his charges to the work tables, actually showed them how this liquor was drawn off from the test-tubes; how it was let out drop by drop on to the specially warmed slides of the microscopes; how the eggs which it contained were inspected for abnormalities, counted and transferred to a porous receptacle; how (and he now took them to watch the operation) this receptacle was immersed in a warm bouillon containing free-swimming spermatozoa--at a minimum concentration of one hundred thousand per cubic centimetre, he insisted; and how, after ten minutes, the container was lifted out of the liquor and its contents re-examined; how, if any of the eggs remained unfertilized, it was again immersed, and, if necessary, yet again; how the fertilized ova went back to the incubators; where the Alphas and Betas remained until definitely bottled; while the Gammas, Deltas and Epsilons were brought out again, after only thirty-six hours, to undergo Bokanovsky's Process.

'Bokanovsky's Process,' repeated the Director, and the students underlined the words in their little note-books.

One egg, one embryo, one adult--normality. But a bokanovskified egg will bud, will proliferate, will divide. From eight to ninety-six buds, and every bud will grow into a perfectly formed embryo, and every embryo into a full-sized adult. Making ninety-six human beings grow where only one grew before. Progress.

'Essentially,' the D.H.C. concluded, 'bokanovskification consists of a series of arrests of development. We check the normal growth and, paradoxically enough, the egg responds by budding.'

Responds by budding. The pencils were busy.

He pointed. On a very slowly moving band a rack-full of test-tubes was entering a large metal box, another rack-full was emerging. Machinery faintly purred. It took eight minutes for the tubes to go through, he told them. Eight minutes of hard X-rays being about as much as an egg can stand. A few died; of the rest, the least susceptible divided into two; most put out four buds; some eight; all were returned to the incubators, where the buds began to develop; then, after two days, were suddenly chilled, chilled and checked. Two, four, eight, the buds in their turn budded; and having budded were dosed almost to death with alcohol; consequently burgeoned again and having budded--bud out of bud out of bud were thereafter--further arrest being generally fatal--left to develop in peace. By which time the original egg was in a fair way to becoming anything from eight to ninety-six embryos--a prodigious improvement, you will agree, on nature. Identical twins--but not in piddling twos and threes as in the old viviparous days, when an egg would sometimes accidentally divide; actually by dozens, by scores at a time.

'Scores,' the Director repeated and flung out his arms, as though he were distributing largesse. 'Scores.'

But one of the students was fool enough to ask where the advantage lay.

'My good boy!' The Director wheeled sharply round on him. 'Can't you see? Can't you see?' He raised a hand; his expression was solemn. 'Bokanovsky's Process is one of the major instruments of social stability!'

Major instruments of social stability.

Standard men and women; in uniform batches. The whole of a small factory staffed with the products of a single bokanovskified egg.

'Ninety-six identical twins working ninety-six identical machines!' The voice was almost tremulous with enthusiasm. 'You really know where you are. For the first time in history.' He quoted the planetary motto. 'Community, Identity, Stability.' Grand words. 'If we could bokanovskify indefinitely the whole problem would be solved.'

Solved by standard Gammas, unvarying Deltas, uniform Epsilons. Millions of identical twins. The principle of mass production at last applied to biology.

'But, alas,' the Director shook his head, 'we *can't* bokanovskify indefinitely.'

Ninety-six seemed to be the limit; seventy-two a good average. From the same ovary and with gametes of the same male to manufacture as many batches of identical twins as possible--that was the best (sadly a second best) that they could do. And even that was difficult.

'For in nature it takes thirty years for two hundred eggs to reach maturity. But our business is to stabilize the population at this moment, here and now. Dribbling out twins over a quarter of a century--what would be the use of that?'

Obviously, no use at all. But Podsnap's Technique had immensely accelerated the process of ripening. They could make sure of at least a hundred and fifty mature eggs within two years. Fertilize and bokanovskify--in other words, multiply by seventy-two--and you get an average of nearly eleven thousand brothers and sisters in a hundred and fifty batches of identical twins, all within two years of the same age.

'And in exceptional cases we can make one ovary yield us over fifteen thousand adult individuals.'

Beckoning to a fair-haired, ruddy young man who happened to be passing at the moment, 'Mr. Foster,' he called. The ruddy young man approached. 'Can you tell us the record for a single ovary, Mr. Foster?'

'Sixteen thousand and twelve in this Centre,' Mr. Foster replied without hesitation. He spoke very quickly, had a vivacious blue eye, and took an evident pleasure in quoting figures. 'Sixteen thousand and twelve; in one hundred and eighty-nine batches of identicals. But of course they've done much better,' he rattled on, 'in some of the tropical Centres. Singapore has often produced over sixteen thousand five hundred; and Mombasa has actually touched the seventeen thousand mark. But then they have unfair advantages. You should see the way a negro ovary responds to pituitary! It's quite astonishing, when you're used to working with European material. Still,' he added, with a laugh (but the light of combat was in his eyes and the lift of his chin was challenging), 'still, we mean to beat them if we can. I'm working on a wonderful Delta-Minus ovary at this moment. Only just eighteen months old. Over twelve thousand seven hundred children already, either decanted or in embryo. And still going strong. We'll beat them yet.'

'That's the spirit I like!' cried the Director, and clapped Mr. Foster on the shoulder. 'Come along with us and give these boys the benefit of your expert knowledge.'

Mr. Foster smiled modestly. 'With pleasure.' They went.

In the Bottling Room all was harmonious bustle and ordered activity. Flaps of fresh sow's peritoneum ready cut to the proper size came shooting up in little lifts from the Organ Store in the sub-basement. Whizz and then, click! the lift-hatches flew open; the Bottle-Liner had only to reach out a hand, take the flap, insert, smooth-down, and before the lined bottle had had time to travel out of reach along the endless band, whizz, click! another flap of peritoneum had shot up from the depths, ready to be slipped into yet another bottle, the next of that slow interminable procession on the band.

Next to the Liners stood the Matriculators. The procession advanced; one by one the eggs were transferred from their test-tubes to the larger containers; deftly the peritoneal lining was slit, the morula dropped into place, the saline solution poured in... and already the bottle had passed, and it was the turn of the labellers. Heredity, date of fertilization, membership of Bokanovsky Group--details were transferred from test-tube to bottle. No longer anonymous, but named, identified, the procession marched slowly on; on through an opening in the wall, slowly on into the Social Predestination Room.

'Eighty-eight cubic metres of card-index,' said Mr. Foster with relish, as they entered.

'Containing *all* the relevant information,' added the Director.

'Brought up to date every morning.'

'And co-ordinated every afternoon.'

'On the basis of which they make their calculations.'

'So many individuals, of such and such quality,' said Mr. Foster.

'Distributed in such and such quantities.'

'The optimum Decanting Rate at any given moment.'

'Unforeseen wastages promptly made good.'

'Promptly,' repeated Mr. Foster. 'If you knew the amount of overtime I had to put in after the last Japanese earthquake!' He laughed good-humouredly and shook his head.

'The Predestinators send in their figures to the Fertilizers.'

'Who give them the embryos they ask for.'

'And the bottles come in here to be predestinated in detail.'

'After which they are sent down to the Embryo Store.'

'Where we now proceed ourselves.'

And opening a door Mr. Foster led the way down a staircase into the basement.

The temperature was still tropical. They descended into a thickening twilight. Two doors and a passage with a double turn ensured the cellar against any possible infiltration of the day.

'Embryos are like photograph film,' said Mr. Foster waggishly, as he pushed open the second door. 'They can only stand red light.'

And in effect the sultry darkness into which the students now followed him was visible and crimson, like the darkness of closed eyes on a summer's afternoon. The bulging flanks of row on receding row and tier above tier of bottles glinted with innumerable rubies, and among the rubies moved the dim red spectres of men and women with purple eyes and all the symptoms of lupus. The hum and rattle of machinery faintly stirred the air.

'Give them a few figures, Mr. Foster,' said the Director, who was tired of talking.

Mr. Foster was only too happy to give them a few figures.

Two hundred and twenty metres long, two hundred wide, ten high. He pointed upwards. Like chickens drinking, the students lifted their eyes towards the distant ceiling.

Three tiers of racks: ground-floor level, first gallery, second gallery.

The spidery steelwork of gallery above gallery faded away in all directions into the dark. Near them three red ghosts were busily unloading demi-johns from a moving staircase.

The escalator from the Social Predestination Room.

Each bottle could be placed on one of fifteen racks, each rack, though you couldn't see it, was a conveyor travelling at the rate of thirty-three and a third centimetres an hour. Two hundred and sixty-seven days at eight metres a day. Two thousand one hundred and thirty-six metres in all. One circuit of the cellar at ground level, one on the first gallery, half on the second, and on the two hundred and sixty-seventh morning, daylight in the Decanting Room. Independent existence--so called.

'But in the interval,' Mr. Foster concluded, 'we've managed to do a lot to them. Oh, a very great deal.' His laugh was knowing and triumphant.

'That's the spirit I like,' said the Director once more. 'Let's walk round. You tell them everything, Mr. Foster.'

Mr. Foster duly told them.

Told them of the growing embryo on its bed of peritoneum. Made them taste the rich blood surrogate on which it fed. Explained why it had to be stimulated with placentin and thyroxin. Told them of the *corpus luteum* extract. Showed them the jets through which at every twelfth metre from zero to 2040 it was automatically injected. Spoke of those gradually increasing doses of pituitary administered during the final ninety-six metres of their course. Described the artificial maternal circulation installed on every bottle at metres 112; showed them the reservoir of blood-surrogate, the centrifugal pump that kept the liquid moving over the placenta and drove it through the synthetic lung and waste-product filter. Referred to the embryo's troublesome tendency to anæmia, to the massive doses of hog's stomach extract and foetal foal's liver with which, in consequence, it had to be supplied.

Showed them the simple mechanism by means of which, during the last two metres out of every eight, all the embryos were simultaneously shaken into familiarity with movement. Hinted at the gravity of the so-called 'trauma of decanting,' and enumerated the precautions taken to minimize, by a suitable training of the bottled embryo, that dangerous shock. Told them of the tests for sex carried out in the neighbourhood of metre 200. Explained the system of labelling--a T for the males, a circle for the females and for those who were destined to become freemartins a question mark, black on a white ground.

'For of course,' said Mr. Foster, 'in the vast majority of cases, fertility is merely a nuisance. One fertile ovary in twelve hundred--that would really be quite sufficient for our purposes. But we want to have a good choice. And of course one must always leave an enormous margin of safety. So we allow as many as thirty per cent. of the female embryos to develop normally. The others get a dose of male sex-hormone every twenty-four metres for the rest of the course. Result: they're decanted as freemartins--structurally quite normal (except,' he had to admit, 'that they *do* have just the slightest tendency to grow beards), but sterile. Guaranteed sterile. Which brings us at last,' continued Mr. Foster, 'out of the realm of mere slavish imitation of nature into the much more interesting world of human invention.'

He rubbed his hands. For, of course, they didn't content themselves with merely hatching out embryos: any cow could do that.

'We also predestine and condition. We decant our babies as socialized human beings, as Alphas or Epsilons, as future sewage workers or future...' He was going to say 'future World Controllers,' but correcting himself, said 'future Directors of Hatcheries' instead.

The D.H.C. acknowledged the compliment with a smile.

They were passing metre 320 on rack eleven. A young Beta-Minus mechanic was busy with screw-driver and spanner on the blood-surrogate pump of a passing bottle. The hum of the electric motor deepened by fractions of a tone as he turned the nuts. Down, down... A final twist, a glance at the revolution-counter, and he was done. He moved two paces down the line and began the same process on the next pump.

'Reducing the number of revolutions per minute,' Mr. Foster explained. 'The surrogate goes round slower; therefore passes through the lung at longer intervals; therefore gives the embryo less oxygen. Nothing like oxygen-shortage for keeping an embryo below par.' Again he rubbed his hands.

'But why do you want to keep the embryo below par?' asked an ingenuous student.

'Ass!' said the Director, breaking a long silence. 'Hasn't it occurred to you that an Epsilon embryo must have an Epsilon environment as well as an Epsilon heredity?'

It evidently hadn't occurred to him. He was covered with confusion.

'The lower the caste,' said Mr. Foster, 'the shorter the oxygen.' The first organ affected was the brain. After that the skeleton. At seventy per cent. of normal oxygen you got dwarfs. At less than seventy, eyeless monsters.

'Who are no use at all,' concluded Mr. Foster.

Whereas (his voice became confidential and eager), if they could discover a technique for shortening the period of maturation what a triumph, what a benefaction to Society!

'Consider the horse.'

They considered it.

Mature at six; the elephant at ten. While at thirteen a man is not yet sexually mature; and is only full grown at twenty. Hence, of course, that fruit of delayed development, the human intelligence.

'But in Epsilons,' said Mr. Foster very justly, 'we don't need human intelligence.'

Didn't need and didn't get it. But though the Epsilon mind was mature at ten, the Epsilon body was not fit to work till eighteen. Long years of superfluous and wasted immaturity. If the physical development could be speeded up till it was as quick, say, as a cow's, what an enormous saving to the Community!

'Enormous!' murmured the students. Mr. Foster's enthusiasm was infectious.

He became rather technical; spoke of the abnormal endocrine co-ordination which made men grow so slowly; postulated a germinal mutation to account for it. Could the effects of this germinal mutation be undone? Could the individual Epsilon embryo be made to revert, by a suitable technique, to the normality of dogs and cows? That was the problem. And it was all but solved.

Pilkington, at Mombasa, had produced individuals who were sexually mature at four and full grown at six and a half. A scientific triumph. But socially useless. Six-year-old men and women were too stupid to do even Epsilon work. And the process was an all-or-nothing one; either you failed to modify at all, or else you modified the whole way. They were still trying to find the ideal compromise between adults of twenty and adults of six. So far without success. Mr. Foster sighed and shook his head.

Their wanderings through the crimson twilight had brought them to the neighbourhood of Metre 170 on Rack 9. From this point onwards Rack 9 was enclosed and the bottles performed the remainder of their journey in a kind of tunnel, interrupted here and there by openings two or three metres wide.

'Heat conditioning,' said Mr. Foster.

Hot tunnels alternated with cool tunnels. Coolness was wedded to discomfort in the form of hard X-rays. By the time they were decanted the embryos had a horror of cold. They were predestined to emigrate to the tropics, to be miners and acetate silk spinners and steel workers. Later on their minds would be made to endorse the judgment of their bodies. 'We condition them to thrive on heat,' concluded Mr. Foster. 'Our colleagues upstairs will teach them to love it.'

'And that,' put in the Director sententiously, 'that is the secret of happiness and virtue--liking what you've *got* to do. All conditioning aims at that: making people like their unescapable social destiny.'

In a gap between two tunnels, a nurse was delicately probing with a long fine syringe into the gelatinous contents of a passing bottle. The students and their guides stood watching her for a few moments in silence.

'Well, Lenina,' said Mr. Foster, when at last she withdrew the syringe and straightened herself up.

The girl turned with a start. One could see that, for all the lupus and the purple eyes, she was uncommonly pretty.

'Henry!' Her smile flashed redly at him--a row of coral teeth.

'Charming, charming,' murmured the Director and, giving her two or three little pats, received in exchange a rather deferential smile for himself.

'What are you giving them?' asked Mr. Foster, making his tone very professional.

'Oh, the usual typhoid and sleeping sickness.'

'Tropical workers start being inoculated at metre 150,' Mr. Foster explained to the students. 'The embryos still have gills. We immunize the fish against the future man's diseases.' Then, turning back to Lenina, 'Ten to five on the roof this afternoon,' he said, 'as usual.'

'Charming,' said the Director once more, and, with a final pat, moved away after the others.

On Rack 10 rows of next generation's chemical workers were being trained in the toleration of lead, caustic soda, tar, chlorine. The first of a batch of two hundred and fifty embryonic rocket-plane engineers was just passing the eleven hundredth metre mark on Rack 3. A special mechanism kept their containers in constant rotation. 'To improve their sense of balance,' Mr. Foster explained. 'Doing repairs on the outside of a rocket in mid air is a ticklish job. We slacken off the circulation when they're right way up, so that they're half starved, and double the flow of surrogate when they're upside down. They learn to associate topsy-turvydom with well-being; in fact, they're only truly happy when they're standing on their heads.'

'And now,' Mr. Foster went on, 'I'd like to show you some very interesting conditioning for Alpha-Plus Intellectuals. We have a big batch of them on Rack 5. First Gallery level,' he called to two boys who had started to go down to the ground floor.

'They're round about metre 900,' he explained. 'You can't really do any useful intellectual conditioning till the foetuses have lost their tails. Follow me.'

But the Director had looked at his watch. 'Ten to three,' he said. 'No time for the intellectual embryos, I'm afraid. We must go up to the Nurseries before the children have finished their afternoon sleep.'

Mr. Foster was disappointed. 'At least one glance at the Decanting Room,' he pleaded.

'Very well, then.' The Director smiled indulgently. 'Just one glance.'

Chapter II

Mr. Foster was left in the Decanting Room. The D.H.C. and his students stepped into the nearest lift and were carried up to the fifth floor.

INFANT NURSERIES. NEO-PAVLOVIAN CONDITIONING ROOMS, announced the notice board.

The Director opened a door. They were in a large bare room, very bright and sunny; for the whole of the southern wall was a single window. Half a dozen nurses, trousered and jacketed in the regulation white viscose-linen uniform, their hair aseptically hidden under white caps, were engaged in setting out bowls of roses in a long row across the floor. Big bowls, packed tight with blossom. Thousands of petals, ripe-blown and silkily smooth, like the cheeks of innumerable little cherubs, but of cherubs, in that bright light, not exclusively pink and Aryan, but also luminously Chinese, also Mexican, also apoplectic with too much blowing of celestial trumpets, also pale as death, pale with the posthumous whiteness of marble.

The nurses stiffened to attention as the D.H.C. came in.

'Set out the books,' he said curtly.

In silence the nurses obeyed his command. Between the rose bowls the books were duly set out--a row of nursery quartos opened invitingly each at some gaily coloured image of beast or fish or bird.

'Now bring in the children.'

They hurried out of the room and returned in a minute or two, each pushing a kind of tall dumb-waiter laden, on all its four wire-netted shelves, with eight-month-old babies, all exactly alike (a Bokanovsky Group, it was evident) and all (since their caste was Delta) dressed in khaki.

'Put them down on the floor.'

The infants were unloaded.

'Now turn them so that they can see the flowers and books.'

Turned, the babies at once fell silent, then began to crawl towards those clusters of sleek colours, those shapes so gay and brilliant on the white pages. As they approached, the sun came out of a momentary eclipse behind a cloud. The roses flamed up as though with a sudden passion from within; a new and profound significance seemed to suffuse the shining pages of the books. From the ranks of the crawling babies came little squeals of excitement, gurgles and twitterings of pleasure.

The Director rubbed his hands. 'Excellent!' he said. 'It might almost have been done on purpose.'

The swiftest crawlers were already at their goal. Small hands reached out uncertainly, touched, grasped, unpetaling the transfigured roses, crumpling the illuminated pages of the books. The Director waited until all were happily busy. Then, 'Watch carefully,' he said. And, lifting his hand, he gave the signal.

The Head Nurse, who was standing by a switchboard at the other end of the room, pressed down a little lever.

There was a violent explosion. Shriller and ever shriller, a siren shrieked. Alarm bells maddeningly sounded.

The children started, screamed; their faces were distorted with terror.

'And now,' the Director shouted (for the noise was deafening), 'now we proceed to rub in the lesson with a mild electric shock.'

He waved his hand again, and the Head Nurse pressed a second lever. The screaming of the babies suddenly changed its tone. There was something desperate, almost insane, about the sharp spasmodic yelps to which they now gave utterance. Their little bodies twitched and stiffened; their limbs moved jerkily as if to the tug of unseen wires.

'We can electrify that whole strip of floor,' bawled the Director in explanation. 'But that's enough,' he signalled to the nurse.

The explosions ceased, the bells stopped ringing, the shriek of the siren died down from tone to tone into silence. The stiffly twitching bodies relaxed, and what had become the sob and yelp of infant maniacs broadened out once more into a normal howl of ordinary terror.

'Offer them the flowers and the books again.'

The nurses obeyed; but at the approach of the roses, at the mere sight of those gaily-coloured images of pussy and cock-a-doodle-doo and baa-baa black sheep, the infants shrank away in horror; the volume of their howling suddenly increased.

'Observe,' said the Director triumphantly, 'observe.'

Books and loud noises, flowers and electric shocks--already in the infant mind these couples were compromisingly linked; and after two hundred repetitions of the same or a similar lesson would be wedded indissolubly. What man has joined, nature is powerless to put asunder.

'They'll grow up with what the psychologists used to call an "instinctive" hatred of books and flowers. Reflexes unalterably conditioned. They'll be safe from books and botany all their lives.' The Director turned to his nurses. 'Take them away again.'

Still yelling, the khaki babies were loaded on to their dumb-waiters and wheeled out, leaving behind them the smell of sour milk and a most welcome silence.

One of the students held up his hand; and though he could see quite well why you couldn't have lower-caste people wasting the Community's time over books, and that there was always the risk of their reading something which might undesirably de-condition one of their reflexes, yet... well, he couldn't understand about the flowers. Why go to the trouble of making it psychologically impossible for Deltas to like flowers?

Patiently the D.H.C. explained. If the children were made to scream at the sight of a rose, that was on grounds of high economic policy. Not so very long ago (a century or thereabouts), Gammas, Deltas, even Epsilons, had been conditioned to like flowers--flowers in particular and wild nature in general. The idea was to make them want to be going out into the country at every available opportunity, and so compel them to consume transport.

'And didn't they consume transport?' asked the student.

'Quite a lot,' the D.H.C. replied. 'But nothing else.'

Primroses and landscapes, he pointed out, have one grave defect: they are gratuitous. A love of nature keeps no factories busy. It was decided to abolish the love of nature, at any rate among the lower classes; to abolish the love of nature, but *not* the tendency to consume transport. For of course it was essential that they should keep on going to the country, even though they hated it. The problem was to find an economically sounder reason for consuming transport than a mere affection for primroses and landscapes. It was duly found.

'We condition the masses to hate the country,' concluded the Director. 'But simultaneously we condition them to love all country sports. At the same time, we see to it that all country sports shall entail the use of elaborate apparatus. So that they consume manufactured articles as well as transport. Hence those electric shocks.'

'I see,' said the student, and was silent, lost in admiration.

There was a silence; then, clearing his throat, 'Once upon a time,' the Director began, 'while Our Ford was still on earth, there was a little boy called Reuben Rabinovitch. Reuben was the child of Polish-speaking parents.' The Director interrupted himself. 'You know what Polish is, I suppose?'

'A dead language.'

'Like French and German,' added another student, officiously showing off his learning.

'And "parent?"'?' questioned the D.H.C.

There was an uneasy silence. Several of the boys blushed. They had not learned to draw the significant but often very fine distinction between smut and pure science. One, at last, had the courage to raise a hand.

'Human beings used to be...' he hesitated; the blood rushed to his cheeks. 'Well, they used to be viviparous.'

'Quite right.' The Director nodded approvingly.

'And when the babies were decanted...'

'"Born",' came the correction.

'Well, then they were the parents--I mean, not the babies, of course; the other ones.' The poor boy was overwhelmed with confusion.

'In brief,' the Director summed up, 'the parents were the father and the mother.' The smut that was really science fell with a crash into the boys' eye-avoiding silence. 'Mother,' he repeated loudly rubbing in the science; and, leaning back in his chair, 'These,' he said gravely, 'are unpleasant facts; I know it. But, then, most historical facts *are* unpleasant.'

He returned to Little Reuben--to Little Reuben, in whose room, one evening, by an oversight, his father and mother (crash, crash!) happened to leave the radio turned on.

('For you must remember that in those days of gross viviparous reproduction, children were always brought up by their parents and not in State Conditioning Centres.')

While the child was asleep, a broadcast programme from London suddenly started to come through; and the next morning, to the astonishment of his crash and crash (the more daring of the boys ventured to grin at one another) Little Reuben woke up repeating word for word a long lecture by that curious old writer ('one of the very few whose works have been permitted to come down to us'), George Bernard Shaw, who was speaking, according to a well-authenticated tradition, about his own genius. To Little Reuben's wink and snigger, this lecture was, of course, perfectly incomprehensible and, imagining that their child had suddenly gone mad, they sent for a doctor. He, fortunately, understood English, recognized the discourse as that which Shaw had broadcasted the previous evening, realized the significance of what had happened, and sent a letter to the medical press about it.

'The principle of sleep-teaching, or hypnopædia, had been discovered.' The D.H.C. made an impressive pause.

The principle had been discovered; but many, many years were to elapse before that principle was usefully applied.

'The case of Little Reuben occurred only twenty-three years after Our Ford's first T-Model was put on the market.' (Here the Director made a sign of the T on his stomach and all the students reverently followed suit.) 'And yet...'

Furiously the students scribbled. '*Hypnopædia, first used officially in A.F. 214. Why not before? Two reason. (a)...*'

'These early experimenters,' the D.H.C. was saying, 'were on the wrong track. They thought that hypnopædia could be made an instrument of intellectual education...'

(A small boy asleep on his right side, the right arm stuck out, the right hand hanging limp over the edge of the bed. Through a round grating in the side of a box a voice speaks softly.

'The Nile is the longest river in Africa and the second in length of all the rivers of the globe. Although falling short of the length of the Mississippi-Missouri, the Nile is at the head of all rivers as regards the length of its basin, which extends through 35 degrees of latitude...'

At breakfast the next morning, 'Tommy,' some one says, 'do you know which is the longest river in Africa?' A shaking of the head. 'But don't you remember something that begins: The Nile is the...'

'The-Nile-is-the-longest-river-in-Africa-and-the   second-in-length-of-all-the-rivers-of-the-globe...' The words come rushing out. 'Although-falling-short-of...'

'Well now, which is the longest river in Africa?'

The eyes are blank. 'I don't know.'

'But the Nile, Tommy.'

'The-Nile-is-the-longest-river-in-Africa-and-second...'

'Then which river is the longest, Tommy?'

Tommy bursts into tears. 'I don't know,' he howls.)

That howl, the Director made it plain, discouraged the earliest investigators. The experiments were abandoned. No further attempt was made to teach children the length of the Nile in their sleep. Quite rightly. You can't learn a science unless you know what it's all about.

'Whereas, if they'd only started on *moral* education,' said the Director, leading the way towards the door. The students followed him, desperately scribbling as they walked and all the way up in the lift. 'Moral education, which ought never, in any circumstances, to be rational.'

'Silence, silence,' whispered a loud-speaker as they stepped out at the fourteenth floor, and 'Silence, silence,' the trumpet mouths indefatigably repeated at intervals down every corridor. The students and even the Director himself rose automatically to the tips of their toes. They were Alphas, of course; but even Alphas have been well conditioned. 'Silence, silence.' All the air of the fourteenth floor was sibilant with the categorical imperative.

Fifty yards of tiptoeing brought them to a door which the Director cautiously opened. They stepped over the threshold into the twilight of a shuttered dormitory. Eighty cots stood in a row against the wall. There was a sound of light regular breathing and a continuous murmur, as of very faint voices remotely whispering.

A nurse rose as they entered and came to attention before the Director.

'What's the lesson this afternoon?' he asked.

'We had Elementary Sex for the first forty minutes,' she answered. 'But now it's switched over to Elementary Class Consciousness.'

The Director walked slowly down the long line of cots. Rosy and relaxed with sleep, eighty little boys and girls lay softly breathing. There was a whisper under every pillow. The D.H.C. halted and, bending over one of the little beds, listened attentively.

'Elementary Class Consciousness, did you say? Let's have it repeated a little louder by the trumpet.'

At the end of the room a loud-speaker projected from the wall. The Director walked up to it and pressed a switch.

'...all wear green,' said a soft but very distinct voice, beginning in the middle of a sentence, 'and Delta Children wear khaki. Oh no, I don't want to play with Delta children. And Epsilons are still worse. They're too stupid to be able to read or write. Besides, they wear black, which is such a beastly colour. I'm *so* glad I'm a Beta.'

There was a pause; then the voice began again.

'Alpha children wear grey. They work much harder than we do, because they're so frightfully clever. I'm really awfully glad I'm a Beta, because I don't work so hard. And then we are much better than the Gammas and Deltas. Gammas are stupid. They all wear green, and Delta children wear khaki. Oh no, I *don't* want to play with Delta children. And Epsilons are still worse. They're too stupid to be able...'

The Director pushed back the switch. The voice was silent. Only its thin ghost continued to mutter from beneath the eighty pillows.

'They'll have that repeated forty or fifty times more before they wake; then again on Thursday, and again on Saturday. A hundred and twenty times three times a week for thirty months. After which they go on to a more advanced lesson.'

Roses and electric shocks, the khaki of Deltas and a whiff of asafoetida--wedded indissolubly before the child can speak. But wordless conditioning is crude and wholesale; cannot bring home the finer distinctions, cannot inculcate the more complex courses of behaviour. For that there must be words, but words without reason. In brief, hypnopædia.

'The greatest moralizing and socializing force of all time.'

The students took it down in their little books. Straight from the horse's mouth.

Once more the Director touched the switch.

'...so frightfully clever,' the soft, insinuating, indefatigable voice was saying. 'I'm really awfully glad I'm a Beta, because...'

Not so much like drops of water, though water, it is true, can wear holes in the hardest granite; rather, drops of liquid sealing-wax, drops that adhere, incrust, incorporate themselves with what they fall on, till finally the rock is all one scarlet blob.

'Till at last the child's mind *is* these suggestions, and the sum of the suggestions *is* the child's mind. And not the child's mind only. The adult's mind too--all his life long. The mind that judges and desires and decides--made up of these suggestions. But all these suggestions are *our* suggestions!' The Director almost shouted in his triumph. 'Suggestions from the State.' He banged the nearest table. 'It therefore follows...'A noise made him turn round. 'Oh, Ford!' he said in another tone, 'I've gone and woken the children.'

Chapter III

Outside, in the garden, it was playtime. Naked in the warm June sunshine, six or seven hundred little boys and girls were running with shrill yells over the lawns, or playing ball games, or squatting silently in twos and threes among the flowering shrubs. The roses were in bloom, two nightingales soliloquized in the boskage, a cuckoo was just going out of tune among the lime trees. The air was drowsy with the murmur of bees and helicopters.

The Director and his students stood for a short time watching a game of Centrifugal Bumble-puppy. Twenty children were grouped in a circle round a chrome-steel tower. A ball thrown up so as to land on the platform at the top of the tower rolled down into the interior, fell on a rapidly revolving disk, was hurled through one or other of the numerous apertures pierced in the cylindrical casing, and had to be caught.

'Strange,' mused the Director, as they turned away, 'strange to think that even in Our Ford's day most games were played without more apparatus than a ball or two and a few sticks and perhaps a bit of netting. Imagine the folly of allowing people to play elaborate games which do nothing whatever to increase consumption. It's madness. Nowadays the Controllers won't approve of any new game unless it can be shown that it requires at least as much apparatus as the most complicated of existing games.' He interrupted himself.

'That's a charming little group,' he said, pointing.

In a little grassy bay between tall clumps of Mediterranean heather, two children, a little boy of about seven and a little girl who might have been a year older, were playing, very gravely and with all the focussed attention of scientists intent on a labour of discovery, a rudimentary sexual game.

'Charming, charming!' the D.H.C. repeated sentimentally.

'Charming,' the boys politely agreed. But their smile was rather patronizing. They had put aside similar childish amusements too recently to be able to watch them now without a touch of contempt. Charming? but it was just a pair of kids fooling about; that was all. Just kids.

'I always think,' the Director was continuing in the same rather maudlin tone, when he was interrupted by a loud boo-hooing.

From a neighbouring shrubbery emerged a nurse, leading by the hand a small boy, who howled as he went. An anxious-looking little girl trotted at her heels.

'What's the matter?' asked the Director.

The nurse shrugged her shoulders. 'Nothing much,' she answered. 'It's just that this little boy seems rather reluctant to join in the ordinary erotic play. I'd noticed it once or twice before. And now again to-day. He started yelling just now...'

'Honestly,' put in the anxious-looking little girl, 'I didn't mean to hurt him or anything. Honestly.'

'Of course you didn't, dear,' said the nurse reassuringly. 'And so,' she went on, turning back to the Director, 'I'm taking him in to see the Assistant Superintendent of Psychology. Just to see if anything's at all abnormal.'

'Quite right,' said the Director. 'Take him in. You stay here, little girl,' he added, as the nurse moved away with her still howling charge. 'What's your name?'

'Polly Trotsky.'

'And a very good name too,' said the Director. 'Run away now and see if you can find some other little boy to play with.'

The child scampered off into the bushes and was lost to sight.

'Exquisite little creature!' said the Director, looking after her. Then, turning to his students, 'What I'm going to tell you now,' he said, 'may sound incredible. But then, when you're not accustomed to history, most facts about the past *do* sound incredible.'

He let out the amazing truth. For a very long period before the time of Our Ford, and even for some generations afterwards, erotic play between children had been regarded as abnormal (there was a roar of laughter); and not only abnormal, actually immoral (no!): and had therefore been rigorously suppressed.

A look of astonished incredulity appeared on the faces of his listeners. Poor little kids not allowed to amuse themselves? They could not believe it.

'Even adolescents,' the D.H.C. was saying, 'even adolescents like yourselves...'

'Not possible!'

'Barring a little surreptitious auto-erotism and homosexuality--absolutely nothing.'

'*Nothing?*'

'In most cases, till they were over twenty years old.'

'Twenty years old?' echoed the students in a chorus of loud disbelief.

'Twenty,' the Director repeated. 'I told you that you'd find it incredible.'

'But what happened?' they asked. 'What were the results?'

'The results were terrible.' A deep resonant voice broke startlingly into the dialogue.

They looked round. On the fringe of the little group stood a stranger--a man of middle height, black-haired, with a hooked nose, full red lips, eyes very piercing and dark. 'Terrible,' he repeated.

The D.H.C. had at that moment sat down on one of the steel and rubber benches conveniently scattered through the gardens; but at the sight of the stranger, he sprang to his feet and darted forward, his hands outstretched, smiling with all his teeth, effusive.

'Controller! What an unexpected pleasure! Boys, what are you thinking of? This is the Controller; this is his fordship, Mustapha Mond.'

****

In the four thousand rooms of the Centre the four thousand electric clocks simultaneously struck four. Discarnate voices called from the trumpet mouths.

'Main Day-shift off duty. Second Day-shift take over. Main Day-shift off...'

In the lift, on their way up to the changing-rooms, Henry Foster and the Assistant Director of Predestination rather pointedly turned their backs on Bernard Marx from the Psychology Bureau: averted themselves from that unsavoury reputation.

The faint hum and rattle of machinery still stirred the crimson air in the Embryo-Store. Shifts might come and go, one lupus-coloured face give place to another; majestically and for ever the conveyors crept forward with their load of future men and women.

Lenina Crowne walked briskly towards the door.

****

His fordship Mustapha Mond! The eyes of the saluting students almost popped out of their heads. Mustapha Mond! The Resident Controller for Western Europe! One of the Ten World Controllers. One of the Ten... and he sat down on the bench with the D.H.C., he was going to stay, to stay, yes, and actually talk to them... straight from the horse's mouth. Straight from the mouth of Ford himself.

Two shrimp-brown children emerged from a neighbouring shrubbery, stared at them for a moment with large, astonished eyes, then returned to their amusements among the leaves.

'You all remember,' said the Controller, in his strong deep voice, 'you all remember, I suppose, that beautiful and inspired saying of Our Ford's: History is bunk. History,' he repeated slowly, 'is bunk.'

He waved his hand; and it was as though, with an invisible feather whisk, he had brushed away a little dust, and the dust was Harappa, was Ur of the Chaldees; some spider-webs, and they were Thebes and Babylon and Cnossos and Mycenae. Whisk, Whisk--and where was Odysseus, where was Job, where were Jupiter and Gotama and Jesus? Whisk--and those specks of antique dirt called Athens and Rome, Jerusalem and the Middle Kingdom--all were gone. Whisk--the place where Italy had been was empty. Whisk, the cathedrals; whisk, whisk, King Lear and the Thoughts of Pascal. Whisk, Passion: whisk, Requiem; whisk, Symphony; whisk...

****

'Going to the Feelies this evening, Henry?' enquired the Assistant Predestinator. 'I hear the new one at the Alhambra is first-rate. There's a love scene on a bearskin rug; they say it's marvellous. Every hair of the bear reproduced. The most amazing tactual effects.'

****

'That's why you're taught no history,' the Controller was saying. 'But now the time has come...'

The D.H.C. looked at him nervously. There were those strange rumours of old forbidden books hidden in a safe in the Controller's study. Bibles, poetry--Ford knew what.

Mustapha Mond intercepted his anxious glance and the corners of his red lips twitched ironically.

'It's all right, Director,' he said in a tone of faint derision, 'I won't corrupt them.'

The D.H.C. was overwhelmed with confusion.

****

Those who feel themselves despised do well to look despising. The smile on Bernard Marx's face was contemptuous. Every hair on the bear indeed!

'I shall make a point of going,' said Henry Foster.

****

Mustapha Mond leaned forward, shook a finger at them. 'Just try to realize it,' he said, and his voice sent a strange thrill quivering along their diaphragms. 'Try to realize what it was like to have a viviparous mother.'

That smutty word again. But none of them dreamed, this time, of smiling.

'Try to imagine what "living with one's family" meant.'

They tried; but obviously without the smallest success.

'And do you know what a "home" was?'

They shook their heads.

****

From her dim crimson cellar Lenina Crowne shot up seventeen stories, turned to the right as she stepped out of the lift, walked down a long corridor and, opening the door marked GIRLS' DRESSING-ROOM, plunged into a deafening chaos of arms and bosoms and underclothing. Torrents of hot water were splashing into or gurgling out of a hundred baths. Rumbling and hissing, eighty vibro-vacuum massage machines were simultaneously kneading and sucking the firm and sunburnt flesh of eighty superb female specimens. Every one was talking at the top of her voice. A Synthetic Music machine was warbling out a super-cornet solo.

'Hullo, Fanny,' said Lenina to the young woman who had the pegs and locker next to hers.

Fanny worked in the Bottling Room, and her surname was also Crowne. But as the two thousand million inhabitants of the planet had only ten thousand names between them, the coincidence was not particularly surprising.

Lenina pulled at her zippers--downwards on the jacket, downwards with a double-handed gesture at the two that held trousers, downwards again to loosen her undergarment. Still wearing her shoes and stockings, she walked off towards the bathrooms.

****

Home, home--a few small rooms, stiflingly over-inhabited by a man, by a periodically teeming woman, by a rabble of boys and girls of all ages. No air, no space; an understerilized prison; darkness, disease, and smells.

(The Controller's evocation was so vivid that one of the boys, more sensitive than the rest, turned pale at the mere description and was on the point of being sick.)

****

Lenina got out of the bath, towelled herself dry, took hold of a long flexible tube plugged into the wall, presented the nozzle to her breast, as though she meant to commit suicide, pressed down the trigger. A blast of warmed air dusted her with the finest talcum powder. Eight different scents and eau-de-Cologne were laid on in little taps over the wash-basin. She turned on the third from the left, dabbled herself with chypre and, carrying her shoes and stockings in her hand, went out to see if one of the vibro-vacuum machines were free.

****

And home was as squalid psychically as physically. Psychically, it was a rabbit hole, a midden, hot with the frictions of tightly packed life, reeking with emotion. What suffocating intimacies, what dangerous, insane, obscene relationships between the members of the family group! Maniacally, the mother brooded over her children (*her* children)... brooded over them like a cat over its kittens; but a cat that could talk, a cat that could say, 'My baby, my baby,' over and over again. 'My baby, and oh, oh, at my breast, the little hands, the hunger, and that unspeakable agonizing pleasure! Till at last my baby sleeps, my baby sleeps with a bubble of white milk at the corner of his mouth. My little baby sleeps...'

'Yes,' said Mustapha Mond, nodding his head, 'you may well shudder.'

****

'Who are you going out with to-night?' Lenina asked, returning from the vibro-vac like a pearl illuminated from within, pinkly glowing.

'Nobody.'

Lenina raised her eyebrows in astonishment.

'I've been feeling rather out of sorts lately,' Fanny explained. 'Dr. Wells advised me to have a Pregnancy Substitute.'

'But, my dear, you're only nineteen. The first Pregnancy Substitute isn't compulsory till twenty-one.'

'I know, dear. But some people are better if they begin earlier. Dr. Wells told me that brunettes with wide pelvises, like me, ought to have their first Pregnancy Substitute at seventeen. So I'm really two years late, not two years early.' She opened the door of her locker and pointed to the row of boxes and labelled phials on the upper shelf.

'SYRUP OF CORPUS LUTEUM.' Lenina read the names aloud. 'OVARIN, GUARANTEED FRESH: NOT TO BE USED AFTER AUGUST 1ST, A.F. 632. MAMMARY GLAND EXTRACT: TO BE TAKEN THREE TIMES DAILY, BEFORE MEALS, WITH A LITTLE WATER. PLACENTIN: 5CC TO BE INJECTED INTRAVENALLY EVERY THIRD DAY... Ugh!' Lenina shuddered. 'How I loathe intravenals, don't you?'

'Yes. But when they do one good...' Fanny was a particularly sensible girl.

****

Our Ford--or Our Freud, as, for some inscrutable reason, he chose to call himself whenever he spoke of psychological matters--Our Freud had been the first to reveal the appalling dangers of family life. The world was full of fathers--was therefore full of misery; full of mothers--therefore of every kind of perversion from sadism to chastity; full of brothers, sisters, uncles, aunts--full of madness and suicide.

'And yet, among the savages of Samoa, in certain islands off the coast of New Guinea...'

The tropical sunshine lay like warm honey on the naked bodies of children tumbling promiscuously among the hibiscus blossoms. Home was in any one of twenty palm-thatched houses. In the Trobriands conception was the work of ancestral ghosts; nobody had ever heard of a father.

'Extremes,' said the Controller, 'meet. For the good reason that they were made to meet.'

****

'Dr. Wells says that a three months' Pregnancy Substitute now will make all the difference to my health for the next three or four years.'

'Well, I hope he's right,' said Lenina. 'But, Fanny, do you really mean to say that for the next three months you're not supposed to...'

'Oh no, dear. Only for a week or two, that's all. I shall spend the evening at the Club playing Musical Bridge. I suppose you're going out?'

Lenina nodded.

'Who with?'

'Henry Foster.'

'Again?' Fanny's kind, rather moon-like face took on an incongruous expression of pained and disapproving astonishment. 'Do you mean to tell me you're *still* going out with Henry Foster?'

****

Mothers and fathers, brothers and sisters. But there were also husbands, wives, lovers. There were also monogamy and romance.

'Though you probably don't know what those are,' said Mustapha Mond.

They shook their heads.

Family, monogamy, romance. Everywhere exclusiveness, everywhere a focussing of interest, a narrow channelling of impulse and energy.

'But every one belongs to every one else,' he concluded, citing the hypnopædic proverb.

The students nodded, emphatically agreeing with a statement which upwards of sixty-two thousand repetitions in the dark had made them accept, not merely as true, but as axiomatic, self-evident, utterly indisputable.

****

'But after all,' Lenina was protesting, 'it's only about four months now since I've been having Henry.'

'*Only* four months! I like that. And what's more,' Fanny went on, pointing an accusing finger, 'there's been nobody else except Henry all that time. Has there?'

Lenina blushed scarlet; but her eyes, the tone of her voice remained defiant. 'No, there hasn't been any one else,' she answered almost truculently. 'And I jolly well don't see why there should have been.'

'Oh, she jolly well doesn't see why there should have been,' Fanny repeated, as though to an invisible listener behind Lenina's left shoulder. Then, with a sudden change of tone, 'But seriously,' she said, 'I really do think you ought to be careful. It's such horribly bad form to go on and on like this with one man. At forty, or thirty-five, it wouldn't be so bad. But at *your* age, Lenina! No, it really won't do. And you know how strongly the D.H.C. objects to anything intense or long-drawn. Four months of Henry Foster, without having another man--why, he'd be furious if he knew...'

****

'Think of water under pressure in a pipe.' They thought of it. 'I pierce it once,' said the Controller. 'What a jet!'

He pierced it twenty times. There were twenty piddling little fountains.

'My baby. My baby...!'

'Mother!' The madness is infectious.

'My love, my one and only, precious, precious...'

Mother, monogamy, romance. High spurts the fountain; fierce and foamy the wild jet. The urge has but a single outlet. My love, my baby. No wonder those poor pre-moderns were mad and wicked and miserable. Their world didn't allow them to take things easily, didn't allow them to be sane, virtuous, happy. What with mothers and lovers, what with the prohibitions they were not conditioned to obey, what with the temptations and the lonely remorses, what with all the diseases and the endless isolating pain, what with the uncertainties and the poverty--they were forced to feel strongly. And feeling strongly (and strongly, what was more, in solitude, in hopelessly individual isolation), how could they be stable?

****

'Of course there's no need to give him up. Have somebody else from time to time, that's all. He has other girls, doesn't he?'

Lenina admitted it.

'Of course he does. Trust Henry Foster to be the perfect gentleman--always correct. And then there's the Director to think of. You know what a stickler...'

Nodding, 'He patted me on the behind this afternoon,' said Lenina.

'There, you see!' Fanny was triumphant. 'That shows what *he* stands for. The strictest conventionality.'

****

'Stability,' said the Controller, 'stability. No civilization without social stability. No social stability without individual stability.' His voice was a trumpet. Listening, they felt larger, warmer.

The machine turns, turns and must keep on turning--for ever. It is death if it stands still. A thousand millions scrabbled the crust of the earth. The wheels began to turn. In a hundred and fifty years there were two thousand millions. Stop all the wheels. In a hundred and fifty weeks there are once more only a thousand millions; a thousand thousand thousand men and women have starved to death.

Wheels must turn steadily, but cannot turn untended. There must be men to tend them, men as steady as the wheels upon their axles, sane men, obedient men, stable in contentment.

Crying: My baby, my mother, my only, only love; groaning: My sin, my terrible God; screaming with pain, muttering with fever, bemoaning old age and poverty--how can they tend the wheels? And if they cannot tend the wheels... The corpses of a thousand thousand thousand men and women would be hard to bury or burn.

****

'And after all,' Fanny's tone was coaxing, 'it's not as though there were anything painful or disagreeable about having one or two men besides Henry. And seeing that, you *ought* to be a little more promiscuous....'

****

'Stability,' insisted the Controller, 'stability. The primal and the ultimate need. Stability. Hence all this.'

With a wave of his hand he indicated the gardens, the huge building of the Conditioning Centre, the naked children furtive in the undergrowth or running across the lawns.

****

Lenina shook her head. 'Somehow,' she mused, 'I hadn't been feeling very keen on promiscuity lately. There are times when one doesn't. Haven't you found that too, Fanny?'

Fanny nodded her sympathy and understanding. 'But one's got to make the effort,' she said sententiously, 'one's got to play the game. After all, every one belongs to every one else.'

'Yes, every one belongs to every one else.' Lenina repeated slowly and, sighing, was silent for a moment; then, taking Fanny's hand, gave it a little squeeze. 'You're quite right, Fanny. As usual. I'll make the effort.'

****

Impulse arrested spills over, and the flood is feeling, the flood is passion, the flood is even madness: it depends on the force of the current, the height and strength of the barrier. The unchecked stream flows smoothly down its appointed channels into a calm well-being. (The embryo is hungry; day in, day out, the blood-surrogate pump unceasingly turns its eight hundred revolutions a minute. The decanted infant howls; at once a nurse appears with a bottle of external secretion. Feeling lurks in that interval of time between desire and its consummation. Shorten that interval, break down all those old unnecessary barriers.)

'Fortunate boys!' said the Controller. 'No pains have been spared to make your lives emotionally easy--to preserve you, so far as that is possible, from having emotions at all.'

'Ford's in his flivver,' murmured the D.H.C. 'All's well with the world.'

****

'Lenina Crowne?' said Henry Foster, echoing the Assistant Predestinator's question as he zipped up his trousers. 'Oh, she's a splendid girl. Wonderfully pneumatic. I'm surprised you haven't had her.'

'I can't think how it is I haven't,' said the Assistant Predestinator. 'I certainly will. At the first opportunity.'

From his place on the opposite side of the changing-room aisle, Bernard Marx overheard what they were saying and turned pale.

****

'And to tell the truth,' said Lenina, 'I'm beginning to get just a tiny bit bored with nothing but Henry every day.' She pulled on her left stocking. 'Do you know Bernard Marx?' she asked in a tone whose excessive casualness was evidently forced.

Fanny looked startled. 'You don't mean to say...?'

'Why not? Bernard's an Alpha-Plus. Besides, he asked me to go to one of the Savage Reservations with him. I've always wanted to see a Savage Reservation.'

'But his reputation?'

'What do I care about his reputation?'

'They say he doesn't like Obstacle Golf.'

'They say, they say,' mocked Lenina.

'And then he spends most of his time by himself--*alone*.' There was horror in Fanny's voice.

'Well, he won't be alone when he's with me. And anyhow, why are people so beastly to him? I think he's rather sweet.' She smiled to herself; how absurdly shy he had been! Frightened almost--as though she were a World Controller and he a Gamma-Minus machine minder.

****

'Consider your own lives,' said Mustapha Mond. 'Has any of you ever encountered an insurmountable obstacle?'

The question was answered by a negative silence.

'Has any of you been compelled to live through a long time-interval between the consciousness of a desire and its fulfilment?'

'Well,' began one of the boys, and hesitated.

'Speak up,' said the D.H.C. 'Don't keep his fordship waiting.'

'I once had to wait nearly four weeks before a girl I wanted would let me have her.'

'And you felt a strong emotion in consequence?'

'Horrible!'

'Horrible; precisely,' said the Controller. 'Our ancestors were so stupid and short-sighted that when the first reformers came along and offered to deliver them from those horrible emotions, they wouldn't have anything to do with them.'

****

'Talking about her as though she were a bit of meat.' Bernard ground his teeth. 'Have her here, have her there. Like mutton. Degrading her to so much mutton. She said she'd think it over, she said she'd give me an answer this week. Oh, Ford, Ford, Ford.' He would have liked to go up to them and hit them in the face--hard, again and again.

'Yes, I really do advise you to try her,' Henry Foster was saying.

****

'Take Ectogenesis. Pfitzner and Kawaguchi had got the whole technique worked out. But would the Governments look at it? No. There was something called Christianity. Women were forced to go on being viviparous.'

****

'He's so ugly!' said Fanny.

'But I rather like his looks.'

'And then so *small*' Fanny made a grimace; smallness was so horribly and typically low-caste.

'I think that's rather sweet,' said Lenina. 'One feels one would like to pet him. You know. Like a cat.'

Fanny was shocked. 'They say somebody made a mistake when he was still in the bottle--thought he was a Gamma and put alcohol into his blood-surrogate. That's why he's so stunted.'

'What nonsense!' Lenina was indignant.

****

'Sleep teaching was actually prohibited in England. There was something called liberalism. Parliament, if you know what that was, passed a law against it. The records survive. Speeches about liberty of the subject. Liberty to be inefficient and miserable. Freedom to be a round peg in a square hole.'

****

'But, my dear chap, you're welcome, I assure you. You're welcome.' Henry Foster patted the Assistant Predestinator on the shoulder. 'Every one belongs to every one else, after all.'

One hundred repetitions three nights a week for four years, thought Bernard Marx, who was a specialist on hypnopædia. Sixty-two thousand four hundred repetitions make one truth. Idiots!

****

'Or the Caste System. Constantly proposed, constantly rejected. There was something called democracy. As though men were more than physico-chemically equal.'

****

'Well, all I can say is that I'm going to accept his invitation.'

****

Bernard hated them, hated them. But they were two, they were large, they were strong.

****

'The Nine Years' War began in A.F. 141.'

****

'Not even if it *were* true about the alcohol in his blood-surrogate.'

****

'Phosgene, chloropicrin, ethyl iodoacetate, diphenylcyanarsine, trichlormethyl chloroformate, dichlorethyl sulphide. Not to mention hydrocyanic acid.'

****

'Which I simply don't believe,' Lenina concluded.

****

'The noise of fourteen thousand aeroplanes advancing in open order. But in the Kurfürstendamm and the Eighth Arrondissement, the explosion of the anthrax bombs is hardly louder than the popping of a paper bag.'

****

'Because I *do* want to see a Savage Reservation.'

****

$CH_3C_6H_2(NO_2)_3+Hg(CNO)_2$=well, what? An enormous hole in the ground, a pile of masonry, some bits of flesh and mucus, a foot, with the boot still on it, flying through the air and landing, flop, in the middle of the geraniums-- the scarlet ones; such a splendid show that summer!

****

'You're hopeless, Lenina, I give you up.'

****

'The Russian technique for infecting water supplies was particularly ingenious.'

****

Back turned to back, Fanny and Lenina continued their changing in silence.

****

'The Nine Years' War, the great Economic Collapse. There was a choice between World Control and destruction. Between stability and...'

****

'Fanny Crowne's a nice girl too,' said the Assistant Predestinator.

****

In the nurseries, the Elementary Class Consciousness lesson was over, the voices were adapting future demand to future industrial supply. 'I do love flying,' they whispered, 'I do love flying, I do love having new clothes, I do love...'

****

'Liberalism, of course, was dead of anthrax, but all the same you couldn't do things by force.'

****

'Not nearly so pneumatic as Lenina. Oh, not nearly.'

****

'But old clothes are beastly,' continued the untiring whisper. 'We always throw away old clothes. Ending is better than mending, ending is better than mending, ending is better...'

****

'Government's an affair of sitting, not hitting. You rule with the brains and the buttocks, never with the fists. For example, there was the conscription of consumption.'

****

'There, I'm ready,' said Lenina; but Fanny remained speechless and averted. 'Let's make peace, Fanny darling.'

****

'Every man, woman and child compelled to consume so much a year. In the interests of industry. The sole result...'

****

'Ending is better than mending. The more stitches, the less riches; the more stitches...'

****

'One of these days,' said Fanny, with dismal emphasis, 'you'll get into trouble.'

****

'Conscientious objection on an enormous scale. Anything not to consume. Back to nature.'

****

'I do love flying, I do love flying.'

****

'Back to culture. Yes, actually to culture. You can't consume much if you sit still and read books.'

****

'Do I look all right?' Lenina asked. Her jacket was made of bottle-green acetate cloth with green viscose fur at the cuffs and collar.

****

'Eight hundred Simple Lifers were mowed down by machine guns at Golders Green.'

****

'Ending is better than mending, ending is better than mending.'

****

Green corduroy shorts and white viscose-woollen stockings turned down below the knee.

****

'Then came the famous British Museum Massacre. Two thousand culture fans gassed with dichlorethyl sulphide.'

****

A green-and-white jockey cap shaded Lenina's eyes; her shoes were bright green and highly polished.

****

'In the end,' said Mustapha Mond, 'the Controllers realized that force was no good. The slower but infinitely surer methods of ectogenesis, Neo-Pavlovian conditioning and hypnopædia...'

****

And round her waist she wore a silver-mounted green morocco-surrogate cartridge belt, bulging (for Lenina was not a freemartin) with the regulation supply of contraceptives.

****

'The discoveries of Pfitzner and Kawaguchi were at last made use of. An intensive propaganda against viviparous reproduction...'

****

'Perfect!' cried Fanny enthusiastically. She could never resist Lenina's charm for long. 'And what a perfectly *sweet* Malthusian belt!'

****

'Accompanied by a campaign against the Past; by the closing of museums, the blowing up of historical monuments (luckily most of them had already been destroyed during the Nine Years' War); by the suppression of all books published before A.F. 150.'

****

'I simply must get one like it,' said Fanny.

****

'There were some things called the pyramids, for example.'

****

'My old black-patent bandolier...'

****

'And a man called Shakespeare. You've never heard of them of course.'

****

'It's an absolute disgrace--that bandolier of mine.'

****

'Such are the advantages of a really scientific education.'

****

'The more stitches the less riches; the more stitches the less...'

****

'The introduction of Our Ford's first T-Model...'

****

'I've had it nearly three months.'

****

'Chosen as the opening date of the new era.'

****

'Ending is better than mending; ending is better...'

****

'There was a thing, as I've said before, called Christianity.'

****

'Ending is better than mending.'

****

'The ethics and philosophy of under-consumption...'

****

'I love new clothes, I love new clothes, I love...'

****

'So essential when there was under-production; but in an age of machines and the fixation of nitrogen--positively a crime against society.'

****

'Henry Foster gave it me.'

****

'All crosses had their tops cut and became T's. There was also a thing called God.'

****

'It's real morocco-surrogate.'

****

'We have the World State now. And Ford's Day celebrations, and Community Sings, and Solidarity Services.'

****

'Ford, how I hate them!' Bernard Marx was thinking.

****

'There was a thing called Heaven; but all the same they used to drink enormous quantities of alcohol.'

****

'Like meat, like so much meat.'

****

'There was a thing called the soul and a thing called immortality.'

****

'Do ask Henry where he got it.'

****

'But they used to take morphia and cocaine.'

****

'And what makes it worse, she thinks of herself as meat.'

****

'Two thousand pharmacologists and bio-chemists were subsidized in A.F. 178.'

****

'He does look glum,' said the Assistant Predestinator, pointing at Bernard Marx.

****

'Six years later it was being produced commercially. The perfect drug.'

****

'Let's bait him.'

****

'Euphoric, narcotic, pleasantly hallucinant.'

****

'Glum, Marx, glum.' The clap on the shoulder made him start, look up. It was that brute Henry Foster. 'What you need is a gramme of *soma*.'

****

'All the advantages of Christianity and alcohol; none of their defects.'

****

'Ford, I should like to kill him!' But all he did was to say, 'No, thank you,' and fend off the proffered tube of tablets.

****

'Take a holiday from reality whenever you like, and come back without so much as a headache or a mythology.'

****

'Take it,' insisted Henry Foster, 'take it.'

****

'Stability was practically assured.'

****

'One cubic centimetre cures ten gloomy sentiments,' said the Assistant Predestinator, citing a piece of homely hypnopædic wisdom.

****

'It only remained to conquer old age.'

****

'Damn you, damn you!' shouted Bernard Marx.

****

'Hoity-toity.'

****

'Gonadal hormones, transfusion of young blood, magnesium salts...'

****

'And do remember that a gramme is better than a damn.' They went out, laughing.

****

'All the physiological stigmata of old age have been abolished. And along with them, of course...'

****

'Don't forget to ask him about that Malthusian belt,' said Fanny.

****

'Along with them all the old man's mental peculiarities. Characters remain constant throughout a whole lifetime.'

****

'...two rounds of Obstacle Golf to get through before dark. I must fly.'

****

'Work, play--at sixty our powers and tastes are what they were at seventeen. Old men in the bad old days used to renounce, retire, take to religion, spend their time reading, thinking--*thinking!*'

****

'Idiots, swine!' Bernard Marx was saying to himself, as he walked down the corridor to the lift.

****

'Now--such is progress--the old men work, the old men copulate, the old men have no time, no leisure from pleasure, not a moment to sit down and think--or if ever by some unlucky chance such a crevice of time should yawn in the solid substance of their distractions, there is always *soma*, delicious *soma*, half a gramme for a half-holiday, a gramme for a week-end, two grammes for a trip to the gorgeous East, three for a dark eternity on the moon; returning whence they find themselves on the other side of the crevice, safe on the solid ground of daily labour and distraction, scampering from feely to feely, from girl to pneumatic girl, from Electro-magnetic Golf Course to...'

****

'Go away, little girl,' shouted the D.H.C. angrily. 'Go away, little boy! Can't you see that his fordship's busy? Go and do your erotic play somewhere else.'

****

'Poor little children!' said the Controller.

****

Slowly, majestically, with a faint humming of machinery, the Conveyors moved forward, thirty-three centimetres an hour. In the red darkness glinted innumerable rubies.

Chapter IV

The lift was crowded with men from the Alpha Changing Rooms, and Lenina's entry was greeted by many friendly nods and smiles. She was a popular girl and, at one time or another, had spent a night with almost all of them.

They were dear boys, she thought, as she returned their salutations. Charming boys! Still, she did wish that George Edzel's ears weren't quite so big (perhaps he'd been given just a spot too much parathyroid at metre 328?). And looking at Benito Hoover, she couldn't help remembering that he was really *too* hairy when he took his clothes off.

Turning, with eyes a little saddened by the recollection of Benito's curly blackness, she saw in a corner the small thin body, the melancholy face of Bernard Marx.

'Bernard!' she stepped up to him. 'I was looking for you.' Her voice rang clear above the hum of the mounting lift. The others looked round curiously. 'I wanted to talk to you about our New Mexico plan.' Out of the tail of her eye she could see Benito Hoover gaping with astonishment. The gape annoyed her. 'Surprised I shouldn't be begging to go with *him* again!' she said to herself. Then aloud, and more warmly than ever, 'I'd simply *love* to come with you for a week in July,' she went on. (Anyhow, she was publicly proving her unfaithfulness to Henry. Fanny ought to be pleased, even though it was Bernard.) 'That is,' Lenina gave him her most deliciously significant smile, 'if you still want to have me.'

Bernard's pale face flushed. 'What on earth for?' she wondered, astonished, but at the same time touched by this strange tribute to her power.

'Hadn't we better talk about it somewhere else?' he stammered, looking horribly uncomfortable.

'As though I'd been saying something shocking,' thought Lenina. 'He couldn't look more upset if I'd made a dirty joke--asked him who his mother was, or something like that.'

'I mean, with all these people about...' He was choked with confusion.

Lenina's laugh was frank and wholly unmalicious. 'How funny you are!' she said; and she quite genuinely did think him funny. 'You'll give me at least a week's warning, won't you,' she went on in another tone. 'I suppose we take the Blue Pacific Rocket? Does it start from the Charing-T Tower? Or is it from Hampstead?'

Before Bernard could answer, the lift came to a standstill.

'Roof!' called a creaking voice.

The liftman was a small simian creature, dressed in the black tunic of an Epsilon-Minus Semi-Moron.

'Roof!'

He flung open the gates. The warm glory of afternoon sunlight made him start and blink his eyes. 'Oh, roof!' he repeated in a voice of rapture. He was as though suddenly and joyfully awakened from a dark annihilating stupor. 'Roof!'

He smiled up with a kind of doggily expectant adoration into the faces of his passengers. Talking and laughing together, they stepped out into the light. The liftman looked after them.

'Roof?' he said once more, questioningly.

Then a bell rang, and from the ceiling of the lift a loud-speaker began, very softly and yet very imperiously, to issue its commands.

'Go down,' it said, 'go down. Floor Eighteen. Go down, go down. Floor Eighteen. Go down, go...'

The liftman slammed the gates, touched a button and instantly dropped back into the droning twilight of the well, the twilight of his own habitual stupor.

It was warm and bright on the roof. The summer afternoon was drowsy with the hum of passing helicopters; and the deeper drone of the rocket-planes hastening, invisible, through the bright sky five or six miles overhead was like a caress on the soft air. Bernard Marx drew a deep breath. He looked up into the sky and round the blue horizon and finally down into Lenina's face.

'Isn't it beautiful!' His voice trembled a little.

She smiled at him with an expression of the most sympathetic understanding. 'Simply perfect for Obstacle Golf,' she answered rapturously. 'And now I must fly, Bernard. Henry gets cross if I keep him waiting. Let me know in good time about the date.' And waving her hand, she ran away across the wide flat roof towards the hangars. Bernard stood watching the retreating twinkle of the white stockings, the sunburnt knees vivaciously bending and unbending, again, again, and the softer rolling of those well-fitted corduroy shorts beneath the bottle-green jacket. His face wore an expression of pain.

'I should say she was pretty,' said a loud and cheery voice just behind him.

Bernard started, and looked round. The chubby red face of Benito Hoover was beaming down at him--beaming with manifest cordiality. Benito was notoriously good-natured. People said of him that he could have got through life without ever touching *soma*. The malice and bad tempers from which other people had to take holidays never afflicted him. Reality for Benito was always sunny.

'Pneumatic too. And how!' Then, in another tone, 'But, I say,' he went on, 'you do look glum! What you need is a gramme of *soma*.' Diving into his right-hand trouser-pocket, Benito produced a phial. 'One cubic centimetre cures ten gloomy... But, I say!'

Bernard had suddenly turned and rushed away.

Benito stared after him. 'What can be the matter with the fellow?' he wondered, and, shaking his head, decided that the story about the alcohol having been put into the poor chap's blood-surrogate must be true. 'Touched his brain, I suppose.'

He put away the *soma* bottle, and taking out a packet of sex-hormone chewing-gum, stuffed a plug into his cheek and walked slowly away towards the hangars, ruminating.

Henry Foster had had his machine wheeled out of its lock-up and, when Lenina arrived, was already seated in the cockpit, waiting.

'Four minutes late,' was all his comment, as she climbed in beside him. He started the engines and threw the helicopter screws into gear. The machine shot vertically into the air. Henry accelerated; the humming of the propeller shrilled from hornet to wasp, from wasp to mosquito; the speedometer showed that they were rising at the best part of two kilometres a minute. London diminished beneath them. The huge table-topped buildings were no more, in a few seconds, than a bed of geometrical mushrooms sprouting from the green of park and garden. In the midst of them, thin-stalked, a taller, slenderer fungus, the Charing-T Tower lifted towards the sky a disk of shining concrete.

Like the vague torsos of fabulous athletes, huge fleshy clouds lolled on the blue air above their heads. Out of one of them suddenly dropped a small scarlet insect, buzzing as it fell.

'There's the Red Rocket,' said Henry, 'just come in from New York.' Looking at his watch, 'Seven minutes behind time,' he added, and shook his head. 'These Atlantic services--they're really scandalously unpunctual.'

He took his foot off the accelerator. The humming of the screws overhead dropped an octave and a half, back through wasp and hornet to bumble-bee, to cockchafer, to stag-beetle. The upward rush of the machine slackened off; a moment later they were hanging motionless in the air. Henry pushed at a lever; there was a click. Slowly at first, then faster and faster, till it was a circular mist before their eyes, the propeller in front of them began to revolve. The wind of a horizontal speed whistled ever more shrilly in the stays. Henry kept his eye on the revolution-counter; when the needle touched the twelve hundred mark, he threw the helicopter screws out of gear. The machine had enough forward momentum to be able to fly on its planes.

Lenina looked down through the window in the floor between her feet. They were flying over the six kilometre zone of park-land that separated Central London from its first ring of satellite suburbs. The green was maggoty with foreshortened life. Forests of Centrifugal Bumble-puppy towers gleamed between the trees. Near Shepherd's Bush two thousand Beta-Minus mixed doubles were playing Riemann-surface tennis. A double row of Escalator Fives Courts lined the main road from Notting Hill to Willesden. In the Ealing stadium a Delta gymnastic display and community sing was in progress.

'What a hideous colour khaki is,' remarked Lenina, voicing the hypnopædic prejudices of her caste.

The buildings of the Hounslow Feely Studio covered seven and a half hectares. Near them a black and khaki army of labourers was busy revitrifying the surface of the Great West Road. One of the huge travelling crucibles was being tapped as they flew over. The molten stone poured out in a stream of dazzling incandescence across the road; the asbestos rollers came and went; at the tail of an insulated watering-cart the steam rose in white clouds.

At Brentford the Television Corporation's factory was like a small town.

'They must be changing the shift,' said Lenina.

Like aphides and ants, the leaf-green Gamma girls, the black Semi-Morons swarmed round the entrances, or stood in queues to take their places in the monorail tram-cars. Mulberry-coloured Beta-Minuses came and went among the crowd. The roof of the main building was alive with the alighting and departure of helicopters.

'My word,' said Lenina, 'I'm glad I'm not a Gamma.'

Ten minutes later they were at Stoke Poges and had started their first round of Obstacle Golf.

2

With eyes for the most part downcast and, if ever they lighted on a fellow creature, at once and furtively averted, Bernard hastened across the roof. He was like a man pursued, but pursued by enemies he does not wish to see, lest they should seem more hostile even than he had supposed, and he himself be made to feel guiltier and even more helplessly alone.

'That horrible Benito Hoover!' And yet the man had meant well enough. Which only made it, in a way, much worse. Those who meant well behaved in the same way as those who meant badly. Even Lenina was making him suffer. He remembered those weeks of timid indecision, during which he had looked and longed and despaired of ever having the courage to ask her. Dared he face the risk of being humiliated by a contemptuous refusal? But if she were to say yes, what rapture! Well, now she had said it and he was still wretched--wretched that she should have thought it such a perfect afternoon for Obstacle Golf, that she should have trotted away to join Henry Foster, that she should have found him funny for not wanting to talk of their most private affairs in public. Wretched, in a word, because she had behaved as any healthy and virtuous English girl ought to behave and not in some other, abnormal, extraordinary way.

He opened the door of his lock-up and called to a lounging couple of Delta-Minus attendants to come and push his machine out on to the roof. The hangars were staffed by a single Bokanovsky Group, and the men were twins, identically small, black and hideous. Bernard gave his orders in the sharp, rather arrogant and even offensive tone of one who does not feel himself too secure in his superiority. To have dealings with members of the lower castes was always, for Bernard, a most distressing experience. For whatever the cause (and the current gossip about the alcohol in his blood-surrogate may very likely--for accidents will happen--have been true) Bernard's physique was hardly better than that of the average Gamma. He stood eight centimetres short of the standard Alpha height and was slender in proportion. Contact with members of the lower castes always reminded him painfully of this physical inadequacy. 'I am I, and wish I wasn't'; his self-consciousness was acute and distressing. Each time he found himself looking on the level, instead of downward, into a Delta's face, he felt humiliated. Would the creature treat him with the respect due to his caste? The question haunted him. Not without reason. For Gammas, Deltas and Epsilons had been to some extent conditioned to associate corporeal mass with social superiority. Indeed, a faint hypnopædic prejudice in favour of size was universal. Hence the laughter of the women to whom he made proposals, the practical joking of his equals among the men. The mockery made him feel an outsider; and feeling an outsider he behaved like one, which increased the prejudice against him and intensified the contempt and hostility aroused by his physical defects. Which in turn increased his sense of being alien and alone. A chronic fear of being slighted made him avoid his equals, made him stand, where his inferiors were concerned, self-consciously on his dignity. How bitterly he envied men like Henry Foster and Benito Hoover! Men who never had to shout at an Epsilon to get an order obeyed; men who took their position for granted; men who moved through the caste system as a fish through the water--so utterly at home as to be unaware either of themselves or of the beneficent and comfortable element in which they had their being.

Slackly, it seemed to him, and with reluctance, the twin attendants wheeled his plane out on the roof.

'Hurry up!' said Bernard irritably. One of them glanced at him. Was that a kind of bestial derision that he detected in those blank grey eyes? 'Hurry up!' he shouted more loudly, and there was an ugly rasp in his voice.

He climbed into the plane and, a minute later was flying southwards, towards the river.

The various Bureaux of Propaganda and the College of Emotional Engineering were housed in a single sixty-story building in Fleet Street. In the basement and on the lower floors were the presses and offices of the three great London newspapers--*The Hourly Radio*, an upper-caste sheet, the pale-green *Gamma Gazette*, and, on khaki paper and in words exclusively of one syllable, *The Delta Mirror*. Then came the Bureaux of Propaganda by Television, by Feeling Picture, and by Synthetic Voice and Music respectively--twenty-two floors of them. Above were the research laboratories and the padded rooms in which the Sound-Track Writers and Synthetic Composers did their delicate work. The top eighteen floors were occupied by the College of Emotional Engineering.

Bernard landed on the roof of Propaganda House and stepped out.

'Ring down to Mr. Helmholtz Watson,' he ordered the Gamma-Plus porter, 'and tell him that Mr. Bernard Marx is waiting for him on the roof.'

He sat down and lit a cigarette.

Helmholtz Watson was writing when the message came down.

'Tell him I'm coming at once,' he said and hung up the receiver. Then, turning to his secretary, 'I'll leave you to put my things away,' he went on in the same official and impersonal tone; and, ignoring her lustrous smile, got up and walked briskly to the door.

He was a powerfully built man, deep-chested, broad-shouldered, massive, and yet quick in his movements, springy and agile. The round strong pillar of his neck supported a beautifully shaped head. His hair was dark and curly, his features strongly marked. In a forcible emphatic way, he was handsome and looked, as his secretary was never tired of repeating, every centimetre an Alpha-Plus. By profession he was a lecturer at the College of Emotional Engineering (Department of Writing) and in the intervals of his educational activities, a working Emotional Engineer. He wrote regularly for *The Hourly Radio*, composed feely scenarios, and had the happiest knack for slogans and hypnopædic rhymes.

'Able,' was the verdict of his superiors. 'Perhaps' (and they would shake their heads, would significantly lower their voices) 'a little *too* able.'

Yes, a little too able; they were right. A mental excess had produced in Helmholtz Watson effects very similar to those which, in Bernard Marx, were the result of a physical defect. Too little bone and brawn had isolated Bernard from his fellow men, and the sense of this apartness, being, by all the current standards, a mental excess, became in its turn a cause of wider separation. That which had made Helmholtz so uncomfortably aware of being himself and all alone was too much ability. What the two men shared was the knowledge that they were individuals. But whereas the physically defective Bernard had suffered all his life from the consciousness of being separate, it was only quite recently that, grown aware of his mental excess, Helmholtz Watson had also become aware of his difference from the people who surrounded him. This Escalator-Squash champion, this indefatigable lover (it was said that he had had six hundred and forty different girls in under four years), this admirable committee man and best mixer had realized quite suddenly that sport, women, communal activities were only, so far as he was concerned, second bests. Really, and at the bottom, he was interested in something else. But in what? In what? That was the problem which Bernard had come to discuss with him--or rather, since it was always Helmholtz who did all the talking, to listen to his friend discussing, yet once more.

Three charming girls from the Bureau of Propaganda by Synthetic Voice waylaid him as he stepped out of the lift.

'Oh, Helmholtz darling, *do* come and have a picnic supper with us on Exmoor.' They clung round him imploringly.

He shook his head, he pushed his way through them. 'No, no.'

'We're not inviting any other man.'

But Helmholtz remained unshaken even by this delightful promise. 'No,' he repeated, 'I'm busy.' And he held resolutely on his course. The girls trailed after him. It was not till he had actually climbed into Bernard's plane and slammed the door that they gave up pursuit. Not without reproaches.

'These women!' he said, as the machine rose into the air. 'These women!' And he shook his head, he frowned. 'Too awful.' Bernard hypocritically agreed, wishing, as he spoke the words, that he could have as many girls as Helmholtz did, and with as little trouble. He was seized with a sudden urgent need to boast. 'I'm taking Lenina Crowne to New Mexico with me,' he said in a tone as casual as he could make it.

'Are you?' said Helmholtz, with a total absence of interest. Then after a little pause, 'This last week or two,' he went on, 'I've been cutting all my committees and all my girls. You can't imagine what a hullabaloo they've been making about it at the College. Still, it's been worth it, I think. The effects...' He hesitated. 'Well, they're odd, they're very odd.'

A physical shortcoming could produce a kind of mental excess. The process, it seemed, was reversible. Mental excess could produce, for its own purposes, the voluntary blindness and deafness of deliberate solitude, the artificial impotence of asceticism.

The rest of the short flight was accomplished in silence. When they had arrived and were comfortably stretched out on the pneumatic sofas in Bernard's room, Helmholtz began again.

Speaking very slowly, 'Did you ever feel,' he asked, 'as though you had something inside you that was only waiting for you to give it a chance to come out? Some sort of extra power that you aren't using--you know, like all the water that goes down the falls instead of through the turbines?' He looked at Bernard questioningly.

'You mean all the emotions one might be feeling if things were different?'

Helmholtz shook his head. 'Not quite. I'm thinking of a queer feeling I sometimes get, a feeling that I've got something important to say and the power to say it--only I don't know what it is, and I can't make any use of the power. If there was some different way of writing... Or else something else to write about...' He was silent; then, 'You see,' he went on at last, 'I'm pretty good at inventing phrases--you know, the sort of words that suddenly make you jump, almost as though you'd sat on a pin, they seem so new and exciting even though they're about something hypnopædically obvious. But that doesn't seem enough. It's not enough for the phrases to be good; what you make with them ought to be good too.'

'But your things are good, Helmholtz.'

'Oh, as far as they go.' Helmholtz shrugged his shoulders. 'But they go such a little way. They aren't important enough, somehow. I feel I could do something much more important. Yes, and more intense, more violent. But what? What is there more important to say? And how can one be violent about the sort of things one's expected to write about? Words can be like X-rays, if you use them properly--they'll go through anything. You read and you're pierced. That's one of the things I try to teach my students--how to write piercingly. But what on earth's the good of being pierced by an article about a Community Sing, or the latest improvement in scent organs? Besides, can you make words really piercing--you know, like the very hardest X-rays--when you're writing about that sort of thing? Can you say something about nothing? That's what it finally boils down to. I try and I try...'

'Hush!' said Bernard suddenly, and lifted a warning finger; they listened. 'I believe there's somebody at the door,' he whispered.

Helmholtz got up, tiptoed across the room, and with a sharp quick movement flung the door wide open. There was, of course, nobody there.

'I'm sorry,' said Bernard, feeling and looking uncomfortably foolish. 'I suppose I've got things on my nerves a bit. When people are suspicious with you, you start being suspicious with them.'

He passed his hand across his eyes, he sighed, his voice became plaintive. He was justifying himself. 'If you knew what I'd had to put up with recently,' he said almost tearfully--and the uprush of his self-pity was like a fountain suddenly released. 'If you only knew!'

Helmholtz Watson listened with a certain sense of discomfort. 'Poor little Bernard!' he said to himself. But at the same time he felt rather ashamed for his friend. He wished Bernard would show a little more pride.

Chapter V

By eight o'clock the light was failing. The loud-speakers in the tower of the Stoke Poges Club House began, in a more than human tenor, to announce the closing of the courses. Lenina and Henry abandoned their game and walked back towards the Club. From the grounds of the Internal and External Secretion Trust came the lowing of those thousands of cattle which provided, with their hormones and their milk, the raw materials for the great factory at Farnham Royal.

An incessant buzzing of helicopters filled the twilight. Every two and a half minutes a bell and the screech of whistles announced the departure of one of the light monorail trains which carried the lower-caste golfers back from their separate course to the metropolis.

Lenina and Henry climbed into their machine and started off. At eight hundred feet Henry slowed down the helicopter screws, and they hung for a minute or two poised above the fading landscape. The forest of Burnham Beeches stretched like a great pool of darkness towards the bright shore of the western sky. Crimson at the horizon, the last of the sunset faded, through orange, upwards into yellow and a pale watery green. Northwards, beyond and above the trees, the Internal and External Secretions factory glared with a fierce electric brilliance from every window of its twenty stories. Beneath them lay the buildings of the Golf Club--the huge lower-caste barracks and, on the other side of a dividing wall, the smaller houses reserved for Alpha and Beta members. The approaches to the monorail station were black with the ant-like pullulation of lower-caste activity. From under the glass vault a lighted train shot out into the open. Following its south-easterly course across the dark plain their eyes were drawn to the majestic buildings of the Slough Crematorium. For the safety of night-flying planes, its four tall chimneys were flood-lighted and tipped with crimson danger signals. It was a landmark.

'Why do the smoke-stacks have those things like balconies round them?' enquired Lenina.

'Phosphorus recovery,' explained Henry telegraphically. 'On their way up the chimney the gases go through four separate treatments. P_2O_5 used to go right out of circulation every time they cremated some one. Now they recover over ninety-eight per cent. of it. More than a kilo and a half per adult corpse. Which makes the best part of four hundred tons of phosphorus every year from England alone.' Henry spoke with a happy pride, rejoicing whole-heartedly in the achievement, as though it had been his own. 'Fine to think we can go on being socially useful even after we're dead. Making plants grow.'

Lenina, meanwhile, had turned her eyes away and was looking perpendicularly downwards at the monorail station. 'Fine,' she agreed. 'But queer that Alphas and Betas won't make any more plants grow than those nasty little Gammas and Deltas and Epsilons down there.'

'All men are physico-chemically equal,' said Henry sententiously. 'Besides, even Epsilons perform indispensable services.'

'Even an Epsilon...' Lenina suddenly remembered an occasion when, as a little girl at school, she had woken up in the middle of the night and become aware, for the first time, of the whispering that had haunted all her sleeps. She saw again the beam of moonlight, the row of small white beds; heard once more the soft, soft voice that said (the words were there, unforgotten, unforgettable after so many night-long repetitions): 'Every one works for every one else. We can't do without any one. Even Epsilons are useful. We couldn't do without Epsilons. Every one works for every one else. We can't do without any one...' Lenina remembered her first shock of fear and surprise; her speculations through half a wakeful hour; and then, under the influence of those endless repetitions, the gradual soothing of her mind, the soothing, the smoothing, the stealthy creeping of sleep....

'I suppose Epsilons don't really mind being Epsilons,' she said aloud.

'Of course they don't. How can they? They don't know what it's like being anything else. We'd mind, of course. But then we've been differently conditioned. Besides, we start with a different heredity.'

'I'm glad I'm not an Epsilon,' said Lenina, with conviction.

'And if you were an Epsilon,' said Henry, 'your conditioning would have made you no less thankful that you weren't a Beta or an Alpha.' He put his forward propeller into gear and headed the machine towards London. Behind them, in the west, the crimson and orange were almost faded; a dark bank of cloud had crept into the zenith. As they flew over the Crematorium, the plane shot upwards on the column of hot air rising from the chimneys, only to fall as suddenly when it passed into the descending chill beyond.

'What a marvellous switchback!' Lenina laughed delightedly.

But Henry's tone was almost, for a moment, melancholy. 'Do you know what that switchback was?' he said. 'It was some human being finally and definitely disappearing. Going up in a squirt of hot gas. It would be curious to know who it was--a man or a woman, an Alpha or an Epsilon....' He sighed. Then, in a resolutely cheerful voice, 'Anyhow,' he concluded, 'there's one thing we can be certain of; whoever he may have been, he was happy when he was alive. Everybody's happy now.'

'Yes, everybody's happy now,' echoed Lenina. They had heard the words repeated a hundred and fifty times every night for twelve years.

Landing on the roof of Henry's forty-story apartment house in Westminster, they went straight down to the dining-hall. There, in a loud and cheerful company, they ate an excellent meal. *Soma* was served with the coffee. Lenina took two half-gramme tablets and Henry three. At twenty past nine they walked across the street to the newly opened Westminster Abbey Cabaret. It was a night almost without clouds, moonless and starry; but of this on the whole depressing fact Lenina and Henry were fortunately unaware. The electric sky-signs effectively shut off the outer darkness. 'CALVIN STOPES AND HIS SIXTEEN SEXOPHONISTS.' From the façade of the new Abbey the giant letters invitingly glared. 'LONDON'S FINEST SCENT AND COLOUR ORGAN. ALL THE LATEST SYNTHETIC MUSIC.'

They entered. The air seemed hot and somehow breathless with the scent of ambergris and sandalwood. On the domed ceiling of the hall, the colour organ had momentarily painted a tropical sunset. The Sixteen Sexophonists were playing an old favourite: 'There ain't no Bottle in all the world like that dear little Bottle of mine.' Four hundred couples were five-stepping round the polished floor. Lenina and Henry were soon the four hundred and first. The sexophones wailed like melodious cats under the moon, moaned in the alto and tenor registers as though the little death were upon them. Rich with a wealth of harmonics, their tremulous chorus mounted towards a climax, louder and ever louder--until at last, with a wave of his hand, the conductor let loose the final shattering note of ethermusic and blew the sixteen merely human blowers clean out of existence. Thunder in A flat major. And then, in all but silence, in all but darkness, there followed a gradual deturgescence, a *diminuendo* sliding gradually, through quarter tones, down, down to a faintly whispered dominant chord that lingered on (while the five-four rhythms still pulsed below) charging the darkened seconds with an intense expectancy. And at last expectancy was fulfilled. There was a sudden explosive sunrise, and simultaneously, the Sixteen burst into song:

Bottle	of	mine,	it's	you	I've	always	wanted!
Bottle	of	mine,	why	was	I	ever	decanted?
Skies		are	blue	inside		of	you,
The		weather's			always		fine;
For							

There	ain't	no	Bottle	in	all	the	world

Like that dear little Bottle of mine.

Five-stepping with the other four hundred round and round Westminster Abbey, Lenina and Henry were yet dancing in another world--the warm, the richly coloured, the infinitely friendly world of *soma*-holiday. How kind, how good-looking, how delightfully amusing every one was! 'Bottle of mine, it's you I've always wanted...' But Lenina and Henry had what they wanted... They were inside, here and now--safely inside with the fine weather, the perennially blue sky. And when, exhausted, the Sixteen had laid by their saxophones and the Synthetic Music apparatus was producing the very latest in slow Malthusian Blues, they might have been twin embryos gently rocking together on the waves of a bottled ocean of blood-surrogate.

'Good-night, dear friends. Good-night, dear friends.' The loud-speakers veiled their commands in a genial and musical politeness. Good-night, dear friends....'

Obediently, with all the others, Lenina and Henry left the building. The depressing stars had travelled quite some way across the heavens. But though the separating screen of the sky-signs had now to a great extent dissolved, the two young people still retained their happy ignorance of the night.

Swallowed half an hour before closing time, that second dose of *soma* had raised a quite impenetrable wall between the actual universe and their minds. Bottled, they crossed the street; bottled, they took the lift up to Henry's room on the twenty-eighth floor. And yet, bottled as she was, and in spite of that second gramme of *soma*, Lenina did not forget to take all the contraceptive precautions prescribed by the regulations. Years of intensive hypnopædia and, from twelve to seventeen, Malthusian drill three times a week had made the taking of these precautions almost as automatic and inevitable as blinking.

'Oh, and that reminds me,' she said, as she came back from the bathroom, 'Fanny Crowne wants to know where you found that lovely green morocco-surrogate cartridge belt you gave me.'

§ 2

Alternate Thursdays were Bernard's Solidarity Service days. After an early dinner at the Aphroditæum (to which Helmholtz had recently been elected under Rule Two) he took leave of his friend and, hailing a taxi on the roof, told the man to fly to the Fordson Community Singery. The machine rose a couple of hundred metres, then headed eastwards, and as it turned, there before Bernard's eyes, gigantically beautiful, was the Singery. Flood-lighted, its three hundred and twenty metres of white Carrara-surrogate gleamed with a snowy incandescence over Ludgate Hill; at each of the four corners of its helicopter platform an immense T shone crimson against the night, and from the mouths of twenty-four vast golden trumpets rumbled a solemn synthetic music.

'Damn, I'm late,' Bernard said to himself as he first caught sight of Big Henry, the Singery clock. And sure enough, as he was paying off his cab, Big Henry sounded the hour. 'Ford,' sang out an immense bass voice from all the golden trumpets. 'Ford, Ford, Ford...' Nine times. Bernard ran for the lift.

The great auditorium for Ford's Day celebrations and other massed Community Sings was at the bottom of the building. Above it, a hundred to each floor, were the seven thousand rooms used by Solidarity Groups for their fortnightly services. Bernard dropped down to floor thirty-three, hurried along the corridor, stood hesitating for a moment outside Room 3210, then, having wound himself up, opened the door and walked in.

Thank Ford! he was not the last. Three chairs of the twelve arranged round the circular table were still unoccupied. He slipped into the nearest of them as inconspicuously as he could and prepared to frown at the yet later comers whenever they should arrive.

Turning towards him, 'What were you playing this afternoon?' the girl on his left enquired. 'Obstacle, or Electro-magnetic?'

Bernard looked at her (Ford! it was Morgana Rothschild) and blushingly had to admit that he had been playing neither. Morgana stared at him with astonishment. There was an awkward silence.

Then pointedly she turned away and addressed herself to the more sporting man on her left.

'A good beginning for a Solidarity Service,' thought Bernard miserably, and foresaw for himself yet another failure to achieve atonement. If only he had given himself time to look round instead of scuttling for the nearest chair! He could have sat between Fifi Bradlaugh and Joanna Diesel. Instead of which he had gone and blindly planted himself next to Morgana. *Morgana!* Ford! Those black eyebrows of hers--that eyebrow, rather--for they met above the nose. Ford! And on his right was Clara Deterding. True, Clara's eyebrows didn't meet. But she was really *too* pneumatic. Whereas Fifi and Joanna were absolutely right. Plump, blonde, not too large... And it was that great lout, Tom Kawaguchi, who now took the seat between them.

The last arrival was Sarojini Engels.

'You're late,' said the President of the Group severely. 'Don't let it happen again.'

Sarojini apologized and slid into her place between Jim Bokanovsky and Herbert Bakunin. The group was now complete, the solidarity circle perfect and without flaw. Man, woman, man, in a ring of endless alternation round the table. Twelve of them ready to be made one, waiting to come together, to be fused, to lose their twelve separate identities in a larger being.

The President stood up, made the sign of the T and, switching on the synthetic music, let loose the soft indefatigable beating of drums and a choir of instruments--near-wind and super-string--that plangently repeated and repeated the brief and unescapably haunting melody of the first Solidarity Hymn. Again, again--and it was not the ear that heard the pulsing rhythm, it was the midriff; the wail and clang of those recurring harmonies haunted, not the mind, but the yearning bowels of compassion.

The President made another sign of the T and sat down. The service had begun. The dedicated *soma* tablets were placed in the centre of the dinner table. The loving cup of strawberry ice-cream *soma* was passed from hand to hand and, with the formula, 'I drink to my annihilation,' twelve times quaffed. Then to the accompaniment of the synthetic orchestra the First Solidarity Hymn was sung.

Ford,	we	are	twelve;	oh,	make	us	one,
Like	drops	within	the		Social		River;
Oh,	make	us	now		together		run

As swiftly as thy shining Flivver.

Twelve yearning stanzas. And then the loving cup was passed a second time. 'I drink to the Greater Being' was now the formula. All drank. Tirelessly the music played. The drums beat. The crying and clashing of the harmonies were an obsession in the melted bowels. The Second Solidarity Hymn was sung.

Come,		Greater		Being,		Social		Friend,
Annihilating								Twelve-in-One!
We	long	to	die,	for	when		we	end,

Our larger life has but begun.

Again twelve stanzas. By this time the *soma* had begun to work. Eyes shone, cheeks were flushed, the inner light of universal benevolence broke out on every face in happy, friendly smiles. Even Bernard felt himself a little melted. When Morgana Rothschild turned and beamed at him, he did his best to beam back. But the eyebrow, that black two-in-one--alas, it was still there; he couldn't ignore it, couldn't, however hard he tried. The melting hadn't gone far enough. Perhaps if he had been sitting between Fifi and Joanna... For the third time the loving cup went round. 'I drink to the imminence of His Coming,' said Morgana Rothschild, whose turn it happened to be to initiate the circular rite. Her tone was loud, exultant. She drank and passed the cup to Bernard. 'I drink to the imminence of His Coming,' he repeated, with a sincere attempt to feel that the coming was imminent; but the eyebrow continued to haunt him, and the Coming, so far as he was concerned, was horribly remote. He drank and handed the cup to Clara Deterding. 'It'll be a failure again,' he said to himself. 'I know it will.' But he went on doing his best to beam.

The loving cup had made its circuit. Lifting his hand, the President gave a signal; the chorus broke out into the third Solidarity Hymn.

Feel	how		the		Greater		Being	comes!
Rejoice		and,		in		rejoicings,		die!
Melt	in		the		music	of	the	drums!

For I am you and you are I.

As verse succeeded verse the voices thrilled with an ever intenser excitement. The sense of the Coming's imminence was like an electric tension in the air. The President switched off the music and, with the final note of the final stanza, there was absolute silence--the silence of stretched expectancy, quivering and creeping with a galvanic life. The President reached out his hand; and suddenly a Voice, a deep strong Voice, more musical than any merely human voice, richer, warmer, more vibrant with love and yearning and compassion, a wonderful, mysterious, supernatural Voice spoke from above their heads. Very slowly, 'Oh, Ford, Ford, Ford,' it said diminishingly and on a descending scale. A sensation of warmth radiated thrillingly out from the solar plexus to every extremity of the bodies of those who listened; tears came into their eyes; their hearts, their bowels seemed to move within them, as though with an independent life. 'Ford!' they were melting, 'Ford!' dissolved, dissolved. Then, in another tone, suddenly, startlingly. 'Listen!' trumpeted the Voice. 'Listen!' They listened. After a pause, sunk to a whisper, but a whisper, somehow, more penetrating than the loudest cry. 'The feet of the Greater Being,' it went on, and repeated the words: 'The feet of the Greater Being.' The whisper almost expired. 'The feet of the Greater Being are on the stairs.' And once more there was silence; and the expectancy, momentarily relaxed, was stretched again, tauter, tauter, almost to the tearing point. The feet of the Greater Being--oh, they heard them, they heard them, coming softly down the stairs, coming nearer and nearer down the invisible stairs. The feet of the Greater Being. And suddenly the tearing point was reached. Her eyes staring, her lips parted, Morgana Rothschild sprang to her feet.

'I hear him,' she cried. 'I hear him.'

'He's coming,' shouted Sarojini Engels.

'Yes, he's coming, I hear him.' Fifi Bradlaugh and Tom Kawaguchi rose simultaneously to their feet.

'Oh, oh, oh!' Joanna inarticulately testified.

'He's coming!' yelled Jim Bokanovsky.

The President leaned forward and, with a touch, released a delirium of cymbals and blown brass, a fever of tom-tomming.

'Oh, he's coming!' screamed Clara Deterding. 'Aie!' and it was as though she were having her throat cut.

Feeling that it was time for him to do something, Bernard also jumped up and shouted: 'I hear him; he's coming.' But it wasn't true. He heard nothing and, for him, nobody was coming. Nobody--in spite of the music, in spite of the mounting excitement. But he waved his arms, he shouted with the best of them; and when the others began to jig and stamp and shuffle, he also jigged and shuffled.

Round they went, a circular procession of dancers, each with hands on the hips of the dancer preceding, round and round, shouting in unison, stamping to the rhythm of the music with their feet, beating it, beating it out with hands on the buttocks in front; twelve pairs of hands beating as one; as one, twelve buttocks slabbily resounding. Twelve as one, twelve as one. 'I hear him, I hear him coming.' The music quickened; faster beat the feet, faster, faster fell the rhythmic hands. And all at once a great synthetic bass boomed out the words which announced the approaching atonement and final consummation of solidarity, the coming of the Twelve-in-One, the incarnation of the Greater Being. 'Orgy-porgy,' it sang, while the tom-toms continued to beat their feverish tattoo:

Orgy-porgy,			Ford		and		fun,
Kiss	the		girls	and	make	them	One.
Boys	at		one	with	girls	at	peace;

Orgy-porgy gives release.

'Orgy-porgy,' the dancers caught up the liturgical refrain, 'Orgy-porgy, Ford and fun, kiss the girls...' And as they sang, the lights began slowly to fade--to fade and at the same time to grow warmer, richer, redder, until at last they were dancing in the crimson twilight of an Embryo Store. 'Orgy-Porgy...' In their blood-coloured and foetal darkness the dancers continued for a while to circulate, to beat and beat out the indefatigable rhythm. 'Orgy-porgy...' Then the circle wavered, broke, fell in partial disintegration on the ring of couches which surrounded--circle enclosing circle-- the table and its planetary chairs. 'Orgy-porgy...' Tenderly the deep Voice crooned and cooed; in the red twilight it was as though some enormous negro dove were hovering benevolently over the now prone or supine dancers.

****

They were standing on the roof; Big Henry had just sung eleven. The night was calm and warm.

'Wasn't it wonderful?' said Fifi Bradlaugh. 'Wasn't it simply wonderful?' She looked at Bernard with an expression of rapture, but of rapture in which there was no trace of agitation or excitement--for to be excited is still to be unsatisfied. Hers was the calm ecstasy of achieved consummation, the peace, not of mere vacant satiety and nothingness, but of balanced life, of energies at rest and in equilibrium. A rich and living peace. For the Solidarity Service had given as well as taken, drawn off only to replenish. She was full, she was made perfect, she was still more than merely herself. 'Didn't you think it was wonderful?' she insisted, looking into Bernard's face with those supernaturally shining eyes.

'Yes, I thought it was wonderful,' he lied and looked away; the sight of her transfigured face was at once an accusation and an ironical reminder of his own separateness. He was as miserably isolated now as he had been when the service began--more isolated by reason of his unreplenished emptiness, his dead satiety. Separate and unatoned, while the others were being fused into the Greater Being; alone even in Morgana's embrace--much more alone, indeed, more hopelessly himself than he had ever been in his life before. He had emerged from that crimson twilight into the common electric glare with a self-consciousness intensified to the pitch of agony. He was utterly miserable, and perhaps (her shining eyes accused him), perhaps it was his own fault. 'Quite wonderful,' he repeated; but the only thing he could think of was Morgana's eyebrow.

Chapter VI

Odd, odd, *odd*, was Lenina's verdict on Bernard Marx. So odd, indeed, that in the course of the succeeding weeks she had wondered more than once whether she shouldn't change her mind about the New Mexico holiday, and go instead to the North Pole with Benito Hoover. The trouble was that she knew the North Pole, had been there with George Edzel only last summer, and what was more, found it pretty grim. Nothing to do, and the hotel too hopelessly old-fashioned--no television laid on in the bedrooms, no scent organ, only the most putrid synthetic music, and not more than twenty-five Escalator-Squash Courts for over two hundred guests. No, decidedly she couldn't face the North Pole again. Added to which, she had only been to America once before. And even then, how inadequately! A cheap week-end in New York--had it been with Jean-Jacques Habibullah or Bokanovsky Jones? She couldn't remember. Anyhow, it was of absolutely no importance. The prospect of flying West again, and for a whole week, was very inviting. Moreover, for at least three days of that week they would be in the Savage Reservation. Not more than half a dozen people in the whole Centre had ever been inside a Savage Reservation. As an Alpha-Plus psychologist, Bernard was one of the few men she knew entitled to a permit. For Lenina, the opportunity was unique. And yet, so unique also was Bernard's oddness, that she had hesitated to take it, had actually thought of risking the Pole again with funny old Benito. At least Benito was normal. Whereas Bernard...

'Alcohol in his blood-surrogate,' was Fanny's explanation of every eccentricity. But Henry, with whom, one evening when they were in bed together, Lenina had rather anxiously discussed her new lover, Henry had compared poor Bernard to a rhinoceros.

'You can't teach a rhinoceros tricks,' he had explained in his brief and vigorous style. 'Some men are almost rhinoceroses; they don't respond properly to conditioning. Poor devils! Bernard's one of them. Luckily for him, he's pretty good at his job. Otherwise the Director would never have kept him. 'However,' he added consolingly, 'I think he's pretty harmless.'

Pretty harmless, perhaps; but also pretty disquieting. That mania, to start with, for doing things in private. Which meant, in practice, not doing anything at all. For what was there that one *could* do in private. (Apart, of course, from going to bed: but one couldn't do that all the time.) Yes, what *was* there? Precious little. The first afternoon they went out together was particularly fine. Lenina had suggested a swim at the Torquay Country Club followed by dinner at the Oxford Union. But Bernard thought there would be too much of a crowd. Then what about a round of Electro-magnetic Golf at St. Andrews? But again, no: Bernard considered that Electro-magnetic Golf was a waste of time.

'Then what's time for?' asked Lenina in some astonishment.

Apparently, for going walks in the Lake District; for that was what he now proposed. Land on the top of Skiddaw and walk for a couple of hours in the heather. 'Alone with you, Lenina.'

'But, Bernard, we shall be alone all night.'

Bernard blushed and looked away. 'I meant, alone for talking,' he mumbled.

'Talking? But what about?' Walking and talking--that seemed a very odd way of spending an afternoon.

In the end she persuaded him, much against his will, to fly over to Amsterdam to see the Semi-Demi-Finals of the Women's Heavyweight Wrestling Championship.

'In a crowd,' he grumbled. 'As usual.' He remained obstinately gloomy the whole afternoon; wouldn't talk to Lenina's friends (of whom they met dozens in the ice-cream *soma* bar between the wrestling bouts); and in spite of his misery absolutely refused to take the half-gramme raspberry sundae which she pressed upon him. 'I'd rather be myself,' he said. 'Myself and nasty. Not somebody else, however jolly.'

'A gramme in time saves nine,' said Lenina, producing a bright treasure of sleep-taught wisdom.

Bernard pushed away the proffered glass impatiently.

'Now don't lose your temper,' she said. 'Remember, one cubic centimetre cures ten gloomy sentiments.'

'Oh, for Ford's sake, be quiet!' he shouted.

Lenina shrugged her shoulders. 'A gramme is always better than a damn,' she concluded with dignity, and drank the sundae herself.

On their way back across the Channel, Bernard insisted on stopping his propeller and hovering on his helicopter screws within a hundred feet of the waves. The weather had taken a change for the worse; a south-westerly wind had sprung up, the sky was cloudy.

'Look,' he commanded.

'But it's horrible,' said Lenina, shrinking back from the window. She was appalled by the rushing emptiness of the night, by the black foam-flecked water heaving beneath them, by the pale face of the moon, so haggard and distracted among the hastening clouds. 'Let's turn on the radio. Quick!' She reached for the dialling knob on the dash-board and turned it at random.

'...skies are blue inside of you,' sang sixteen tremoloing falsettos, 'the weather's always...'

Then a hiccough and silence. Bernard had switched off the current.

'I want to look at the sea in peace,' he said. 'One can't even look with that beastly noise going on.'

'But it's lovely. And I don't want to look.'

'But I do,' he insisted. 'It makes me feel as though...' he hesitated, searching for words with which to express himself, 'as though I were more *me*, if you see what I mean. More on my own, not so completely a part of something else. Not just a cell in the social body. Doesn't it make you feel like that, Lenina?'

But Lenina was crying. 'It's horrible, it's horrible,' she kept repeating. 'And how can you talk like that about not wanting to be a part of the social body? After all, every one works for every one else. We can't do without any one. Even Epsilons...'

'Yes, I know,' said Bernard derisively. '"Even Epsilons are useful"! So am I. And I damned well wish I weren't!'

Lenina was shocked by his blasphemy. 'Bernard!' she protested in a voice of amazed distress. 'How can you?'

In a different key, 'How can I?' he repeated meditatively. 'No, the real problem is: How is it that I can't, or rather-- because, after all, I know quite well why I can't--what would it be like if I could, if I were free--not enslaved by my conditioning.'

'But, Bernard, you're saying the most awful things.'

'Don't you wish you were free, Lenina?'

'I don't know what you mean. I am free. Free to have the most wonderful time. Everybody's happy nowadays.'

He laughed, 'Yes, "Everybody's happy nowadays." We begin giving the children that at five. But wouldn't you like to be free to be happy in some other way, Lenina? In your own way, for example; not in everybody else's way.'

'I don't know what you mean,' she repeated. Then, turning to him, 'Oh, do let's go back, Bernard,' she besought; 'I do so hate it here.'

'Don't you like being with me?'

'But of course, Bernard! It's this horrible place.'

'I thought we'd be more... more *together* here--with nothing but the sea and moon. More together than in that crowd, or even in my rooms. Don't you understand that?'

'I don't understand anything,' she said with decision, determined to preserve her incomprehension intact. 'Nothing. Least of all,' she continued in another tone, 'why you don't take *soma* when you have these dreadful ideas of yours. You'd forget all about them. And instead of feeling miserable, you'd be jolly. *So* jolly,' she repeated and smiled, for all the puzzled anxiety in her eyes, with what was meant to be an inviting and voluptuous cajolery.

He looked at her in silence, his face unresponsive and very grave--looked at her intently. After a few seconds Lenina's eyes flinched away; she uttered a nervous little laugh, tried to think of something to say and couldn't. The silence prolonged itself.

When Bernard spoke at last, it was in a small tired voice. 'All right then,' he said, 'we'll go back.' And stepping hard on the accelerator, he sent the machine rocketing up into the sky. At four thousand he started his propeller. They flew in silence for a minute or two. Then, suddenly, Bernard began to laugh. Rather oddly, Lenina thought; but still, it was laughter.

'Feeling better?' she ventured to ask.

For answer, he lifted one hand from the controls and, slipping his arm round her, began to fondle her breasts.

'Thank Ford,' she said to herself, 'he's all right again.'

Half an hour later they were back in his rooms. Bernard swallowed four tablets of *soma* at a gulp, turned on the radio and television and began to undress.

'Well,' Lenina enquired, with significant archness when they met next afternoon on the roof, 'did you think it was fun yesterday?'

Bernard nodded. They climbed into the plane. A little jolt, and they were off.

'Every one says I'm awfully pneumatic,' said Lenina reflectively, patting her own legs.

'Awfully.' But there was an expression of pain in Bernard's eyes. 'Like meat,' he was thinking.

She looked up with a certain anxiety. 'But you don't think I'm *too* plump, do you?'

He shook his head. Like so much meat.

'You think I'm all right.' Another nod. 'In every way?'

'Perfect,' he said aloud. And inwardly, 'She thinks of herself that way. She doesn't mind being meat.'

Lenina smiled triumphantly. But her satisfaction was premature.

'All the same,' he went on, after a little pause, 'I still rather wish it had all ended differently.'

'Differently?' Were there other endings?

'I didn't want it to end with our going to bed,' he specified.

Lenina was astonished.

'Not at once, not the first day.'

'But then what...?'

He began to talk a lot of incomprehensible and dangerous nonsense. Lenina did her best to stop the ears of her mind; but every now and then a phrase would insist on becoming audible. '...to try the effect of arresting my impulses,' she heard him say. The words seemed to touch a spring in her mind.

'Never put off till to-morrow the fun you can have to-day,' she said gravely.

'Two hundred repetitions, twice a week from fourteen to sixteen and a half,' was all his comment. The mad bad talk rambled on. 'I want to know what passion is,' she heard him saying. 'I want to feel something strongly.'

'When the individual feels, the community reels,' Lenina pronounced.

'Well, why shouldn't it reel a bit?'

'Bernard!'

But Bernard remained unabashed.

'Adults intellectually and during working hours,' he went on. 'Infants where feeling and desire are concerned.'

'Our Ford loved infants.'

Ignoring the interruption, 'It suddenly struck me the other day,' continued Bernard, 'that it might be possible to be an adult all the time.'

'I don't understand.' Lenina's tone was firm.

'I know you don't. And that's why we went to bed together yesterday--like infants--instead of being adults and waiting.'

'But it was fun,' Lenina insisted. 'Wasn't it?'

'Oh, the greatest fun,' he answered, but in a voice so mournful, with an expression so profoundly miserable, that Lenina felt all her triumph suddenly evaporate. Perhaps he had found her too plump, after all.

'I told you so,' was all that Fanny said, when Lenina came and made her confidences. 'It's the alcohol they put in his surrogate.'

'All the same,' Lenina insisted. 'I do like him. He has such awfully nice hands. And the way he moves his shoulders--that's very attractive.' She sighed. 'But I wish he weren't so odd.'

§ 2

Halting for a moment outside the door of the Director's room, Bernard drew a deep breath and squared his shoulders, bracing himself to meet the dislike and disapproval which he was certain of finding within. He knocked and entered.

'A permit for you to initial, Director,' he said as airily as possible, and laid the paper on the writing-table.

The Director glanced at him sourly. But the stamp of the World Controller's Office was at the head of the paper and the signature of Mustapha Mond, bold and black, across the bottom. Everything was perfectly in order. The Director had no choice. He pencilled his initials--two small pale letters abject at the feet of Mustapha Mond----and was about to return the paper without a word of comment or genial Ford-speed, when his eye was caught by something written in the body of the permit.

'For the New Mexican Reservation?' he said, and his tone, the face he lifted to Bernard, expressed a kind of agitated astonishment.

Surprised by his surprise, Bernard nodded. There was a silence.

The Director leaned back in his chair, frowning. 'How long ago was it?' he said, speaking more to himself than to Bernard. 'Twenty years, I suppose. Nearer twenty-five. I must have been your age...' He sighed and shook his head.

Bernard felt extremely uncomfortable. A man so conventional, so scrupulously correct as the Director--and to commit so gross a solecism! It made him want to hide his face, to run out of the room. Not that he himself saw anything intrinsically objectionable in people talking about the remote past; that was one of those hypnopædic prejudices he had (so he imagined) completely got rid of. What made him feel shy was the knowledge that the Director disapproved--disapproved and yet had been betrayed into doing the forbidden thing. Under what inward compulsion? Through his discomfort Bernard eagerly listened.

'I had the same idea as you,' the Director was saying. 'Wanted to have a look at the savages. Got a permit for New Mexico and went there for my summer holiday. With the girl I was having at the moment. She was a Beta-Minus, and I think' (he shut his eyes). 'I think she had yellow hair. Anyhow, she was pneumatic, particularly pneumatic; I remember that. Well, we went there, and we looked at the savages, and we rode about on horses and all that. And then--it was almost the last day of my leave--then... well, she got lost. We'd gone riding up one of those revolting mountains, and it was horribly hot and oppressive, and after lunch we went to sleep. Or at least I did. She must have gone for a walk, alone. At any rate, when I woke up, she wasn't there. And the most frightful thunderstorm I've ever seen was just bursting on us. And it poured and roared and flashed; and the horses broke loose and ran away; and I fell down, trying to catch them, and hurt my knee, so that I could hardly walk. Still, I searched and I shouted and I searched. But there was no sign of her. Then I thought she must have gone back to the rest-house by herself. So I crawled down into the valley by the way we had come. My knee was agonizingly painful, and I'd lost my *soma*. It took me hours. I didn't get back to the rest-house till after midnight. And she wasn't there; she wasn't there,' the Director repeated. There was a silence. 'Well,' he resumed at last, 'the next day there was a search. But we couldn't find her. She must have fallen into a gulley somewhere; or been eaten by a mountain lion. Ford knows. Anyhow it was horrible. It upset me very much at the time. More than it ought to have done, I dare say. Because, after all, it's the sort of accident that might have happened to any one; and, of course, the social body persists although the component cells may change.' But this sleep-taught consolation did not seem to be very effective. Shaking his head, 'I actually dream about it sometimes,' the Director went on in a low voice. 'Dream of being woken up by that peal of thunder and finding her gone; dream of searching and searching for her under the trees.' He lapsed into the silence of reminiscence.

'You must have had a terrible shock,' said Bernard, almost enviously.

At the sound of his voice the Director started into a guilty realization of where he was; shot a glance at Bernard, and averting his eyes, blushed darkly; looked at him again with sudden suspicion and, angrily on his dignity, 'Don't imagine,' he said, 'that I'd had any indecorous relation with the girl. Nothing emotional, nothing long-drawn. It was all perfectly healthy and normal.' He handed Bernard the permit. 'I really don't know why I bored you with this trivial anecdote.' Furious with himself for having given away a discreditable secret, he vented his rage on Bernard. The look in his eyes was now frankly malignant. 'And I should like to take this opportunity, Mr. Marx,' he went on, 'of saying that I'm not at all pleased with the reports I receive of your behaviour outside working hours. You may say that this is not my business. But it is. I have the good name of the Centre to think of. My workers must be above suspicion, particularly those of the highest castes. Alphas are so conditioned that they do not *have* to be infantile in their emotional behaviour. But that is all the more reason for their making a special effort to conform. It is their duty to be infantile, even against their inclination. And so, Mr. Marx, I give you fair warning.' The Director's voice vibrated with an indignation that had now become wholly righteous and impersonal--was the expression of the disapproval of Society itself. 'If ever I hear again of any lapse from a proper standard of infantile decorum, I shall ask for your transference to a Sub-Centre--preferably to Iceland. Good morning.' And swivelling round in his chair, he picked up his pen and began to write.

'That'll teach him,' he said to himself. But he was mistaken. For Bernard left the room with a swagger, exulting, as he banged the door behind him, in the thought that he stood alone, embattled against the order of things; elated by the intoxicating consciousness of his individual significance and importance. Even the thought of persecution left him undismayed, was rather tonic than depressing. He felt strong enough to meet and overcome affliction, strong enough to face even Iceland. And this confidence was the greater for his not for a moment really believing that he would be called upon to face anything at all. People simply weren't transferred for things like that. Iceland was just a threat. A most stimulating and life-giving threat. Walking along the corridor, he actually whistled.

Heroic was the account he gave that evening of his interview with the D.H.C. 'Whereupon,' it concluded, 'I simply told him to go to the Bottomless Past and marched out of the room. And that was that.' He looked at Helmholtz Watson expectantly, awaiting his due reward of sympathy, encouragement, admiration. But no word came. Helmholtz sat silent, staring at the floor.

He liked Bernard; he was grateful to him for being the only man of his acquaintance with whom he could talk about the subjects he felt to be important. Nevertheless, there were things in Bernard which he hated. This boasting, for example. And the outbursts of an abject self-pity with which it alternated. And his deplorable habit of being bold after the event, and full, in absence, of the most extraordinary presence of mind. He hated these things--just because he liked Bernard. The seconds passed. Helmholtz continued to stare at the floor. And suddenly Bernard blushed and turned away.

§ 3

The journey was quite uneventful. The Blue Pacific Rocket was two and a half minutes early at New Orleans, lost four minutes in a tornado over Texas, but flew into a favourable air current at Longitude 95 West, and was able to land at Santa Fé less than forty seconds behind schedule time.

'Forty seconds on a six and a half hour flight. Not so bad,' Lenina conceded.

They slept that night at Santa Fé. The hotel was excellent--incomparably better, for example, than that horrible Aurora Bora Palace in which Lenina had suffered so much the previous summer. Liquid air, television, vibro-vacuum massage, radio, boiling caffeine solution, hot contraceptives, and eight different kinds of scent were laid on in every bedroom. The synthetic music plant was working as they entered the hall and left nothing to be desired. A notice in the lift announced that there were sixty Escalator-Squash-Racquet Courts in the hotel, and that Obstacle and Electro-magnetic Golf could both be played in the park.

'But it sounds simply too lovely,' cried Lenina. I almost wish we could stay here. Sixty Escalator-Squash Courts...'

'There won't be any in the Reservation,' Bernard warned her. 'And no scent, no television, no hot water, even. If you feel you can't stand it, stay here till I come back.'

Lenina was quite offended. 'Of course I can stand it. I only said it was lovely here because... well, because progress *is* lovely, isn't it?'

'Five hundred repetitions once a week from thirteen to seventeen,' said Bernard wearily, as though to himself.

'What did you say?'

'I said that progress was lovely. That's why you mustn't come to the Reservation unless you really want to.'

'But I do want to.'

'Very well, then,' said Bernard; and it was almost a threat.

Their permit required the signature of the Warden of the Reservation, at whose office next morning they duly presented themselves. An Epsilon-Plus negro porter took in Bernard's card, and they were admitted almost immediately.

The Warden was a blond and brachycephalic Alpha-Minus, short, red, moon-faced, and broad-shouldered, with a loud booming voice, very well adapted to the utterance of hypnopædic wisdom. He was a mine of irrelevant information and unasked-for good advice. Once started, he went on and on--boomingly.

'...five hundred and sixty thousand square kilometres, divided into four distinct Sub-Reservations, each surrounded by a high-tension wire fence.'

At this moment, and for no apparent reason, Bernard suddenly remembered that he had left the eau-de-Cologne tap in his bathroom wide open and running.

'...supplied with current from the Grand Canyon hydro-electric station.'

'Cost me a fortune by the time I get back.' With his mind's eye, Bernard saw the needle on the scent meter creeping round and round, ant-like, indefatigably. 'Quickly telephone to Helmholtz Watson.'

'...upwards of five thousand kilometres of fencing at sixty thousand volts.'

'You don't say so,' said Lenina politely, not knowing in the least what the Warden had said, but taking her cue from his dramatic pause. When the Warden started booming, she had inconspicuously swallowed half a gramme of *soma*, with the result that she could now sit, serenely not listening, thinking of nothing at all, but with her large blue eyes fixed on the Warden's face in an expression of rapt attention.

'To touch the fence is instant death,' pronounced the Warden solemnly. 'There is no escape from a Savage Reservation.'

The word 'escape' was suggestive. 'Perhaps,' said Bernard, half rising, 'we ought to think of going.' The little black needle was scurrying, an insect, nibbling through time, eating into his money.

'No escape,' repeated the Warden, waving him back into his chair; and as the permit was not yet countersigned, Bernard had no choice but to obey. 'Those who are born in the Reservation--and remember, my dear young lady,' he added, leering obscenely at Lenina, and speaking in an improper whisper, 'remember that, in the Reservation, children still *are* born, yes, actually born, revolting as that may seem...' (He hoped that this reference to a shameful subject would make Lenina blush; but she only smiled with simulated intelligence and said, 'You don't say so!' Disappointed, the Warden began again.) 'Those, I repeat, who are born in the Reservation are destined to die there.'

Destined to die... A decilitre of eau-de-Cologne every minute. Six litres an hour. 'Perhaps,' Bernard tried again, 'we ought...'

Leaning forward, the Director tapped the table with his forefinger. 'You ask me how many people live in the Reservation. And I reply'--triumphantly--'I reply that we do not know. We can only guess.'

'You don't say so.'

'My dear young lady, I do say so.'

Six times twenty-four--no, it would be nearer six times thirty-six. Bernard was pale and trembling with impatience. But inexorably the booming continued.

'...about sixty thousand Indians and half-breeds... absolute savages... our inspectors occasionally visit... otherwise, no communication whatever with the civilized world... still preserve their repulsive habits and customs... marriage, if you know what that is, my dear young lady; families... no conditioning... monstrous superstitions... Christianity and totemism and ancestor worship... extinct languages, such as Zuñi and Spanish and Athapascan... pumas, porcupines and other ferocious animals... infectious diseases... priests... venomous lizards...'

'You don't say so?'

They got away at last. Bernard dashed to the telephone. Quick, quick; but it took him nearly three minutes to get on to Helmholtz Watson. 'We might be among the savages already,' he complained. 'Damned incompetence!'

'Have a gramme,' suggested Lenina.

He refused, preferring his anger. And at last, thank Ford, he was through and, yes, it was Helmholtz; Helmholtz, to whom he explained what had happened, and who promised to go round at once, at once, and turn off the tap, yes, at once, but took this opportunity to tell him what the D.H.C. had said, in public, yesterday evening...

'What? He's looking out for some one to take my place?' Bernard's voice was agonized. 'So it's actually decided? Did he mention Iceland? You say he did? Ford! Iceland...' He hung up the receiver and turned back to Lenina. His face was pale, his expression utterly dejected.

'What's the matter?' she asked.

'The matter?' He dropped heavily into a chair. 'I'm going to be sent to Iceland.'

Often in the past he had wondered what it would be like to be subjected (*soma*-less and with nothing but his own inward resources to rely on) to some great trial, some pain, some persecution; he had even longed for affliction. As recently as a week ago, in the Director's office, he had imagined himself courageously resisting, stoically accepting suffering without a word. The Director's threats had actually elated him, made him feel larger than life. But that, as he now realized, was because he had not taken the threats quite seriously; he had not believed that, when it came to the point, the D.H.C. would ever do anything. Now that it looked as though the threats were really to be fulfilled, Bernard was appalled. Of that imagined stoicism, that theoretical courage, not a trace was left.

He raged against himself--what a fool!--against the Director--how unfair not to give him that other chance, that other chance which, he now had no doubt at all, he had always intended to take. And Iceland, Iceland...

Lenina shook her head. 'Was and will make me ill,' she quoted, 'I take a gramme and only am.'

In the end she persuaded him to swallow four tablets of *soma*. Five minutes later roots and fruits were abolished; the flower of the present rosily blossomed. A message from the porter announced that, at the Warden's orders, a Reservation Guard had come round with a plane and was waiting on the roof of the hotel. They went up at once. An octoroon in Gamma-green uniform saluted and proceeded to recite the morning's programme.

A bird's-eye view of ten or a dozen of the principal pueblos, then a landing for lunch in the valley of Malpais. The rest-house was comfortable there, and up at the pueblo the savages would probably be celebrating their summer festival. It would be the best place to spend the night.

They took their seats in the plane and set off. Ten minutes later they were crossing the frontier that separated civilization from savagery. Uphill and down, across the deserts of salt or sand, through forests, into the violet depth of canyons, over crag and peak and table-topped mesa, the fence marched on and on, irresistibly the straight line, the geometrical symbol of triumphant human purpose. And at its foot, here and there, a mosaic of white bones, a still unrotted carcase dark on the tawny ground marked the place where deer or steer, puma or porcupine or coyote, or the greedy turkey buzzards drawn down by the whiff of carrion and fulminated as though by a poetic justice, had come too close to the destroying wires.

'They never learn,' said the green-uniformed pilot, pointing down at the skeletons on the ground below them. 'And they never will learn,' he added and laughed, as though he had somehow scored a personal triumph over the electrocuted animals.

Bernard also laughed; after two grammes of *soma* the joke seemed, for some reason, good. Laughed and then, almost immediately, dropped off to sleep and, sleeping, was carried over Taos and Tesuque; over Nambe and Picuris and Pojoaque, over Sia and Cochiti, over Laguna and Acoma and the Enchanted Mesa, over Zuñi and Cibola and Ojo Caliente, and woke at last to find the machine standing on the ground, Lenina carrying the suit-cases into a small square house, and the Gamma-green octoroon talking incomprehensibly with a young Indian.

'Malpais,' explained the pilot, as Bernard stepped out. 'This is the rest-house. And there's a dance this afternoon at the pueblo. He'll take you there.' He pointed to the sullen young savage. 'Funny, I expect.' He grinned. 'Everything they do is funny.' And with that he climbed into the plane and started up the engines. 'Back to-morrow. And remember,' he added reassuringly to Lenina, 'they're perfectly tame; savages won't do you any harm. They've got enough experience of gas bombs to know that they mustn't play any tricks.' Still laughing, he threw the helicopter screws into gear, accelerated, and was gone.

Chapter VII

The mesa was like a ship becalmed in a strait of lion-coloured dust. The channel wound between precipitous banks, and slanting from one wall to the other across the valley ran a streak of green--the river and its fields. On the prow of that stone ship in the centre of the strait, and seemingly a part of it, a shaped and geometrical outcrop of the naked rock, stood the pueblo of Malpais. Block above block, each story smaller than the one below, the tall houses rose like stepped and amputated pyramids into the blue sky. At their feet lay a straggle of low buildings, a criss-cross of walls; and on three sides the precipices fell sheer into the plain. A few columns of smoke mounted perpendicularly into the windless air and were lost.

'Queer,' said Lenina. 'Very queer.' It was her ordinary word of condemnation. 'I don't like it. And I don't like that man.' She pointed to the Indian guide who had been appointed to take them up to the pueblo. Her feeling was evidently reciprocated; the very back of the man, as he walked along before them, was hostile, sullenly contemptuous.

'Besides,' she lowered her voice, 'he smells.'

Bernard did not attempt to deny it. They walked on.

Suddenly it was as though the whole air had come alive and were pulsing, pulsing with the indefatigable movement of blood. Up there, in Malpais, the drums were being beaten. Their feet fell in with the rhythm of that mysterious heart; they quickened their pace. Their path led them to the foot of the precipice. The sides of the great mesa ship towered over them, three hundred feet to the gunwale.

'I wish we could have brought the plane,' said Lenina, looking up resentfully at the blank impending rock-face. 'I hate walking. And you feel so small when you're on the ground at the bottom of a hill.'

They walked along for some way in the shadow of the mesa, rounded a projection, and there, in a water-worn ravine, was the way up the companion ladder. They climbed. It was a very steep path that zigzagged from side to side of the gulley. Sometimes the pulsing of the drums was all but inaudible, at others they seemed to be beating only just round the corner.

When they were half-way up, an eagle flew past so close to them that the wind of his wings blew chill on their faces. In a crevice of the rock lay a pile of bones. It was all oppressively queer, and the Indian smelt stronger and stronger. They emerged at last from the ravine into the full sunlight. The top of the mesa was a flat deck of stone.

'Like the Charing-T Tower,' was Lenina's comment. But she was not allowed to enjoy her discovery of this reassuring resemblance for long. A padding of soft feet made them turn round. Naked from throat to navel, their dark-brown bodies painted with white lines ('like asphalt tennis courts,' Lenina was later to explain), their faces inhuman with daubings of scarlet, black and ochre, two Indians came running along the path. Their black hair was braided with fox fur and red flannel. Cloaks of turkey feathers fluttered from their shoulders; huge feather diadems exploded gaudily round their heads. With every step they took came the clink and rattle of their silver bracelets, their heavy necklaces of bone and turquoise beads. They came on without a word, running quietly in their deerskin moccasins. One of them was holding a feather brush; the other carried, in either hand, what looked at a distance like three or four pieces of thick rope. One of the ropes writhed uneasily, and suddenly Lenina saw that they were snakes.

The men came nearer and nearer; their dark eyes looked at her, but without giving any sign of recognition, any smallest sign that they had seen her or were aware of her existence. The writhing snake hung limp again with the rest. The men passed.

'I don't like it,' said Lenina. 'I don't like it.'

She liked even less what awaited her at the entrance to the pueblo, where their guide had left them while he went inside for instructions. The dirt, to start with, the piles of rubbish, the dust, the dogs, the flies. Her face wrinkled up into a grimace of disgust. She held her handkerchief to her nose.

'But how can they live like this?' she broke out in a voice of indignant incredulity. (It wasn't possible.)

Bernard shrugged his shoulders philosophically. 'Anyhow,' he said, 'they've been doing it for the last five or six thousand years. So I suppose they must be used to it by now.'

'But cleanliness is next to fordliness,' she insisted.

'Yes, and civilization is sterilization,' Bernard went on, concluding on a tone of irony the second hypnopædic lesson in elementary hygiene. 'But these people have never heard of Our Ford, and they aren't civilized. So there's no point in...'

'Oh!' She gripped his arm. 'Look.'

An almost naked Indian was very slowly climbing down the ladder from the first-floor terrace of a neighbouring house--rung after rung, with the tremulous caution of extreme old age. His face was profoundly wrinkled and black, like a mask of obsidian. The toothless mouth had fallen in. At the corners of the lips, and on each side of the chin a few long bristles gleamed almost white against the dark skin. The long unbraided hair hung down in grey wisps round his face. His body was bent and emaciated to the bone, almost fleshless. Very slowly he came down, pausing at each rung before he ventured another step.

'What's the matter with him?' whispered Lenina. Her eyes were wide with horror and amazement.

'He's old, that's all,' Bernard answered as carelessly as he could. He too was startled; but he made an effort to seem unmoved.

'Old?' she repeated. 'But the Director's old; lots of people are old; they're not like that.'

'That's because we don't allow them to be like that. We preserve them from diseases. We keep their internal secretions artificially balanced at a youthful equilibrium. We don't permit their magnesium-calcium ratio to fall below what it was at thirty. We give them transfusions of young blood. We keep their metabolism permanently stimulated. So, of course, they don't look like that. Partly,' he added, 'because most of them die long before they reach this old creature's age. Youth almost unimpaired till sixty, and then, crack! the end.'

But Lenina was not listening. She was watching the old man. Slowly, slowly he came down. His feet touched the ground. He turned. In their deep-sunken orbits his eyes were still extraordinarily bright. They looked at her for a long moment expressionlessly, without surprise, as though she had not been there at all. Then slowly, with bent back, the old man hobbled past them and was gone.

'But it's terrible,' Lenina whispered. 'It's awful. We ought not to have come here.' She felt in her pocket for her *soma*--only to discover that, by some unprecedented oversight, she had left the bottle down at the rest-house. Bernard's pockets were also empty.

Lenina was left to face the horrors of Malpais unaided. They came crowding in on her thick and fast. The spectacle of two young women giving the breast to their babies made her blush and turn away her face. She had never seen anything so indecent in her life. And what made it worse was that, instead of tactfully ignoring it, Bernard proceeded to make open comments on this revoltingly viviparous scene. Ashamed, now that the effects of the *soma* had worn off, of the weakness he had displayed that morning in the hotel, he went out of his way to show himself strong and unorthodox.

'What a wonderfully intimate relationship,' he said, deliberately outrageous. 'And what an intensity of feeling it must generate! I often think one may have missed something in not having had a mother. And perhaps you've missed something in not *being* a mother, Lenina. Imagine yourself sitting there with a little baby of your own....'

'Bernard! How can you?' The passage of an old woman with ophthalmia and a disease of the skin distracted her from her indignation.

'Let's go away,' she begged. 'I don't like it.'

But at this moment their guide came back and, beckoning to them to follow, led the way down the narrow street between the houses. They rounded a corner. A dead dog was lying on a rubbish heap; a woman with a goitre was looking for lice in the hair of a small girl. Their guide halted at the foot of a ladder, raised his hand perpendicularly, then darted it horizontally forward. They did what he mutely commanded--climbed the ladder and walked through the doorway, to which it gave access, into a long narrow room, rather dark and smelling of smoke and cooked grease and long-worn, long-unwashed clothes. At the further end of the room was another doorway, through which came a shaft of sunlight and the noise, very loud and close, of the drums.

They stepped across the threshold and found themselves on a wide terrace. Below them, shut in by the tall houses, was the village square, crowded with Indians. Bright blankets, and feathers in black hair, and the glint of turquoise, and dark skins shining with heat. Lenina put her handkerchief to her nose again. In the open space at the centre of the square were two circular platforms of masonry and trampled clay--the roofs, it was evident, of underground chambers; for in the centre of each platform was an open hatchway, with a ladder emerging from the lower darkness. A sound of subterranean flute-playing came up and was almost lost in the steady remorseless persistence of the drums.

Lenina liked the drums. Shutting her eyes she abandoned herself to their soft repeated thunder, allowed it to invade her consciousness more and more completely, till at last there was nothing left in the world but that one deep pulse of sound. It reminded her reassuringly of the synthetic noises made at Solidarity Services and Ford's Day celebrations. 'Orgy-porgy,' she whispered to herself. These drums beat out just the same rhythms.

There was a sudden startling burst of singing--hundreds of male voices crying out fiercely in harsh metallic unison. A few long notes and silence, the thunderous silence of the drums; then shrill, in a neighing treble, the women's answer. Then again the drums; and once more the men's deep savage affirmation of their manhood.

Queer--yes. The place was queer, so was the music, so were the clothes and the goitres and the skin diseases and the old people. But the performance itself--there seemed to be nothing specially queer about that.

'It reminds me of a lower-caste Community Sing,' she told Bernard.

But a little later it was reminding her a good deal less of that innocuous function. For suddenly there had swarmed up from those round chambers underground a ghastly troop of monsters. Hideously masked or painted out of all semblance of humanity, they had tramped out a strange limping dance round the square; round and again round, singing as they went, round and round--each time a little faster; and the drums had changed and quickened their rhythm, so that it became like the pulsing of fever in the ears; and the crowd had begun to sing with the dancers, louder and louder; and first one woman had shrieked, and then another and another, as though they were being killed; and then suddenly the leader of the dancers broke out of the line, ran to a big wooden chest which was standing at one end of the square, raised the lid and pulled out a pair of black snakes. A great yell went up from the crowd, and all the other dancers ran towards him with outstretched hands. He tossed the snakes to the first-comers, then dipped back into the chest for more. More and more, black snakes and brown and mottled--he flung them out. And then the dance began again on a different rhythm. Round and round they went with their snakes, snakily, with a soft undulating movement at the knees and hips. Round and round. Then the leader gave a signal, and one after another, all the snakes were flung down in the middle of the square; an old man came up from underground and sprinkled them with corn meal, and from the other hatchway came a woman and sprinkled them with water from a black jar. Then the old man lifted his hand and, startlingly, terrifyingly, there was absolute silence. The drums stopped beating, life seemed to have come to an end. The old man pointed towards the two hatchways that gave entrance to the lower world. And slowly, raised by invisible hands from below, there emerged from the one a painted image of an eagle, from the other that of a man, naked, and nailed to a cross. They hung there, seemingly self-sustained, as though watching. The old man clapped his hands. Naked but for a white cotton breech-cloth, a boy of about eighteen stepped out of the crowd and stood before him, his hands crossed over his chest, his head bowed. The old man made the sign of the cross over him and turned away. Slowly, the boy began to walk round the writhing heap of snakes. He had completed the first circuit and was half-way through the second when, from among the dancers, a tall man wearing the mask of a coyote and holding in his hand a whip of plaited leather, advanced towards him. The boy moved on as though unaware of the other's existence. The coyote-man raised his whip; there was a long moment of expectancy, then a swift movement, the whistle of the lash and its loud flat-sounding impact on the flesh. The boy's body quivered; but he made no sound, he walked on at the same slow, steady pace. The coyote struck again, again; and at every blow at first a gasp and then a deep groan went up from the crowd. The boy walked on. Twice, thrice, four times round he went. The blood was streaming. Five times round, six times round. Suddenly Lenina covered her face with her hands and began to sob. 'Oh, stop them, stop them!' she implored. But the whip fell and fell inexorably. Seven times round. Then all at once the boy staggered and, still without a sound, pitched forward on to his face. Bending over him, the old man touched his back with a long white feather, held it up for a moment, crimson, for the people to see, then shook it thrice over the snakes. A few drops fell, and suddenly the drums broke out again into a panic of hurrying notes; there was a great shout. The dancers rushed forward, picked up the snakes and ran out of the square. Men, women, children, all the crowd ran after them. A minute later the square was empty, only the boy remained, prone where he had fallen, quite still. Three old women came out of one of the houses, and with some difficulty lifted him and carried him in. The eagle and the man on the cross kept guard for a little while over the empty pueblo; then, as though they had seen enough, sank slowly down through their hatchways, out of sight, into the nether world.

Lenina was still sobbing. 'Too awful,' she kept repeating, and all Bernard's consolations were in vain. 'Too awful! That blood!' She shuddered. 'Oh, I wish I had my *soma*.'

There was the sound of feet in the inner room.

Lenina did not move, but sat with her face in her hands, unseeing, apart. Only Bernard turned round.

The dress of the young man who now stepped out on to the terrace was Indian; but his plaited hair was straw-coloured, his eyes a pale blue, and his skin a white skin, bronzed.

'Hullo. Good-morrow,' said the stranger, in faultless but peculiar English. 'You're civilized, aren't you? You come from the Other Place, outside the Reservation?'

'Who on earth...?' Bernard began in astonishment.

The young man sighed and shook his head. 'A most unhappy gentleman.' And, pointing to the bloodstains in the centre of the square, 'Do you see that damned spot?' he asked in a voice that trembled with emotion.

'A gramme is better than a damn,' said Lenina mechanically from behind her hands. 'I wish I had my *soma*!'

'*I* ought to have been there.' The young man went on. 'Why wouldn't they let me be the sacrifice? I'd have gone round ten times--twelve, fifteen. Palowhtiwa only got as far as seven. They could have had twice as much blood from me. The multitudinous seas incarnadine.' He flung out his arms in a lavish gesture; then, despairingly, let them fall again. 'But they wouldn't let me. They disliked me for my complexion. It's always been like that. Always.' Tears stood in the young man's eyes; he was ashamed and turned away.

Astonishment made Lenina forget the deprivation of *soma*. She uncovered her face and, for the first time, looked at the stranger. 'Do you mean to say that you *wanted* to be hit with that whip?'

Still averted from her, the young man made a sign of affirmation. 'For the sake of the pueblo--to make the rain come and the corn grow. And to please Pookong and Jesus. And then to show that I can bear pain without crying out. Yes,' and his voice suddenly took on a new resonance, he turned with a proud squaring of the shoulders, a proud, defiant lifting of the chin, 'to show that I'm a man... Oh!' He gave a gasp and was silent, gaping. He had seen, for the first time in his life, the face of a girl whose cheeks were not the colour of chocolate or dogskin, whose hair was auburn and permanently waved, and whose expression (amazing novelty!) was one of benevolent interest. Lenina was smiling at him; such a nice-looking boy, she was thinking, and a really beautiful body. The blood rushed up into the young man's face; he dropped his eyes, raised them again for a moment only to find her still smiling at him, and was so much overcome that he had to turn away and pretend to be looking very hard at something on the other side of the square.

Bernard's questions made a diversion. Who? How? When? From where? Keeping his eyes fixed on Bernard's face (for so passionately did he long to see Lenina smiling that he simply dared not look at her), the young man tried to explain himself. Linda and he--Linda was his mother (the word made Lenina look uncomfortable)--were strangers in the Reservation. Linda had come from the Other Place long ago, before he was born, with a man who was his father. (Bernard pricked up his ears.) She had gone walking alone in those mountains over there to the North, had fallen down a steep place and hurt her head. ('Go on, go on,' said Bernard excitedly.) Some hunters from Malpais had found her and brought her to the pueblo. As for the man who was his father, Linda had never seen him again. His name was Tomakin. (Yes, 'Thomas' was the D.H.C.'s first name.) He must have flown away, back to the Other Place, away without her--a bad, unkind, unnatural man.

'And so I was born in Malpais,' he concluded. 'In Malpais.' And he shook his head.

****

The squalor of that little house on the outskirts of the pueblo!

A space of dust and rubbish separated it from the village. Two famine-stricken dogs were nosing obscenely in the garbage at its door. Inside, when they entered, the twilight stank and was loud with flies.

'Linda!' the young man called.

From the inner room a rather hoarse female voice said, 'Coming.'

They waited. In bowls on the floor were the remains of a meal, perhaps of several meals.

The door opened. A very stout blonde squaw stepped across the threshold and stood looking at the strangers, staring incredulously, her mouth open. Lenina noticed with disgust that two of the front teeth were missing. And the colour of the ones that remained... She shuddered. It was worse than the old man. So fat. And all the lines in her face, the flabbiness, the wrinkles. And the sagging cheeks, with those purplish blotches. And the red veins on her nose, the bloodshot eyes. And that neck--that neck; and the blanket she wore over her head--ragged and filthy. And under the brown sack-shaped tunic those enormous breasts, the bulge of the stomach, the hips. Oh, much worse than the old man, much worse! And suddenly the creature burst out in a torrent of speech, rushed at her with outstretched arms and--Ford! Ford! it was too revolting, in another moment she'd be sick--pressed her against the bulge, the bosom, and began to kiss her. Ford! to *kiss*, slobberingly, and smelt too horrible, obviously never had a bath, and simply reeked of that beastly stuff that was put into Delta and Epsilon bottles (no, it wasn't true about Bernard), positively stank of alcohol. She broke away as quickly as she could.

A blubbered and distorted face confronted her; the creature was crying.

'Oh, my dear, my dear.' The torrent of words flowed sobbingly. 'If you knew how glad--after all these years! A civilized face. Yes, and civilized clothes. Because I thought I should never see a piece of real acetate silk again.' She fingered the sleeve of Lenina's shirt. The nails were black. 'And those adorable viscose velveteen shorts! Do you know, dear, I've still got my old clothes, the ones I came in, put away in a box. I'll show them you afterwards. Though, of course, the acetate has all gone into holes. But such a lovely white bandolier--though I must say your green morocco is even lovelier. Not that it did *me* much good, that bandolier.' Her tears began to flow again. 'I suppose John told you. What I had to suffer--and not a gramme of *soma* to be had. Only a drink of *mescal* every now and then, when Popé used to bring it. Popé is a boy I used to know. But it makes you feel so bad afterwards, the *mescal* does, and you're sick with the *peyotl*; besides, it always made that awful feeling of being ashamed much worse the next day. And I *was* so ashamed. Just think of it: me, a Beta--having a baby, put yourself in my place.' (The mere suggestion made Lenina shudder.) 'Though it wasn't my fault, I swear; because I still don't know how it happened, seeing that I did all the Malthusian drill--you know, by numbers, One, two, three, four, always, I swear it; but all the same it happened; and of course there wasn't anything like an Abortion Centre here. Is it still down in Chelsea, by the way?' she asked. Lenina nodded. 'And still flood-lighted on Tuesdays and Fridays?' Lenina nodded again. 'That lovely pink glass tower!' Poor Linda lifted her face and with closed eyes ecstatically contemplated the bright remembered image. 'And the river at night,' she whispered. Great tears oozed slowly out from between her tight-shut eyelids. 'And flying back in the evening from Stoke Poges. And then a hot bath and vibro-vacuum massage... But there.' She drew a deep breath, shook her head, opened her eyes again, sniffed once or twice, then blew her nose on her fingers and wiped them on the skirt of her tunic. 'Oh, I'm so sorry,' she said in response to Lenina's involuntary grimace of disgust. 'I oughtn't to have done that. I'm sorry. But what *are* you to do when there aren't any handkerchiefs? I remember how it used to upset me, all that dirt, and nothing being aseptic. I had an awful cut on my head when they first brought me here. You can't imagine what they used to put on it. Filth, just filth. "Civilization is Sterilization," I used to say to them. And "Streptocock-Gee to Banbury-T, to see a fine bathroom and W.C." as though they were children. But of course they didn't understand. How should they? And in the end I suppose I got used to it. And anyhow, how *can* you keep things clean when there isn't hot water laid on? And look at these clothes. This beastly wool isn't like acetate. It lasts and lasts. And you're supposed to mend it if it gets torn. But I'm a Beta; I worked in the Fertilizing Room; nobody ever taught me to do anything like that. It wasn't my business. Besides, it never used to be right to mend clothes. Throw them away when they've got holes in them and buy new. "The more stitches, the less riches." Isn't that right? Mending's anti-social. But it's all different here. It's like living with lunatics. Everything they do is mad.' She looked round; saw John and Bernard had left them and were walking up and down in the dust and garbage outside the house; but, none the less confidentially lowering her voice, and leaning, while Lenina stiffened and shrank, so close that the blown reek of embryo-poison stirred the hair on her cheek. 'For instance,' she hoarsely whispered, 'take the way they have one another here. Mad, I tell you, absolutely mad. Everybody belongs to every one else--don't they? don't they?' she insisted, tugging at Lenina's sleeve. Lenina nodded her averted head, let out the breath she had been holding and managed to draw another one, relatively untainted. 'Well, here,' the other went on, 'nobody's supposed to belong to more than one person. And if you have people in the ordinary way, the others think you're wicked and anti-social. They hate and despise you. Once a lot of women came and made a scene because their men came to see me. Well, why not? And then they rushed at me... No, it was too awful. I can't tell you about it.' Linda covered her face with her hands and shuddered. 'They're so hateful, the women here. Mad, mad and cruel. And of course they don't know anything about Malthusian drill, or bottles, or decanting, or anything of that sort. So they're having children all the time--like dogs. It's too revolting. And to think that I... Oh, Ford, Ford, Ford! And yet John *was* a great comfort to me. I don't know what I should have done without him. Even though he did get so upset whenever a man... Quite as a tiny boy, even. Once (but that was when he was bigger) he tried to kill poor Waihusiwa--or was it Popé?--just because I used to have them sometimes. Because I never *could* make him understand that that was what civilized people ought to do. Being mad's infectious, I believe. Anyhow, John seems to have caught it from the Indians. Because, of course, he was with them a lot. Even though they always were so beastly to him and wouldn't let him do all the things the other boys did. Which was a good thing in a way, because it made it easier for me to condition him a little. Though you've no idea how difficult that is. There's so much one doesn't know; it wasn't my business to know. I mean, when a child asks you how a helicopter works or who made the world--well, what are you to answer if you're a Beta and have always worked in the Fertilizing Room? What *are* you to answer?'

Chapter VIII

Outside, in the dust and among the garbage (there were four dogs now), Bernard and John were walking slowly up and down.

'So hard for me to realize,' Bernard was saying, 'to reconstruct. As though we were living on different planets, in different centuries. A mother, and all this dirt, and gods, and old age, and disease...' He shook his head. 'It's almost inconceivable. I shall never understand unless you explain.'

'Explain what?'

'This.' He indicated the pueblo. 'That.' And it was the little house outside the village. 'Everything. All your life.'

'But what is there to say?'

'From the beginning. As far back as you can remember.'

'As far back as I can remember.' John frowned. There was a long silence.

****

It was very hot. They had eaten a lot of tortillas and sweet corn. Linda said, 'Come and lie down, Baby.' They lay down together in the big bed. 'Sing,' and Linda sang. Sang 'Streptocock-Gee to Banbury-T' and 'Bye, Baby Banting, soon you'll need decanting.' Her voice got fainter and fainter...

There was a loud noise, and he woke with a start. A man was standing by the bed, enormous, frightening. He was saying something to Linda, and Linda was laughing. She had pulled the blanket up to her chin, but the man pulled it down again. His hair was like two black ropes, and round his arm was a lovely silver bracelet with blue stones in it. He liked the bracelet; but all the same, he was frightened; he hid his face against Linda's body. Linda put her hand on him and he felt safer. In those other words he did not understand so well, she said to the man, 'Not with John here.' The man looked at him, then again at Linda, and said a few words in a soft voice. Linda said, 'No.' But the man bent over the bed towards him and his face was huge, terrible; the black ropes of hair touched the blanket. 'No,' Linda said again, and he felt her hand squeezing him more tightly. 'No, no!' But the man took hold of one of his arms, and it hurt. He screamed. The man put out his other hand and lifted him up. Linda was still holding him, still saying 'No, no.' The man said something short and angry, and suddenly her hands were gone. 'Linda, Linda.' He kicked and wriggled; but the man carried him across to the door, opened it, put him down on the floor in the middle of the other room, and went away, shutting the door behind him. He got up, he ran to the door. Standing on tiptoe he could just reach the big wooden latch. He lifted it and pushed; but the door wouldn't open. 'Linda,' he shouted. She didn't answer.

****

He remembered a huge room, rather dark; and there were big wooden things with strings fastened to them, and lots of women standing round them--making blankets, Linda said. Linda told him to sit in the corner with the other children, while she went and helped the women. He played with the little boys for a long time. Suddenly people started talking very loud, and there were the women pushing Linda away, and Linda was crying. She went to the door and he ran after her. He asked her why they were angry. 'Because I broke something,' she said. And then she got angry too. 'How should I know how to do their beastly weaving?' she said. 'Beastly savages.' He asked her what savages were. When they got back to their house, Popé was waiting at the door, and he came in with them. He had a big gourd full of stuff that looked like water; only it wasn't water, but something with a bad smell that burnt your mouth and made you cough. Linda drank some and Popé drank some, and then Linda laughed a lot and talked very loud; and then she and Popé went into the other room. When Popé went away, he went into the room. Linda was in bed and so fast asleep that he couldn't wake her.

Popé used to come often. He said the stuff in the gourd was called *mescal*; but Linda said it ought to be called *soma*; only it made you feel ill afterwards. He hated Popé. He hated them all--all the men who came to see Linda. One afternoon, when he had been playing with the other children--it was cold, he remembered, and there was snow on the mountains--he came back to the house and heard angry voices in the bedroom. They were women's voices, and they said words he didn't understand; but he knew they were dreadful words. Then suddenly, crash! something was upset; he heard people moving about quickly, and there was another crash and then a noise like hitting a mule, only not so bony; then Linda screamed. 'Oh, don't, don't, don't!' she said. He ran in. There were three women in dark blankets. Linda was on the bed. One of the women was holding her wrists. Another was lying across her legs, so that she couldn't kick. The third was hitting her with a whip. Once, twice, three times; and each time Linda screamed. Crying, he tugged at the fringe of the woman's blanket. 'Please, please.' With her free hand she held him away. The whip came down again, and again Linda screamed. He caught hold of the woman's enormous brown hand between his own and bit it with all his might. She cried out, wrenched her hand free, and gave him such a push that he fell down. While he was lying on the ground she hit him three times with the whip. It hurt more than anything he had ever felt--like fire. The whip whistled again, fell. But this time it was Linda who screamed.

'But why did they want to hurt you, Linda?' he asked that night. He was crying, because the red marks of the whip on his back still hurt so terribly. But he was also crying because people were so beastly and unfair, and because he was only a little boy and couldn't do anything against them. Linda was crying too. She was grown up, but she wasn't big enough to fight against three of them. It wasn't fair for her either. 'Why did they want to hurt you, Linda?'

'I don't know. How should I know?' It was difficult to hear what she said, because she was lying on her stomach and her face was in the pillow. 'They say those men are *their* men,' she went on; and she did not seem to be talking to him at all; she seemed to be talking with some one inside herself. A long talk which he didn't understand; and in the end she started crying louder than ever.

'Oh, don't cry, Linda. Don't cry.'

He pressed himself against her. He put his arm round her neck. Linda cried out. 'Oh, be careful. My shoulder! Oh!' and she pushed him away, hard. His head banged against the wall. 'Little idiot!' she shouted; and then, suddenly, she began to slap him. Slap, slap...

'Linda,' he cried out. 'Oh, mother, don't!'

'I'm not your mother. I won't be your mother.'

'But, Linda... Oh!' She slapped him on the cheek.

'Turned into a savage,' she shouted. 'Having young ones like an animal.... If it hadn't been for you, I might have gone to the Inspector, I might have got away. But not with a baby. That would have been too shameful.'

He saw that she was going to hit him again, and lifted his arm to guard his face. 'Oh don't, Linda, please don't.'

'Little beast!' She pulled down his arm; his face was uncovered.

'Don't, Linda.' He shut his eyes, expecting the blow.

But she didn't hit him. After a little time, he opened his eyes again and saw that she was looking at him. He tried to smile at her. Suddenly she put her arms round him and kissed him again and again.

****

Sometimes, for several days, Linda didn't get up at all. She lay in bed and was sad. Or else she drank the stuff that Popé brought and laughed a great deal and went to sleep. Sometimes she was sick. Often she forgot to wash him, and there was nothing to eat except cold tortillas. He remembered the first time she found those little animals in his hair, how she screamed and screamed.

****

The happiest times were when she told him about the Other Place. 'And you really can go flying, whenever you like?'

'Whenever you like.' And she would tell him about the lovely music that came out of a box, and all the nice games you could play, and the delicious things to eat and drink, and the light that came when you pressed a little thing in the wall, and the pictures that you could hear and feel and smell, as well as see, and another box for making nice smells, and the pink and green and blue and silver houses as high as mountains, and everybody happy and no one ever sad or angry, and every one belonging to every one else, and the boxes where you could see and hear what was happening at the other side of the world, and babies in lovely clean bottles--everything so clean, and no nasty smells, no dirt at all--and people never lonely, but living together and being so jolly and happy, like the summer dances here in Malpais, but much happier, and the happiness being there every day, every day.... He listened by the hour. And sometimes, when he and the other children were tired with too much playing, one of the old men of the pueblo would talk to them, in those other words, of the great Transformer of the World, and of the long fight between Right Hand and Left Hand, between Wet and Dry; of Awonawilona, who made a great fog by thinking in the night, and then made the whole world out of the fog; of Earth Mother and Sky Father; of Ahaiyuta and Marsailema, the twins of War and Chance; of Jesus and Pookong; of Mary and Etsanatlehi, the woman who makes herself young again; of the Black Stone at Laguna and the Great Eagle and Our Lady of Acoma. Strange stories, all the more wonderful to him for being told in the other words and so not fully understood. Lying in bed, he would think of Heaven and London and Our Lady of Acoma and the rows and rows of babies in clean bottles and Jesus flying up and Linda flying up and the great Director of World Hatcheries and Awonawilona.

****

Lots of men came to see Linda. The boys began to point their fingers at him. In the strange other words they said that Linda was bad; they called her names he did not understand, but that he knew were bad names. One day they sang a song about her, again and again. He threw stones at them. They threw back; a sharp stone cut his cheek. The blood wouldn't stop; he was covered with blood.

****

Linda taught him to read. With a piece of charcoal she drew pictures on the wall--an animal sitting down, a baby inside a bottle; then she wrote letters. THE CAT IS ON THE MAT. THE TOT IS IN THE POT. He learned quickly and easily. When he knew how to read all the words she wrote on the wall, Linda opened her big wooden box and pulled out from under those funny little red trousers she never wore a thin little book. He had often seen it before. 'When you're bigger,' she had said, 'you can read it.' Well, now he was big enough. He was proud. 'I'm afraid you won't find it very exciting,' she said. 'But it's the only thing I have.' She sighed. 'If only you could see the lovely reading machines we used to have in London!' He began reading. *The Chemical and Bacteriological Conditioning of the Embryo. Practical Instructions for Beta Embryo-Store Workers*. It took him a quarter of an hour to read the title alone. He threw the book on the floor. 'Beastly, beastly book!' he said, and began to cry.

****

The boys still sang their horrible song about Linda. Sometimes, too, they laughed at him for being so ragged. When he tore his clothes, Linda did not know how to mend them. In the Other Place, she told him, people threw away clothes with holes in them and got new ones. 'Rags, rags!' the boys used to shout at him. 'But I can read,' he said to himself, 'and they can't. They don't even know what reading is.' It was fairly easy, if he thought hard enough about the reading, to pretend that he didn't mind when they made fun of him. He asked Linda to give him the book again.

The more the boys pointed and sang, the harder he read. Soon he could read all the words quite well. Even the longest. But what did they mean? He asked Linda; but even when she could answer it didn't seem to make it very clear. And generally she couldn't answer at all.

'What are chemicals?' he would ask.

'Oh, stuff like magnesium salts, and alcohol for keeping the Deltas and Epsilons small and backward, and calcium carbonate for bones, and all that sort of thing.'

'But how do you make chemicals, Linda? Where do they come from?'

'Well, I don't know. You get them out of bottles. And when the bottles are empty, you send up to the Chemical Store for more. It's the Chemical Store people who make them, I suppose. Or else they send to the factory for them. I don't know. I never did any chemistry. My job was always with the embryos.'

It was the same with everything else he asked about. Linda never seemed to know. The old men of the pueblo had much more definite answers.

'The seed of men and all creatures, the seed of the sun and the seed of earth and the seed of the sky--Awonawilona made them all out of the Fog of Increase. Now the world has four wombs; and he laid the seeds in the lowest of the four wombs. And gradually the seeds began to grow...'

****

One day (John calculated later that it must have been soon after his twelfth birthday) he came home and found a book that he had never seen before lying on the floor in the bedroom. It was a thick book and looked very old. The binding had been eaten by mice; some of its pages were loose and crumpled. He picked it up, looked at the title-page: the book was called *The Complete Works of William Shakespeare*.

Linda was lying on the bed, sipping that horrible stinking *mescal* out of a cup. 'Popé brought it,' she said. Her voice was thick and hoarse like somebody else's voice. 'It was lying in one of the chests of the Antelope Kiva. It's supposed to have been there for hundreds of years. I expect it's true, because I looked at it, and it seemed to be full of nonsense. Uncivilized. Still, it'll be good enough for you to practise your reading on.' She took a last sip, set the cup down on the floor beside the bed, turned over on her side, hiccoughed once or twice and went to sleep.

He opened the book at random.

	Nay,		but		to		live
In	the	rank	sweat	of	an	enseamed	bed,
Stew'd	in	corruption,	honeying	and	making		love
Over the nasty sty...							

The strange words rolled through his mind; rumbled, like talking thunder; like the drums at the summer dances, if the drums could have spoken; like the men singing the Corn Song, beautiful, beautiful, so that you cried; like old Mitsima saying magic over his feathers and his carved sticks and his bits of bone and stone--*kiathla tsilu silokwe silokwe silokwe. Kiai silu silu, tsithl*--but better than Mitsima's magic, because it meant more, because it talked to *him*; talked wonderfully and only half-understandably, a terrible beautiful magic, about Linda; about Linda lying there snoring, with the empty cup on the floor beside the bed; about Linda and Popé, Linda and Popé.

****

He hated Popé more and more. A man can smile and smile and be a villain. Remorseless, treacherous, lecherous, kindless villain. What did the words exactly mean? He only half knew. But their magic was strong and went on rumbling in his head, and somehow it was as though he had never really hated Popé before; never really hated him because he had never been able to say how much he hated him. But now he had these words, these words like drums and singing and magic. These words and the strange, strange story out of which they were taken (he couldn't make head or tail of it, but it was wonderful, wonderful all the same)--they gave him a reason for hating Popé; and they made his hatred more real; they even made Popé himself more real.

One day, when he came in from playing, the door of the inner room was open, and he saw them lying together on the bed, asleep--white Linda and Popé almost black beside her, with one arm under her shoulders and the other dark hand on her breast, and one of the plaits of his long hair lying across her throat, like a black snake trying to strangle her. Popé's gourd and a cup were standing on the floor near the bed. Linda was snoring.

His heart seemed to have disappeared and left a hole. He was empty. Empty, and cold, and rather sick, and giddy. He leaned against the wall to steady himself. Remorseless, treacherous, lecherous... Like drums, like the men singing for the corn, like magic, the words repeated and repeated themselves in his head. From being cold he was suddenly hot. His cheeks burnt with the rush of blood, the room swam and darkened before his eyes. He ground his teeth. 'I'll kill him, I'll kill him, I'll kill him,' he kept saying. And suddenly there were more words.

When   he   is   drunk   asleep,   or   in   his   rage
Or in the incestuous pleasure of his bed...

The magic was on his side, the magic explained and gave orders. He stepped back into the outer room. 'When he is drunk asleep...' The knife for the meat was lying on the floor near the fireplace. He picked it up and tiptoed to the door again. 'When he is drunk asleep, drunk asleep...' He ran across the room and stabbed--oh, the blood!--stabbed again, as Popé heaved out of his sleep, lifted his hand to stab once more, but found his wrist caught, held and--oh, oh!--twisted. He couldn't move, he was trapped, and there were Popé's small black eyes, very close, staring into his own. He looked away. There were two cuts on Popé's left shoulder. 'Oh, look at the blood!' Linda was crying. 'Look at the blood!' She had never been able to bear the sight of blood. Popé lifted his other hand--to strike him, he thought. He stiffened to receive the blow. But the hand only took him under the chin and turned his face, so that he had to look again into Popé's eyes. For a long time, for hours and hours. And suddenly--he couldn't help it--he began to cry. Popé burst out laughing. 'Go,' he said, in the other Indian words. 'Go, my brave Ahaiyuta.' He ran out into the other room to hide his tears.

****

'You are fifteen,' said old Mitsima, in the Indian words. 'Now I may teach you to work the clay.'

Squatting by the river, they worked together.

'First of all,' said Mitsima, taking a lump of the wetted clay between his hands, 'we make a little moon.' The old man squeezed the lump into a disk, then bent up the edges; the moon became a shallow cup.

Slowly and unskilfully he imitated the old man's delicate gestures.

'A moon, a cup, and now a snake.' Mitsima rolled out another piece of clay into a long flexible cylinder, hooped it into a circle and pressed it on to the rim of the cup. 'Then another snake. And another. And another.' Round by round, Mitsima built up the sides of the pot; it was narrow, it bulged, it narrowed again towards the neck. Mitsima squeezed and patted, stroked and scraped; and there at last it stood, in shape the familiar water-pot of Malpais, but creamy white instead of black, and still soft to the touch. The crooked parody of Mitsima's, his own stood beside it. Looking at the two pots, he had to laugh.

'But the next one will be better,' he said, and began to moisten another piece of clay.

To fashion, to give form, to feel his fingers gaining in skill and power--this gave him an extraordinary pleasure. 'A, B, C, Vitamin D,' he sang to himself as he worked, 'The fat's in the liver, the cod's in the sea.' And Mitsima also sang--a song about killing a bear. They worked all day, and all day he was filled with an intense, absorbing happiness.

'Next winter,' said old Mitsima, 'I will teach you to make the bow.'

****

He stood for a long time outside the house; and at last the ceremonies within were finished. The door opened; they came out. Kothlu came first, his right hand outstretched and tightly closed, as though over some precious jewel. Her clenched hand similarly outstretched, Kiakimé followed. They walked in silence, and in silence, behind them, came the brothers and sisters and cousins and all the troop of old people.

They walked out of the pueblo, across the mesa. At the edge of the cliff they halted, facing the early morning sun. Kothlu opened his hand. A pinch of corn meal lay white on the palm; he breathed on it, murmured a few words, then threw it, a handful of white dust, towards the sun. Kiakimé did the same. Then Kiakimé's father stepped forward, and holding up a feathered prayer stick, made a long prayer, then threw the stick after the corn meal.

'It is finished,' said old Mitsima in a loud voice. 'They are married.'

'Well,' said Linda, as they turned away, 'all I can say is, it does seem a lot of fuss to make about so little. In civilized countries, when a boy wants to have a girl, he just... But where *are* you going, John?'

He paid no attention to her calling, but ran on, away, away, anywhere to be by himself.

It is finished. Old Mitsima's words repeated themselves in his mind. Finished, finished... In silence and from a long way off, but violently, desperately, hopelessly, he had loved Kiakimé. And now it was finished. He was sixteen.

****

At the full moon, in the Antelope Kiva, secrets would be told, secrets would be done and borne. They would go down, boys, into the kiva and come out again, men. The boys were all afraid and at the same time impatient. And at last it was the day. The sun went down, the moon rose. He went with the others. Men were standing, dark, at the entrance to the kiva; the ladder went down into the red lighted depths. Already the leading boys had begun to climb down. Suddenly one of the men stepped forward, caught him by the arm, and pulled him out of the ranks. He broke free and dodged back into his place among the others. This time the man struck him, pulled his hair. 'Not for you, white-hair!' 'Not for the son of the she-dog,' said one of the other men. The boys laughed. 'Go!' And as he still hovered on the fringes of the group, 'Go!' the men shouted again. One of them bent down, took a stone, threw it. 'Go, go, go!' There was a shower of stones. Bleeding, he ran away into the darkness. From the red-lit kiva came the noise of singing. The last of the boys had climbed down the ladder. He was all alone.

All alone, outside the pueblo, on the bare plain of the mesa. The rock was like bleached bones in the moonlight. Down in the valley, the coyotes were howling at the moon. The bruises hurt him, the cuts were still bleeding; but it was not for pain that he sobbed; it was because he was all alone, because he had been driven out, alone, into this skeleton world of rocks and moonlight. At the edge of the precipice he sat down. The moon was behind him; he looked down into the black shadow of the mesa, into the black shadow of death. He had only to take one step, one little jump.... He held out his right hand in the moonlight. From the cut on his wrist the blood was still oozing. Every few seconds a drop fell, dark, almost colourless in the dead light. Drop, drop, drop. To-morrow and to-morrow and to-morrow...

He had discovered Time and Death and God.

'Alone, always alone,' the young man was saying.

The words awoke a plaintive echo in Bernard's mind. Alone, alone... 'So am I,' he said, on a gush of confidingness. 'Terribly alone.'

'Are you?' John looked surprised. 'I thought that in the Other Place... I mean, Linda always said that nobody was ever alone there.'

Bernard blushed uncomfortably. 'You see,' he said, mumbling and with averted eyes, 'I'm rather different from most people, I suppose. If one happens to be decanted different...'

'Yes, that's just it.' The young man nodded. 'If one's different, one's bound to be lonely. They're beastly to one. Do you know, they shut me out of absolutely everything? When the other boys were sent out to spend the night on the mountains--you know, when you have to dream which your sacred animal is--they wouldn't let me go with the others; they wouldn't tell me any of the secrets. I did it by myself, though,' he added. 'Didn't eat anything for five days and then went out one night alone into those mountains there.' He pointed.

Patronizingly, Bernard smiled. 'And did you dream of anything?' he asked.

The other nodded. 'But I mustn't tell you what.' He was silent for a little; then, in a low voice, 'Once,' he went on, 'I did something that none of the others did: I stood against a rock in the middle of the day, in summer, with my arms out, like Jesus on the cross.'

'What on earth for?'

'I wanted to know what it was like being crucified. Hanging there in the sun...'

'But why?'

'Why? Well...' He hesitated. 'Because I felt I ought to. If Jesus could stand it. And then, if one has done something wrong... Besides, I was unhappy; that was another reason.'

'It seems a funny way of curing your unhappiness,' said Bernard. But on second thoughts he decided that there was, after all, some sense in it. Better than taking *soma*....

'I fainted after a time,' said the young man. 'Fell down on my face. Do you see the mark where I cut myself?' He lifted the thick yellow hair from his forehead. The scar showed, pale and puckered, on his right temple.

Bernard looked, and then quickly, with a little shudder, averted his eyes. His conditioning had made him not so much pitiful as profoundly squeamish. The mere suggestion of illness or wounds was to him not only horrifying, but even repulsive and rather disgusting. Like dirt, or deformity, or old age. Hastily he changed the subject.

'I wonder if you'd like to come back to London with us?' he asked, making the first move in a campaign whose strategy he had been secretly elaborating ever since, in the little house, he had realized who the 'father' of this young savage must be. 'Would you like that?'

The young man's face lit up. 'Do you really mean it?'

'Of course; if I can get permission, that is.'

'Linda too?'

'Well...' He hesitated doubtfully. That revolting creature! No, it was impossible. Unless, unless... It suddenly occurred to Bernard that her very revoltingness might prove an enormous asset. 'But of course!' he cried, making up for his first hesitations with an excess of noisy cordiality.

The young man drew a deep breath. 'To think it should be coming true--what I've dreamt of all my life. Do you remember what Miranda says?'

'Who's Miranda?'

But the young man had evidently not heard the question. 'O wonder!' he was saying; and his eyes shone, his face was brightly flushed. 'How many goodly creatures are there here! How beauteous mankind is!' The flush suddenly deepened; he was thinking of Lenina, of an angel in bottle-green viscose, lustrous with youth and skin food, plump, benevolently smiling. His voice faltered. 'O brave new world,' he began, then suddenly interrupted himself; the blood had left his cheeks; he was as pale as paper. 'Are you married to her?' he asked.

'Am I what?'

'Married. You know--for ever. They say "for ever" in the Indian words; it can't be broken.'

'Ford, no!' Bernard couldn't help laughing.

John also laughed, but for another reason--laughed for pure joy.

'O brave new world,' he repeated. 'O brave new world that has such people in it. Let's start at once.'

'You have a most peculiar way of talking sometimes,' said Bernard, staring at the young man in perplexed astonishment. 'And, anyhow, hadn't you better wait till you actually see the new world?'

Chapter IX

Lenina felt herself entitled, after this day of queerness and horror, to a complete and absolute holiday. As soon as they got back to the rest-house, she swallowed six half-gramme tablets of *soma*, lay down on her bed, and within ten minutes had embarked for lunar eternity. It would be eighteen hours at the least before she was in time again.

Bernard meanwhile lay pensive and wide-eyed in the dark. It was long after midnight before he fell asleep. Long after midnight; but his insomnia had not been fruitless; he had a plan.

Punctually, on the following morning, at ten o'clock, the green-uniformed octoroon stepped out of his helicopter. Bernard was waiting for him among the agaves.

'Miss Crowne's gone on *soma*-holiday,' he explained. 'Can hardly be back before five. Which leaves us seven hours.'

He could fly to Santa Fé, do all the business he had to do, and be in Malpais again long before she woke up.

'She'll be quite safe here by herself?'

'Safe as helicopters,' the octoroon assured him.

They climbed into the machine and started off at once. At ten thirty-four they landed on the roof of the Santa Fé Post Office; at ten thirty-seven Bernard had got through to the World Controller's Office in Whitehall; at ten thirty-nine he was speaking to his fordship's fourth personal secretary; at ten forty-four he was repeating his story to the first secretary, and at ten forty-seven and a half it was the deep, resonant voice of Mustapha Mond himself that sounded in his ears.

'I ventured to think,' stammered Bernard, 'that your fordship might find the matter of sufficient scientific interest...'

'Yes, I do find it of sufficient scientific interest,' said the deep voice. 'Bring these two individuals back to London with you.'

'Your fordship is aware that I shall need a special permit...'

'The necessary orders,' said Mustapha Mond, 'are being sent to the Warden of the Reservation at this moment. You will proceed at once to the Warden's Office. Good-morning, Mr. Marx.'

There was silence. Bernard hung up the receiver and hurried up to the roof.

'Warden's Office,' he said to the Gamma-green octoroon.

At ten fifty-four Bernard was shaking hands with the Warden.

'Delighted, Mr. Marx, delighted.' His boom was deferential. 'We have just received special orders...'

'I know,' said Bernard, interrupting him. 'I was talking to his fordship on the phone a moment ago.' His bored tone implied that he was in the habit of talking to his fordship every day of the week. He dropped into a chair. 'If you'll kindly take all the necessary steps as soon as possible. As soon as possible,' he emphatically repeated. He was thoroughly enjoying himself.

At eleven three he had all the necessary papers in his pocket.

'So long,' he said patronizingly to the Warden, who had accompanied him as far as the lift gates. 'So long.'

He walked across to the hotel, had a bath, a vibro-vac massage, and an electrolytic shave, listened in to the morning's news, looked in for half an hour on the televisor, ate a leisured luncheon, and at half-past two flew back with the octoroon to Malpais.

****

The young man stood outside the rest-house.

'Bernard,' he called. 'Bernard!' There was no answer.

Noiseless on his deerskin moccasins, he ran up the steps and tried the door. The door was locked.

They were gone! Gone! It was the most terrible thing that had ever happened to him. She had asked him to come and see them, and now they were gone. He sat down on the steps and cried.

Half an hour later it occurred to him to look through the window. The first thing he saw was a green suit-case, with the initials L. C. painted on the lid. Joy flared up like fire within him. He picked up a stone. The smashed glass tinkled on the floor. A moment later he was inside the room. He opened the green suit-case; and all at once he was breathing Lenina's perfume, filling his lungs with her essential being. His heart beat wildly; for a moment he was almost faint. Then, bending over the precious box, he touched, he lifted into the light, he examined. The zippers on Lenina's spare pair of viscose velveteen shorts were at first a puzzle, then, solved, a delight. Zip, and then zip; zip, and then zip; he was enchanted. Her green slippers were the most beautiful things he had ever seen. He unfolded a pair of zippicamiknicks, blushed, put them hastily away again; but kissed a perfumed acetate handkerchief and wound a scarf round his neck. Opening a box, he spilt a cloud of scented powder. His hands were floury with the stuff. He wiped them on his chest, on his shoulders, on his bare arms. Delicious perfume! He shut his eyes; he rubbed his cheek against his own powdered arm. Touch of smooth skin against his face, scent in his nostrils of musky dust--her real presence. 'Lenina,' he whispered. 'Lenina!'

A noise made him start, made him guiltily turn. He crammed up his thieveries into the suit-case and shut the lid; then listened again, looked. Not a sign of life, not a sound. And yet he had certainly heard something--something like a sigh, something like the creak of a board. He tiptoed to the door and, cautiously opening it, found himself looking on to a broad landing. On the opposite side of the landing was another door, ajar. He stepped out, pushed, peeped.

There, on a low bed, the sheet flung back, dressed in a pair of pink one-piece zippyjamas, lay Lenina, fast asleep and so beautiful in the midst of her curls, so touchingly childish with her pink toes and her grave sleeping face, so trustful in the helplessness of her limp hands and melted limbs, that the tears came to his eyes.

With an infinity of quite unnecessary precautions--for nothing short of a pisto-shot could have called Lenina back from her *soma*-holiday before the appointed time--he entered the room, he knelt on the floor beside the bed. He gazed, he clasped his hands, his lips moved. 'Her eyes,' he murmured,

'Her   eyes,   her   hair,   her   cheek,   her   gait,   her   voice;
Handlest   in   thy   discourse,   O!   that   her   hand,

| In | whose | comparison | all | whites | are | ink |
| Writing | their | own | reproach; | to | whose | soft | seizure |

The cygnet's down is harsh...'

A fly buzzed round her; he waved it away. 'Flies,' he remembered,

'On	the	white	wonder	of	dear	Juliet's	hand,	may	seize
And	steal	immortal	blessing	from	her	lips,
Who,	even	in	pure	and	vestal	modesty,

Still blush, as thinking their own kisses sin.'

Very slowly, with the hesitating gesture of one who reaches forward to stroke a shy and possibly rather dangerous bird, he put out his hand. It hung there trembling, within an inch of those limp fingers, on the verge of contact. Did he dare? Dare to profane with his unworthiest hand that... No he didn't. The bird was too dangerous. His hand dropped back. How beautiful she was! How beautiful!

Then suddenly he found himself reflecting that he had only to take hold of the zipper at her neck and give one long, strong pull.... He shut his eyes, he shook his head with the gesture of a dog shaking its ears as it emerges from the water. Detestable thought! He was ashamed of himself. Pure and vestal modesty...

There was a humming in the air. Another fly trying to steal immortal blessings? A wasp? He looked, saw nothing. The humming grew louder and louder, localized itself as being outside the shuttered windows. The plane! In a panic, he scrambled to his feet and ran into the other room, vaulted through the open window, and hurrying along the path between the tall agaves was in time to receive Bernard Marx as he climbed out of the helicopter.

Chapter X

The hands of all the four thousand electric clocks in all the Bloomsbury Centre's four thousand rooms marked twenty-seven minutes past two. 'This hive of industry,' as the Director was fond of calling it, was in the full buzz of work. Every one was busy, everything in ordered motion. Under the microscopes, their long tails furiously lashing, spermatozoa were burrowing head first into eggs; and, fertilized, the eggs were expanding, dividing, or if bokanovskified, budding and breaking up into whole populations of separate embryos. From the Social Predestination Room the escalators went rumbling down into the basement, and there, in the crimson darkness, stewingly warm on their cushion of peritoneum and gorged with blood-surrogate and hormones, the foetuses grew and grew or, poisoned, languished into a stunted Epsilonhood. With a faint hum and rattle the moving racks crawled imperceptibly through the weeks and the recapitulated æons to where, in the Decanting Room, the newly-unbottled babes uttered their first yell of horror and amazement.

The dynamos purred in the sub-basement, the lifts rushed up and down. On all the eleven floors of Nurseries it was feeding time. From eighteen hundred bottles eighteen hundred carefully labelled infants were simultaneously sucking down their pint of pasteurized external secretion.

Above them, in ten successive layers of dormitory, the little boys and girls who were still young enough to need an afternoon sleep were as busy as every one else, though they did not know it, listening unconsciously to hypnopædic lessons in hygiene and sociability, in class-consciousness and the toddler's love-life. Above these again were the playrooms where, the weather having turned to rain, nine hundred older children were amusing themselves with bricks and clay modelling, hunt-the-zipper, and erotic play.

Buzz, buzz! the hive was humming, busily, joyfully. Blithe was the singing of the young girls over their test-tubes, the Predestinators whistled as they worked, and in the Decanting Room what glorious jokes were cracked above the empty bottles! But the Director's face, as he entered the Fertilizing Room with Henry Foster, was grave, wooden with severity.

'A public example,' he was saying. 'In this room, because it contains more high-caste workers than any other in the Centre. I have told him to meet me here at half-past two.'

'He does his work very well,' put in Henry, with hypocritical generosity.

'I know. But that's all the more reason for severity. His intellectual eminence carries with it corresponding moral responsibilities. The greater a man's talents, the greater his power to lead astray. It is better that one should suffer than that many should be corrupted. Consider the matter dispassionately, Mr. Foster, and you will see that no offence is so heinous as unorthodoxy of behaviour. Murder kills only the individual--and, after all, what is an individual?' With a sweeping gesture he indicated the rows of microscopes, the test-tubes, the incubators. 'We can make a new one with the greatest ease--as many as we like. Unorthodoxy threatens more than the life of a mere individual; it strikes at Society itself. Yes, at Society itself,' he repeated. 'Ah, but here he comes.'

Bernard had entered the room and was advancing between the rows of fertilizers towards them. A veneer of jaunty self-confidence thinly concealed his nervousness. The voice in which he said, 'Good-morning, Director,' was absurdly too loud; that in which, correcting his mistake, he said, 'You asked me to come and speak to you here,' ridiculously soft, a squeak.

'Yes, Mr. Marx,' said the Director portentously. 'I did ask you to come to me here. You returned from your holiday last night, I understand.'

'Yes,' Bernard answered.

'Yes-s,' repeated the Director, lingering, a serpent, on the 's.' Then, suddenly raising his voice, 'Ladies and gentlemen,' he trumpeted, 'ladies and gentlemen.'

The singing of the girls over their test-tubes, the preoccupied whistling of the Microscopists, suddenly ceased. There was a profound silence; every one looked round.

'Ladies and gentlemen,' the Director repeated once more, 'excuse me for thus interrupting your labours. A painful duty constrains me. The security and stability of Society are in danger. Yes, in danger, ladies and gentlemen. This man,' he pointed accusingly at Bernard, 'this man who stands before you here, this Alpha-Plus to whom so much has been given, and from whom, in consequence, so much must be expected, this colleague of yours--or should I anticipate and say this ex-colleague?--has grossly betrayed the trust imposed in him. By his heretical views on sport and *soma*, by the scandalous unorthodoxy of his sex-life, by his refusal to obey the teachings of Our Ford and behave out of office hours "like a babe in a bottle"' (here the Director made the sign of the T), 'he has proved himself an enemy of Society, a subverter, ladies and gentlemen, of all Order and Stability, a conspirator against Civilization itself. For this reason I propose to dismiss him, to dismiss him with ignominy from the post he has held in this Centre; I propose forthwith to apply for his transference to a Sub-Centre of the lowest order and, that his punishment may serve the best interest of Society, as far as possible removed from any important Centre of population. In Iceland he will have small opportunity to lead others astray by his unfordly example.' The Director paused; then, folding his arms, he turned impressively to Bernard. 'Marx,' he said, 'can you show any reason why I should not now execute the judgment passed upon you?'

'Yes, I can,' Bernard answered in a very loud voice.

Somewhat taken aback, but still majestically, 'Then show it,' said the Director.

'Certainly. But it's in the passage. One moment.' Bernard hurried to the door and threw it open. 'Come in,' he commanded, and the reason came in and showed itself.

There was a gasp, a murmur of astonishment and horror; a young girl screamed; standing on a chair to get a better view some one upset two test-tubes full of spermatozoa. Bloated, sagging, and among those firm youthful bodies, those undistorted faces, a strange and terrifying monster of middle-agedness, Linda advanced into the room, coquettishly smiling her broken and discoloured smile, and rolling as she walked, with what was meant to be a voluptuous undulation, her enormous haunches. Bernard walked beside her.

'There he is,' he said, pointing at the Director.

'Did you think I didn't recognize him?' Linda asked indignantly; then, turning to the Director, 'Of course I knew you; Tomakin, I should have known you anywhere, among a thousand. But perhaps you've forgotten me. Don't you remember? Don't you remember, Tomakin? Your Linda.' She stood looking at him, her head on one side, still smiling, but with a smile that became progressively, in face of the Director's expression of petrified disgust, less and less self-confident, that wavered and finally went out. 'Don't you remember, Tomakin?' she repeated in a voice that trembled. Her eyes were anxious, agonized. The blotched and sagging face twitched grotesquely into the grimace of extreme grief. 'Tomakin!' She held out her arms. Some one began to titter.

'What's the meaning,' began the Director, 'of this monstrous...'

'Tomakin!' She ran forward, her blanket trailing behind her, threw her arms round his neck, hid her face on his chest.

A howl of laughter went up irrepressibly.

'...this monstrous practical joke,' the Director shouted.

Red in the face, he tried to disengage himself from her embrace. Desperately she clung. 'But I'm Linda, I'm Linda.' The laughter drowned her voice. 'You made me have a baby,' she screamed above the uproar. There was a sudden and appalling hush; eyes floated uncomfortably, not knowing where to look. The Director went suddenly pale, stopped struggling and stood, his hands on her wrists, staring down at her, horrified. 'Yes, a baby--and I was its mother.' She flung the obscenity like a challenge into the outraged silence; then, suddenly breaking away from him, ashamed, ashamed, covered her face with her hands, sobbing. 'It wasn't my fault, Tomakin. Because I always did my drill, didn't I? Didn't I? Always... I don't know how... If you knew how awful, Tomakin... But he was a comfort to me, all the same.' Turning towards the door, 'John!' she called. 'John!'

He came in at once, paused for a moment just inside the door, looked round, then soft on his moccasined feet strode quickly across the room, fell on his knees in front of the Director, and said in a clear voice: 'My father!'

The word (for 'father' was not so much obscene as--with its connotation of something at one remove from the loathsomeness and moral obliquity of child-bearing--merely gross, a scatological rather than a pornographic impropriety), the comically smutty word relieved what had become a quite intolerable tension. Laughter broke out, enormous, almost hysterical, peal after peal, as though it would never stop. My father--and it was the Director! My *father!* Oh, Ford, oh Ford! That was really too good. The whooping and the roaring renewed themselves, faces seemed on the point of disintegration, tears were streaming. Six more test-tubes of spermatozoa were upset. My *father!*

Pale, wild-eyed, the Director glared about him in an agony of bewildered humiliation.

My *father!* The laughter, which had shown signs of dying away, broke out again more loudly than ever. He put his hands over his ears and rushed out of the room.

Chapter XI

After the scene in the Fertilizing Room, all upper-caste London was wild to see this delicious creature who had fallen on his knees before the Director of Hatcheries and Conditioning--or rather the ex-Director, for the poor man had resigned immediately afterwards and never set foot inside the Centre again--had flopped down and called him (the joke was almost too good to be true!) 'my father.' Linda, on the contrary, cut no ice; nobody had the smallest desire to see Linda. To say one was a mother--that was past a joke: it was an obscenity. Moreover, she wasn't a real savage, had been hatched out of a bottle and conditioned like any one else: so couldn't have really quaint ideas. Finally--and this was by far the strongest reason for people's not wanting to see poor Linda--there was her appearance. Fat; having lost her youth; with bad teeth, and a blotched complexion, and that figure (Ford!)--you simply couldn't look at her without feeling sick, yes, positively sick. So the best people were quite determined *not* to see Linda. And Linda, for her part, had no desire to see them. The return to civilization was for her the return to *soma*, was the possibility of lying in bed and taking holiday after holiday, without ever having to come back to a headache or a fit of vomiting, without ever being made to feel as you always felt after *peyotl*, as though you'd done something so shamefully anti-social that you could never hold up your head again. *Soma* played none of these unpleasant tricks. The holiday it gave was perfect and, if the morning after was disagreeable, it was so, not intrinsically, but only by comparison with the joys of the holiday. The remedy was to make the holiday continuous. Greedily she clamoured for ever larger, ever more frequent doses. Dr. Shaw at first demurred; then let her have what she wanted. She took as much as twenty grammes a day.

'Which will finish her off in a month or two,' the doctor confided to Bernard. 'One day the respiratory centre will be paralysed. No more breathing. Finished. And a good thing too. If we could rejuvenate, of course it would be different. But we can't.'

Surprisingly, as every one thought (for on *soma*-holiday Linda was most conveniently out of the way), John raised objections.

'But aren't you shortening her life by giving her so much?'

'In one sense, yes,' Dr. Shaw admitted. 'But in another we're actually lengthening it.' The young man stared, uncomprehending. '*Soma* may make you lose a few years in time,' the doctor went on. 'But think of the enormous, immeasurable durations it can give you out of time. Every *soma*-holiday is a bit of what our ancestors used to call eternity.'

John began to understand. 'Eternity was in our lips and eyes,' he murmured.

'Eh?'

'Nothing,'

'Of course,' Dr. Shaw went on, 'you can't allow people to go popping off into eternity if they've got any serious work to do. But as she hasn't got any serious work...'

'All the same,' John persisted, 'I don't believe it's right.'

The doctor shrugged his shoulders. 'Well, of course, if you prefer to have her screaming mad all the time...'

In the end John was forced to give in. Linda got her *soma*. Thenceforward she remained in her little room on the thirty-seventh floor of Bernard's apartment house, in bed, with the radio and television always on, and the patchouli tap just dripping, and the *soma* tablets within reach of her hand--there she remained; and yet wasn't there at all, was all the time away, infinitely far away, on holiday; on holiday in some other world, where the music of the radio was a labyrinth of sonorous colours, a sliding, palpitating labyrinth, that led (by what beautifully inevitable windings) to a bright centre of absolute conviction; where the dancing images of the television box were the performers in some indescribably delicious all-singing feely; where the dripping patchouli was more than scent--was the sun, was a million sexophones, was Popé making love, only much more so, incomparably more, and without end.

'No, we can't rejuvenate. But I'm very glad,' Dr. Shaw had concluded, 'to have had this opportunity to see an example of senility in a human being. Thank you so much for calling me in.' He shook Bernard warmly by the hand.

It was John, then, they were all after. And as it was only through Bernard, his accredited guardian, that John could be seen, Bernard now found himself, for the first time in his life, treated not merely normally, but as a person of outstanding importance. There was no more talk of the alcohol in his blood-surrogate, no gibes at his personal appearance. Henry Foster went out of his way to be friendly; Benito Hoover made him a present of six packets of sex-hormone chewing-gum; the Assistant Predestinator came and cadged almost abjectly for an invitation to one of Bernard's evening parties. As for the women, Bernard had only to hint at the possibility of an invitation, and he could have whichever of them he liked.

'Bernard's asked me to meet the Savage next Wednesday,' Fanny announced triumphantly.

'I'm so glad,' said Lenina. 'And now you must admit that you were wrong about Bernard. Don't you think he's really rather sweet?'

Fanny nodded. 'And I must say,' she said, 'I was quite agreeably surprised.'

The Chief Bottler, the Director of Predestination, three Deputy Assistant Fertilizer-Generals, the Professor of Feelies in the College of Emotional Engineering, the Dean of the Westminster Community Singery, the Supervisor of Bokanovskification--the list of Bernard's notabilities was interminable.

'And I had six girls last week,' he confided to Helmholtz Watson. 'One on Monday, two on Tuesday, two more on Friday, and one on Saturday. And if I'd had the time or the inclination, there were at least a dozen more who were only too anxious...'

Helmholtz listened to his boastings in a silence so gloomily disapproving that Bernard was offended.

'You're envious,' he said.

Helmholtz shook his head. 'I'm rather sad, that's all,' he answered.

Bernard went off in a huff. Never, he told himself, never would he speak to Helmholtz again.

The days passed. Success went fizzily to Bernard's head, and in the process completely reconciled him (as any good intoxicant should do) to a world which, up till then, he had found very unsatisfactory. In so far as it recognized him as important, the order of things was good. But, reconciled by his success, he yet refused to forgo the privilege of criticizing this order. For the act of criticizing heightened his sense of importance, made him feel larger. Moreover, he did genuinely believe that there were things to criticize. (At the same time, he genuinely liked being a success and having all the girls he wanted.) Before those who now, for the sake of the Savage, paid their court to him, Bernard would parade a carping unorthodoxy. He was politely listened to. But behind his back people shook their heads. 'That young man will come to a bad end,' they said, prophesying the more confidently in that they themselves would in due course personally see to it that the end was bad. 'He won't find another Savage to help him out a second time,' they said. Meanwhile, however, there was the first Savage; they were polite. And because they were polite, Bernard felt positively gigantic--gigantic and at the same time light with elation, lighter than air.

****

'Lighter than air,' said Bernard, pointing upwards.

Like a pearl in the sky, high, high above them, the Weather Department's captive balloon shone rosily in the sunshine.

'...the said Savage,' so ran Bernard's instructions, 'to be shown civilized life in all its aspects....'

He was being shown a bird's-eye view of it at present, a bird's-eye view from the platform of the Charing-T Tower. The Station Master and the Resident Meteorologist were acting as guides. But it was Bernard who did most of the talking. Intoxicated, he was behaving as though, at the very least, he were a visiting World Controller. Lighter than air.

The Bombay Green Rocket dropped out of the sky. The passengers alighted. Eight identical Dravidian twins in khaki looked out of the eight portholes of the cabin--the stewards.

'Twelve hundred and fifty kilometres an hour,' said the Station Master impressively. 'What do you think of that, Mr. Savage?'

John thought it very nice. 'Still,' he said, 'Ariel could put a girdle round the earth in forty minutes.'

****

'The Savage,' wrote Bernard in his report to Mustapha Mond, 'shows surprisingly little astonishment at, or awe of, civilized inventions. This is partly due, no doubt, to the fact that he has heard them talked about by the woman Linda, his m----.'

(Mustapha Mond frowned. 'Does the fool think I'm too squeamish to see the word written out at full length?')

'Partly on his interest being focussed on what he calls "the soul," which he persists as regarding as an entity independent of the physical environment; whereas, as I tried to point out to him...'

The Controller skipped the next sentences and was just about to turn the page in search of something more interestingly concrete, when his eye was caught by a series of quite extraordinary phrases. '...though I must admit,' he read, 'that I agree with the Savage in finding civilized infantility too easy or, as he puts it, not expensive enough; and I would like to take this opportunity of drawing your fordship's attention to...'

Mustapha Mond's anger gave place almost at once to mirth. The idea of this creature solemnly lecturing him--*him*--about the social order was really too grotesque. The man must have gone mad. 'I ought to give him a lesson,' he said to himself; then threw back his head and laughed aloud. For the moment, at any rate, the lesson would not be given.

****

It was a small factory of lighting-sets for helicopters, a branch of the Electrical Equipment Corporation. They were met on the roof itself (for that circular letter of recommendation from the Controller was magical in its effects) by the Chief Technician and the Human Element Manager. They walked downstairs into the factory.

'Each process,' explained the Human Element Manager, 'is carried out, so far as possible, by a single Bokanovsky Group.'

And, in effect, eighty-three almost noseless black brachycephalic Deltas were cold-pressing. The fifty-six four-spindle chucking and turning machines were being manipulated by fifty-six aquiline and ginger Gammas. One hundred and seven heat-conditioned Epsilon Senegalese were working in the foundry. Thirty-three Delta females, long-headed, sandy, with narrow pelvises, and all within 20 millimetres of 1 metre 69 centimetres tall, were cutting screws. In the assembling room, the dynamos were being put together by two sets of Gamma-Plus dwarfs. The two low work-tables faced one another; between them crawled the conveyor with its load of separate parts; forty-seven blond heads were confronted by forty-seven brown ones. Forty-seven snubs by forty-seven hooks; forty-seven receding by forty-seven prognathous chins. The completed mechanisms were inspected by eighteen identical curly auburn girls in Gamma green, packed in crates by thirty-four short-legged, left-handed male Delta-Minuses, and loaded into the waiting trucks and lorries by sixty-three blue-eyed, flaxen and freckled Epsilon Semi-Morons.

'O brave new world...' By some malice of his memory the Savage found himself repeating Miranda's words. 'O brave new world that has such people in it.'

'And I assure you,' the Human Element Manager concluded, as they left the factory, 'we hardly ever have any trouble with our workers. We always find...'

But the Savage had suddenly broken away from his companions and was violently retching, behind a clump of laurels, as though the solid earth had been a helicopter in an air pocket.

****

'The Savage,' wrote Bernard, 'refuses to take *soma*, and seems much distressed because the woman Linda, his m----, remains permanently on holiday. It is worthy of note that, in spite of his m----'s senility and the extreme repulsiveness of her appearance, the Savage frequently goes to see her and appears to be much attached to her--an interesting example of the way in which early conditioning can be made to modify and even run counter to natural impulses (in this case, the impulse to recoil from an unpleasant object).'

****

At Eton they alighted on the roof of Upper School. On the opposite side of School Yard, the fifty-two stories of Lupton's Tower gleamed white in the sunshine. College on their left and, on their right, the School Community Singery reared their venerable piles of ferro-concrete and vita-glass. In the centre of the quadrangle stood the quaint old chrome-steel statue of Our Ford.

Dr. Gaffney, the Provost, and Miss Keate, the Head Mistress, received them as they stepped out of the plane.

'Do you have many twins here?' the Savage asked rather apprehensively, as they set out on their tour of inspection.

'Oh no,' the Provost answered. 'Eton is reserved exclusively for upper-caste boys and girls. One egg, one adult. It makes education more difficult, of course. But as they'll be called upon to take responsibilities and deal with unexpected emergencies, it can't be helped.' He sighed.

Bernard, meanwhile, had taken a strong fancy to Miss Keate. 'If you're free any Monday, Wednesday, or Friday evening,' he was saying. Jerking his thumb towards the Savage, 'He's curious, you know,' Bernard added. 'Quaint.'

Miss Keate smiled (and her smile was really charming, he thought); said Thank you; would be delighted to come to one of his parties. The Provost opened a door.

Five minutes in that Alpha-Double-Plus classroom left John a trifle bewildered.

'What *is* elementary relativity?' he whispered to Bernard. Bernard tried to explain, then thought better of it and suggested that they should go to some other classroom.

From behind a door in the corridor leading to the Beta-Minus geography room, a ringing soprano voice called, 'One, two, three, four,' and then, with a weary impatience, 'As you were.'

'Malthusian Drill,' explained the Head Mistress. 'Most of our girls are freemartins, of course. I'm a freemartin myself.' She smiled at Bernard. 'But we have about eight hundred unsterilized ones who need constant drilling.'

In the Beta-Minus geography room John learnt that 'a savage reservation is a place which, owing to unfavourable climatic or geological conditions, or poverty of natural resources, has not been worth the expense of civilizing.' A click; the room was darkened; and suddenly, on the screen above the Master's head, there were the *Penitentes* of Acoma prostrating themselves before Our Lady, and wailing as John had heard them wail, confessing their sins before Jesus on the cross, before the eagle image of Pookong. The young Etonians fairly shouted with laughter. Still wailing, the *Penitentes* rose to their feet, stripped off their upper garments and, with knotted whips, began to beat themselves, blow after blow. Redoubled, the laughter drowned even the amplified record of their groans.

'But why do they laugh?' asked the Savage in a pained bewilderment.

'Why?' The Provost turned towards him a still broadly grinning face. '*Why?* But because it's so extraordinarily funny.'

In the cinematographic twilight, Bernard risked a gesture which, in the past, even total darkness would hardly have emboldened him to make. Strong in his new importance, he put his arm round the Head Mistress's waist. It yielded, willowily. He was just about to snatch a kiss or two and perhaps a gentle pinch, when the shutters clicked open again.

'Perhaps we had better go on,' said Miss Keate, and moved towards the door.

'And this,' said the Provost a moment later, 'is the Hypnopædic Control Room.'

Hundreds of synthetic music boxes, one for each dormitory, stood ranged in shelves round three sides of the room; pigeon-holed on the fourth were the paper sound-track rolls on which the various hypnopædic lessons were printed.

'You slip the roll in here,' explained Bernard, interrupting Dr. Gaffney, 'press down this switch...'

'No, that one,' corrected the Provost, annoyed.

'That one, then. The roll unwinds. The selenium cells transform the light impulses into sound waves, and...'

'And there you are,' Dr. Gaffney concluded.

'Do they read Shakespeare?' asked the Savage as they walked, on their way to the Bio-chemical Laboratories, past the School Library.

'Certainly not,' said the Head Mistress, blushing.

'Our library,' said Dr. Gaffney, 'contains only books of reference. If our young people need distraction, they can get it at the feelies. We don't encourage them to indulge in any solitary amusements.'

Five bus-loads of boys and girls, singing or in a silent embracement, rolled past them over the vitrified highway.

'Just returned,' explained Dr. Gaffney, while Bernard, whispering, made an appointment with the Head Mistress for that very evening, 'from the Slough Crematorium. Death conditioning begins at eighteen months. Every tot spends two mornings a week in a Hospital for the Dying. All the best toys are kept there, and they get chocolate cream on death days. They learn to take dying as a matter of course.'

'Like any other physiological process,' put in the Head Mistress professionally.

Eight o'clock at the Savoy. It was all arranged.

****

On their way back to London they stopped at the Television Corporation's factory at Brentford.

'Do you mind waiting here a moment while I go and telephone?' asked Bernard.

The Savage waited and watched. The Main Day-Shift was just going off duty. Crowds of lower-caste workers were queued-up in front of the monorail station--seven or eight hundred Gamma, Delta and Epsilon men and women, with not more than a dozen faces and statures between them. To each of them, with his or her ticket, the booking clerk pushed over a little cardboard pillbox. The long caterpillar of men and women moved slowly forward.

'What's in those' (remembering *The Merchant of Venice*), 'those caskets?' the Savage enquired when Bernard had rejoined him.

'The day's *soma* ration,' Bernard answered, rather indistinctly; for he was masticating a piece of Benito Hoover's chewing-gum. 'They get it after their work's over. Four half-gramme tablets. Six on Saturdays.'

He took John's arm affectionately and they walked back towards the helicopter.

****

Lenina came singing into the Changing Room.

'You seem very pleased with yourself,' said Fanny.

'I *am* pleased,' she answered. Zip! 'Bernard rang up half an hour ago.' Zip, zip! She stepped out of her shorts. 'He has an unexpected engagement.' Zip! 'Asked me if I'd take the Savage to the feelies this evening. I must fly.' She hurried away towards the bathroom.

'She's a lucky girl,' Fanny said to herself as she watched Lenina go.

There was no envy in the comment; good-natured Fanny was merely stating a fact. Lenina *was* lucky; lucky in having shared with Bernard a generous portion of the Savage's immense celebrity, lucky in reflecting from her insignificant person the moment's supremely fashionable glory. Had not the Secretary of the Young Women's Fordian Association asked her to give a lecture about her experiences? Had she not been invited to the Annual Dinner of the Aphroditæum Club? Had she not already appeared in the Feelytone News--visibly, audibly and tactually appeared to countless millions all over the planet?

Hardly less flattering had been the attentions paid her by conspicuous individuals. The Resident World Controller's Second Secretary had asked her to dinner and breakfast. She had spent one week-end with the Ford Chief-Justice, and another with the Arch-Community-Songster of Canterbury. The President of the Internal and

External Secretions Corporation was perpetually on the phone, and she had been to Deauville with the Deputy-Governor of the Bank of Europe.

'It's wonderful, of course. And yet in a way,' she had confessed to Fanny, 'I feel as though I were getting something on false pretences. Because, of course, the first thing they all want to know is what it's like to make love to a Savage. And I have to say I don't know.' She shook her head. 'Most of the men don't believe me, of course. But it's true. I wish it weren't,' she added sadly and sighed. 'He's terribly good-looking; don't you think so?'

'But doesn't he like you?' asked Fanny.

'Sometimes I think he does and sometimes I think he doesn't. He always does his best to avoid me; goes out of the room when I come in; won't touch me; won't even look at me. But sometimes if I turn round suddenly, I catch him staring; and then--well, you know how men look when they like you.'

Yes, Fanny knew.

'I can't make it out,' said Lenina.

She couldn't make it out; and not only was bewildered; was also rather upset.

'Because, you see, Fanny, *I* like him.'

Liked him more and more. Well, now there'd be a real chance, she thought, as she scented herself after her bath. Dab, dab, dab--a real chance. Her high spirits overflowed in song.

'Hug	me	till	you	drug	me,	honey;
Kiss	me	till	I'm	in	a	coma:
Hug	me,	honey,		snuggly		bunny;

Love's as good as *soma*.'

****

The scent organ was playing a delightfully refreshing Herbal Capriccio--rippling arpeggios of thyme and lavender, of rosemary, basil, myrtle, tarragon; a series of daring modulations through the spice keys into ambergris; and a slow return through sandalwood, camphor, cedar and new-mown hay (with occasional subtle touches of discord--a whiff of kidney pudding, the faintest suspicion of pig's dung) back to the simple aromatics with which the piece began. The final blast of thyme died away; there was a round of applause; the lights went up. In the synthetic music machine the sound-track roll began to unwind. It was a trio for hyper-violin, super-'cello and oboe-surrogate that now filled the air with its agreeable languor. Thirty or forty bars--and then, against this instrumental background, a much more than human voice began to warble; now throaty, now from the head, now hollow as a flute, now charged with yearning harmonics, it effortlessly passed from Gaspard Forster's low record on the very frontiers of musical tone to a trilled bat-note high above the highest C to which (in 1770, at the Ducal opera of Parma, and to the astonishment of Mozart) Lucrezia Ajugari, alone of all the singers in history, once piercingly gave utterance.

Sunk in their pneumatic stalls, Lenina and the Savage sniffed and listened. It was now the turn also for eyes and skin.

The house lights went down; fiery letters stood out solid and as though self-supported in the darkness. THREE WEEKS IN A HELICOPTER. AN ALL-SUPER-SINGING, SYNTHETIC-TALKING, COLOURED, STEREOSCOPIC FEELY. WITH SYNCHRONIZED SCENT-ORGAN ACCOMPANIMENT.

'Take hold of those metal knobs on the arms of your chair,' whispered Lenina. 'Otherwise you won't get any of the feely effects.'

The Savage did as he was told.

Those fiery letters, meanwhile, had disappeared; there were ten seconds of complete darkness; then suddenly, dazzling and incomparably more solid-looking than they would have seemed in actual flesh and blood, far more real than reality, there stood the stereoscopic images, locked in one another's arms, of a gigantic negro and a golden-haired young brachycephalic Beta-Plus female.

The Savage started. That sensation on his lips! He lifted a hand to his mouth; the titillation ceased; let his hand fall back on the metal knob; it began again. The scent organ, meanwhile, breathed pure musk. Expiringly, a sound-track super-dove cooed 'Oo-oh'; and vibrating only thirty-two times a second, a deeper than African bass made answer: 'Aa-aah.' 'Ooh-ah! Ooh-ah!' the stereoscopic lips came together again, and once more the facial erogenous zones of the six thousand spectators in the Alhambra tingled with almost intolerable galvanic pleasure. 'Ooh...'

The plot of the film was extremely simple. A few minutes after the first Ooh's and Aah's (a duet having been sung and a little love made on that famous bearskin, every hair of which--the Assistant Predestinator was perfectly right--could be separately and distinctly felt), the negro had a helicopter accident, fell on his head. Thump! what a twinge through the forehead! A chorus of *ow's* and *aie's* went up from the audience.

The concussion knocked all the negro's conditioning into a cocked hat. He developed for the Beta blonde an exclusive and maniacal passion. She protested. He persisted. There were struggles, pursuits, an assault on a rival, finally a sensational kidnapping. The Beta blonde was ravished away into the sky and kept there, hovering, for three weeks in a wildly anti-social *tête-à-tête* with the black madman. Finally, after a whole series of adventures and much aerial acrobacy, three handsome young Alphas succeeded in rescuing her. The negro was packed off to an Adult Re-conditioning Centre and the film ended happily and decorously, with the Beta blonde becoming the mistress of all her three rescuers. They interrupted themselves for a moment to sing a synthetic quartet, with full super-orchestral accompaniment and gardenias on the scent organ. Then the bearskin made a final appearance and, amid a blare of sexophones, the last stereoscopic kiss faded into darkness, the last electric titillation died on the lips like a dying moth that quivers, quivers, ever more feebly, ever more faintly, and at last is quite, quite still.

But for Lenina the moth did not completely die. Even after the lights had gone up, while they were shuffling slowly along with the crowd towards the lifts, its ghost still fluttered against her lips, still traced fine shuddering roads of anxiety and pleasure across her skin. Her cheeks were flushed, her eyes dewily bright, her breath came deeply. She caught hold of the Savage's arm and pressed it, limp, against her side. He looked down at her for a moment, pale, pained, desiring, and ashamed of his desire. He was not worthy, not... Their eyes for a moment met. What treasures hers promised! A queen's ransom of temperament. Hastily he looked away, disengaged his imprisoned arm. He was obscurely terrified lest she should cease to be something he could feel himself unworthy of.

'I don't think you ought to see things like that,' he said, making haste to transfer from Lenina herself to the surrounding circumstances the blame for any past or possible future lapse from perfection.

'Things like what, John?'

'Like this horrible film.'

'Horrible?' Lenina was genuinely astonished. 'But I thought it was lovely.'

'It was base,' he said indignantly, 'it was ignoble.'

She shook her head. 'I don't know what you mean.' Why was he so queer? Why did he go out of his way to spoil things?

In the taxicopter he hardly even looked at her. Bound by strong vows that had never been pronounced, obedient to laws that had long since ceased to run, he sat averted and in silence. Sometimes, as though a finger had plucked at some taut, almost breaking string, his whole body would shake with a sudden nervous start.

The taxicopter landed on the roof of Lenina's apartment house. 'At last,' she thought exultantly as she stepped out of the cab. At last--even though he *had* been so queer just now. Standing under a lamp, she peered into her hand-mirror. At last. Yes, her nose *was* a bit shiny. She shook the loose powder from her puff. While he was paying off the taxi--there would just be time. She rubbed at the shininess, thinking: 'He's terribly good-looking. No need for him to be shy like Bernard. And yet... Any other man would have done it long ago. Well, now at last.' That fragment of a face in the little round mirror suddenly smiled at her.

'Good-night,' said a strangled voice behind her. Lenina wheeled round. He was standing in the doorway of the cab, his eyes fixed, staring; had evidently been staring all this time while she was powdering her nose, waiting--but what for? or hesitating, trying to make up his mind, and all the time thinking, thinking--she could not imagine what extraordinary thoughts. 'Good-night, Lenina,' he repeated, and made a strange grimacing attempt to smile.

'But, John... I thought you were... I mean, aren't you?...'

He shut the door and bent forward to say something to the driver. The cab shot up into the air.

Looking down through the window in the floor, the Savage could see Lenina's upturned face, pale in the bluish light of the lamps. The mouth was open, she was calling. Her foreshortened figure rushed away from him; the diminishing square of the roof seemed to be falling through the darkness.

Five minutes later he was back in his room. From its hiding-place he took out his mouse-nibbled volume, turned with religious care its stained and crumpled pages, and began to read *Othello*. Othello, he remembered, was like the hero of *Three Weeks in a Helicopter*--a black man.

Drying her eyes, Lenina walked across the roof to the lift. On her way down to the twenty-seventh floor she pulled out her *soma* bottle. One gramme, she decided, would not be enough; hers had been more than a one-gramme affliction. But if she took two grammes, she ran the risk of not waking up in time to-morrow morning. She compromised and, into her cupped left palm, shook out three half-gramme tablets.

Chapter XII

Bernard had to shout through the locked door; the Savage would not open.

'But everybody's there, waiting for you.'

'Let them wait,' came back the muffled voice through the door.

'But you know quite well, John' (how difficult it is to sound persuasive at the top of one's voice!), 'I asked them on purpose to meet you.'

'You ought to have asked *me* first whether I wanted to meet *them*.'

'But you always came before, John.'

'That's precisely why I don't want to come again.'

'Just to please me,' Bernard bellowingly wheedled. 'Won't you come to please me?'

'No.'

'Do you seriously mean it?'

'Yes.'

Despairingly, 'But what shall I do?' Bernard wailed.

'Go to hell!' bawled the exasperated voice from within.

'But the Arch-Community-Songster of Canterbury is there to-night.' Bernard was almost in tears.

'*Ai yaa tákwa!*' It was only in Zuñi that the Savage could adequately express what he felt about the Arch-Community-Songster. '*Háni!*' he added as an afterthought; and then (with what derisive ferocity!): '*Sons éso tse-ná.*' And he spat on the ground, as Popé might have done.

In the end Bernard had to slink back, diminished, to his rooms and inform the impatient assembly that the Savage would not be appearing that evening. The news was received with indignation. The men were furious at having been tricked into behaving politely to this insignificant fellow with the unsavoury reputation and the heretical opinions. The higher their position in the hierarchy, the deeper their resentment.

'To play such a joke on me,' the Arch-Songster kept repeating, 'on *me*!'

As for the women, they indignantly felt that they had been had on false pretences--had by a wretched little man who had had alcohol poured into his bottle by mistake--by a creature with a Gamma-Minus physique. It was an outrage, and they said so, more and more loudly. The Head Mistress of Eton was particularly scathing.

Lenina alone said nothing. Pale, her blue eyes clouded with an unwonted melancholy, she sat in a corner, cut off from those who surrounded her by an emotion which they did not share. She had come to the party filled with a strange feeling of anxious exultation. 'In a few minutes,' she had said to herself, as she entered the room, 'I shall be seeing him, talking to him, telling him' (for she had come with her mind made up) 'that I like him--more than anybody I've ever known. And then perhaps he'll say...'

What would he say? The blood had rushed to her cheeks.

'Why was he so strange the other night, after the feelies? So queer. And yet I'm absolutely sure he really does rather like me. I'm sure...'

It was at this moment that Bernard had made his announcement; the Savage wasn't coming to the party.

Lenina suddenly felt all the sensations normally experienced at the beginning of a Violent Passion Surrogate treatment--a sense of dreadful emptiness, a breathless apprehension, a nausea. Her heart seemed to stop beating.

'Perhaps it's because he doesn't like me,' she said to herself. And at once this possibility became an established certainty: John had refused to come because he didn't like her. He didn't like her....

'It really is a bit *too* thick,' the Head Mistress of Eton was saying to the Director of Crematoria and Phosphorus Reclamation. 'When I think that I actually...'

'Yes,' came the voice of Fanny Crowne, 'it's absolutely true about the alcohol. Some one I know knew some one who was working in the Embryo Store at the time. She said to my friend, and my friend said to me...'

'Too bad, too bad,' said Henry Foster, sympathizing with the Arch-Community-Songster. 'It may interest you to know that our ex-Director was on the point of transferring him to Iceland.'

Pierced by every word that was spoken, the tight balloon of Bernard's happy self-confidence was leaking from a thousand wounds. Pale, distraught, abject and agitated, he moved among his guests, stammering incoherent apologies, assuring them that next time the Savage would certainly be there, begging them to sit down and take a carotine sandwich, a slice of vitamin A *pâté*, a glass of champagne-surrogate. They duly ate, but ignored him; drank and were either rude to his face or talked to one another about him, loudly and offensively as though he had not been there.

'And now, my friends,' said the Arch-Community-Songster of Canterbury, in that beautiful ringing voice with which he led the proceedings at Ford's Day Celebrations, 'Now, my friends, I think perhaps the time has come...' He rose, put down his glass, brushed from his purple viscose waistcoat the crumbs of a considerable collation, and walked towards the door.

Bernard darted forward to intercept him.

'Must you really, Arch-Songster?... It's very early still. I'd hoped you would...'

Yes, what hadn't he hoped, when Lenina confidentially told him that the Arch-Community-Songster would accept an invitation if it were sent. 'He's really rather sweet, you know.' And she had shown Bernard the little golden zipper-fastening in the form of a T which the Arch-Songster had given her as a memento of the week-end she had spent at the Diocesan Singery. *To meet the Arch-Community-Songster of Canterbury and Mr. Savage.* Bernard had proclaimed his triumph on every invitation card. But the Savage had chosen this evening of all evenings to lock himself up in his room, to shout '*Háni!*' and even (it was lucky that Bernard didn't understand Zuñi) '*Sons éso tse-ná!*' What should have been the crowning moment of Bernard's whole career had turned out to be the moment of his greatest humiliation.

'I'd so much hoped...' he stammeringly repeated, looking up at the great dignitary with pleading and distracted eyes.

'My young friend,' said the Arch-Community-Songster in a tone of loud and solemn severity; there was a general silence. 'Let me give you a word of advice.' He wagged his finger at Bernard. 'Before it's too late. A word of good advice.' (His voice became sepulchral.) 'Mend your ways, my young friend, mend your ways.' He made the sign of the T over him and turned away. 'Lenina, my dear,' he called in another tone. 'Come with me.'

Obediently, but unsmiling and (wholly insensible of the honour done to her) without elation, Lenina walked after him, out of the room. The other guests followed at a respectful interval. The last of them slammed the door. Bernard was all alone.

Punctured, utterly deflated, he dropped into a chair and, covering his face with his hands, began to weep. A few minutes later, however, he thought better of it and took four tablets of *soma*.

****

Upstairs in his room the Savage was reading *Romeo and Juliet*.

****

Lenina and the Arch-Community-Songster stepped out on to the roof of the Singery. 'Hurry up, my young friend--I mean, Lenina,' called the Arch-Songster impatiently from the lift gates. Lenina, who had lingered for a moment to look at the moon, dropped her eyes and came hurrying across the roof to rejoin him.

****

'A New Theory of Biology' was the title of the paper which Mustapha Mond had just finished reading. He sat for some time, meditatively frowning, then picked up his pen and wrote across the title-page. 'The author's mathematical treatment of the conception of purpose is novel and highly ingenious, but heretical and, so far as the present social order is concerned, dangerous and potentially subversive. *Not to be published.*' He underlined the words. 'The author will be kept under supervision. His transference to the Marine Biological Station of St. Helena may become necessary.' A pity, he thought, as he signed his name. It was a masterly piece of work. But once you began admitting explanations in terms of purpose--well, you didn't know what the result might be. It was the sort of idea that might easily de-condition the more unsettled minds among the higher castes--make them lose their faith in happiness as the Sovereign Good and take to believing, instead, that the goal was somewhere beyond, somewhere outside the present human sphere; that the purpose of life was not the maintenance of well-being, but some intensification and refining of consciousness, some enlargement of knowledge. Which was, the Controller reflected, quite possibly true. But not, in the present circumstance, admissible. He picked up his pen again, and under the words '*Not to be published*' drew a second line, thicker and blacker than the first; then sighed. 'What fun it would be,' he thought, 'if one didn't have to think about happiness!'

****

With closed eyes, his face shining with rapture, John was softly declaiming to vacancy:

'O, she doth teach the torches to burn bright!
It seems she hangs upon the cheek of night
Like a rich jewel in an Ethiop's ear;
Beauty too rich for use, for earth too dear....'

****

The golden T lay shining on Lenina's bosom. Sportively, the Arch-Community-Songster caught hold of it, sportively he pulled, pulled. 'I think,' said Lenina suddenly, breaking a long silence, 'I'd better take a couple of grammes of *soma*.'

****

Bernard, by this time, was fast asleep and smiling at the private paradise of his dreams. Smiling, smiling. But inexorably, every thirty seconds, the minute hand of the electric clock above his bed jumped forward with an almost imperceptible click. Click, click, click, click... And it was morning. Bernard was back among the miseries of space and time. It was in the lowest spirits that he taxied across to his work at the Conditioning Centre. The intoxication of success had evaporated; he was soberly his old self; and by contrast with the temporary balloon of these last weeks, the old self seemed unprecedentedly heavier than the surrounding atmosphere.

To this deflated Bernard the Savage showed himself unexpectedly sympathetic.

'You're more like what you were at Malpais,' he said, when Bernard had told him his plaintive story. 'Do you remember when we first talked together? Outside the little house. You're like what you were then.'

'Because I'm unhappy again; that's why.'

'Well, I'd rather be unhappy than have the sort of false, lying happiness you were having here.'

'I like that,' said Bernard bitterly. 'When it's you who were the cause of it all. Refusing to come to my party and so turning them all against me!' He knew that what he was saying was absurd in its injustice; he admitted inwardly, and at last even aloud, the truth of all that the Savage now said about the worthlessness of friends who could be turned upon so slight a provocation into persecuting enemies. But in spite of this knowledge and these admissions, in spite of the fact that his friend's support and sympathy were now his only comfort, Bernard continued perversely to nourish, along with his quite genuine affection, a secret grievance against the Savage, to meditate a campaign of small revenges to be wreaked upon him. Nourishing a grievance against the Arch-Community-Songster was useless; there was no possibility of being revenged on the Chief Bottler or the Assistant Predestinator. As a victim, the Savage possessed, for Bernard, this enormous superiority over the others: that he was accessible. One of the principal functions of a friend is to suffer (in a milder and symbolic form) the punishments that we should like, but are unable, to inflict upon our enemies.

Bernard's other victim-friend was Helmholtz. When, discomfited, he came and asked once more for the friendship which in his prosperity he had not thought it worth his while to preserve, Helmholtz gave it; and gave it without a reproach, without a comment, as though he had forgotten that there had ever been a quarrel. Touched, Bernard felt himself at the same time humiliated by this magnanimity--a magnanimity the more extraordinary and therefore the more humiliating in that it owed nothing to *soma* and everything to Helmholtz's character. It was the Helmholtz of daily life who forgot and forgave, not the Helmholtz of a half-gramme holiday. Bernard was duly grateful (it was an enormous comfort to have his friend again) and also duly resentful (it would be a pleasure to take some revenge on Helmholtz for his generosity.)

At their first meeting after the estrangement, Bernard poured out the tale of his miseries and accepted consolation. It was not till some days later that he learned, to his surprise and with a twinge of shame, that he was not the only one who had been in trouble. Helmholtz had also come into conflict with Authority.

'It was over some rhymes,' he explained. 'I was giving my usual course of Advanced Emotional Engineering for Third Year Students. Twelve lectures, of which the seventh is about rhymes. "On the Use of Rhymes in Moral Propaganda and Advertisement," to be precise. I always illustrate my lecture with a lot of technical examples. This time I thought I'd give them one I'd just written myself. Pure madness, of course; but I couldn't resist it.' He laughed. 'I was curious to see what their reactions would be. Besides,' he added more gravely, 'I wanted to do a bit of propaganda; I was trying to engineer them into feeling as I'd felt when I wrote the rhymes. Ford!' He laughed again.

'What an outcry there was! The Principal had me up and threatened to hand me the immediate sack. I'm a marked man.'

'But what were your rhymes?' Bernard asked.

'They were about being alone.'

Bernard's eyebrows went up.

'I'll recite them to you, if you like.' And Helmholtz began:

'Yesterday's committee,
Sticks, but a broken drum,
Midnight in the City,
Flutes in a vacuum,
Shut lips, sleeping faces,
Every stopped machine,
The dumb and littered places
Where crowds have been--
All silences rejoice,
Weep (loudly or low),
Speak--but with the voice
Of whom, I do not know.
Absence, say, of Susan's,
Absence of Egeria's
Arms and respective bosoms,
Lips and, ah, posteriors,
Slowly form a presence;
Whose? and, I ask, of what
So absurd an essence,
That something, which is not,
Nevertheless should populate
Empty night more solidly
Than that with which we copulate,
Why should it seem so squalidly?

Well, I gave them that as an example, and they reported me to the Principal.'

'I'm not surprised,' said Bernard. 'It's flatly against all their sleep-teaching. Remember, they've had at least a quarter of a million warnings against solitude.'

'I know. But I thought I'd like to see what the effect would be.'

'Well, you've seen now.'

Helmholtz only laughed. 'I feel,' he said, after a silence, 'as though I were just beginning to have something to write about. As though I were beginning to be able to use that power I feel I've got inside me--that extra, latent power. Something seems to be coming to me.' In spite of all his troubles, he seemed, Bernard thought, profoundly happy.

Helmholtz and the Savage took to one another at once. So cordially indeed that Bernard felt a sharp pang of jealousy. In all these weeks he had never come to so close an intimacy with the Savage as Helmholtz immediately achieved. Watching them, listening to their talk, he found himself sometimes resentfully wishing that he had never brought them together. He was ashamed of his jealousy and alternately made efforts of will and took *soma* to keep himself from feeling it. But the efforts were not very successful; and between the *soma*-holidays there were, of necessity, intervals. The odious sentiment kept on returning.

At his third meeting with the Savage, Helmholtz recited his rhymes on Solitude.

'What do you think of them?' he asked when he had done.

The Savage shook his head. 'Listen to *this*,' was his answer; and unlocking the drawer in which he kept his mouse-eaten book, he opened and read:

'Let   the   bird   of   loudest   lay,
On   the   sole   Arabian   tree,
Herald sad and trumpet be...'

Helmholtz listened with a growing excitement. At 'sole Arabian tree' he started; at 'thou shrieking harbinger' he smiled with sudden pleasure; at 'every fowl of tyrant wing' the blood rushed up into his cheeks; but at 'defunctive music' he turned pale and trembled with an unprecedented emotion. The Savage read on:

'Property   was   thus   appall'd,
That   the   self   was   not   the   same;
Single   nature's   double   name
Neither   two   nor   one   was   call'd.

Reason   in   itself   confounded
Saw division grow together...'

'Orgy-porgy!' said Bernard, interrupting the reading with a loud, unpleasant laugh. 'It's just a Solidarity Service hymn.' He was revenging himself on his two friends for liking one another more than they liked him.

In the course of their next two or three meetings he frequently repeated this little act of vengeance. It was simple and, since both Helmholtz and the Savage were dreadfully pained by the shattering and defilement of a favourite poetic crystal, extremely effective. In the end, Helmholtz threatened to kick him out of the room if he dared to interrupt again. And yet, strangely enough, the next interruption, the most disgraceful of all, came from Helmholtz himself.

The Savage was reading *Romeo and Juliet* aloud--reading (for all the time he was seeing himself as Romeo and Lenina as Juliet) with an intense and quivering passion. Helmholtz had listened to the scene of the lovers' first meeting with a puzzled interest. The scene in the orchard had delighted him with its poetry; but the sentiments expressed had made him smile. Getting into such a state about having a girl--it seemed rather ridiculous. But, taken detail by verbal detail, what a superb piece of emotional engineering! 'That old fellow,' he said, 'he makes our best propaganda technicians look absolutely silly.' The Savage smiled triumphantly and resumed his reading. All went tolerably well until, in the last scene of the third act, Capulet and Lady Capulet began to bully Juliet to marry Paris. Helmholtz had been restless throughout the entire scene; but when, pathetically mimed by the Savage, Juliet cried out:

'Is   there   no   pity   sitting   in   the   clouds,
That   sees   into   the   bottom   of   my   grief?
O,   sweet   my   mother,   cast   me   not   away!
Delay   this   marriage   for   a   month,   a   week;
Or,   if   you   do   not,   make   the   bridal   bed
In that dim monument where Tybalt lies...'

when Juliet said this, Helmholtz broke out in an explosion of uncontrollable guffawing.

The mother and father (grotesque obscenity) forcing the daughter to have some one she didn't want! And the idiotic girl not saying that she was having some one else whom (for the moment, at any rate) she preferred! In its smutty absurdity the situation was irresistibly comical. He had managed, with a heroic effort, to hold down the mounting pressure of his hilarity; but 'sweet mother' (in the Savage's tremulous tone of anguish) and the reference to Tybalt lying dead, but evidently uncremated and wasting his phosphorus on a dim monument, were too much for him. He laughed and laughed till the tears streamed down his face--quenchlessly laughed while, pale with a sense of outrage, the Savage looked at him over the top of his book and then, as the laughter still continued, closed it indignantly, got up and, with the gesture of one who removes his pearl from before swine, locked it away in its drawer.

'And yet,' said Helmholtz when, having recovered breath enough to apologize, he had mollified the Savage into listening to his explanations, 'I know quite well that one needs ridiculous, mad situations like that; one can't write really well about anything else. Why was that old fellow such a marvellous propaganda technician? Because he had so many insane, excruciating things to get excited about. You've got to be hurt and upset; otherwise you can't think of the really good, penetrating, X-rayish phrases. But fathers and mothers!' He shook his head. 'You can't expect me to keep a straight face about fathers and mothers. And who's going to get excited about a boy having a girl or not having her?' (The Savage winced; but Helmholtz, who was staring pensively at the floor, saw nothing.) 'No,' he concluded, with a sigh, 'it won't do. We need some other kind of madness and violence. But what? What? Where can one find it?' He was silent; then, shaking his head, 'I don't know,' he said at last, 'I don't know.'

Chapter XIII

Henry Foster loomed up through the twilight of the Embryo Store.

'Like to come to a feely this evening?'

Lenina shook her head without speaking.

'Going out with some one else?' It interested him to know which of his friends was being had by which other. 'Is it Benito?' he questioned.

She shook her head again.

Henry detected the weariness in those purple eyes, the pallor beneath that glaze of lupus, the sadness at the corners of the unsmiling crimson mouth. 'You're not feeling ill, are you?' he asked, a trifle anxiously, afraid that she might be suffering from one of the few remaining infectious diseases.

Yet once more Lenina shook her head.

'Anyhow, you ought to go and see the doctor,' said Henry. 'A doctor a day keeps the jim-jams away,' he added heartily, driving home his hypnopædic adage with a clap on the shoulder. 'Perhaps you need a Pregnancy Substitute,' he suggested. 'Or else an extra-strong V.P.S. treatment. Sometimes, you know, the standard passion-surrogate isn't quite...'

'Oh, for Ford's sake,' said Lenina, breaking her stubborn silence, 'shut up!' And she turned back to her neglected embryos.

A V.P.S. treatment indeed! She would have laughed, if she hadn't been on the point of crying. As though she hadn't got enough V.P. of her own! She sighed profoundly as she refilled her syringe. 'John,' she murmured to herself, 'John...' Then 'My Ford,' she wondered, 'have I given this one its sleeping-sickness injection, or haven't I?' She simply couldn't remember. In the end, she decided not to run the risk of letting it have a second dose, and moved down the line to the next bottle.

Twenty-two years eight months and four days from that moment, a promising young Alpha-Minus administrator at Mwanza-Mwanza was to die of trypanosomiasis--the first case for over half a century. Sighing, Lenina went on with her work.

An hour later, in the Changing Room, Fanny was energetically protesting. 'But it's absurd to let yourself get into a state like this. Simply absurd,' she repeated. 'And what about? A man--*one* man.'

'But he's the one I want.'

'As though there weren't millions of other men in the world.'

'But I don't want them.'

'How can you know till you've tried?'

'I have tried.'

'But how many?' asked Fanny, shrugging her shoulders contemptuously. 'One, two?'

'Dozens. But,' shaking her head, 'it wasn't any good,' she added.

'Well, you must persevere,' said Fanny sententiously. But it was obvious that her confidence in her own prescriptions had been shaken. 'Nothing can be achieved without perseverance.'

'But meanwhile...'

'Don't think of him.'

'I can't help it.'

'Take *soma*, then.'

'I do.'

'Well, go on.'

'But in the intervals I still like him. I shall always like him.'

'Well, if that's the case,' said Fanny, with decision, 'why don't you just go and take him. Whether he wants it or no.'

'But if you knew how terribly *queer* he was!'

'All the more reason for taking a firm line.'

'It's all very well to *say* that.'

'Don't stand any nonsense. Act.' Fanny's voice was a trumpet; she might have been a Y.W.F.A. lecturer giving an evening talk to adolescent Beta-Minuses. 'Yes, act--at once. Do it now.'

'I'd be scared,' said Lenina.

'Well, you've only got to take half a gramme of *soma* first. And now I'm going to have my bath.' She marched off, trailing her towel.

****

The bell rang, and the Savage, who was impatiently hoping that Helmholtz would come that afternoon (for having at last made up his mind to talk to Helmholtz about Lenina, he could not bear to postpone his confidences a moment longer), jumped up and ran to the door.

'I had a premonition it was you, Helmholtz,' he shouted as he opened.

On the threshold, in a white acetate-satin sailor suit, and with a round white cap rakishly tilted over her left ear, stood Lenina.

'Oh!' said the Savage, as though some one had struck him a heavy blow.

Half a gramme had been enough to make Lenina forget her fears and her embarrassments. 'Hullo, John,' she said, smiling, and walked past him into the room. Automatically he closed the door and followed her. Lenina sat down. There was a long silence.

'You don't seem very glad to see me, John,' she said at last.

'Not glad?' The Savage looked at her reproachfully; then suddenly fell on his knees before her and, taking Lenina's hand, reverently kissed it. 'Not glad? Oh, if you only knew,' he whispered, and, venturing to raise his eyes to her face, 'Admired Lenina,' he went on, 'indeed the top of admiration, worth what's dearest in the world.' She smiled at him with a luscious tenderness. 'Oh, you so perfect' (she was leaning towards him with parted lips), 'so perfect and so peerless are created' (nearer and nearer) 'of every creature's best.' Still nearer. The Savage suddenly scrambled to his feet. 'That's why,' he said, speaking with averted face,' I wanted to *do* something first... I mean, to show I was worthy of you. Not that I could ever really be that. But at any rate to show I wasn't absolutely *un*worthy. I wanted to do *something*.'

'Why should you think it necessary...' Lenina began, but left the sentence unfinished. There was a note of irritation in her voice. When one has leant forward, nearer and nearer, with parted lips--only to find oneself, quite suddenly, as a clumsy oaf scrambles to his feet, leaning towards nothing at all--well, there is a reason, even with half a gramme of *soma* circulating in one's blood-stream, a genuine reason for annoyance.

'At Malpais,' the Savage was incoherently mumbling, 'you had to bring her the skin of a mountain lion--I mean, when you wanted to marry some one. Or else a wolf.'

'There aren't any lions in England,' Lenina almost snapped.

'And even if there were,' the Savage added, with sudden contemptuous resentment, 'people would kill them out of helicopters, I suppose, with poison gas or something. I wouldn't do *that*, Lenina.' He squared his shoulders, he ventured to look at her and was met with a stare of annoyed incomprehension. Confused, 'I'll do anything,' he went on, more and more incoherently. 'Anything you tell me. There be some sports are painful--you know. But their labour delight in them sets off. That's what I feel. I mean I'd sweep the floor if you wanted.'

'But we've got vacuum cleaners here,' said Lenina in bewilderment. 'It isn't necessary.'

'No, of course it isn't *necessary*. But some kinds of baseness are nobly undergone. I'd like to undergo something nobly. Don't you see?'

'But if there *are* vacuum cleaners...'

'That's not the point.'

'And Epsilon Semi-Morons to work them,' she went on, 'well, really, *why*?'

'Why? But for you, for *you*. Just to show that I...'

'And what on earth vacuum cleaners have got to do with lions...'

'To show how much...'

'Or lions with being glad to see *me*...' She was getting more and more exasperated.

'How much I love you, Lenina,' he brought out almost desperately.

An emblem of the inner tide of startled elation, the blood rushed up into Lenina's cheeks. 'Do you mean it, John?'

'But I hadn't meant to say so,' cried the Savage, clasping his hands in a kind of agony. 'Not until... Listen, Lenina; in Malpais people get married.'

'Get what?' The irritation had begun to creep back into her voice. What was he talking about now?

'For always. They make a promise to live together for always.'

'What a horrible idea!' Lenina was genuinely shocked.

'Outliving beauty's outward, with a mind that doth renew swifter than blood decays.'

'*What?*'

'It's like that in Shakespeare too. "If thou dost break her virgin knot before all sanctimonious ceremonies may with full and holy rite..."'

'For Ford's sake, John, talk sense. I can't understand a word you say. First it's vacuum cleaners; then it's knots. You're driving me crazy.' She jumped up and, as though afraid that he might run away from her physically, as well as with his mind, caught him by the wrist. 'Answer me this question: do you really like me, or don't you?'

There was a moment's silence; then, in a very low voice, 'I love you more than anything in the world,' he said.

'Then why on earth didn't you say so?' she cried, and so intense was her exasperation that she drove her sharp nails into the skin of his wrist. 'Instead of drivelling away about knots and vacuum cleaners and lions, and making me miserable for weeks and weeks.'

She released his hand and flung it angrily away from her.

'If I didn't like you so much,' she said, 'I'd be furious with you.'

And suddenly her arms were round his neck; he felt her lips soft against his own. So deliciously soft, so warm and electric that inevitably he found himself thinking of the embraces in *Three Weeks in a Helicopter*. Ooh! ooh! the stereoscopic blonde and aah! the more than real blackamoor. Horror, horror, horror... he tried to disengage himself; but Lenina tightened her embrace.

'Why didn't you say so?' she whispered, drawing back her face to look at him. Her eyes were tenderly reproachful.

'The murkiest den, the most opportune place' (the voice of conscience thundered poetically), 'the strongest suggestion our worser genius can, shall never melt mine honour into lust. Never, never!' he resolved.

'You silly boy!' she was saying. 'I wanted you so much. And if you wanted me too, why didn't you?...'

'But, Lenina...' he began protesting; and as she immediately untwined her arms, as she stepped away from him, he thought, for a moment, that she had taken his unspoken hint. But when she unbuckled her white patent cartridge belt and hung it carefully over the back of a chair, he began to suspect that he had been mistaken.

'Lenina!' he repeated apprehensively.

She put her hand to her neck and gave a long vertical pull; her white sailor's blouse was ripped to the hem; suspicion condensed into a too, too solid certainty. 'Lenina, what *are* you doing?'

Zip, zip! Her answer was wordless. She stepped out of her bell-bottomed trousers. Her zippicamiknicks were a pale shell pink. The Arch-Community-Songster's golden T dangled at her breast.

'For those milk paps that through the window bars bore at men's eyes...' The singing, thundering, magical words made her seem doubly dangerous, doubly alluring. Soft, soft, but how piercing! boring and drilling into reason, tunnelling through resolution. 'The strongest oaths are straw to the fire i' the blood. Be more abstemious, or else...'

Zip! The rounded pinkness fell apart like a neatly divided apple. A wriggle of the arms, a lifting first of the right foot, then the left: the zippicamiknicks were lying lifeless and as though deflated on the floor.

Still wearing her shoes and socks, and her rakishly tilted round white cap, she advanced towards him. 'Darling. *Darling!* If only you'd said so before!' She held out her arms.

But instead of also saying 'Darling!' and holding out *his* arms, the Savage retreated in terror, flapping his hands at her as though he were trying to scare away some intruding and dangerous animal. Four backward steps, and he was brought to bay against the wall.

'Sweet!' said Lenina and, laying her hands on his shoulders, pressed herself against him. 'Put your arms round me,' she commanded. 'Hug me till you drug me, honey.' She too had poetry at her command, knew words that sang and were spells and beat drums. 'Kiss me'; she closed her eyes, she let her voice sink to a sleepy murmur, 'kiss me till I'm in a coma. Hug me, honey, snuggly...'

The Savage caught her by the wrists, tore her hands from his shoulders, thrust her roughly away at arm's length.

'Ow, you're hurting me, you're... oh!' She was suddenly silent. Terror had made her forget the pain. Opening her eyes, she had seen his face--no, not *his* face, a ferocious stranger's, pale, distorted, twitching with some insane, inexplicable fury. Aghast, 'But what is it, John?' she whispered. He did not answer, but only stared into her face with those mad eyes. The hands that held her wrists were trembling. He breathed deeply and irregularly. Faint almost to imperceptibility, but appalling, she suddenly heard the grinding of his teeth. 'What is it?' she almost screamed.

And as though awakened by her cry he caught her by the shoulders and shook her. 'Whore!' he shouted. 'Whore! Impudent strumpet!'

'Oh, don't, do-on't,' she protested in a voice made grotesquely tremulous by his shaking.

'Whore!'

'Plea-ease.'

'Damned whore!'

'A gra-amme is be-etter...' she began.

The Savage pushed her away with such force that she staggered and fell. 'Go,' he shouted, standing over her menacingly, 'get out of my sight or I'll kill you.' He clenched his fists.

Lenina raised her arm to cover her face. 'No, please don't, John...'

'Hurry up. Quick!'

One arm still raised, and following his every movement with a terrified eye, she scrambled to her feet and still crouching, still covering her head, made a dash for the bathroom.

The noise of that prodigious slap by which her departure was accelerated was like a pistol-shot.

'Ow!' Lenina bounded forward.

Safely locked into the bathroom, she had leisure to take stock of her injuries. Standing with her back to the mirror, she twisted her head. Looking over her left shoulder she could see the imprint of an open hand standing out distinct and crimson on the pearly flesh. Gingerly she rubbed the wounded spot.

Outside, in the other room, the Savage was striding up and down, marching, marching to the drums and music of magical words. 'The wren goes to't, and the small gilded fly does lecher in my sight.' Maddeningly they rumbled in his ears. 'The fitchew nor the soiled horse goes to't with a more riotous appetite. Down from the waist they are Centaurs, though women all above. But to the girdle do the gods inherit. Beneath is all the fiends'. There's hell, there's darkness, there is the sulphurous pit, burning, scalding, stench, consumption; fie, fie, fie, pah, pah! Give me an ounce of civet, good apothecary, to sweeten my imagination.'

'John!' ventured a small ingratiating voice from the bathroom. 'John!'

'O thou weed, who art so lovely fair and smell'st so sweet that the sense aches at thee. Was this most goodly book made to write "whore" upon? Heaven stops the nose at it...'

But her perfume still hung about him, his jacket was white with the powder that had scented her velvety body. 'Impudent strumpet, impudent strumpet, impudent strumpet.' The inexorable rhythm beat itself out. 'Impudent...'

'John, do you think I might have my clothes?'

He picked up the bell-bottomed trousers, the blouse, the zippicamiknicks.

'Open!' he ordered, kicking the door.

'No, I won't.' The voice was frightened and defiant.

'Well, how do you expect me to give them to you?'

'Push them through the ventilator over the door.'

He did what she suggested and returned to his uneasy pacing of the room. 'Impudent strumpet, impudent strumpet. The devil Luxury with his fat rump and potato finger...'

'John.'

He would not answer. 'Fat rump and potato finger.'

'John.'

'What is it?' he asked gruffly.

'I wonder if you'd mind giving me my Malthusian belt.'

Lenina sat listening to the footsteps in the other room, wondering, as she listened, how long he was likely to go tramping up and down like that; whether she would have to wait until he left the flat; or if it would be safe, after allowing his madness a reasonable time to subside, to open the bathroom door and make a dash for it.

She was interrupted in the midst of these uneasy speculations by the sound of the telephone bell ringing in the other room. Abruptly the tramping ceased. She heard the voice of the Savage parleying with silence.

'Hullo.'

......

'Yes.'

......

'If I do not usurp myself, I am.'

......

'Yes, didn't you hear me say so? Mr. Savage speaking.'

......

'What? Who's ill? Of course it interests me.'

......

'But is it serious? Is she really bad? I'll go at once....'

......

'Not in her rooms any more? Where has she been taken?'

......

'Oh, my God! What's the address?'

......

'Three Park Lane--is that it? Three? Thanks.'

Lenina heard the click of the replaced receiver, then hurrying steps. A door slammed. There was silence. Was he really gone?

With an infinity of precautions she opened the door a quarter of an inch; peeped through the crack; was encouraged by the view of emptiness; opened a little further, and put her whole head out; finally tiptoed into the room; stood for a few seconds with strongly beating heart, listening, listening; then darted to the front door, opened, slipped through, slammed, ran. It was not till she was in the lift and actually dropping down the well that she began to feel herself secure.

Chapter XIV

The Park Lane Hospital for the Dying was a sixty-story tower of primrose tiles. As the Savage stepped out of his taxicopter a convoy of gaily-coloured aerial hearses rose whirring from the roof and darted away across the Park, westwards, bound for the Slough Crematorium. At the lift gates the presiding porter gave him the information he required, and he dropped down to Ward 81 (a Galloping Senility ward, the porter explained) on the seventeenth floor.

It was a large room bright with sunshine and yellow paint, and containing twenty beds, all occupied. Linda was dying in company--in company and with all the modern conveniences. The air was continuously alive with gay synthetic melodies. At the foot of every bed, confronting its moribund occupant, was a television box. Television was left on, a running tap, from morning till night. Every quarter of an hour the prevailing perfume of the room was automatically changed. 'We try,' explained the nurse, who had taken charge of the Savage at the door, 'we try to create a thoroughly pleasant atmosphere here--something between a first-class hotel and a feely-palace, if you take my meaning.'

'Where is she?' asked the Savage, ignoring these polite explanations.

The nurse was offended. 'You *are* in a hurry,' she said.

'Is there any hope?' he asked.

'You mean, of her not dying?' (He nodded.) 'No, of course there isn't. When somebody's sent here, there's no...' Startled by the expression of distress on his pale face, she suddenly broke off. 'Why, whatever is the matter?' she asked. She was not accustomed to this kind of thing in visitors. (Not that there were many visitors anyhow: or any reason why there should be many visitors.) 'You're not feeling ill, are you?'

He shook his head. 'She's my mother,' he said in a scarcely audible voice.

The nurse glanced at him with startled, horrified eyes; then quickly looked away. From throat to temple she was all one hot blush.

'Take me to her,' said the Savage, making an effort to speak in an ordinary tone.

Still blushing, she led the way down the ward. Faces still fresh and unwithered (for senility galloped so hard that it had no time to age the cheeks--only the heart and brain) turned as they passed. Their progress was followed by the blank, incurious eyes of second infancy. The Savage shuddered as he looked.

Linda was lying in the last of the long row of beds, next to the wall. Propped up on pillows, she was watching the Semi-finals of the South American Riemann-Surface Tennis Championship, which were being played in silent and diminished reproduction on the screen of the television box at the foot of the bed. Hither and thither across their square of illumined glass the little figures noiselessly darted, like fish in an aquarium--the silent but agitated inhabitants of another world.

Linda looked on, vaguely and uncomprehendingly smiling. Her pale, bloated face wore an expression of imbecile happiness. Every now and then her eyelids closed, and for a few seconds she seemed to be dozing. Then with a little start she would wake up again--wake up to the aquarium antics of the Tennis Champions, to the Super-Vox-Wurlitzeriana rendering of 'Hug me till you drug me, honey,' to the warm draught of verbena that came blowing through the ventilator above her head--would wake to these things, or rather to a dream of which these things, transformed and embellished by the *soma* in her blood, were the marvellous constituents, and smile once more her broken and discoloured smile of infantile contentment.

'Well, I must go,' said the nurse. 'I've got my batch of children coming. Besides, there's Number 3.' She pointed up the ward. 'Might go off any minute now. Well, make yourself comfortable.' She walked briskly away.

The Savage sat down beside the bed.

'Linda,' he whispered, taking her hand.

At the sound of her name, she turned. Her vague eyes brightened with recognition. She squeezed his hand, she smiled, her lips moved; then quite suddenly her head fell forward. She was asleep. He sat watching her--seeking through the tired flesh, seeking and finding that young, bright face which had stooped over his childhood in Malpais, remembering (and he closed his eyes) her voice, her movements, all the events of their life together. 'Streptocock-Gee to Banbury-T...' How beautiful her singing had been! And those childish rhymes, how magically strange and mysterious!

A,   B,   C,   vitamin   D:
The fat's in the liver, the cod's in the sea.

He felt the hot tears welling up behind his eyelids as he recalled the words and Linda's voice as she repeated them. And then the reading lessons; The tot is in the pot, the cat is on the mat; and the Elementary Instructions for Beta Workers in the Embryo Store. And long evenings by the fire or, in summer time, on the roof of the little house, when she told him those stories about the Other Place, outside the Reservation: that beautiful, beautiful Other Place, whose memory, as of a heaven, a paradise of goodness and loveliness, he still kept whole and intact, undefiled by contact with the reality of this real London, these actual civilized men and women.

A sudden noise of shrill voices made him open his eyes and, after hastily brushing away the tears, look round. What seemed an interminable stream of identical eight-year-old male twins was pouring into the room. Twin after twin, twin after twin, they came--a nightmare. Their faces, their repeated face--for there was only one between the lot of them--puggishly stared, all nostrils and pale goggling eyes. Their uniform was khaki. All their mouths hung open. Squealing and chattering they entered. In a moment, it seemed, the ward was maggoty with them. They swarmed between the beds, clambered over, crawled under, peeped into the television boxes, made faces at the patients.

Linda astonished and rather alarmed them. A group stood clustered at the foot of her bed, staring with the frightened and stupid curiosity of animals suddenly confronted by the unknown.

'Oh, look, look!' They spoke in low, scared voices. 'Whatever is the matter with her? Why is she so fat?'

They had never seen a face like hers before--had never seen a face that was not youthful and taut-skinned, a body that had ceased to be slim and upright. All these moribund sexagenarians had the appearance of childish girls. At forty-four, Linda seemed, by contrast, a monster of flaccid and distorted senility.

'Isn't she awful?' came the whispered comments. 'Look at her teeth!'

Suddenly from under the bed a pug-faced twin popped up between John's chair and the wall, and began peering into Linda's sleeping face.

'I say...' he began; but his sentence ended prematurely in a squeal. The Savage had seized him by the collar, lifted him clear over the chair and, with a smart box on the ears, sent him howling away.

His yells brought the Head Nurse hurrying to the rescue.

'What have you been doing to him?' she demanded fiercely. 'I won't have you striking the children.'

'Well, then, keep them away from this bed.' The Savage's voice was trembling with indignation. 'What are these filthy little brats doing here at all? It's disgraceful!'

'Disgraceful? But what do you mean? They're being death-conditioned. And I tell you,' she warned him truculently, 'if I have any more of your interference with their conditioning, I'll send for the porters and have you thrown out.'

The Savage rose to his feet and took a couple of steps towards her. His movements and the expression on his face were so menacing that the nurse fell back in terror. With a great effort he checked himself and, without speaking, turned away and sat down again by the bed.

Reassured, but with a dignity that was a trifle shrill and uncertain, 'I've warned you,' said the nurse, 'so mind.' Still, she led the too inquisitive twins away and made them join in the game of hunt-the-zipper, which had been organized by one of her colleagues at the other end of the room.

'Run along now and have your cup of caffeine solution, dear,' she said to the other nurse. The exercise of authority restored her confidence, made her feel better. 'Now, children!' she called.

Linda had stirred uneasily, had opened her eyes for a moment, looked vaguely around, and then once more dropped off to sleep. Sitting beside her, the Savage tried hard to recapture his mood of a few minutes before. 'A, B, C, vitamin D,' he repeated to himself, as though the words were a spell that would restore the dead past to life. But the spell was ineffective. Obstinately the beautiful memories refused to rise; there was only a hateful resurrection of jealousies and uglinesses and miseries. Popé with the blood trickling down from his cut shoulder; and Linda hideously asleep, and the flies buzzing round the spilt *mescal* on the floor beside the bed; and the boys calling those names as she passed.... Ah, no, no! He shut his eyes, he shook his head in strenuous denial of these memories. 'A, B, C, vitamin D...' He tried to think of those times when he sat on her knees and she put her arms about him and sang, over and over again, rocking him, rocking him to sleep. 'A, B, C, vitamin D, vitamin D, vitamin D...'

The Super-Vox-Wurlitzeriana had risen to a sobbing crescendo; and suddenly the verbena gave place, in the scent-circulating system, to an intense patchouli. Linda stirred, woke up, stared for a few seconds bewilderedly at the Semi-finalists, then, lifting her face, sniffed once or twice at the newly perfumed air and suddenly smiled--a smile of childish ecstasy.

'Popé!' she murmured, and closed her eyes. 'Oh, I do so like it, I do...' She sighed and let herself sink back into the pillows.

'But, Linda!' The Savage spoke imploringly. 'Don't you know me?' He had tried so hard, had done his very best; why wouldn't she allow him to forget? He squeezed her limp hand almost with violence, as though he would force her to come back from this dream of ignoble pleasures, from these base and hateful memories--back into the present, back into reality: the appalling present, the awful reality--but sublime, but significant, but desperately important precisely because of the imminence of that which made them so fearful. 'Don't you know me, Linda?'

He felt the faint answering pressure of her hand. The tears started into his eyes. He bent over her and kissed her.

Her lips moved. 'Popé!' she whispered again, and it was as though he had had a pailful of ordure thrown in his face.

Anger suddenly boiled up in him. Balked for the second time, the passion of his grief had found another outlet, was transformed into a passion of agonized rage.

'But I'm John!' he shouted. 'I'm John!' And in his furious misery he actually caught her by the shoulder and shook her.

Linda's eyes fluttered open; she saw him, knew him--'John!'--but situated the real face, the real and violent hands, in an imaginary world--among the inward and private equivalents of patchouli and the Super-Wurlitzer, among the transfigured memories and the strangely transposed sensations that constituted the universe of her dream. She knew him for John, her son, but fancied him an intruder into that paradisal Malpais where she had been spending her *soma*-holiday with Popé. He was angry because she liked Popé, he was shaking her because Popé was there in the bed--as though there were something wrong, as though all civilized people didn't do the same? 'Every one belongs to every...' Her voice suddenly died into an almost inaudible breathless croaking, her mouth fell open: she made a desperate effort to fill her lungs with air. But it was as though she had forgotten how to breathe. She tried to cry out--but no sound came; only the terror of her staring eyes revealed what she was suffering. Her hands went to her throat, then clawed at the air--the air she could no longer breathe, the air that, for her, had ceased to exist.

The Savage was on his feet, bent over her. 'What is it, Linda? What is it?' His voice was imploring; it was as though he were begging to be reassured.

The look she gave him was charged with an unspeakable terror--with terror and, it seemed to him, reproach. She tried to raise herself in bed, but fell back on to the pillows. Her face was horribly distorted, her lips blue.

The Savage turned and ran up the ward.

'Quick, quick!' he shouted. 'Quick!'

Standing in the centre of a ring of zipper-hunting twins, the Head Nurse looked round. The first moment's astonishment gave place almost instantly to disapproval. 'Don't shout! Think of the little ones,' she said, frowning. 'You might decondition... But what are you doing?' He had broken through the ring. 'Be careful!' A child was yelling.

'Quick, quick!' He caught her by the sleeve, dragged her after him. 'Quick! Something's happened. I've killed her.'

By the time they were back at the end of the ward Linda was dead.

The Savage stood for a moment in frozen silence, then fell on his knees beside the bed and, covering his face with his hands, sobbed uncontrollably.

The nurse stood irresolute, looking now at the kneeling figure by the bed (the scandalous exhibition!) and now (poor children!) at the twins who had stopped their hunting of the zipper and were staring from the other end of the ward, staring with all their eyes and nostrils at the shocking scene that was being enacted round Bed 20. Should she speak to him? try to bring him back to a sense of decency? remind him of where he was? of what fatal mischief he might do to these poor innocents? Undoing all their wholesome death-conditioning with this disgusting outcry--as though death were something terrible, as though any one mattered as much as all that! It might give them the most disastrous ideas about the subject, might upset them into reacting in the entirely wrong, the utterly anti-social way.

She stepped forward, she touched him on the shoulder. 'Can't you behave?' she said in a low, angry voice. But, looking round, she saw that half a dozen twins were already on their feet and advancing down the ward. The circle was disintegrating. In another moment... No, the risk was too great; the whole Group might be put back six or seven months in its conditioning. She hurried back towards her menaced charges.

'Now, who wants a chocolate éclair?' she asked in a loud, cheerful tone.

'Me!' yelled the entire Bokanovsky Group in chorus. Bed 20 was completely forgotten.

'Oh, God, God, God...' the Savage kept repeating to himself. In the chaos of grief and remorse that filled his mind it was the one articulate word. 'God!' he whispered it aloud. 'God...'

'Whatever *is* he saying?' said a voice, very near, distinct and shrill through the warblings of the Super-Wurlitzer.

The Savage violently started and, uncovering his face, looked round. Five khaki twins, each with the stump of a long éclair in his right hand, and their identical faces variously smeared with liquid chocolate, were standing in a row, puggily goggling at him.

They met his eyes and simultaneously grinned. One of them pointed with his éclair butt.

'Is she dead?' he asked.

The Savage stared at them for a moment in silence. Then, in silence he rose to his feet, in silence slowly walked towards the door.

'Is she dead?' repeated the inquisitive twin trotting at his side.

The Savage looked down at him and still without speaking pushed him away. The twin fell on the floor and at once began to howl. The Savage did not even look round.

Chapter XV

The menial staff of the Park Lane Hospital for the Dying consisted of one hundred and sixty-two Deltas divided into two Bokanovsky Groups of eighty-four red-headed female and seventy-eight dark dolichocephalic male twins, respectively. At six, when their working day was over, the two Groups assembled in the vestibule of the Hospital and were served by the Deputy Sub-Bursar with their *soma* ration.

From the lift the Savage stepped out into the midst of them. But his mind was elsewhere--with death, with his grief, and his remorse; mechanically, without consciousness of what he was doing, he began to shoulder his way through the crowd.

'Who are you pushing? Where do you think you're going?'

High, low, from a multitude of separate throats, only two voices squeaked or growled. Repeated indefinitely, as though by a train of mirrors, two faces, one a hairless and freckled moon haloed in orange, the other a thin, beaked bird-mask, stubbly with two days' beard, turned angrily towards him. Their words and, in his ribs, the sharp nudging of elbows, broke through his unawareness. He woke once more to external reality, looked round him, knew what he saw--knew it, with a sinking sense of horror and disgust, for the recurrent delirium of his days and nights, the nightmare of swarming indistinguishable sameness. Twins, twins.... Like maggots they had swarmed defilingly over the mystery of Linda's death. Maggots again, but larger, full grown, they now crawled across his grief and his repentance. He halted and, with bewildered and horrified eyes, stared round him at the khaki mob, in the midst of which, overtopping it by a full head, he stood. 'How many goodly creatures are there here!' The singing words mocked him derisively. 'How beauteous mankind is! O brave new world...'

'*Soma* distribution!' shouted a loud voice. 'In good order, please. Hurry up there.'

A door had been opened, a table and chair carried into the vestibule. The voice was that of a jaunty young Alpha, who had entered carrying a black iron cash-box. A murmur of satisfaction went up from the expectant twins. They forgot all about the Savage. Their attention was now focussed on the black cash-box, which the young man had placed on the table, and was now in process of unlocking. The lid was lifted.

'Oo-oh!' said all the hundred and sixty-two simultaneously, as though they were looking at fireworks.

The young man took out a handful of tiny pillboxes. 'Now,' he said peremptorily, 'step forward, please. One at a time, and no shoving.'

One at a time, with no shoving, the twins stepped forward. First two males, then a female, then another male, then three females, then...

The Savage stood looking on. 'O brave new world, O brave new world...' In his mind the singing words seemed to change their tone. They had mocked him through his misery and remorse, mocked him with how hideous a note of cynical derision! Fiendishly laughing, they had insisted on the low squalor, the nauseous ugliness of the nightmare. Now, suddenly, they trumpeted a call to arms. 'O brave new world!' Miranda was proclaiming the possibility of loveliness, the possibility of transforming even the nightmare into something fine and noble. 'O brave new world!' It was a challenge, a command.

'No shoving there, now!' shouted the Deputy Sub-Bursar in a fury. He slammed down the lid of his cash-box. 'I shall stop the distribution unless I have good behaviour.'

The Deltas muttered, jostled one another a little, and then were still. The threat had been effective. Deprivation of *soma*--appalling thought!

'That's better' said the young man, and reopened his cash-box.

Linda had been a slave, Linda had died; others should live in freedom, and the world be made beautiful. A reparation, a duty. And suddenly it was luminously clear to the Savage what he must do; it was as though a shutter had been opened, a curtain drawn back.

'Now,' said the Deputy-Bursar.

Another khaki female stepped forward.

'Stop!' called the Savage in a loud and ringing voice. 'Stop!'

He pushed his way to the table; the Deltas stared at him with astonishment.

'Ford!' said the Deputy Sub-Bursar, below his breath. 'It's the Savage.' He felt scared.

'Listen, I beg you,' cried the Savage earnestly. 'Lend me your ears...' He had never spoken in public before, and found it very difficult to express what he wanted to say. 'Don't take that horrible stuff. It's poison, it's poison.'

'I say, Mr. Savage,' said the Deputy Sub-Bursar, smiling propitiatingly. 'Would you mind letting me...'

'Poison to soul as well as body.'

'Yes, but let me get on with my distribution, won't you? There's a good fellow.' With the cautious tenderness of one who strokes a notoriously vicious animal, he patted the Savage's arm. 'Just let me...'

'Never!' cried the Savage.

'But look here, old man...'

'Throw it all away, that horrible poison.'

The words 'Throw it all away' pierced through the enfolding layers of incomprehension to the quick of the Deltas' consciousness. An angry murmur went up from the crowd.

'I come to bring you freedom,' said the Savage, turning back towards the twins. 'I come...'

The Deputy Sub-Bursar heard no more; he had slipped out of the vestibule and was looking up a number in the telephone book.

****

'Not in his own rooms,' Bernard summed up. 'Not in mine, not in yours. Not at the Aphroditæum; not at the Centre or the College. Where can he have got to?'

Helmholtz shrugged his shoulders. They had come back from their work expecting to find the Savage waiting for them at one or other of their usual meeting-places, and there was no sign of the fellow. Which was annoying, as they had meant to nip across to Biarritz in Helmholtz's four-seater sporticopter. They'd be late for dinner if he didn't come soon.

'We'll give him five more minutes,' said Helmholtz. 'If he doesn't turn up by then, we'll...'

The ringing of the telephone bell interrupted him. He picked up the receiver. 'Hullo. Speaking.' Then, after a long interval of listening, 'Ford in Flivver!' he swore. 'I'll come at once.'

'What is it?' Bernard asked.

'A fellow I know at the Park Lane Hospital,' said Helmholtz. 'The Savage is there. Seems to have gone mad. Anyhow, it's urgent. Will you come with me?'

Together they hurried along the corridor to the lifts.

****

'But do you like being slaves?' the Savage was saying as they entered the Hospital. His face was flushed, his eyes bright with ardour and indignation. 'Do you like being babies? Yes, babies. Mewling and puking,' he added, exasperated by their bestial stupidity into throwing insults at those he had come to save. The insults bounced off their carapace of thick stupidity; they stared at him with a blank expression of dull and sullen resentment in their eyes. 'Yes, puking!' he fairly shouted. Grief and remorse, compassion and duty--all were forgotten now and, as it were, absorbed into an intense overpowering hatred of these less than human monsters. 'Don't you want to be free and men? Don't you even understand what manhood and freedom are?' Rage was making him fluent; the words came easily, in a rush. 'Don't you?' he repeated, but got no answer to his question. 'Very well, then,' he went on grimly. 'I'll teach you; I'll *make* you be free whether you want to or not.' And pushing open a window that looked on to the inner court of the Hospital, he began to throw the little pill-boxes of *soma* tablets in handfuls out into the area.

For a moment the khaki mob was silent, petrified, at the spectacle of this wanton sacrilege, with amazement and horror.

'He's mad,' whispered Bernard, staring with wide open eyes. 'They'll kill him. They'll...' A great shout suddenly went up from the mob; a wave of movement drove it menacingly towards the Savage. 'Ford help him!' said Bernard, and averted his eyes.

'Ford helps those who help themselves.' And with a laugh, actually a laugh of exultation, Helmholtz Watson pushed his way through the crowd.

'Free, free!' the Savage shouted, and with one hand continued to throw the *soma* into the area while, with the other, he punched the indistinguishable faces of his assailants. 'Free!' And suddenly there was Helmholtz at his side--'Good old Helmholtz!'--also punching--'Men at last!'--and in the interval also throwing the poison out by handfuls through the open window. 'Yes, men! men!' and there was no more poison left. He picked up the cash-box and showed them its black emptiness. 'You're free!'

Howling, the Deltas charged with a redoubled fury.

Hesitant on the fringes of the battle, 'They're done for,' said Bernard and, urged by a sudden impulse, ran forward to help them; then thought better of it and halted; then, ashamed, stepped forward again; then again thought better of it, and was standing in an agony of humiliated indecision--thinking that *they* might be killed if he didn't help them, and that *he* might be killed if he did--when (Ford be praised!), goggle-eyed and swine-snouted in their gas-masks, in ran the police.

Bernard dashed to meet them. He waved his arms; and it was action, he was doing something. He shouted 'Help!' several times, more and more loudly so as to give himself the illusion of helping. 'Help! *Help!* HELP!'

The policemen pushed him out of the way and got on with their work. Three men with spraying machines buckled to their shoulders pumped thick clouds of *soma* vapour into the air. Two more were busy round the portable Synthetic Music Box. Carrying water pistols charged with a powerful anæsthetic, four others had pushed their way into the crowd and were methodically laying out, squirt by squirt, the more ferocious of the fighters.

'Quick, quick!' yelled Bernard. 'They'll be killed if you don't hurry. They'll... Oh!' Annoyed by his chatter, one of the policemen had given him a shot from his water pistol. Bernard stood for a second or two wambling unsteadily on legs that seemed to have lost their bones, their tendons, their muscles, to have become mere sticks of jelly, and at last not even jelly--water: he tumbled in a heap on the floor.

Suddenly, from out of the Synthetic Music Box a Voice began to speak. The Voice of Reason, the Voice of Good Feeling. The sound-track roll was unwinding itself in Synthetic Anti-Riot Speech Number Two (Medium Strength). Straight from the depths of a non-existent heart, 'My friends, my friends!' said the Voice so pathetically, with a note of such infinitely tender reproach that, behind their gas-masks, even the policemen's eyes were momentarily dimmed with tears, 'what is the meaning of this? Why aren't you all being happy and good together. Happy and good,' the Voice repeated. 'At peace, at peace.' It trembled, sank into a whisper and momentarily expired. 'Oh, I do want you to be happy,' it began, with a yearning earnestness. 'I do so want you to be good! Please, please be good and...'

Two minutes later the Voice and the *soma* vapour had produced their effect. In tears, the Deltas were kissing and hugging one another--half a dozen twins at a time in a comprehensive embrace. Even Helmholtz and the Savage were almost crying. A fresh supply of pill-boxes was brought in from the Bursary; a new distribution was hastily made and, to the sound of the Voice's richly affectionate, baritone valedictions, the twins dispersed, blubbering as though their hearts would break. 'Good-bye, my dearest, dearest friends, Ford keep you! Good-bye, my dearest, dearest friends. Ford keep you. Good-bye, my dearest, dearest...'

When the last of the Deltas had gone the policeman switched off the current. The angelic Voice fell silent.

'Will you come quietly?' asked the Sergeant, 'or must we anæsthetize?' He pointed his water pistol menacingly.

'Oh, we'll come quietly,' the Savage answered, dabbing alternately a cut lip, a scratched neck, and a bitten left hand.

Still keeping his handkerchief to his bleeding nose, Helmholtz nodded in confirmation.

Awake and having recovered the use of his legs, Bernard had chosen this moment to move as inconspicuously as he could towards the door.

'Hi, you there,' called the Sergeant, and a swine-masked policeman hurried across the room and laid a hand on the young man's shoulder.

Bernard turned with an expression of indignant innocence. Escaping? He hadn't dreamed of such a thing. 'Though what on earth you want *me* for,' he said to the Sergeant, 'I really can't imagine.'

'You're a friend of the prisoners, aren't you?'

'Well...' said Bernard, and hesitated. No, he really couldn't deny it. 'Why shouldn't I be?' he asked.

'Come on, then,' said the Sergeant, and led the way towards the door and the waiting police car.

Chapter XVI

The room into which the three were ushered was the Controller's study.

'His fordship will be down in a moment.' The Gamma butler left them to themselves.

Helmholtz laughed aloud.

'It's more like a caffeine-solution party than a trial,' he said, and let himself fall into the most luxurious of the pneumatic arm-chairs. 'Cheer up, Bernard,' he added, catching sight of his friend's green unhappy face. But Bernard would not be cheered; without answering, without even looking at Helmholtz, he went and sat down on the most uncomfortable chair in the room, carefully chosen in the obscure hope of somehow deprecating the wrath of the higher powers.

The Savage meanwhile wandered restlessly round the room, peering with a vague superficial inquisitiveness at the books in the shelves, at the sound-track rolls and the reading-machine bobbins in their numbered pigeon-holes. On the table under the window lay a massive volume bound in limp black leather-surrogate, and stamped with large golden T's. He picked it up and opened it. MY LIFE AND WORK, BY OUR FORD. The book had been published at Detroit by the Society for the Propagation of Fordian Knowledge. Idly he turned the pages, read a sentence here, a paragraph there, and had just come to the conclusion that the book didn't interest him, when the door opened, and the Resident World Controller for Western Europe walked briskly into the room.

Mustapha Mond shook hands with all three of them; but it was to the Savage that he addressed himself. 'So you don't much like civilization, Mr. Savage,' he said.

The Savage looked at him. He had been prepared to lie, to bluster, to remain sullenly unresponsive; but, reassured by the good-humoured intelligence of the Controller's face, he decided to tell the truth, straightforwardly. 'No.' He shook his head.

Bernard started and looked horrified. What would the Controller think? To be labelled as the friend of a man who said that he didn't like civilization--said it openly and, of all people, to the Controller--it was terrible. 'But, John,' he began. A look from Mustapha Mond reduced him to an abject silence.

'Of course,' the Savage went on to admit, 'there are some very nice things. All that music in the air, for instance...'

'Sometimes a thousand twangling instruments will hum about my ears, and sometimes voices.'

The Savage's face lit up with a sudden pleasure. 'Have you read it too?' he asked. 'I thought nobody knew about that book here, in England.'

'Almost nobody. I'm one of the very few. It's prohibited, you see. But as I make the laws here, I can also break them. With impunity, Mr. Marx,' he added, turning to Bernard. 'Which I'm afraid you *can't* do.'

Bernard sank into a yet more hopeless misery.

'But why is it prohibited?' asked the Savage. In the excitement of meeting a man who had read Shakespeare he had momentarily forgotten everything else.

The Controller shrugged his shoulders. 'Because it's old; that's the chief reason. We haven't any use for old things here.'

'Even when they're beautiful?'

'Particularly when they're beautiful. Beauty's attractive, and we don't want people to be attracted by old things. We want them to like the new ones.'

'But the new ones are so stupid and horrible. Those plays, where there's nothing but helicopters flying about and you *feel* the people kissing.' He made a grimace. 'Goats and monkeys!' Only in Othello's words could he find an adequate vehicle for his contempt and hatred.

'Nice tame animals, anyhow,' the Controller murmured parenthetically.

'Why don't you let them see *Othello* instead?'

'I've told you; it's old. Besides, they couldn't understand it.'

Yes, that was true. He remembered how Helmholtz had laughed at *Romeo and Juliet*. 'Well, then,' he said, after a pause, 'something new that's like *Othello*, and that they could understand.'

'That's what we've all been wanting to write,' said Helmholtz, breaking a long silence.

'And it's what you never will write,' said the Controller. 'Because, if it were really like *Othello* nobody could understand it, however new it might be. And if it were new, it couldn't possibly be like *Othello*.'

'Why not?'

'Yes, why not?' Helmholtz repeated. He too was forgetting the unpleasant realities of the situation. Green with anxiety and apprehension, only Bernard remembered them; the others ignored him. 'Why not?'

'Because our world is not the same as Othello's world. You can't make flivvers without steel--and you can't make tragedies without social instability. The world's stable now. People are happy; they get what they want, and they never want what they can't get. They're well off; they're safe; they're never ill; they're not afraid of death; they're blissfully ignorant of passion and old age; they're plagued with no mothers or fathers; they've got no wives, or children, or lovers to feel strongly about; they're so conditioned that they practically can't help behaving as they ought to behave. And if anything should go wrong, there's *soma*. Which you go and chuck out of the window in the name of liberty, Mr. Savage. *Liberty!*' He laughed. 'Expecting Deltas to know what liberty is! And now expecting them to understand *Othello*! My good boy!'

The Savage was silent for a little. 'All the same,' he insisted obstinately, '*Othello*'s good, *Othello*'s better than those feelies.'

'Of course it is,' the Controller agreed. 'But that's the price we have to pay for stability. You've got to choose between happiness and what people used to call high art. We've sacrificed the high art. We have the feelies and the scent organ instead.'

'But they don't mean anything.'

'They mean themselves; they mean a lot of agreeable sensations to the audience.'

'But they're... they're told by an idiot.'

The Controller laughed. 'You're not being very polite to your friend, Mr. Watson. One of our most distinguished Emotional Engineers...'

'But he's right,' said Helmholtz gloomily. 'Because it *is* idiotic. Writing when there's nothing to say...'

'Precisely. But that requires the most enormous ingenuity. You're making flivvers out of the absolute minimum of steel--works of art out of practically nothing but pure sensation.'

The Savage shook his head. 'It all seems to me quite horrible.'

'Of course it does. Actual happiness always looks pretty squalid in comparison with the over-compensations for misery. And, of course, stability isn't nearly so spectacular as instability. And being contented has none of the glamour of a good fight against misfortune, none of the picturesqueness of a struggle with temptation, or a fatal overthrow by passion or doubt. Happiness is never grand.'

'I suppose not,' said the Savage after a silence. 'But need it be quite so bad as those twins?' He passed his hand over his eyes as though he were trying to wipe away the remembered image of those long rows of identical midgets at the assembling tables, those queued-up twin-herds at the entrance to the Brentford monorail station, those human maggots swarming round Linda's bed of death, the endlessly repeated face of his assailants. He looked at his bandaged left hand and shuddered. 'Horrible!'

'But how useful! I see you don't like our Bokanovsky Groups; but, I assure you, they're the foundation on which everything else is built. They're the gyroscope that stabilizes the rocket plane of state on its unswerving course.' The deep voice thrillingly vibrated; the gesticulating hand implied all space and the onrush of the irresistible machine. Mustapha Mond's oratory was almost up to synthetic standards.

'I was wondering,' said the Savage, 'why you had them at all--seeing that you can get whatever you want out of those bottles. Why don't you make everybody an Alpha Double Plus while you're about it?'

Mustapha Mond laughed. 'Because we have no wish to have our throats cut,' he answered. 'We believe in happiness and stability. A society of Alphas couldn't fail to be unstable and miserable. Imagine a factory staffed by Alphas--that is to say by separate and unrelated individuals of good heredity and conditioned so as to be capable (within limits) of making a free choice and assuming responsibilities. Imagine it!' he repeated.

The Savage tried to imagine it, not very successfully.

'It's an absurdity. An Alpha-decanted, Alpha-conditioned man would go mad if he had to do Epsilon Semi-Moron work--go mad, or start smashing things up. Alphas can be completely socialized--but only on condition that you make them do Alpha work. Only an Epsilon can be expected to make Epsilon sacrifices, for the good reason that for him they aren't sacrifices; they're the line of least resistance. His conditioning has laid down rails along which he's got to run. He can't help himself; he's foredoomed. Even after decanting, he's still inside a bottle--an invisible bottle of infantile and embryonic fixations. Each one of us, of course,' the Controller meditatively continued, 'goes through life inside a bottle. But if we happen to be Alphas, our bottles are, relatively speaking, enormous. We should suffer acutely if we were confined in a narrower space. You cannot pour upper-caste champagne-surrogate into lower-caste bottles. It's obvious theoretically. But it has also been proved in actual practice. The result of the Cyprus experiment was convincing.'

'What was that?' asked the Savage.

Mustapha Mond smiled. 'Well, you can call it an experiment in rebottling if you like. It began in A.F. 473. The Controllers had the island of Cyprus cleared of all its existing inhabitants and re-colonized with a specially prepared batch of twenty-two thousand Alphas. All agricultural and industrial equipment was handed over to them and they were left to manage their own affairs. The result exactly fulfilled all the theoretical predictions. The land wasn't properly worked; there were strikes in all the factories; the laws were set at naught, orders disobeyed; all the people detailed for a spell of low-grade work were perpetually intriguing for high-grade jobs, and all the people with high-grade jobs were counter-intriguing at all costs to stay where they were. Within six years they were having a first-class civil war. When nineteen out of the twenty-two thousand had been killed, the survivors unanimously petitioned the World Controllers to resume the government of the island. Which they did. And that was the end of the only society of Alphas that the world has ever seen.'

The Savage sighed, profoundly.

'The optimum population,' said Mustapha Mond, 'is modelled on the iceberg--eight-ninths below the water line, one-ninth above.'

'And they're happy below the water line?'

'Happier than above it. Happier than your friends here, for example.' He pointed.

'In spite of that awful work?'

'Awful? *They* don't find it so. On the contrary, they like it. It's light, it's childishly simple. No strain on the mind or the muscles. Seven and a half hours of mild, unexhausting labour, and then the *soma* ration and games and unrestricted copulation and the feelies. What more can they ask for? True,' he added, 'they might ask for shorter hours. And of course we could give them shorter hours. Technically, it would be perfectly simple to reduce all lower-caste working hours to three or four a day. But would they be any the happier for that? No, they wouldn't. The experiment was tried, more than a century and a half ago. The whole of Ireland was put on to the four-hour day. What was the result? Unrest and a large increase in the consumption of *soma*; that was all. Those three and a half hours of extra leisure were so far from being a source of happiness, that people felt constrained to take a holiday from them. The Inventions Office is stuffed with plans for labour-saving processes. Thousands of them.' Mustapha Mond made a lavish gesture. 'And why don't we put them into execution? For the sake of the labourers; it would be sheer cruelty to afflict them with excessive leisure. It's the same with agriculture. We could synthesize every morsel of food, if we wanted to. But we don't. We prefer to keep a third of the population on the land. For their own sakes--because it takes *longer* to get food out of the land than out of a factory. Besides, we have our stability to think of. We don't want to change. Every change is a menace to stability. That's another reason why we're so chary of applying new inventions. Every discovery in pure science is potentially subversive; even science must sometimes be treated as a possible enemy. Yes, even science.'

Science? The Savage frowned. He knew the word. But what it exactly signified he could not say. Shakespeare and the old men of the pueblo had never mentioned science, and from Linda he had only gathered the vaguest hints: science was something you made helicopters with, something that caused you to laugh at the Corn Dances, something that prevented you from being wrinkled and losing your teeth. He made a desperate effort to take the Controller's meaning.

'Yes,' Mustapha Mond was saying, 'that's another item in the cost of stability. It isn't only art that's incompatible with happiness; it's also science. Science is dangerous; we have to keep it most carefully chained and muzzled.'

'What?' said Helmholtz, in astonishment. 'But we're always saying that science is everything. It's a hypnopædic platitude.'

'Three times a week between thirteen and seventeen,' put in Bernard.

'And all the science propaganda we do at the College...'

'Yes; but what sort of science?' asked Mustapha Mond sarcastically. 'You've had no scientific training, so you can't judge. I was a pretty good physicist in my time. Too good--good enough to realize that all our science is just a cookery book, with an orthodox theory of cooking that nobody's allowed to question, and a list of recipes that mustn't be added to except by special permission from the head cook. I'm the head cook now. But I was an inquisitive young scullion once. I started doing a bit of cooking on my own. Unorthodox cooking, illicit cooking. A bit of real science, in fact.' He was silent.

'What happened?' asked Helmholtz Watson.

The Controller sighed. 'Very nearly what's going to happen to you young men. I was on the point of being sent to an island.'

The words galvanized Bernard into a violent and unseemly activity. 'Send *me* to an island?' He jumped up, ran across the room, and stood gesticulating in front of the Controller. 'You can't send *me*. I haven't done anything. It was the others. I swear it was the others.' He pointed accusingly to Helmholtz and the Savage. 'Oh, please don't send me to Iceland. I promise I'll do what I ought to do. Give me another chance. Please give me another chance.' The tears began to flow. 'I tell you, it's their fault,' he sobbed. 'And not to Iceland. Oh, please, your fordship, please...' And in a paroxysm of abjection he threw himself on his knees before the Controller. Mustapha Mond tried to make him get up; but Bernard persisted in his grovelling; the stream of words poured out inexhaustibly. In the end the Controller had to ring for his fourth secretary.

'Bring three men,' he ordered, 'and take Mr. Marx into a bedroom. Give him a good *soma* vaporization and then put him to bed and leave him.'

The fourth secretary went out and returned with three green-uniformed twin footmen. Still shouting and sobbing, Bernard was carried out.

'One would think he was going to have his throat cut,' said the Controller, as the door closed. 'Whereas, if he had the smallest sense, he'd understand that his punishment is really a reward. He's being sent to an island. That's to say, he's being sent to a place where he'll meet the most interesting set of men and women to be found anywhere in the world. All the people who, for one reason or another, have got too self-consciously individual to fit into community-life. All the people who aren't satisfied with orthodoxy, who've got independent ideas of their own. Every one, in a word, who's any one. I almost envy you, Mr. Watson.'

Helmholtz laughed. 'Then why aren't you on an island yourself?'

'Because, finally, I preferred this,' the Controller answered. 'I was given the choice: to be sent to an island, where I could have got on with my pure science, or to be taken on to the Controllers' Council with the prospect of succeeding in due course to an actual Controllership. I chose this and let the science go.' After a little silence, 'Sometimes,' he added, 'I rather regret the science. Happiness is a hard master--particularly other people's happiness. A much harder master, if one isn't conditioned to accept it unquestioningly, than truth.' He sighed, fell silent again, then continued in a brisker tone. 'Well, duty's duty. One can't consult one's own preferences. I'm interested in truth, I like science. But truth's a menace, science is a public danger. As dangerous as it's been beneficent. It has given us the stablest equilibrium in history. China's was hopelessly insecure by comparison; even the primitive matriarchies weren't steadier than we are. Thanks, I repeat, to science. But we can't allow science to undo its own good work. That's why we so carefully limit the scope of its researches--that's why I almost got sent to an island. We don't allow it to deal with any but the most immediate problems of the moment. All other enquiries are most sedulously discouraged. It's curious,' he went on after a little pause, 'to read what people in the time of Our Ford used to write about scientific progress. They seemed to have imagined that it could be allowed to go on indefinitely, regardless of everything else. Knowledge was the highest good, truth the supreme value; all the rest was secondary and subordinate. True, ideas were beginning to change even then. Our Ford himself did a great deal to shift the emphasis from truth and beauty to comfort and happiness. Mass production demanded the shift. Universal happiness keeps the wheels steadily turning; truth and beauty can't. And, of course, whenever the masses seized political power, then it was happiness rather than truth and beauty that mattered. Still, in spite of everything, unrestricted scientific research was still permitted. People still went on talking about truth and beauty as though they were the sovereign goods. Right up to the time of the Nine Years' War. *That* made them change their tune all right. What's the point of truth or beauty or knowledge when the anthrax bombs are popping all around you? That was when science first began to be controlled--after the Nine Years' War. People were ready to have even their appetites controlled then. Anything for a quiet life. We've gone on controlling ever since. It hasn't been very good for truth, of course. But it's been very good for happiness. One can't have something for nothing. Happiness has got to be paid for. You're paying for it, Mr. Watson--paying because you happen to be too much interested in beauty. I was too much interested in truth; I paid too.'

'But *you* didn't go to an island,' said the Savage, breaking a long silence.

The Controller smiled. 'That's how I paid. By choosing to serve happiness. Other people's--not mine. It's lucky,' he added, after a pause, 'that there are such a lot of islands in the world. I don't know what we should do without them. Put you all in the lethal chamber, I suppose. By the way, Mr. Watson, would you like a tropical climate? The Marquesas, for example; or Samoa? Or something rather more bracing?'

Helmholtz rose from his pneumatic chair. 'I should like a thoroughly bad climate,' he answered. 'I believe one would write better if the climate were bad. If there were a lot of wind and storms, for example...'

The Controller nodded his approbation. 'I like your spirit, Mr. Watson. I like it very much indeed. As much as I officially disapprove of it.' He smiled. 'What about the Falkland Islands?'

'Yes, I think that will do,' Helmholtz answered. 'And now, if you don't mind, I'll go and see how poor Bernard's getting on.'

Chapter XVII

'Art, science--you seem to have paid a fairly high price for your happiness,' said the Savage, when they were alone. 'Anything else?'

'Well, religion, of course,' replied the Controller. 'There used to be something called God--before the Nine Years' War. But I was forgetting; you know all about God, I suppose.'

'Well...' The Savage hesitated. He would have liked to say something about solitude, about night, about the mesa lying pale under the moon, about the precipice, the plunge into shadowy darkness, about death. He would have liked to speak; but there were no words. Not even in Shakespeare.

The Controller, meanwhile, had crossed to the other side of the room and was unlocking a large safe let into the wall between the bookshelves. The heavy door swung open. Rummaging in the darkness within, 'It's a subject,' he said, 'that has always had a great interest for me.' He pulled out a thick black volume. 'You've never read this, for example.'

The Savage took it. '*The Holy Bible, containing the Old and New Testaments*,' he read aloud from the title-page.

'Nor this.' It was a small book and had lost its cover.

'*The Imitation of Christ*.'

'Nor this.' He handed out another volume.

'*The Varieties of Religious Experience*. By William James.'

'And I've got plenty more,' Mustapha Mond continued, resuming his seat. 'A whole collection of pornographic old books. God in the safe and Ford on the shelves.' He pointed with a laugh to his avowed library--to the shelves of books, the racks full of reading-machine bobbins and sound-track rolls.

'But if you know about God, why don't you tell them?' asked the Savage indignantly. 'Why don't you give them these books about God?'

'For the same reason as we don't give them *Othello*: they're old; they're about God hundreds of years ago. Not about God now.'

'But God doesn't change.'

'Men do, though.'

'What difference does that make?'

'All the difference in the world,' said Mustapha Mond. He got up again and walked to the safe. 'There was a man called Cardinal Newman,' he said. 'A cardinal,' he exclaimed parenthetically, 'was a kind of Arch-Community-Songster.'

'"I, Pandulph, of fair Milan cardinal." I've read about them in Shakespeare.'

'Of course you have. Well, as I was saying, there was a man called Cardinal Newman. Ah, here's the book.' He pulled it out. 'And while I'm about it I'll take this one too. It's by a man called Maine de Biran. He was a philosopher, if you know what that was.'

'A man who dreams of fewer things than there are in heaven and earth,' said the Savage promptly.

'Quite so. I'll read you one of the things he *did* dream of in a moment. Meanwhile, listen to what this old Arch-Community-Songster said.' He opened the book at the place marked by a slip of paper and began to read. '"We are not our own any more than what we possess is our own. We did not make ourselves, we cannot be supreme over ourselves. We are not our own masters. We are God's property. Is it not our happiness thus to view the matter? Is it any happiness, or any comfort, to consider that we *are* our own? It may be thought so by the young and prosperous. These may think it a great thing to have everything, as they suppose, their own way--to depend on no one--to have to think of nothing out of sight, to be without the irksomeness of continual acknowledgment, continual prayer, continual reference of what they do to the will of another. But as time goes on, they, as all men, will find that independence was not made for man--that it is an unnatural state--will do for a while, but will not carry us on safely to the end..."' Mustapha Mond paused, put down the first book and, picking up the other, turned over the pages. 'Take this, for example,' he said, and in his deep voice once more began to read: '"A man grows old; he feels in himself that radical sense of weakness, of listlessness, of discomfort, which accompanies the advance of age; and, feeling thus, imagines himself merely sick, lulling his fears with the notion that this distressing condition is due to some particular cause, from which, as from an illness, he hopes to recover. Vain imaginings! That sickness is old age; and a horrible disease it is. They say that it is the fear of death and of what comes after death that makes men turn to religion as they advance in years. But my own experience has given me the conviction that, quite apart from any such terrors or imaginings, the religious sentiment tends to develop as we grow older; to develop because, as the passions grow calm, as the fancy and sensibilities are less excited and less excitable, our reason becomes less troubled in its working, less obscured by the images, desires and distractions, in which it used to be absorbed; whereupon God emerges as from behind a cloud; our soul feels, sees, turns towards the source of all light; turns naturally and inevitably; for now that all that gave to the world of sensations its life and charm has begun to leak away from us, now that phenomenal existence is no more bolstered up by impressions from within or from without, we feel the need to lean on something that abides, something that will never play us false--a reality, an absolute and everlasting truth. Yes, we inevitably turn to God; for this religious sentiment is of its nature so pure, so delightful to the soul that experiences it, that it makes up to us for all our other losses."' Mustapha Mond shut the book and leaned back in his chair. 'One of the numerous things in heaven and earth that these philosophers didn't dream about was this' (he waved his hand), 'us, the modern world. "You can only be independent of God while you've got youth and prosperity; independence won't take you safely to the end." Well, we've now got youth and prosperity right up to the end. What follows? Evidently, that we can be independent of God. "The religious sentiment will compensate us for all our losses." But there aren't any losses for us to compensate; religious sentiment is superfluous. And why should we go hunting for a substitute for youthful desires, when youthful desires never fail? A substitute for distractions, when we go on enjoying all the old fooleries to the very last? What need have we of repose when our minds and bodies continue to delight in activity? of consolation, when we have *soma*? of something immovable, when there is the social order?'

'Then you think there is no God?'

'No, I think there quite probably is one.'

'Then why?...'

Mustapha Mond checked him. 'But he manifests himself in different ways to different men. In pre-modern times he manifested himself as the being that's described in these books. Now...'

'How does he manifest himself now?' asked the Savage.

'Well, he manifests himself as an absence; as though he weren't there at all.'

'That's your fault.'

'Call it the fault of civilization. God isn't compatible with machinery and scientific medicine and universal happiness. You must make your choice. Our civilization has chosen machinery and medicine and happiness. That's why I have to keep these books locked up in the safe. They're smut. People would be shocked if...'

The Savage interrupted him. 'But isn't it *natural* to feel there's a God?'

'You might as well ask if it's natural to do up one's trousers with zippers,' said the Controller sarcastically. 'You remind me of another of those old fellows called Bradley. He defined philosophy as the finding of bad reason for what one believes by instinct. As if one believed anything by instinct! One believes things because one has been conditioned to believe them. Finding bad reasons for what one believes for other bad reasons--that's philosophy. People believe in God because they've been conditioned to believe in God.'

'But all the same,' insisted the Savage, 'it is natural to believe in God when you're alone--quite alone, in the night, thinking about death...'

'But people never are alone now,' said Mustapha Mond. 'We make them hate solitude; and we arrange their lives so that it's almost impossible for them ever to have it.'

The Savage nodded gloomily. At Malpais he had suffered because they had shut him out from the communal activities of the pueblo, in civilized London he was suffering because he could never escape from those communal activities, never be quietly alone.

'Do you remember that bit in *King Lear*?' said the Savage at last: '"The gods are just, and of our pleasant vices make instruments to plague us; the dark and vicious place where thee he got cost him his eyes," and Edmund answers--you remember, he's wounded, he's dying--"Thou hast spoken right; 'tis true. The wheel is come full circle; I am here." What about that, now? Doesn't there seem to be a God managing things, punishing, rewarding?'

'Well, does there?' questioned the Controller in his turn. 'You can indulge in any number of pleasant vices with a freemartin and run no risks of having your eyes put out by your son's mistress. "The wheel is come full circle; I am here." But where would Edmund be nowadays? Sitting in a pneumatic chair, with his arm round a girl's waist, sucking away at his sex-hormone chewing-gum and looking at the feelies. The gods are just. No doubt. But their code of law is dictated, in the last resort, by the people who organize society; Providence takes its cue from men.'

'Are you sure?' asked the Savage. 'Are you quite sure that the Edmund in that pneumatic chair hasn't been just as heavily punished as the Edmund who's wounded and bleeding to death? The gods are just. Haven't they used his pleasant vices as an instrument to degrade him?'

'Degrade him from what position? As a happy, hard-working, goods-consuming citizen he's perfect. Of course, if you choose some other standard than ours, then perhaps you might say he was degraded. But you've got to stick to one set of postulates. You can't play Electro-magnetic Golf according to the rules of Centrifugal Bumble-puppy.'

'But value dwells not in particular will,' said the Savage. 'It holds his estimate and dignity as well wherein 'tis precious of itself as in the prizer.'

'Come, come,' protested Mustapha Mond, 'that's going rather far, isn't it?'

'If you allowed yourselves to think of God, you wouldn't allow yourselves to be degraded by pleasant vices. You'd have a reason for bearing things patiently, for doing things with courage. I've seen it with the Indians.'

'I'm sure you have,' said Mustapha Mond. 'But then we aren't Indians. There isn't any need for a civilized man to bear anything that's seriously unpleasant. And as for doing things--Ford forbid that he should get the idea into his head. It would upset the whole social order if men started doing things on their own.'

'What about self-denial, then? If you had a God, you'd have a reason for self-denial.'

'But industrial civilization is only possible when there's no self-denial. Self-indulgence up to the very limits imposed by hygiene and economics. Otherwise the wheels stop turning.'

'You'd have a reason for chastity!' said the Savage, blushing a little as he spoke the words.

'But chastity means passion, chastity means neurasthenia. And passion and neurasthenia mean instability. And instability means the end of civilization. You can't have a lasting civilization without plenty of pleasant vices.'

'But God's the reason for everything noble and fine and heroic. If you had a God...'

'My dear young friend,' said Mustapha Mond, 'civilization has absolutely no need of nobility or heroism. These things are symptoms of political inefficiency. In a properly organized society like ours, nobody has any opportunities for being noble or heroic. Conditions have got to be thoroughly unstable before the occasion can arise. Where there are wars, where there are divided allegiances, where there are temptations to be resisted, objects of love to be fought for or defended--there, obviously, nobility and heroism have some sense. But there aren't any wars nowadays. The greatest care is taken to prevent you from loving any one too much. There's no such thing as a divided allegiance; you're so conditioned that you can't help doing what you ought to do. And what you ought to do is on the whole so pleasant, so many of the natural impulses are allowed free play, that there really aren't any temptations to resist. And if ever, by some unlucky chance, anything unpleasant should somehow happen, why, there's always *soma* to give you a holiday from the facts. And there's always *soma* to calm your anger, to reconcile you to your enemies, to make you patient and long-suffering. In the past you could only accomplish these things by making a great effort and after years of hard moral training. Now, you swallow two or three half-gramme tablets, and there you are. Anybody can be virtuous now. You can carry at least half your morality about in a bottle. Christianity without tears--that's what *soma* is.'

'But the tears are necessary. Don't you remember what Othello said? "If after every tempest come such calms, may the winds blow till they have wakened death." There's a story one of the old Indians used to tell us, about the Girl of Mátsaki. The young men who wanted to marry her had to do a morning's hoeing in her garden. It seemed easy; but there were flies and mosquitoes, magic ones. Most of the young men simply couldn't stand the biting and stinging. But the one that could--he got the girl.'

'Charming! But in civilized countries,' said the Controller, 'you can have girls without hoeing for them; and there aren't any flies or mosquitoes to sting you. We got rid of them all centuries ago.'

The Savage nodded, frowning. 'You got rid of them. Yes, that's just like you. Getting rid of everything unpleasant instead of learning to put up with it. Whether 'tis nobler in the mind to suffer the slings and arrows of outrageous fortune, or to take arms against a sea of troubles and by opposing end them.... But you don't do either. Neither suffer nor oppose. You just abolish the slings and arrows. It's too easy.'

He was suddenly silent, thinking of his mother. In her room on the thirty-seventh floor, Linda had floated in a sea of singing lights and perfumed caresses--floated away, out of space, out of time, out of the prison of her memories, her habits, her aged and bloated body. And Tomakin, ex-Director of Hatcheries and Conditioning, Tomakin was still on holiday--on holiday from humiliation and pain, in a world where he could not hear those words, that derisive laughter, could not see that hideous face, feel those moist and flabby arms round his neck, in a beautiful world...

'What you need,' the Savage went on, 'is something *with* tears for a change. Nothing costs enough here.'

('Twelve and a half million dollars,' Henry Foster had protested when the Savage told him that. 'Twelve and a half million--that's what the new Conditioning Centre cost. Not a cent less.')

'Exposing what is mortal and unsure to all that fortune, death and danger dare, even for an egg-shell. Isn't there something in that?' he asked, looking up at Mustapha Mond. 'Quite apart from God--though of course God would be a reason for it. Isn't there something in living dangerously?'

'There's a great deal in it,' the Controller replied. 'Men and women must have their adrenals stimulated from time to time.'

'What?' questioned the Savage, uncomprehending.

'It's one of the conditions of perfect health. That's why we've made the V.P.S. treatments compulsory.'

'V.P.S.?'

'Violent Passion Surrogate. Regularly once a month. We flood the whole system with adrenin. It's the complete physiological equivalent of fear and rage. All the tonic effects of murdering Desdemona and being murdered by Othello, without any of the inconveniences.'

'But I like the inconveniences.'

'We don't,' said the Controller. 'We prefer to do things comfortably.'

'But I don't want comfort. I want God, I want poetry, I want real danger, I want freedom, I want goodness. I want sin.'

'In fact,' said Mustapha Mond, 'you're claiming the right to be unhappy.'

'All right, then,' said the Savage defiantly, 'I'm claiming the right to be unhappy.'

'Not to mention the right to grow old and ugly and impotent; the right to have syphilis and cancer; the right to have too little to eat; the right to be lousy; the right to live in constant apprehension of what may happen to-morrow; the right to catch typhoid; the right to be tortured by unspeakable pains of every kind.'

There was a long silence.

'I claim them all,' said the Savage at last.

Mustapha Mond shrugged his shoulders. 'You're welcome,' he said.

Chapter XVIII

The door was ajar; they entered.

'John!'

From the bathroom came an unpleasant and characteristic sound.

'Is there anything the matter?' Helmholtz called.

There was no answer. The unpleasant sound was repeated, twice; there was silence. Then, with a click, the bathroom door opened and, very pale, the Savage emerged.

'I say,' Helmholtz exclaimed solicitously, 'you *do* look ill, John!'

'Did you eat something that didn't agree with you?' asked Bernard.

The Savage nodded. 'I ate civilization.'

'What?'

'It poisoned me; I was defiled. And then,' he added, in a lower tone, 'I ate my own wickedness.'

'Yes, but what exactly?... I mean, just now you were...'

'Now I am purified,' said the Savage. 'I drank some mustard and warm water.'

The others stared at him in astonishment. 'Do you mean to say that you were doing it on purpose?' asked Bernard.

'That's how the Indians always purify themselves.' He sat down and, sighing, passed his hand across his forehead. 'I shall rest for a few minutes,' he said. 'I'm rather tired.'

'Well, I'm not surprised,' said Helmholtz. After a silence, 'We've come to say good-bye,' he went on in another tone. 'We're off to-morrow morning.'

'Yes, we're off to-morrow,' said Bernard, on whose face the Savage remarked a new expression of determined resignation. 'And by the way, John,' he continued, leaning forward in his chair and laying a hand on the Savage's knee, 'I want to say how sorry I am about everything that happened yesterday.' He blushed. 'How ashamed,' he went on, in spite of the unsteadiness of his voice, 'how really...'

The Savage cut him short and, taking his hand, affectionately pressed it.

'Helmholtz was wonderful to me,' Bernard resumed, after a little pause. 'If it hadn't been for him, I should...'

'Now, now,' Helmholtz protested.

There was a silence. In spite of their sadness--because of it, even; for their sadness was the symptom of their love for one another--the three young men were happy.

'I went to see the Controller this morning,' said the Savage at last.

'What for?'

'To ask if I mightn't go to the islands with you.'

'And what did he say?' asked Helmholtz eagerly.

The Savage shook his head. 'He wouldn't let me.'

'Why not?'

'He said he wanted to go on with the experiment. But I'm damned,' the Savage added, with sudden fury, 'I'm damned if I'll go on being experimented with. Not for all the Controllers in the world. *I* shall go away to-morrow too.'

'But where?' the others asked in unison.

The Savage shrugged his shoulders. 'Anywhere. I don't care. So long as I can be alone.'

****

From Guildford the down-line followed the Wey valley to Godalming, then, over Milford and Witley, proceeded to Haslemere and on through Petersfield towards Portsmouth. Roughly parallel to it, the up-line passed over Worplesden, Tongham, Puttenham, Elstead and Grayshott. Between the Hog's Back and Hindhead there were points where the two lines were not more than six or seven kilometres apart. The distance was too small for careless flyers--particularly at night and when they had taken half a gramme too much. There had been accidents. Serious ones. It had been decided to deflect the up-line a few kilometres to the west. Between Grayshott and Tongham four abandoned air-lighthouses marked the course of the old Portsmouth-to-London road. The skies above them were silent and deserted. It was over Selborne, Borden and Farnham that the helicopters now ceaselessly hummed and roared.

The Savage had chosen as his hermitage the old lighthouse which stood on the crest of the hill between Puttenham and Elstead. The building was of ferro-concrete and in excellent condition--almost too comfortable, the Savage had thought when he first explored the place, almost too civilizedly luxurious. He pacified his conscience by promising himself a compensatingly harder self-discipline, purifications the more complete and thorough. His first night in the hermitage was, deliberately, a sleepless one. He spent the hours on his knees praying, now to that Heaven from which the guilty Claudius had begged forgiveness, now in Zuñi to Awonawilona, now to Jesus and Pookong, now to his own guardian animal, the eagle. From time to time he stretched out his arms as though he were on the cross, and held them thus through long minutes of an ache that gradually increased till it became a tremulous and excruciating agony; held them, in voluntary crucifixion, while he repeated, through clenched teeth (the sweat, meanwhile, pouring down his face), 'Oh, forgive me! Oh, make me pure! Oh, help me to be good!' again and again, till he was on the point of fainting from the pain.

When morning came, he felt he had earned the right to inhabit the lighthouse: yes, even though there still *was* glass in most of the windows, even though the view from the platform *was* so fine. For the very reason why he had chosen the lighthouse had become almost instantly a reason for going somewhere else. He had decided to live there because the view was so beautiful, because, from his vantage point, he seemed to be looking out on to the incarnation of a divine being. But who was he to be pampered with the daily and hourly sight of loveliness? Who was he to be living in the visible presence of God? All he deserved to live in was some filthy sty, some blind hole in the ground. Stiff and still aching after his long night of pain, but for that very reason inwardly reassured, he climbed up to the platform of his tower, he looked out over the bright sunrise world which he had regained the right to inhabit. On the north the view was bounded by the long chalk ridge of the Hog's Back, from behind whose eastern extremity rose the towers of the seven skyscrapers which constituted Guildford. Seeing them, the Savage made a grimace; but he was to become reconciled to them in course of time; for at night they twinkled gaily with geometrical constellations, or else, flood-lighted, pointed their luminous fingers (with a gesture whose significance nobody in England but the Savage now understood) solemnly towards the plumbless mysteries of heaven.

In the valley which separated the Hog's Back from the sandy hill on which the lighthouse stood, Puttenham was a modest little village nine stories high, with silos, a poultry farm, and a small vitamin-D factory. On the other side of the lighthouse, towards the south, the ground fell away in long slopes of heather to a chain of ponds.

Beyond them, above the intervening woods, rose the fourteen-story tower of Elstead. Dim in the hazy English air, Hindhead and Selborne invited the eye into a blue romantic distance. But it was not alone the distance that had attracted the Savage to his lighthouse; the near was as seductive as the far. The woods, the open stretches of heather and yellow gorse, the clumps of Scotch firs, the shining ponds with their overhanging birch trees, their water lilies, their beds of rushes--these were beautiful and, to an eye accustomed to the aridities of the American desert, astonishing. And then the solitude! Whole days passed during which he never saw a human being. The lighthouse was only a quarter of an hour's flight from the Charing-T Tower; but the hills of Malpais were hardly more deserted than this Surrey heath. The crowds that daily left London left it only to play Electro-magnetic Golf or Tennis. Puttenham possessed no links; the nearest Riemann-surfaces were at Guildford. Flowers and a landscape were the only attractions here. And so, as there was no good reason for coming, nobody came. During the first days the Savage lived alone and undisturbed.

Of the money which, on his first arrival, John had received for his personal expenses, most had been spent on his equipment. Before leaving London he had bought four viscose-woollen blankets, rope and string, nails, glue, a few tools, matches (though he intended in due course to make a fire drill), some pots and pans, two dozen packets of seeds, and ten kilogrammes of wheat flour. 'No, *not* synthetic starch and cotton-waste flour-substitute,' he had insisted. 'Even though it is more nourishing.' But when it came to pan-glandular biscuits and vitaminized beef-surrogate, he had not been able to resist the shopman's persuasion. Looking at the tins now, he bitterly reproached himself for his weakness. Loathsome civilized stuff! He had made up his mind that he would never eat it, even if he were starving. 'That'll teach them,' he thought vindictively. It would also teach him.

He counted his money. The little that remained would be enough, he hoped, to tide him over the winter. By next spring, his garden would be producing enough to make him independent of the outside world. Meanwhile, there would always be game. He had seen plenty of rabbits, and there were water-fowl on the ponds. He set to work at once to make a bow and arrows.

There were ash trees near the lighthouse and, for arrow shafts, a whole copse full of beautifully straight hazel saplings. He began by felling a young ash, cut out six feet of unbranched stem, stripped off the bark and, paring by paring, shaved away the white wood, as old Mitsima had taught him, until he had a stave of his own height, stiff at the thickened centre, lively and quick at the slender tips. The work gave him an intense pleasure. After those weeks of idleness in London, with nothing to do, whenever he wanted anything, but to press a switch or turn a handle, it was pure delight to be doing something that demanded skill and patience.

He had almost finished whittling the stave into shape, when he realized with a start that he was singing--*singing*! It was as though, stumbling upon himself from the outside, he had suddenly caught himself out, taken himself flagrantly at fault. Guiltily he blushed. After all, it was not to sing and enjoy himself that he had come here. It was to escape further contamination by the filth of civilized life; it was to be purified and made good; it was actively to make amends. He realized to his dismay that, absorbed in the whittling of his bow, he had forgotten what he had sworn to himself he would constantly remember--poor Linda, and his own murderous unkindness to her, and those loathsome twins, swarming like lice across the mystery of her death, insulting, with their presence, not merely his own grief and repentance, but the very gods themselves. He had sworn to remember, he had sworn unceasingly to make amends. And here was he, sitting happily over his bow-stave, singing, actually singing....

He went indoors, opened the box of mustard, and put some water to boil on the fire.

Half an hour later, three Delta-Minus land-workers from one of the Puttenham Bokanovsky Groups happened to be driving to Elstead and, at the top of the hill, were astonished to see a young man standing outside the abandoned lighthouse stripped to the waist and hitting himself with a whip of knotted cords. His back was horizontally streaked with crimson, and from weal to weal ran thin trickles of blood. The driver of the lorry pulled up at the side of the road and, with his two companions, stared open-mouthed at the extraordinary spectacle. One, two, three--they counted the strokes. After the eighth, the young man interrupted his self-punishment to run to the wood's edge and there be violently sick. When he had finished, he picked up the whip and began hitting himself again. Nine, ten, eleven, twelve...

'Ford!' whispered the driver. And his twins were of the same opinion.

'Fordey!' they said.

Three days later, like turkey buzzards settling on a corpse, the reporters came.

Dried and hardened over a slow fire of green wood, the bow was ready. The Savage was busy on his arrows. Thirty hazel sticks had been whittled and dried, tipped with sharp nails, carefully nocked. He had made a raid one night on the Puttenham poultry farm, and now had feathers enough to equip a whole armoury. It was at work upon the feathering of his shafts that the first of the reporters found him. Noiseless on his pneumatic shoes, the man came up behind him.

'Good-morning, Mr. Savage,' he said. 'I am the representative of *The Hourly Radio*.'

Startled as though by the bite of a snake, the Savage sprang to his feet, scattering arrows, feathers, glue-pot and brush in all directions.

'I beg your pardon,' said the reporter, with genuine compunction. 'I had no intention...' He touched his hat--the aluminium stove-pipe hat in which he carried his wireless receiver and transmitter. 'Excuse my not taking it off,' he said. 'It's a bit heavy. Well, as I was saying, I am the representative of *The Hourly...*'

'What do you want?' asked the Savage, scowling. The reporter returned his most ingratiating smile.

'Well, of course, our readers would be profoundly interested...' He put his head on one side, his smile became almost coquettish. 'Just a few words from you, Mr. Savage.' And rapidly, with a series of ritual gestures, he uncoiled two wires connected to the portable battery buckled round his waist; plugged them simultaneously into the sides of his aluminium hat; touched a spring on the crown--and antennæ shot up into the air; touched another spring on the peak of the brim--and, like a jack-in-the-box, out jumped a microphone and hung there, quivering, six inches in front of his nose; pulled down a pair of receivers over his ears; pressed a switch on the left side of the hat--and from within came a faint waspy buzzing; turned a knob on the right--and the buzzing was interrupted by a stethoscopic wheeze and crackle, by hiccoughs and sudden squeaks. 'Hullo,' he said to the microphone, 'hullo, hullo...' A bell suddenly rang inside his hat. 'Is that you, Edzel? Primo Mellon speaking. Yes, I've got hold of him. Mr. Savage will now take the microphone and say a few words. Won't you, Mr. Savage?' He looked up at the Savage with another of those winning smiles of his. 'Just tell our readers why you came here. What made you leave London (hold on, Edzel!) so very suddenly. And, of course, that whip.' (The Savage started. How did they know about the whip?) 'We're all crazy to know about the whip. And then something about Civilization. You know the sort of stuff. "What I think of the Civilized Girl." Just a few words, a very few...'

The Savage obeyed with a disconcerting literalness. Five words he uttered and no more--five words, the same as those he had said to Bernard about the Arch-Community-Songster of Canterbury. '*Háni! Sons éso tse-ná!*' And seizing the reporter by the shoulder, he spun him round (the young man revealed himself invitingly well-covered), aimed and, with all the force and accuracy of a champion foot-and-mouth-baller, delivered a most prodigious kick.

Eight minutes later, a new edition of *The Hourly Radio* was on sale in the streets of London. 'HOURLY RADIO REPORTER HAS COCCYX KICKED BY MYSTERY SAVAGE,' ran the headlines on the front page. 'SENSATION IN SURREY.'

'Sensation even in London,' thought the reporter when, on his return, he read the words. And a very painful sensation, what was more. He sat down gingerly to his luncheon.

Undeterred by that cautionary bruise on their colleague's coccyx, four other reporters, representing the New York *Times*, the Frankfurt *Four-Dimensional Continuum, The Fordian Science Monitor*, and *The Delta Mirror*, called that afternoon at the lighthouse and met with receptions of progressively increasing violence.

From a safe distance and still rubbing his buttocks, 'Benighted fool!' shouted the man from *The Fordian Science Monitor*, 'why don't you take *soma*?'

'Get away!' The Savage shook his fist.

The other retreated a few steps, then turned round again. 'Evil's an unreality if you take a couple of grammes.'

'*Kohakwa iyathtokyai!*' The tone was menacingly derisive.

'Pain's a delusion.'

'Oh, is it?' said the Savage and, picking up a thick hazel switch, strode forward.

The man from *The Fordian Science Monitor* made a dash for his helicopter.

After that the Savage was left for a time in peace. A few helicopters came and hovered inquisitively round the tower. He shot an arrow into the importunately nearest of them. It pierced the aluminium floor of the cabin; there was a shrill yell, and the machine went rocketing up into the air with all the acceleration that its super-charger could give it. The others, in future, kept their distance respectfully. Ignoring their tiresome humming (he likened himself in his imagination to one of the suitors of the Maiden of Mátsaki, unmoved and persistent among the winged vermin), the Savage dug at what was to be his garden. After a time the vermin evidently became bored and flew away; for hours at a stretch the sky above his head was empty and, but for the larks, silent.

The weather was breathlessly hot, there was thunder in the air. He had dug all the morning and was resting, stretched out along the floor. And suddenly the thought of Lenina was a real presence, naked and tangible, saying 'Sweet!' and 'Put your arms round me!'--in shoes and socks, perfumed. Impudent strumpet! But oh, oh, her arms round his neck, the lifting of her breasts, her mouth! Eternity was in our lips and eyes. Lenina... No, no, no! He sprang to his feet and, half naked as he was, ran out of the house. At the edge of the heath stood a clump of hoary juniper bushes. He flung himself against them, he embraced, not the smooth body of his desires, but an armful of green spikes. Sharp, with a thousand points, they pricked him. He tried to think of poor Linda, breathless and dumb, with her clutching hands and the unutterable terror in her eyes. Poor Linda whom he had sworn to remember. But it was still the presence of Lenina that haunted him. Lenina whom he had promised to forget. Even through the stab and sting of the juniper needles, his wincing flesh was aware of her, unescapably real. 'Sweet, sweet... And if you wanted me too, why didn't you...'

The whip was hanging on a nail by the door, ready to hand against the arrival of reporters. In a frenzy the Savage ran back to the house, seized it, whirled it. The knotted cords bit into his flesh.

'Strumpet! Strumpet!' he shouted at every blow as though it were Lenina (and how frantically, without knowing it, he wished it were!), white, warm, scented, infamous Lenina that he was flogging thus. 'Strumpet!' And then, in a voice of despair, 'Oh, Linda, forgive me. Forgive me, God. I'm bad. I'm wicked. I'm... No, no, you strumpet, you strumpet!'

From his carefully constructed hide in the wood three hundred metres away, Darwin Bonaparte, the Feely Corporation's most expert big-game photographer, had watched the whole proceedings. Patience and skill had been rewarded. He had spent three days sitting inside the bole of an artificial oak tree, three nights crawling on his belly through the heather, hiding microphones in gorse bushes, burying wires in the soft grey sand. Seventy-two hours of profound discomfort. But now the great moment had come--the greatest, Darwin Bonaparte had time to reflect, as he moved among his instruments, the greatest since his taking of the famous all-howling stereoscopic feely of the gorillas' wedding. 'Splendid,' he said to himself, as the Savage started his astonishing performance. 'Splendid!' He kept his telescopic cameras carefully aimed--glued to their moving objective; clapped on a higher power to get a close-up of the frantic and distorted face (admirable!); switched over, for half a minute, to slow motion (an exquisitely comical effect, he promised himself); listened in, meanwhile, to the blows, the groans, the wild and raving words that were being recorded on the sound-track at the edge of his film, tried the effect of a little amplification (yes, that was decidedly better); was delighted to hear, in a momentary lull, the shrill singing of a lark; wished the Savage would turn round so that he could get a good close-up of the blood on his back--and almost instantly (what astonishing luck!) the accommodating fellow did turn round, and he was able to take a perfect close-up.

'Well, that was grand!' he said to himself when it was all over. 'Really grand!' He mopped his face. When they had put in the feely effects at the studio, it would be a wonderful film. Almost as good, thought Darwin Bonaparte, as the *Sperm Whale's Love-Life*--and that, by Ford, was saying a good deal!

Twelve days later *The Savage of Surrey* had been released and could be seen, heard and felt in every first-class feely-palace in Western Europe.

The effect of Darwin Bonaparte's film was immediate and enormous. On the afternoon which followed the evening of its release, John's rustic solitude was suddenly broken by the arrival overhead of a great swarm of helicopters.

He was digging in his garden--digging, too, in his own mind, laboriously turning up the substance of his thought. Death--and he drove in his spade once, and again, and yet again. And all our yesterdays have lighted fools the way to dusty death. A convincing thunder rumbled through the words. He lifted another spadeful of earth. Why had Linda died? Why had she been allowed to become gradually less than human and at last... He shuddered. A good kissing carrion. He planted his foot on his spade and stamped it fiercely into the tough ground. As flies to wanton boys are we to the gods; they kill us for their sport. Thunder again; words that proclaimed themselves true--truer somehow than truth itself. And yet that same Gloucester had called them ever-gentle gods. Besides, thy best of rest is sleep, and that thou oft provok'st; yet grossly fear'st thy death which is no more. No more than sleep. Sleep. Perchance to dream. His spade struck against a stone; he stooped to pick it up. For in that sleep of death, what dreams?...

A humming overhead had become a roar; and suddenly he was in shadow, there was something between the sun and him. He looked up, startled, from his digging, from his thoughts; looked up in a dazzled bewilderment, his mind still wandering in that other world of truer-than-truth, still focussed on the immensities of death and deity; looked up and saw, close above him, the swarm of hovering machines. Like locusts they came, hung poised, descended all around him on the heather. And from out of the bellies of these giant grasshoppers stepped men in white viscose-flannels, women (for the weather was hot) in acetate-shantung pyjamas or velveteen shorts and sleeveless, half-unzipped singlets--one couple from each. In a few minutes there were dozens of them, standing in a wide circle round the lighthouse, staring, laughing, clicking their cameras, throwing (as to an ape) pea-nuts, packets of sex-hormone chewing-gum, pan-glandular *petits beurres*. And every moment--for across the Hog's Back the stream of traffic now flowed unceasingly--their numbers increased. As in a nightmare, the dozens became scores, the scores hundreds.

The Savage had retreated towards cover, and now, in the posture of an animal at bay, stood with his back to the wall of the lighthouse, staring from face to face in speechless horror, like a man out of his senses.

From this stupor he was aroused to a more immediate sense of reality by the impact on his cheek of a well-aimed packet of chewing-gum. A shock of startling pain--and he was broad awake, awake and fiercely angry.

'Go away!' he shouted.

The ape had spoken; there was a burst of laughter and hand-clapping. 'Good old Savage! Hurrah, hurrah!' And through the babel he heard cries of: 'Whip, whip, the whip!'

Acting on the word's suggestion, he seized the bunch of knotted cords from its nail behind the door and shook it at his tormentors.

There was a yell of ironical applause.

Menacingly he advanced towards them. A woman cried out in fear. The line wavered at its most immediately threatened point, then stiffened again, stood firm. The consciousness of being in overwhelming force had given these sightseers a courage which the Savage had not expected of them. Taken aback, he halted and looked round.

'Why don't you leave me alone?' There was an almost plaintive note in his anger.

'Have a few magnesium-salted almonds!' said the man who, if the Savage were to advance, would be the first to be attacked. He held out a packet. 'They're really very good, you know,' he added, with a rather nervous smile of propitiation. 'And the magnesium salts will help to keep you young.'

The Savage ignored his offer. 'What do you want with me?' he asked, turning from one grinning face to another. 'What do you want with me?'

'The whip,' answered a hundred voices confusedly. 'Do the whipping stunt. Let's see the whipping stunt.'

Then, in unison and on a slow, heavy rhythm, 'We--want--the whip,' shouted a group at the end of the line. 'We--want--the whip.'

Others at once took up the cry, and the phrase was repeated, parrot-fashion, again and again, with an ever-growing volume of sound, until, by the seventh or eighth reiteration, no other word was being spoken. 'We--want--the whip.'

They were all crying together; and, intoxicated by the noise, the unanimity, the sense of rhythmical atonement, they might, it seemed, have gone on for hours--almost indefinitely. But at about the twenty-fifth repetition the proceedings were startlingly interrupted. Yet another helicopter had arrived from across the Hog's Back, hung poised above the crowd, then dropped within a few yards of where the Savage was standing, in the open space between the line of sightseers and the lighthouse. The roar of the air screws momentarily drowned the shouting; then, as the machine touched the ground and the engines were turned off: 'We--want--the whip; we--want--the whip,' broke out again in the same loud, insistent monotone.

The door of the helicopter opened, and out stepped, first a fair and ruddy-faced young man, then, in green velveteen shorts, white shirt, and jockey cap, a young woman.

At the sight of the young woman, the Savage started, recoiled, turned pale.

The young woman stood, smiling at him--an uncertain, imploring, almost abject smile. The seconds passed. Her lips moved, she was saying something; but the sound of her voice was covered by the loud reiterated refrain of the sightseers.

'We--want--the whip! We--want--the whip!'

The young woman pressed both hands to her left side, and on that peach-bright, doll-beautiful face of hers appeared a strangely incongruous expression of yearning distress. Her blue eyes seemed to grow larger, brighter; and suddenly two tears rolled down her cheeks. Inaudibly, she spoke again; then, with a quick, impassioned gesture stretched out her arms towards the Savage, stepped forward.

'We--want--the whip! We--want...'

And all of a sudden they had what they wanted.

'Strumpet!' The Savage had rushed at her like a madman. 'Fitchew!' Like a madman, he was slashing at her with his whip of small cords.

Terrified, she had turned to flee, had tripped and fallen in the heather. 'Henry, Henry!' she shouted. But her ruddy-faced companion had bolted out of harm's way behind the helicopter.

With a whoop of delighted excitement the line broke; there was a convergent stampede towards that magnetic centre of attraction. Pain was a fascinating horror.

'Fry, lechery, fry!' Frenzied, the Savage slashed again.

Hungrily they gathered round, pushing and scrambling like swine about the trough.

'Oh, the flesh!' The Savage ground his teeth. This time it was on his shoulders that the whip descended. 'Kill it, kill it!'

Drawn by the fascination of the horror of pain and, from within, impelled by that habit of cooperation, that desire for unanimity and atonement, which their conditioning had so ineradicably implanted in them, they began to mime the frenzy of his gestures, striking at one another as the Savage struck at his own rebellious flesh, or at that plump incarnation of turpitude writhing in the heather at his feet.

'Kill it, kill it, kill it...' the Savage went on shouting.

Then suddenly somebody started singing 'Orgy-porgy,' and in a moment they had all caught up the refrain and, singing, had begun to dance. Orgy-porgy, round and round and round, beating one another in six-eight time. Orgy-porgy...

It was after midnight when the last of the helicopters took its flight. Stupefied by *soma*, and exhausted by a long-drawn frenzy of sensuality, the Savage lay sleeping in the heather. The sun was already high when he awoke. He lay for a moment, blinking in owlish incomprehension at the light; then suddenly remembered--everything.

'Oh, my God, my God!' He covered his eyes with his hand.

****

That evening the swarm of helicopters that came buzzing across the Hog's Back was a dark cloud ten kilometres long. The description of last night's orgy of atonement had been in all the papers.

'Savage!' called the first arrivals, as they alighted from their machine. 'Mr. Savage!'

There was no answer.

The door of the lighthouse was ajar. They pushed it open and walked into a shuttered twilight. Through an archway on the further side of the room they could see the bottom of the staircase that led up to the higher floors. Just under the crown of the arch dangled a pair of feet.

'Mr. Savage!'

Slowly, very slowly, like two unhurried compass needles, the feet turned towards the right; north, north-east, east, south-east, south, south-south-west; then paused, and, after a few seconds, turned as unhurriedly back towards the left. South-southwest, south, south-east, east...

This page has been left intentionally blank

BRAVE NEW WORLD REVISITED

I Over-Population

In 1931, when *Brave New World* was being written, I was convinced that there was still plenty of time. The completely organized society, the scientific caste system, the abolition of free will by methodical conditioning, the servitude made acceptable by regular doses of chemically induced happiness, the orthodoxies drummed in by nightly courses of sleep-teaching—these things were coming all right, but not in my time, not even in the time of my grandchildren. I forget the exact date of the events recorded in *Brave New World*; but it was somewhere in the sixth, or seventh century A.F. (After Ford). We who were living in the second quarter of the twentieth century A.D. were the inhabitants, admittedly, of a gruesome kind of universe; but the nightmare of those depression years was radically different from the nightmare of the future, described in *Brave New World*. Ours was a nightmare of too little order; theirs, in the seventh century A.F., of too much. In the process of passing from one extreme to the other, there would be a long interval, so I imagined, during which the more fortunate third of the human race would make the best of both worlds—the disorderly world of liberalism and the much too orderly Brave New World where perfect efficiency left no room for freedom or personal initiative.

Twenty-seven years later, in this third quarter of the twentieth century A.D., and long before the end of the first century A.F., I feel a good deal less optimistic than I did when I was writing *Brave New World*. The prophecies made in 1931 are coming true much sooner than I thought they would. The blessed interval between too little order and the nightmare of too much has not begun and shows no sign of beginning. In the West, it is true, individual men and women still enjoy a large measure of freedom. But even in those countries that have a tradition of democratic government, this freedom and even the desire for this freedom seem to be on the wane. In the rest of the world freedom for individuals has already gone, or is manifestly about to go. The nightmare of total organization, which I had situated in the seventh century After Ford, has emerged from the safe, remote future and is now awaiting us, just around the next corner.

George Orwell's *1984* was a magnified projection into the future of a present that contained Stalinism and an immediate past that had witnessed the flowering of Nazism. *Brave New World* was written before the rise of Hitler to supreme power in Germany and when the Russian tyrant had not yet got into his stride. In 1931 systematic terrorism was not the obsessive contemporary fact which it had become in 1948, and the future dictatorship of my imaginary world was a good deal less brutal than the future dictatorship so brilliantly portrayed by Orwell. In the context of 1948, *1984* seemed dreadfully convincing. But tyrants, after all, are mortal and circumstances change. Recent developments in Russia and recent advances in science and technology have robbed Orwell's book of some of its gruesome verisimilitude. A nuclear war will, of course, make nonsense of everybody's predictions. But, assuming for the moment that the Great Powers can somehow refrain from destroying us, we can say that it now looks as though the odds were more in favor of something like *Brave New World* than of something like *1984*.

In the light of what we have recently learned about animal behavior in general, and human behavior in particular, it has become clear that control through the punishment of undesirable behavior is less effective, in the long run, than control through the reinforcement of desirable behavior by rewards, and that government through terror works on the whole less well than government through the non-violent manipulation of the environment and of the thoughts and feelings of individual men, women and children. Punishment temporarily puts a stop to undesirable behavior, but does not permanently reduce the victim's tendency to indulge in it. Moreover, the psycho-physical by-products of punishment may be just as undesirable as the behavior for which an individual has been punished. Psychotherapy is largely concerned with the debilitating or anti-social consequences of past punishments.

The society described in *1984* is a society controlled almost exclusively by punishment and the fear of punishment. In the imaginary world of my own fable punishment is infrequent and generally mild. The nearly perfect control exercised by the government is achieved by systematic reinforcement of desirable behavior, by many kinds of nearly non-violent manipulation, both physical and psychological, and by genetic standardization. Babies in bottles and the centralized control of reproduction are not perhaps impossible; but it is quite clear that for a long time to come we shall remain a viviparous species breeding at random. For practical purposes genetic standardization may be ruled out. Societies will continue to be controlled postnatally—by punishment, as in the past, and to an ever increasing extent by the more effective methods of reward and scientific manipulation.

In Russia the old-fashioned, *1984*-style dictatorship of Stalin has begun to give way to a more up-to-date form of tyranny. In the upper levels of the Soviets' hierarchical society the reinforcement of desirable behavior has begun to replace the older methods of control through the punishment of undesirable behavior. Engineers and scientists, teachers and administrators, are handsomely paid for good work and so moderately taxed that they are under a constant incentive to do better and so be more highly rewarded. In certain areas they are at liberty to think and do more or less what they like. Punishment awaits them only when they stray beyond their prescribed limits into the realms of ideology and politics. It is because they have been granted a measure of professional freedom that Russian teachers, scientists and technicians have achieved such remarkable successes. Those who live near the base of the Soviet pyramid enjoy none of the privileges accorded to the lucky or specially gifted minority. Their wages are meager and they pay, in the form of high prices, a disproportionately large share of the taxes. The area in which they can do as they please is extremely restricted, and their rulers control them more by punishment and the threat of punishment than through non-violent manipulation or the reinforcement of desirable behavior by reward. The Soviet system combines elements of *1984* with elements that are prophetic of what went on among the higher castes in *Brave New World*.

Meanwhile impersonal forces over which we have almost no control seem to be pushing us all in the direction of the Brave New Worldian nightmare; and this impersonal pushing is being consciously accelerated by representatives of commercial and political organizations who have developed a number of new techniques for manipulating, in the interest of some minority, the thoughts and feelings of the masses. The techniques of manipulation will be discussed in later chapters. For the moment let us confine our attention to those impersonal forces which are now making the world so extremely unsafe for democracy, so very inhospitable to individual freedom. What are these forces? And why has the nightmare, which I had projected into the seventh century A.F., made so swift an advance in our direction? The answer to these questions must begin where the life of even the most highly civilized society has its beginnings—on the level of biology.

On the first Christmas Day the population of our planet was about two hundred and fifty millions—less than half the population of modern China. Sixteen centuries later, when the Pilgrim Fathers landed at Plymouth Rock, human numbers had climbed to a little more than five hundred millions. By the time of the signing of the Declaration of Independence, world population had passed the seven hundred million mark. In 1931, when I was writing *Brave New World*, it stood at just under two billions. Today, only twenty-seven years later, there are two billion eight hundred thousand of us. And tomorrow—what? Penicillin, DDT and clean water are cheap commodities, whose effects on public health are out of all proportion to their cost. Even the poorest government is rich enough to provide its subjects with a substantial measure of death control. Birth control is a very different matter. Death control is something which can be provided for a whole people by a few technicians working in the pay of a benevolent government. Birth control depends on the co-operation of an entire people. It must be practiced by countless individuals, from whom it demands more intelligence and will power than most of the world's teeming illiterates possess, and (where chemical or mechanical methods of contraception are used) an expenditure of more money than most of these millions can now afford. Moreover, there are nowhere any religious traditions in favor of unrestricted death, whereas religious and social traditions in favor of unrestricted reproduction are widespread. For all these reasons, death control is achieved very easily, birth control is achieved with great difficulty. Death rates have therefore fallen in recent years with startling suddenness. But birth rates have either remained at their old high level or, if they have fallen, have fallen very little and at a very slow rate. In consequence, human numbers are now increasing more rapidly than at any time in the history of the species.

Moreover, the yearly increases are themselves increasing. They increase regularly, according to the rules of compound interest; and they also increase irregularly with every application, by a technologically backward society of the principles of Public Health. At the present time the annual increase in world population runs to about forty-three millions. This means that every four years mankind adds to its numbers the equivalent of the present population of the United States, every eight and a half years the equivalent of the present population of India. At the rate of increase prevailing between the birth of Christ and the death of Queen Elizabeth I, it took sixteen centuries for the population of the earth to double. At the present rate it will double in less than half a century. And this fantastically rapid doubling of our numbers will be taking place on a planet whose most desirable and productive areas are already densely populated, whose soils are being eroded by the frantic efforts of bad farmers to raise more food, and whose easily available mineral capital is being squandered with the reckless extravagance of a drunken sailor getting rid of his accumulated pay.

In the Brave New World of my fable, the problem of human numbers in their relation to natural resources had been effectively solved. An optimum figure for world population had been calculated and numbers were maintained at this figure (a little under two billions, if I remember rightly) generation after generation. In the real contemporary world, the population problem has not been solved. On the contrary it is becoming graver and more formidable with every passing year. It is against this grim biological background that all the political, economic, cultural and psychological dramas of our time are being played out. As the twentieth century wears on, as the new billions are added to the existing billions (there will be more than five and a half billions of us by the time my granddaughter is fifty), this biological background will advance, ever more insistently, ever more menacingly, toward the front and center of the historical stage. The problem of rapidly increasing numbers in relation to natural resources, to social stability and to the well-being of individuals—this is now the central problem of mankind; and it will remain the central problem certainly for another century, and perhaps for several centuries thereafter. A new age is supposed to have begun on October 4, 1957. But actually, in the present context, all our exuberant post-Sputnik talk is irrelevant and even nonsensical. So far as the masses of mankind are concerned, the coming time will not be the Space Age; it will be the Age of Over-population. We can parody the words of the old song and ask,

Will   the   space   that   you're   so   rich   in
Light   a   fire   in   the   kitchen,
Or the little god of space turn the spit, spit, spit?

The answer, it is obvious, is in the negative. A settlement on the moon may be of some military advantage to the nation that does the settling. But it will do nothing whatever to make life more tolerable, during the fifty years that it will take our present population to double, for the earth's undernourished and proliferating billions. And even if, at some future date, emigration to Mars should become feasible, even if any considerable number of men and women were desperate enough to choose a new life under conditions comparable to those prevailing on a mountain twice as high as Mount Everest, what difference would that make? In the course of the last four centuries quite a number of people sailed from the Old World to the New. But neither their departure nor the returning flow of food and raw materials could solve the problems of the Old World. Similarly the shipping of a few surplus humans to Mars (at a cost, for transportation and development, of several million dollars a head) will do nothing to solve the problem of mounting population pressures on our own planet. Unsolved, that problem will render insoluble all our other problems. Worse still, it will create conditions in which individual freedom and the social decencies of the democratic way of life will become impossible, almost unthinkable. Not all dictatorships arise in the same way. There are many roads to Brave New World; but perhaps the straightest and the broadest of them is the road we are traveling today, the road that leads through gigantic numbers and accelerating increases. Let us briefly review the reasons for this close correlation between too many people, too rapidly multiplying, and the formulation of authoritarian philosophies, the rise of totalitarian systems of government.

As large and increasing numbers press more heavily upon available resources, the economic position of the society undergoing this ordeal becomes ever more precarious. This is especially true of those underdeveloped regions, where a sudden lowering of the death rate by means of DDT, penicillin and clean water has not been accompanied by a corresponding fall in the birth rate. In parts of Asia and in most of Central and South America populations are increasing so fast that they will double themselves in little more than twenty years. If the production of food and manufactured articles, of houses, schools and teachers, could be increased at a greater rate than human numbers, it would be possible to improve the wretched lot of those who live in these underdeveloped and over-populated countries. But unfortunately these countries lack not merely agricultural machinery and an industrial plant capable of turning out this machinery, but also the capital required to create such a plant. Capital is what is left over after the primary needs of a population have been satisfied. But the primary needs of most of the people in underdeveloped countries are never fully satisfied. At the end of each year almost nothing is left over, and there is therefore almost no capital available for creating the industrial and agricultural plant, by means of which the people's needs might be satisfied. Moreover, there is, in all these underdeveloped countries, a serious shortage of the trained manpower without which a modern industrial and agricultural plant cannot be operated. The present educational facilities are inadequate; so are the resources, financial and cultural, for improving the existing facilities as fast as the situation demands. Meanwhile the population of some of these underdeveloped countries is increasing at the rate of 3 per cent per annum.

Their tragic situation is discussed in an important book, published in 1957—*The Next Hundred Years*, by Professors Harrison Brown, James Bonner and John Weir of the California Institute of Technology. How is mankind coping with the problem of rapidly increasing numbers? Not very successfully. "The evidence suggests rather strongly that in most underdeveloped countries the lot of the average individual has worsened appreciably in the last half century. People have become more poorly fed. There are fewer available goods per person. And practically every attempt to improve the situation has been nullified by the relentless pressure of continued population growth."

Whenever the economic life of a nation becomes precarious, the central government is forced to assume additional responsibilities for the general welfare. It must work out elaborate plans for dealing with a critical situation; it must impose ever greater restrictions upon the activities of its subjects; and if, as is very likely, worsening economic conditions result in political unrest, or open rebellion, the central government must intervene to preserve public order and its own authority. More and more power is thus concentrated in the hands of the executives and their bureaucratic managers. But the nature of power is such that even those who have not sought it, but have had it forced upon them, tend to acquire a taste for more. "Lead us not into temptation," we pray—and with good reason; for when human beings are tempted too enticingly or too long, they generally yield. A democratic constitution is a device for preventing the local rulers from yielding to those particularly dangerous temptations that arise when too much power is concentrated in too few hands. Such a constitution works pretty well where, as in Britain or the United States, there is a traditional respect for constitutional procedures. Where the republican or limited monarchical tradition is weak, the best of constitutions will not prevent ambitious politicians from succumbing with glee and gusto to the temptations of power. And in any country where numbers have begun to press heavily upon available resources, these temptations cannot fail to arise. Over-population leads to economic insecurity and social unrest. Unrest and insecurity lead to more control by central governments and an increase of their power. In the absence of a constitutional tradition, this increased power will probably be exercised in a dictatorial fashion. Even if Communism had never been invented, this would be likely to happen. But Communism has been invented. Given this fact, the probability of over-population leading through unrest to dictatorship becomes a virtual certainty. It is a pretty safe bet that, twenty years from now, all the world's over-populated and underdeveloped countries will be under some form of totalitarian rule—probably by the Communist party.

How will this development affect the over-populated, but highly industrialized and still democratic countries of Europe? If the newly formed dictatorships were hostile to them, and if the normal flow of raw materials from the underdeveloped countries were deliberately interrupted, the nations of the West would find themselves in a very bad way indeed. Their industrial system would break down, and the highly developed technology, which up till now has permitted them to sustain a population much greater than that which could be supported by locally available resources, would no longer protect them against the consequences of having too many people in too small a territory. If this should happen, the enormous powers forced by unfavorable conditions upon central governments may come to be used in the spirit of totalitarian dictatorship.

The United States is not at present an over-populated country. If, however, the population continues to increase at the present rate (which is higher than that of India's increase, though happily a good deal lower than the rate now current in Mexico or Guatemala), the problem of numbers in relation to available resources might well become troublesome by the beginning of the twenty-first century. For the moment over-population is not a direct threat to the personal freedom of Americans. It remains, however, an indirect threat, a menace at one remove. If over-population should drive the underdeveloped countries into totalitarianism, and if these new dictatorships should ally themselves with Russia, then the military position of the United States would become less secure and the preparations for defense and retaliation would have to be intensified. But liberty, as we all know, cannot flourish in a country that is permanently on a war footing, or even a near-war footing. Permanent crisis justifies permanent control of everybody and everything by the agencies of the central government. And permanent crisis is what we have to expect in a world in which over-population is producing a state of things, in which dictatorship under Communist auspices becomes almost inevitable.

II Quantity, Quality, Morality

In the Brave New World of my fantasy eugenics and dysgenics were practiced systematically. In one set of bottles biologically superior ova, fertilized by biologically superior sperm, were given the best possible prenatal treatment and were finally decanted as Betas, Alphas and even Alpha Pluses. In another, much more numerous set of bottles, biologically inferior ova, fertilized by biologically inferior sperm, were subjected to the Bokanovsky Process (ninety-six identical twins out of a single egg) and treated prenatally with alcohol and other protein poisons. The creatures finally decanted were almost subhuman; but they were capable of performing unskilled work and, when properly conditioned, detensioned by free and frequent access to the opposite sex, constantly distracted by gratuitous entertainment and reinforced in their good behavior patterns by daily doses of soma, could be counted on to give no trouble to their superiors.

In this second half of the twentieth century we do nothing systematic about our breeding; but in our random and unregulated way we are not only over-populating our planet, we are also, it would seem, making sure that these greater numbers shall be of biologically poorer quality. In the bad old days children with considerable, or even with slight, hereditary defects rarely survived. Today, thanks to sanitation, modern pharmacology and the social conscience, most of the children born with hereditary defects reach maturity and multiply their kind. Under the conditions now prevailing, every advance in medicine will tend to be offset by a corresponding advance in the survival rate of individuals cursed by some genetic insufficiency. In spite of new wonder drugs and better treatment (indeed, in a certain sense, precisely because of these things), the physical health of the general population will show no improvement, and may even deteriorate. And along with a decline of average healthiness there may well go a decline in average intelligence. Indeed, some competent authorities are convinced that such a decline has already taken place and is continuing. "Under conditions that are both soft and unregulated," writes Dr. W. H. Sheldon, "our best stock tends to be outbred by stock that is inferior to it in every respect.... It is the fashion in some academic circles to assure students that the alarm over differential birth-rates is unfounded; that these problems are merely economic, or merely educational, or merely religious, or merely cultural or something of the sort. This is Pollyanna optimism. Reproductive delinquency is biological and basic." And he adds that "nobody knows just how far the average IQ in this country [the U.S.A.] has declined since 1916, when Terman attempted to standardize the meaning of IQ 100."

In an underdeveloped and over-populated country, where four-fifths of the people get less than two thousand calories a day and one-fifth enjoys an adequate diet, can democratic institutions arise spontaneously? Or if they should be imposed from outside or from above, can they possibly survive?

And now let us consider the case of the rich, industrialized and democratic society, in which, owing to the random but effective practice of dysgenics, IQ's and physical vigor are on the decline. For how long can such a society maintain its traditions of individual liberty and democratic government? Fifty or a hundred years from now our children will learn the answer to this question.

Meanwhile we find ourselves confronted by a most disturbing moral problem. We know that the pursuit of good ends does not justify the employment of bad means. But what about those situations, now of such frequent occurrence, in which good means have end results which turn out to be bad?

For example, we go to a tropical island and with the aid of DDT we stamp out malaria and, in two or three years, save hundreds of thousands of lives. This is obviously good. But the hundreds of thousands of human beings thus saved, and the millions whom they beget and bring to birth, cannot be adequately clothed, housed, educated or even fed out of the island's available resources. Quick death by malaria has been abolished; but life made miserable by undernourishment and over-crowding is now the rule, and slow death by outright starvation threatens ever greater numbers.

And what about the congenitally insufficient organisms, whom our medicine and our social services now preserve so that they may propagate their kind? To help the unfortunate is obviously good. But the wholesale transmission to our descendants of the results of unfavorable mutations, and the progressive contamination of the genetic pool from which the members of our species will have to draw, are no less obviously bad. We are on the horns of an ethical dilemma, and to find the middle way will require all our intelligence and all our good will.

III Over-Organization

The shortest and broadest road to the nightmare of Brave New World leads, as I have pointed out, through over-population and the accelerating increase of human numbers—twenty-eight hundred millions today, fifty-five hundred millions by the turn of the century, with most of humanity facing the choice between anarchy and totalitarian control. But the increasing pressure of numbers upon available resources is not the only force propelling us in the direction of totalitarianism. This blind biological enemy of freedom is allied with immensely powerful forces generated by the very advances in technology of which we are most proud. Justifiably proud, it may be added; for these advances are the fruits of genius and persistent hard work, of logic, imagination and self-denial—in a word, of moral and intellectual virtues for which one can feel nothing but admiration. But the Nature of Things is such that nobody in this world ever gets anything for nothing. These amazing and admirable advances have had to be paid for. Indeed, like last year's washing machine, they are still being paid for—and each installment is higher than the last. Many historians, many sociologists and psychologists have written at length, and with a deep concern, about the price that Western man has had to pay and will go on paying for technological progress. They point out, for example, that democracy can hardly be expected to flourish in societies where political and economic power is being progressively concentrated and centralized. But the progress of technology has led and is still leading to just such a concentration and centralization of power. As the machinery of mass production is made more efficient it tends to become more complex and more expensive—and so less available to the enterpriser of limited means. Moreover, mass production cannot work without mass distribution; but mass distribution raises problems which only the largest producers can satisfactorily solve. In a world of mass production and mass distribution the Little Man, with his inadequate stock of working capital, is at a grave disadvantage. In competition with the Big Man, he loses his money and finally his very existence as an independent producer; the Big Man has gobbled him up. As the Little Men disappear, more and more economic power comes to be wielded by fewer and fewer people. Under a dictatorship the Big Business, made possible by advancing technology and the consequent ruin of Little Business, is controlled by the State—that is to say, by a small group of party leaders and the soldiers, policemen and civil servants who carry out their orders. In a capitalist democracy, such as the United States, it is controlled by what Professor C. Wright Mills has called the Power Elite. This Power Elite directly employs several millions of the country's working force in its factories, offices and stores, controls many millions more by lending them the money to buy its products, and, through its ownership of the media of mass communication, influences the thoughts, the feelings and the actions of virtually everybody. To parody the words of Winston Churchill, never have so many been manipulated so much by so few. We are far indeed from Jefferson's ideal of a genuinely free society composed of a hierarchy of self-governing units—"the elementary republics of the wards, the county republics, the State republics and the Republic of the Union, forming a gradation of authorities."

We see, then, that modern technology has led to the concentration of economic and political power, and to the development of a society controlled (ruthlessly in the totalitarian states, politely and inconspicuously in the democracies) by Big Business and Big Government. But societies are composed of individuals and are good only insofar as they help individuals to realize their potentialities and to lead a happy and creative life. How have individuals been affected by the technological advances of recent years? Here is the answer to this question given by a philosopher-psychiatrist, Dr. Erich Fromm:

Our contemporary Western society, in spite of its material, intellectual and political progress, is increasingly less conducive to mental health, and tends to undermine the inner security, happiness, reason and the capacity for love in the individual; it tends to turn him into an automaton who pays for his human failure with increasing mental sickness, and with despair hidden under a frantic drive for work and so-called pleasure.

Our "increasing mental sickness" may find expression in neurotic symptoms. These symptoms are conspicuous and extremely distressing. But "let us beware," says Dr. Fromm, "of defining mental hygiene as the prevention of symptoms. Symptoms as such are not our enemy, but our friend; where there are symptoms there is conflict, and conflict always indicates that the forces of life which strive for integration and happiness are still fighting." The really hopeless victims of mental illness are to be found among those who appear to be most normal. "Many of them are normal because they are so well adjusted to our mode of existence, because their human voice has been silenced so early in their lives, that they do not even struggle or suffer or develop symptoms as the neurotic does." They are normal not in what may be called the absolute sense of the word; they are normal only in relation to a profoundly abnormal society. Their perfect adjustment to that abnormal society is a measure of their mental sickness. These millions of abnormally normal people, living without fuss in a society to which, if they were fully human beings, they ought not to be adjusted, still cherish "the illusion of individuality," but in fact they have been to a great extent deindividualized. Their conformity is developing into something like uniformity. But "uniformity and freedom are incompatible. Uniformity and mental health are incompatible too.... Man is not made to be an automaton, and if he becomes one, the basis for mental health is destroyed."

In the course of evolution nature has gone to endless trouble to see that every individual is unlike every other individual. We reproduce our kind by bringing the father's genes into contact with the mother's. These hereditary factors may be combined in an almost infinite number of ways. Physically and mentally, each one of us is unique. Any culture which, in the interests of efficiency or in the name of some political or religious dogma, seeks to standardize the human individual, commits an outrage against man's biological nature.

Science may be defined as the reduction of multiplicity to unity. It seeks to explain the endlessly diverse phenomena of nature by ignoring the uniqueness of particular events, concentrating on what they have in common and finally abstracting some kind of "law," in terms of which they make sense and can be effectively dealt with. For examples, apples fall from the tree and the moon moves across the sky. People had been observing these facts from time immemorial. With Gertrude Stein they were convinced that an apple is an apple is an apple, whereas the moon is the moon is the moon. It remained for Isaac Newton to perceive what these very dissimilar phenomena had in common, and to formulate a theory of gravitation in terms of which certain aspects of the behavior of apples, of the heavenly bodies and indeed of everything else in the physical universe could be explained and dealt with in terms of a single system of ideas. In the same spirit the artist takes the innumerable diversities and uniquenesses of the outer world and his own imagination and gives them meaning within an orderly system of plastic, literary or musical patterns. The wish to impose order upon confusion, to bring harmony out of dissonance and unity out of multiplicity is a kind of intellectual instinct, a primary and fundamental urge of the mind. Within the realms of science, art and philosophy the workings of what I may call this "Will to Order" are mainly beneficent. True, the Will to Order has produced many premature syntheses based upon insufficient evidence, many absurd systems of metaphysics and theology, much pedantic mistaking of notions for realities, of symbols and abstractions for the data of immediate experience. But these errors, however regrettable, do not do much harm, at any rate directly—though it sometimes happens that a bad philosophical system may do harm indirectly, by being used as a justification for senseless and inhuman actions. It is in the social sphere, in the realm of politics and economics, that the Will to Order becomes really dangerous.

Here the theoretical reduction of unmanageable multiplicity to comprehensible unity becomes the practical reduction of human diversity to subhuman uniformity, of freedom to servitude. In politics the equivalent of a fully developed scientific theory or philosophical system is a totalitarian dictatorship. In economics, the equivalent of a beautifully composed work of art is the smoothly running factory in which the workers are perfectly adjusted to the machines. The Will to Order can make tyrants out of those who merely aspire to clear up a mess. The beauty of tidiness is used as a justification for despotism.

Organization is indispensable; for liberty arises and has meaning only within a self-regulating community of freely co-operating individuals. But, though indispensable, organization can also be fatal. Too much organization transforms men and women into automata, suffocates the creative spirit and abolishes the very possibility of freedom. As usual, the only safe course is in the middle, between the extremes of *laissez-faire* at one end of the scale and of total control at the other.

During the past century the successive advances in technology have been accompanied by corresponding advances in organization. Complicated machinery has had to be matched by complicated social arrangements, designed to work as smoothly and efficiently as the new instruments of production. In order to fit into these organizations, individuals have had to deindividualize themselves, have had to deny their native diversity and conform to a standard pattern, have had to do their best to become automata.

The dehumanizing effects of over-organization are reinforced by the dehumanizing effects of over-population. Industry, as it expands, draws an ever greater proportion of humanity's increasing numbers into large cities. But life in large cities is not conducive to mental health (the highest incidence of schizophrenia, we are told, occurs among the swarming inhabitants of industrial slums); nor does it foster the kind of responsible freedom within small self-governing groups, which is the first condition of a genuine democracy. City life is anonymous and, as it were, abstract. People are related to one another, not as total personalities, but as the embodiments of economic functions or, when they are not at work, as irresponsible seekers of entertainment. Subjected to this kind of life, individuals tend to feel lonely and insignificant. Their existence ceases to have any point or meaning.

Biologically speaking, man is a moderately gregarious, not a completely social animal—a creature more like a wolf, let us say, or an elephant, than like a bee or an ant. In their original form human societies bore no resemblance to the hive or the ant heap; they were merely packs. Civilization is, among other things, the process by which primitive packs are transformed into an analogue, crude and mechanical, of the social insects' organic communities. At the present time the pressures of over-population and technological change are accelerating this process. The termitary has come to seem a realizable and even, in some eyes, a desirable ideal. Needless to say, the ideal will never in fact be realized. A great gulf separates the social insect from the not too gregarious, big-brained mammal; and even though the mammal should do his best to imitate the insect, the gulf would remain. However hard they try, men cannot create a social organism, they can only create an organization. In the process of trying to create an organism they will merely create a totalitarian despotism.

Brave New World presents a fanciful and somewhat ribald picture of a society, in which the attempt to re-create human beings in the likeness of termites has been pushed almost to the limits of the possible. That we are being propelled in the direction of Brave New World is obvious. But no less obvious is the fact that we can, if we so desire, refuse to co-operate with the blind forces that are propelling us. For the moment, however, the wish to resist does not seem to be very strong or very widespread. As Mr. William Whyte has shown in his remarkable book, *The Organization Man*, a new Social Ethic is replacing our traditional ethical system—the system in which the individual is primary. The key words in this Social Ethic are "adjustment," "adaptation," "socially orientated behavior," "belongingness," "acquisition of social skills," "team work," "group living," "group loyalty," "group dynamics," "group thinking," "group creativity." Its basic assumption is that the social whole has greater worth and significance than its individual parts, that inborn biological differences should be sacrificed to cultural uniformity, that the rights of the collectivity take precedence over what the eighteenth century called the Rights of Man. According to the Social Ethic, Jesus was completely wrong in asserting that the Sabbath was made for man. On the contrary, man was made for the Sabbath, and must sacrifice his inherited idiosyncrasies and pretend to be the kind of standardized good mixer that organizers of group activity regard as ideal for their purposes. This ideal man is the man who displays "dynamic conformity" (delicious phrase!) and an intense loyalty to the group, an unflagging desire to subordinate himself, to belong. And the ideal man must have an ideal wife, highly gregarious, infinitely adaptable and not merely resigned to the fact that her husband's first loyalty is to the Corporation, but actively loyal on her own account. "He for God only," as Milton said of Adam and Eve, "she for God in him." And in one important respect the wife of the ideal organization man is a good deal worse off than our First Mother. She and Adam were permitted by the Lord to be completely uninhibited in the matter of "youthful dalliance."

> *Nor turned, I ween,*
> *Adam from his fair spouse, nor Eve the rites*
> *Mysterious of connubial love refused*

Today, according to a writer in the *Harvard Business Review*, the wife of the man who is trying to live up to the ideal proposed by the Social Ethic, "must not demand too much of her husband's time and interest. Because of his single-minded concentration on his job, even his sexual activity must be relegated to a secondary place." The monk makes vows of poverty, obedience and chastity. The organization man is allowed to be rich, but promises obedience ("he accepts authority without resentment, he looks up to his superiors"—*Mussolini ha sempre ragione*) and he must be prepared, for the greater glory of the organization that employs him, to forswear even conjugal love.

It is worth remarking that, in *1984*, the members of the Party are compelled to conform to a sexual ethic of more than Puritan severity. In *Brave New World*, on the other hand, all are permitted to indulge their sexual impulses without let or hindrance. The society described in Orwell's fable is a society permanently at war, and the aim of its rulers is first, of course, to exercise power for its own delightful sake and, second, to keep their subjects in that state of constant tension which a state of constant war demands of those who wage it. By crusading against sexuality the bosses are able to maintain the required tension in their followers and at the same time can satisfy their lust for power in a most gratifying way. The society described in *Brave New World* is a world-state, in which war has been eliminated and where the first aim of the rulers is at all costs to keep their subjects from making trouble. This they achieve by (among other methods) legalizing a degree of sexual freedom (made possible by the abolition of the family) that practically guarantees the Brave New Worlders against any form of destructive (or creative) emotional tension. In *1984* the lust for power is satisfied by inflicting pain; in *Brave New World*, by inflicting a hardly less humiliating pleasure.

The current Social Ethic, it is obvious, is merely a justification after the fact of the less desirable consequences of over-organization. It represents a pathetic attempt to make a virtue of necessity, to extract a positive value from an unpleasant datum. It is a very unrealistic, and therefore very dangerous, system of morality. The social whole, whose value is assumed to be greater than that of its component parts, is not an organism in the sense that a hive or a termitary may be thought of as an organism. It is merely an organization, a piece of social machinery. There can be no value except in relation to life and awareness. An organization is neither conscious nor alive. Its value is instrumental and derivative. It is not good in itself; it is good only to the extent that it promotes the good of the individuals who are the parts of the collective whole. To give organizations precedence over persons is to subordinate ends to means. What happens when ends are subordinated to means was clearly demonstrated by Hitler and Stalin. Under their hideous rule personal ends were subordinated to organizational means by a mixture of violence and propaganda, systematic terror and the systematic manipulation of minds. In the more efficient dictatorships of tomorrow there will probably be much less violence than under Hitler and Stalin. The future dictator's subjects will be painlessly regimented by a corps of highly trained social engineers. "The challenge of social engineering in our time," writes an enthusiastic advocate of this new science, "is like the challenge of technical engineering fifty years ago. If the first half of the twentieth century was the era of the technical engineers, the second half may well be the era of the social engineers"—and the twenty-first century, I suppose, will be the era of World Controllers, the scientific caste system and Brave New World. To the question *quis cusodiet custodes?*— Who will mount guard over our guardians, who will engineer the engineers?—the answer is a bland denial that they need any supervision. There seems to be a touching belief among certain Ph.D.'s in sociology that Ph.D.'s in sociology will never be corrupted by power. Like Sir Galahad's, their strength is as the strength of ten because their heart is pure—and their heart is pure because they are scientists and have taken six thousand hours of social studies.

Alas, higher education is not necessarily a guarantee of higher virtue, or higher political wisdom. And to these misgivings on ethical and psychological grounds must be added misgivings of a purely scientific character. Can we accept the theories on which the social engineers base their practice, and in terms of which they justify their manipulations of human beings? For example, Professor Elton Mayo tells us categorically that "man's desire to be continuously associated in work with his fellows is a strong, if not the strongest human characteristic." This, I would say, is manifestly untrue. Some people have the kind of desire described by Mayo; others do not. It is a matter of temperament and inherited constitution. Any social organization based upon the assumption that "man" (whoever "man" may be) desires to be continuously associated with his fellows would be, for many individual men and women, a bed of Procrustes. Only by being amputated or stretched upon the rack could they be adjusted to it.

Again, how romantically misleading are the lyrical accounts of the Middle Ages with which many contemporary theorists of social relations adorn their works! "Membership in a guild, manorial estate or village protected medieval man throughout his life and gave him peace and serenity." Protected him from what, we may ask. Certainly not from remorseless bullying at the hands of his superiors. And along with all that "peace and serenity" there was, throughout the Middle Ages, an enormous amount of chronic frustration, acute unhappiness and a passionate resentment against the rigid, hierarchical system that permitted no vertical movement up the social ladder and, for those who were bound to the land, very little horizontal movement in space. The impersonal forces of over-population and over-organization, and the social engineers who are trying to direct these forces, are pushing us in the direction of a new medieval system. This revival will be made more acceptable than the original by such Brave-New-Worldian amenities as infant conditioning, sleep-teaching and drug-induced euphoria; but, for the majority of men and women, it will still be a kind of servitude.

IV Propaganda in a Democratic Society

"The doctrines of Europe," Jefferson wrote, "were that men in numerous associations cannot be restrained within the limits of order and justice, except by forces physical and moral wielded over them by authorities independent of their will.... We (the founders of the new American democracy) believe that man was a rational animal, endowed by nature with rights, and with an innate sense of justice, and that he could be restrained from wrong, and protected in right, by moderate powers, confided to persons of his own choice and held to their duties by dependence on his own will." To post-Freudian ears, this kind of language seems touchingly quaint and ingenuous. Human beings are a good deal less rational and innately just than the optimists of the eighteenth century supposed. On the other hand they are neither so morally blind nor so hopelessly unreasonable as the pessimists of the twentieth would have us believe. In spite of the Id and the Unconscious, in spite of endemic neurosis and the prevalence of low IQ's, most men and women are probably decent enough and sensible enough to be trusted with the direction of their own destinies.

Democratic institutions are devices for reconciling social order with individual freedom and initiative, and for making the immediate power of a country's rulers subject to the ultimate power of the ruled. The fact that, in western Europe and America, these devices have worked, all things considered, not too badly is proof enough that the eighteenth-century optimists were not entirely wrong. Given a fair chance, human beings can govern themselves, and govern themselves better, though perhaps with less mechanical efficiency, than they can be governed by "authorities independent of their will." Given a fair chance, I repeat; for the fair chance is an indispensable prerequisite. No people that passes abruptly from a state of subservience under the rule of a despot to the completely unfamiliar state of political independence can be said to have a fair chance of making democratic institutions work. Again, no people in a precarious economic condition has a fair chance of being able to govern itself democratically. Liberalism flourishes in an atmosphere of prosperity and declines as declining prosperity makes it necessary for the government to intervene ever more frequently and drastically in the affairs of its subjects. Over-population and over-organization are two conditions which, as I have already pointed out, deprive a society of a fair chance of making democratic institutions work effectively. We see, then, that there are certain historical, economic, demographic and technological conditions which make it very hard for Jefferson's rational animals, endowed by nature with inalienable rights and an innate sense of justice, to exercise their reason, claim their rights and act justly within a democratically organized society. We in the West have been supremely fortunate in having been given our fair chance of making the great experiment in self-government. Unfortunately it now looks as though, owing to recent changes in our circumstances, this infinitely precious fair chance were being, little by little, taken away from us. And this, of course, is not the whole story. These blind impersonal forces are not the only enemies of individual liberty and democratic institutions. There are also forces of another, less abstract character, forces that can be deliberately used by power-seeking individuals whose aim is to establish partial or complete control over their fellows. Fifty years ago, when I was a boy, it seemed completely self-evident that the bad old days were over, that torture and massacre, slavery, and the persecution of heretics, were things of the past. Among people who wore top hats, traveled in trains, and took a bath every morning such horrors were simply out of the question. After all, we were living in the twentieth century. A few years later these people who took daily baths and went to church in top hats were committing atrocities on a scale undreamed of by the benighted Africans and Asiatics. In the light of recent history it would be foolish to suppose that this sort of thing cannot happen again. It can and, no doubt, it will. But in the immediate future there is some reason to believe that the punitive methods of *1984* will give place to the reinforcements and manipulations of *Brave New World*.

There are two kinds of propaganda—rational propaganda in favor of action that is consonant with the enlightened self-interest of those who make it and those to whom it is addressed, and non-rational propaganda that is not consonant with anybody's enlightened self-interest, but is dictated by, and appeals to, passion. Where the actions of individuals are concerned there are motives more exalted than enlightened self-interest, but where collective action has to be taken in the fields of politics and economics, enlightened self-interest is probably the highest of effective motives. If politicians and their constituents always acted to promote their own or their country's long-range self-interest, this world would be an earthly paradise. As it is, they often act against their own interests, merely to gratify their least creditable passions; the world, in consequence, is a place of misery. Propaganda in favor of action that is consonant with enlightened self-interest appeals to reason by means of logical arguments based upon the best available evidence fully and honestly set forth. Propaganda in favor of action dictated by the impulses that are below self-interest offers false, garbled or incomplete evidence, avoids logical argument and seeks to influence its victims by the mere repetition of catchwords, by the furious denunciation of foreign or domestic scapegoats, and by cunningly associating the lowest passions with the highest ideals, so that atrocities come to be perpetrated in the name of God and the most cynical kind of *Realpolitik* is treated as a matter of religious principle and patriotic duty.

In John Dewey's words, "a renewal of faith in common human nature, in its potentialities in general, and in its power in particular to respond to reason and truth, is a surer bulwark against totalitarianism than a demonstration of material success or a devout worship of special legal and political forms." The power to respond to reason and truth exists in all of us. But so, unfortunately, does the tendency to respond to unreason and falsehood—particularly in those cases where the falsehood evokes some enjoyable emotion, or where the appeal to unreason strikes some answering chord in the primitive, subhuman depths of our being. In certain fields of activity men have learned to respond to reason and truth pretty consistently. The authors of learned articles do not appeal to the passions of their fellow scientists and technologists. They set forth what, to the best of their knowledge, is the truth about some particular aspect of reality, they use reason to explain the facts they have observed and they support their point of view with arguments that appeal to reason in other people. All this is fairly easy in the fields of physical science and technology. It is much more difficult in the fields of politics and religion and ethics. Here the relevant facts often elude us. As for the meaning of the facts, that of course depends upon the particular system of ideas, in terms of which you choose to interpret them. And these are not the only difficulties that confront the rational truth-seeker. In public and in private life, it often happens that there is simply no time to collect the relevant facts or to weigh their significance. We are forced to act on insufficient evidence and by a light considerably less steady than that of logic. With the best will in the world, we cannot always be completely truthful or consistently rational. All that is in our power is to be as truthful and rational as circumstances permit us to be, and to respond as well as we can to the limited truth and imperfect reasonings offered for our consideration by others.

"If a nation expects to be ignorant and free," said Jefferson, "it expects what never was and never will be.... The people cannot be safe without information. Where the press is free, and every man able to read, all is safe." Across the Atlantic another passionate believer in reason was thinking about the same time, in almost precisely similar terms. Here is what John Stuart Mill wrote of his father, the utilitarian philosopher, James Mill: "So complete was his reliance upon the influence of reason over the minds of mankind, whenever it is allowed to reach them, that he felt as if all would be gained, if the whole population were able to read, and if all sorts of opinions were allowed to be addressed to them by word or in writing, and if by the suffrage they could nominate a legislature to give effect to the opinions they had adopted." *All is safe, all would be gained!* Once more we hear the note of eighteenth-century optimism. Jefferson, it is true, was a realist as well as an optimist. He knew by bitter experience that the freedom of the press can be shamefully abused. "Nothing," he declared, "can now be believed which is seen in a newspaper." And yet, he insisted (and we can only agree with him), "within the pale of truth, the press is a noble institution, equally the friend of science and civil liberty." Mass communication, in a word, is neither good nor bad; it is simply a force and, like any other force, it can be used either well or ill. Used in one way, the press, the radio and the cinema are indispensable to the survival of democracy. Used in another way, they are among the most powerful weapons in the dictator's armory. In the field of mass communications as in almost every other field of enterprise, technological progress has hurt the Little Man and helped the Big Man. As lately as fifty years ago, every democratic country could boast of a great number of small journals and local newspapers. Thousands of country editors expressed thousands of independent opinions. Somewhere or other almost anybody could get almost anything printed. Today the press is still legally free; but most of the little papers have disappeared. The cost of woodpulp, of modern printing machinery and of syndicated news is too high for the Little Man. In the totalitarian East there is political censorship, and the media of mass communication are controlled by the State. In the democratic West there is economic censorship and the media of mass communication are controlled by members of the Power Elite. Censorship by rising costs and the concentration of communication power in the hands of a few big concerns is less objectionable than State ownership and government propaganda; but certainly it is not something of which a Jeffersonian democrat could possibly approve.

In regard to propaganda the early advocates of universal literacy and a free press envisaged only two possibilities: the propaganda might be true, or it might be false. They did not foresee what in fact has happened, above all in our Western capitalist democracies—the development of a vast mass communications industry, concerned in the main neither with the true nor the false, but with the unreal, the more or less totally irrelevant. In a word, they failed to take into account man's almost infinite appetite for distractions.

In the past most people never got a chance of fully satisfying this appetite. They might long for distractions, but the distractions were not provided. Christmas came but once a year, feasts were "solemn and rare," there were few readers and very little to read, and the nearest approach to a neighborhood movie theater was the parish church, where the performances, though frequent, were somewhat monotonous. For conditions even remotely comparable to those now prevailing we must return to imperial Rome, where the populace was kept in good humor by frequent, gratuitous doses of many kinds of entertainment—from poetical dramas to gladiatorial fights, from recitations of Virgil to all-out boxing, from concerts to military reviews and public executions. But even in Rome there was nothing like the non-stop distraction now provided by newspapers and magazines, by radio, television and the cinema. In *Brave New World* non-stop distractions of the most fascinating nature (the feelies, orgy-porgy, centrifugal bumblepuppy) are deliberately used as instruments of policy, for the purpose of preventing people from paying too much attention to the realities of the social and political situation. The other world of religion is different from the other world of entertainment; but they resemble one another in being most decidedly "not of this world." Both are distractions and, if lived in too continuously, both can become, in Marx's phrase, "the opium of the people" and so a threat to freedom. Only the vigilant can maintain their liberties, and only those who are constantly and intelligently on the spot can hope to govern themselves effectively by democratic procedures. A society, most of whose members spend a great part of their time, not on the spot, not here and now and in the calculable future, but somewhere else, in the irrelevant other worlds of sport and soap opera, of mythology and metaphysical fantasy, will find it hard to resist the encroachments of those who would manipulate and control it.

In their propaganda today's dictators rely for the most part on repetition, suppression and rationalization—the repetition of catchwords which they wish to be accepted as true, the suppression of facts which they wish to be ignored, the arousal and rationalization of passions which may be used in the interests of the Party or the State. As the art and science of manipulation come to be better understood, the dictators of the future will doubtless learn to combine these techniques with the non-stop distractions which, in the West, are now threatening to drown in a sea of irrelevance the rational propaganda essential to the maintenance of individual liberty and the survival of democratic institutions.

V Propaganda Under a Dictatorship

At his trial after the Second World War, Hitler's Minister for Armaments, Albert Speer, delivered a long speech in which, with remarkable acuteness, he described the Nazi tyranny and analyzed its methods. "Hitler's dictatorship," he said, "differed in one fundamental point from all its predecessors in history. It was the first dictatorship in the present period of modern technical development, a dictatorship which made complete use of all technical means for the domination of its own country. Through technical devices like the radio and the loud-speaker, eighty million people were deprived of independent thought. It was thereby possible to subject them to the will of one man.... Earlier dictators needed highly qualified assistants even at the lowest level—men who could think and act independently. The totalitarian system in the period of modern technical development can dispense with such men; thanks to modern methods of communication, it is possible to mechanize the lower leadership. As a result of this there has arisen the new type of the uncritical recipient of orders."

In the Brave New World of my prophetic fable technology had advanced far beyond the point it had reached in Hitler's day; consequently the recipients of orders were far less critical than their Nazi counterparts, far more obedient to the order-giving elite. Moreover, they had been genetically standardized and postnatally conditioned to perform their subordinate functions, and could therefore be depended upon to behave almost as predictably as machines. As we shall see in a later chapter, this conditioning of "the lower leadership" is already going on under the Communist dictatorships. The Chinese and the Russians are not relying merely on the indirect effects of advancing technology; they are working directly on the psychophysical organisms of their lower leaders, subjecting minds and bodies to a system of ruthless and, from all accounts, highly effective conditioning. "Many a man," said Speer, "has been haunted by the nightmare that one day nations might be dominated by technical means. That nightmare was almost realized in Hitler's totalitarian system." Almost, but not quite. The Nazis did not have time— and perhaps did not have the intelligence and the necessary knowledge—to brainwash and condition their lower leadership. This, it may be, is one of the reasons why they failed.

Since Hitler's day the armory of technical devices at the disposal of the would-be dictator has been considerably enlarged. As well as the radio, the loudspeaker, the moving picture camera and the rotary press, the contemporary propagandist can make use of television to broadcast the image as well as the voice of his client, and can record both image and voice on spools of magnetic tape. Thanks to technological progress, Big Brother can now be almost as omnipresent as God. Nor is it only on the technical front that the hand of the would-be dictator has been strengthened. Since Hitler's day a great deal of work has been carried out in those fields of applied psychology and neurology which are the special province of the propagandist, the indoctrinator and the brainwasher. In the past these specialists in the art of changing people's minds were empiricists. By a method of trial and error they had worked out a number of techniques and procedures, which they used very effectively without, however, knowing precisely why they were effective. Today the art of mind-control is in process of becoming a science. The practitioners of this science know what they are doing and why. They are guided in their work by theories and hypotheses solidly established on a massive foundation of experimental evidence. Thanks to the new insights and the new techniques made possible by these insights, the nightmare that was "all but realized in Hitler's totalitarian system" may soon be completely realizable.

But before we discuss these new insights and techniques let us take a look at the nightmare that so nearly came true in Nazi Germany. What were the methods used by Hitler and Goebbels for "depriving eighty million people of independent thought and subjecting them to the will of one man"? And what was the theory of human nature upon which those terrifyingly successful methods were based? These questions can be answered, for the most part, in Hitler's own words. And what remarkably clear and astute words they are! When he writes about such vast abstractions as Race and History and Providence, Hitler is strictly unreadable. But when he writes about the German masses and the methods he used for dominating and directing them, his style changes. Nonsense gives place to sense, bombast to a hard-boiled and cynical lucidity. In his philosophical lucubrations Hitler was either cloudily daydreaming or reproducing other people's half-baked notions. In his comments on crowds and propaganda he was writing of things he knew by firsthand experience. In the words of his ablest biographer, Mr. Alan Bullock, "Hitler was the greatest demagogue in history." Those who add, "only a demagogue," fail to appreciate the nature of political power in an age of mass politics. As he himself said, "To be a leader means to be able to move the masses." Hitler's aim was first to move the masses and then, having pried them loose from their traditional loyalties and moralities, to impose upon them (with the hypnotized consent of the majority) a new authoritarian order of his own devising. "Hitler," wrote Hermann Rauschning in 1939, "has a deep respect for the Catholic church and the Jesuit order; not because of their Christian doctrine, but because of the 'machinery' they have elaborated and controlled, their hierarchical system, their extremely clever tactics, their knowledge of human nature and their wise use of human weaknesses in ruling over believers." Ecclesiasticism without Christianity, the discipline of a monastic rule, not for God's sake or in order to achieve personal salvation, but for the sake of the State and for the greater glory and power of the demagogue turned Leader—this was the goal toward which the systematic moving of the masses was to lead.

Let us see what Hitler thought of the masses he moved and how he did the moving. The first principle from which he started was a value judgment: the masses are utterly contemptible. They are incapable of abstract thinking and uninterested in any fact outside the circle of their immediate experience. Their behavior is determined, not by knowledge and reason, but by feelings and unconscious drives. It is in these drives and feelings that "the roots of their positive as well as their negative attitudes are implanted." To be successful a propagandist must learn how to manipulate these instincts and emotions. "The driving force which has brought about the most tremendous revolutions on this earth has never been a body of scientific teaching which has gained power over the masses, but always a devotion which has inspired them, and often a kind of hysteria which has urged them into action. Whoever wishes to win over the masses must know the key that will open the door of their hearts." ... In post-Freudian jargon, of their unconscious.

Hitler made his strongest appeal to those members of the lower middle classes who had been ruined by the inflation of 1923, and then ruined all over again by the depression of 1929 and the following years. "The masses" of whom he speaks were these bewildered, frustrated and chronically anxious millions. To make them more masslike, more homogeneously subhuman, he assembled them, by the thousands and the tens of thousands, in vast halls and arenas, where individuals could lose their personal identity, even their elementary humanity, and be merged with the crowd. A man or woman makes direct contact with society in two ways: as a member of some familial, professional or religious group, or as a member of a crowd. Groups are capable of being as moral and intelligent as the individuals who form them; a crowd is chaotic, has no purpose of its own and is capable of anything except intelligent action and realistic thinking. Assembled in a crowd, people lose their powers of reasoning and their capacity for moral choice. Their suggestibility is increased to the point where they cease to have any judgment or will of their own. They become very excitable, they lose all sense of individual or collective responsibility, they are subject to sudden accesses of rage, enthusiasm and panic. In a word, a man in a crowd behaves as though he had swallowed a large dose of some powerful intoxicant. He is a victim of what I have called "herd-poisoning." Like alcohol, herd-poison is an active, extraverted drug. The crowd-intoxicated individual escapes from responsibility, intelligence and morality into a kind of frantic, animal mindlessness.

During his long career as an agitator, Hitler had studied the effects of herd-poison and had learned how to exploit them for his own purposes. He had discovered that the orator can appeal to those "hidden forces" which motivate men's actions, much more effectively than can the writer. Reading is a private, not a collective activity. The writer speaks only to individuals, sitting by themselves in a state of normal sobriety. The orator speaks to masses of individuals, already well primed with herd-poison. They are at his mercy and, if he knows his business, he can do what he likes with them. As an orator, Hitler knew his business supremely well. He was able, in his own words, "to follow the lead of the great mass in such a way that from the living emotion of his hearers the apt word which he needed would be suggested to him and in its turn this would go straight to the heart of his hearers." Otto Strasser called him "a loud-speaker, proclaiming the most secret desires, the least admissible instincts, the sufferings and personal revolts of a whole nation." Twenty years before Madison Avenue embarked upon "Motivational Research," Hitler was systematically exploring and exploiting the secret fears and hopes, the cravings, anxieties and frustrations of the German masses. It is by manipulating "hidden forces" that the advertising experts induce us to buy their wares—a tooth-paste, a brand of cigarettes, a political candidate. And it is by appealing to the same hidden forces—and to others too dangerous for Madison Avenue to meddle with—that Hitler induced the German masses to buy themselves a Fuehrer, an insane philosophy and the Second World War.

Unlike the masses, intellectuals have a taste for rationality and an interest in facts. Their critical habit of mind makes them resistant to the kind of propaganda that works so well on the majority. Among the masses "instinct is supreme, and from instinct comes faith.... While the healthy common folk instinctively close their ranks to form a community of the people" (under a Leader, it goes without saying) "intellectuals run this way and that, like hens in a poultry yard. With them one cannot make history; they cannot be used as elements composing a community." Intellectuals are the kind of people who demand evidence and are shocked by logical inconsistencies and fallacies. They regard over-simplification as the original sin of the mind and have no use for the slogans, the unqualified assertions and sweeping generalizations which are the propagandist's stock in trade. "All effective propaganda," Hitler wrote, "must be confined to a few bare necessities and then must be expressed in a few stereotyped formulas." These stereotyped formulas must be constantly repeated, for "only constant repetition will finally succeed in imprinting an idea upon the memory of a crowd." Philosophy teaches us to feel uncertain about the things that seem to us self-evident. Propaganda, on the other hand, teaches us to accept as self-evident matters about which it would be reasonable to suspend our judgment or to feel doubt. The aim of the demagogue is to create social coherence under his own leadership. But, as Bertrand Russell has pointed out, "systems of dogma without empirical foundations, such as scholasticism, Marxism and fascism, have the advantage of producing a great deal of social coherence among their disciples." The demagogic propagandist must therefore be consistently dogmatic. All his statements are made without qualification. There are no grays in his picture of the world; everything is either diabolically black or celestially white. In Hitler's words, the propagandist should adopt "a systematically one-sided attitude towards every problem that has to be dealt with." He must never admit that he might be wrong or that people with a different point of view might be even partially right. Opponents should not be argued with; they should be attacked, shouted down, or, if they become too much of a nuisance, liquidated. The morally squeamish intellectual may be shocked by this kind of thing. But the masses are always convinced that "right is on the side of the active aggressor."

Such, then, was Hitler's opinion of humanity in the mass. It was a very low opinion. Was it also an incorrect opinion? The tree is known by its fruits, and a theory of human nature which inspired the kind of techniques that proved so horribly effective must contain at least an element of truth. Virtue and intelligence belong to human beings as individuals freely associating with other individuals in small groups. So do sin and stupidity. But the subhuman mindlessness to which the demagogue makes his appeal, the moral imbecility on which he relies when he goads his victims into action, are characteristic not of men and women as individuals, but of men and women in masses. Mindlessness and moral idiocy are not characteristically human attributes; they are symptoms of herd-poisoning. In all the world's higher religions, salvation and enlightenment are for individuals. The kingdom of heaven is within the mind of a person, not within the collective mindlessness of a crowd. Christ promised to be present where two or three are gathered together. He did not say anything about being present where thousands are intoxicating one another with herd-poison. Under the Nazis enormous numbers of people were compelled to spend an enormous amount of time marching in serried ranks from point A to point B and back again to point A. "This keeping of the whole population on the march seemed to be a senseless waste of time and energy. Only much later," adds Hermann Rauschning, "was there revealed in it a subtle intention based on a well-judged adjustment of ends and means. Marching diverts men's thoughts. Marching kills thought. Marching makes an end of individuality. Marching is the indispensable magic stroke performed in order to accustom the people to a mechanical, quasi-ritualistic activity until it becomes second nature."

From his point of view and at the level where he had chosen to do his dreadful work, Hitler was perfectly correct in his estimate of human nature. To those of us who look at men and women as individuals rather than as members of crowds, or of regimented collectives, he seems hideously wrong. In an age of accelerating over-population, of accelerating over-organization and ever more efficient means of mass communication, how can we preserve the integrity and reassert the value of the human individual? This is a question that can still be asked and perhaps effectively answered. A generation from now it may be too late to find an answer and perhaps impossible, in the stifling collective climate of that future time, even to ask the question.

VI The Arts of Selling

The survival of democracy depends on the ability of large numbers of people to make realistic choices in the light of adequate information. A dictatorship, on the other hand, maintains itself by censoring or distorting the facts, and by appealing, not to reason, not to enlightened self-interest, but to passion and prejudice, to the powerful "hidden forces," as Hitler called them, present in the unconscious depths of every human mind.

In the West, democratic principles are proclaimed and many able and conscientious publicists do their best to supply electors with adequate information and to persuade them, by rational argument, to make realistic choices in the light of that information. All this is greatly to the good. But unfortunately propaganda in the Western democracies, above all in America, has two faces and a divided personality. In charge of the editorial department there is often a democratic Dr. Jekyll—a propagandist who would be very happy to prove that John Dewey had been right about the ability of human nature to respond to truth and reason. But this worthy man controls only a part of the machinery of mass communication. In charge of advertising we find an anti-democratic, because anti-rational, Mr. Hyde—or rather a Dr. Hyde, for Hyde is now a Ph.D. in psychology and has a master's degree as well in the social sciences. This Dr. Hyde would be very unhappy indeed if everybody always lived up to John Dewey's faith in human nature. Truth and reason are Jekyll's affair, not his. Hyde is a motivation analyst, and his business is to study human weaknesses and failings, to investigate those unconscious desires and fears by which so much of men's conscious thinking and overt doing is determined. And he does this, not in the spirit of the moralist who would like to make people better, or of the physician who would like to improve their health, but simply in order to find out the best way to take advantage of their ignorance and to exploit their irrationality for the pecuniary benefit of his employers. But after all, it may be argued, "capitalism is dead, consumerism is king"—and consumerism requires the services of expert salesmen versed in all the arts (including the more insidious arts) of persuasion. Under a free enterprise system commercial propaganda by any and every means is absolutely indispensable. But the indispensable is not necessarily the desirable. What is demonstrably good in the sphere of economics may be far from good for men and women as voters or even as human beings. An earlier, more moralistic generation would have been profoundly shocked by the bland cynicism of the motivation analysts. Today we read a book like Mr. Vance Packard's *The Hidden Persuaders*, and are more amused than horrified, more resigned than indignant. Given Freud, given Behaviorism, given the mass producer's chronically desperate need for mass consumption, this is the sort of thing that is only to be expected. But what, we may ask, is the sort of thing that is to be expected in the future? Are Hyde's activities compatible in the long run with Jekyll's? Can a campaign in favor of rationality be successful in the teeth of another and even more vigorous campaign in favor of irrationality? These are questions which, for the moment, I shall not attempt to answer, but shall leave hanging, so to speak, as a backdrop to our discussion of the methods of mass persuasion in a technologically advanced democratic society.

The task of the commercial propagandist in a democracy is in some ways easier and in some ways more difficult than that of a political propagandist employed by an established dictator or a dictator in the making. It is easier inasmuch as almost everyone starts out with a prejudice in favor of beer, cigarettes and iceboxes, whereas almost nobody starts out with a prejudice in favor of tyrants. It is more difficult inasmuch as the commercial propagandist is not permitted, by the rules of his particular game, to appeal to the more savage instincts of his public. The advertiser of dairy products would dearly love to tell his readers and listeners that all their troubles are caused by the machinations of a gang of godless international margarine manufacturers, and that it is their patriotic duty to march out and burn the oppressors' factories. This sort of thing, however, is ruled out, and he must be content with a milder approach. But the mild approach is less exciting than the approach through verbal or physical violence. In the long run, anger and hatred are self-defeating emotions. But in the short run they pay high dividends in the form of psychological and even (since they release large quantities of adrenalin and noradrenalin) physiological satisfaction. People may start out with an initial prejudice against tyrants; but when tyrants or would-be tyrants treat them to adrenalin-releasing propaganda about the wickedness of their enemies—particularly of enemies weak enough to be persecuted—they are ready to follow him with enthusiasm. In his speeches Hitler kept repeating such words as "hatred," "force," "ruthless," "crush," "smash"; and he would accompany these violent words with even more violent gestures. He would yell, he would scream, his veins would swell, his face would turn purple. Strong emotion (as every actor and dramatist knows) is in the highest degree contagious. Infected by the malignant frenzy of the orator, the audience would groan and sob and scream in an orgy of uninhibited passion. And these orgies were so enjoyable that most of those who had experienced them eagerly came back for more. Almost all of us long for peace and freedom; but very few of us have much enthusiasm for the thoughts, feelings and actions that make for peace and freedom. Conversely almost nobody wants war or tyranny; but a great many people find an intense pleasure in the thoughts, feelings and actions that make for war and tyranny. These thoughts, feelings and actions are too dangerous to be exploited for commercial purposes. Accepting this handicap, the advertising man must do the best he can with the less intoxicating emotions, the quieter forms of irrationality.

Effective rational propaganda becomes possible only when there is a clear understanding, on the part of all concerned, of the nature of symbols and of their relations to the things and events symbolized. Irrational propaganda depends for its effectiveness on a general failure to understand the nature of symbols. Simple-minded people tend to equate the symbol with what it stands for, to attribute to things and events some of the qualities expressed by the words in terms of which the propagandist has chosen, for his own purposes, to talk about them. Consider a simple example. Most cosmetics are made of lanolin, which is a mixture of purified wool fat and water beaten up into an emulsion. This emulsion has many valuable properties: it penetrates the skin, it does not become rancid, it is mildly antiseptic and so forth. But the commercial propagandists do not speak about the genuine virtues of the emulsion. They give it some picturesquely voluptuous name, talk ecstatically and misleadingly about feminine beauty and show pictures of gorgeous blondes nourishing their tissues with skin food. "The cosmetic manufacturers," one of their number has written, "are not selling lanolin, they are selling hope." For this hope, this fraudulent implication of a promise that they will be transfigured, women will pay ten or twenty times the value of the emulsion which the propagandists have so skilfully related, by means of misleading symbols, to a deep-seated and almost universal feminine wish—the wish to be more attractive to members of the opposite sex. The principles underlying this kind of propaganda are extremely simple. Find some common desire, some widespread unconscious fear or anxiety; think out some way to relate this wish or fear to the product you have to sell; then build a bridge of verbal or pictorial symbols over which your customer can pass from fact to compensatory dream, and from the dream to the illusion that your product, when purchased, will make the dream come true. "We no longer buy oranges, we buy vitality. We do not buy just an auto, we buy prestige." And so with all the rest. In toothpaste, for example, we buy, not a mere cleanser and antiseptic, but release from the fear of being sexually repulsive. In vodka and whisky we are not buying a protoplasmic poison which, in small doses, may depress the nervous system in a psychologically valuable way; we are buying friendliness and good fellowship, the warmth of Dingley Dell and the brilliance of the Mermaid Tavern. With our laxatives we buy the health of a Greek god, the radiance of one of Diana's nymphs. With the monthly best seller we acquire culture, the envy of our less literate neighbors and the respect of the sophisticated. In every case the motivation analyst has found some deep-seated wish or fear, whose energy can be used to move the consumer to part with cash and so, indirectly, to turn the wheels of industry. Stored in the minds and bodies of countless individuals, this potential energy is released by, and transmitted along, a line of symbols carefully laid out so as to bypass rationality and obscure the real issue.

Sometimes the symbols take effect by being disproportionately impressive, haunting and fascinating in their own right. Of this kind are the rites and pomps of religion. These "beauties of holiness" strengthen faith where it already exists and, where there is no faith, contribute to conversion. Appealing, as they do, only to the aesthetic sense, they guarantee neither the truth nor the ethical value of the doctrines with which they have been, quite arbitrarily, associated. As a matter of plain historical fact, the beauties of holiness have often been matched and indeed surpassed by the beauties of unholiness. Under Hitler, for example, the yearly Nuremberg rallies were masterpieces of ritual and theatrical art. "I had spent six years in St. Petersburg before the war in the best days of the old Russian ballet," writes Sir Nevile Henderson, the British ambassador to Hitler's Germany, "but for grandiose beauty I have never seen any ballet to compare with the Nuremberg rally." One thinks of Keats—"beauty is truth, truth beauty." Alas, the identity exists only on some ultimate, supramundane level. On the levels of politics and theology, beauty is perfectly compatible with nonsense and tyranny. Which is very fortunate; for if beauty were incompatible with nonsense and tyranny, there would be precious little art in the world. The masterpieces of painting, sculpture and architecture were produced as religious or political propaganda, for the greater glory of a god, a government or a priesthood. But most kings and priests have been despotic and all religions have been riddled with superstition. Genius has been the servant of tyranny and art has advertised the merits of the local cult. Time, as it passes, separates the good art from the bad metaphysics. Can we learn to make this separation, not after the event, but while it is actually taking place? That is the question.

In commercial propaganda the principle of the disproportionately fascinating symbol is clearly understood. Every propagandist has his Art Department, and attempts are constantly being made to beautify the billboards with striking posters, the advertising pages of magazines with lively drawings and photographs. There are no masterpieces; for masterpieces appeal only to a limited audience, and the commercial propagandist is out to captivate the majority. For him, the ideal is a moderate excellence. Those who like this not too good, but sufficiently striking, art may be expected to like the products with which it has been associated and for which it symbolically stands.

Another disproportionately fascinating symbol is the Singing Commercial. Singing Commercials are a recent invention; but the Singing Theological and the Singing Devotional—the hymn and the psalm—are as old as religion itself. Singing Militaries, or marching songs, are coeval with war, and Singing Patriotics, the precursors of our national anthems, were doubtless used to promote group solidarity, to emphasize the distinction between "us" and "them," by the wandering bands of paleolithic hunters and food gatherers. To most people music is intrinsically attractive. Moreover, melodies tend to ingrain themselves in the listener's mind. A tune will haunt the memory during the whole of a lifetime. Here, for example, is a quite uninteresting statement or value judgment. As it stands nobody will pay attention to it. But now set the words to a catchy and easily remembered tune. Immediately they become words of power. Moreover, the words will tend automatically to repeat themselves every time the melody is heard or spontaneously remembered. Orpheus has entered into an alliance with Pavlov—the power of sound with the conditioned reflex. For the commercial propagandist, as for his colleagues in the fields of politics and religion, music possesses yet another advantage. Nonsense which it would be shameful for a reasonable being to write, speak or hear spoken can be sung or listened to by that same rational being with pleasure and even with a kind of intellectual conviction. Can we learn to separate the pleasure of singing or of listening to song from the all too human tendency to believe in the propaganda which the song is putting over? That again is the question.

Thanks to compulsory education and the rotary press, the propagandist has been able, for many years past, to convey his messages to virtually every adult in every civilized country. Today, thanks to radio and television, he is in the happy position of being able to communicate even with unschooled adults and not yet literate children.

Children, as might be expected, are highly susceptible to propaganda. They are ignorant of the world and its ways, and therefore completely unsuspecting. Their critical faculties are undeveloped. The youngest of them have not yet reached the age of reason and the older ones lack the experience on which their new-found rationality can effectively work. In Europe, conscripts used to be playfully referred to as "cannon fodder." Their little brothers and sisters have now become radio fodder and television fodder. In my childhood we were taught to sing nursery rhymes and, in pious households, hymns. Today the little ones warble the Singing Commercials. Which is better— "Rheingold is my beer, the dry beer," or "Hey diddle-diddle, the cat and the fiddle"? "Abide with me" or "You'll wonder where the yellow went, when you brush your teeth with Pepsodent"? Who knows?

"I don't say that children should be forced to harass their parents into buying products they've seen advertised on television, but at the same time I cannot close my eyes to the fact that it's being done every day." So writes the star of one of the many programs beamed to a juvenile audience. "Children," he adds, "are living, talking records of what we tell them every day." And in due course these living, talking records of television commercials will grow up, earn money and buy the products of industry. "Think," writes Mr. Clyde Miller ecstatically, "think of what it can mean to your firm in profits if you can condition a million or ten million children, who will grow up into adults trained to buy your product, as soldiers are trained in advance when they hear the trigger words, Forward March!" Yes, just think of it! And at the same time remember that the dictators and the would-be dictators have been thinking about this sort of thing for years, and that millions, tens of millions, hundreds of millions of children are in process of growing up to buy the local despot's ideological product and, like well-trained soldiers, to respond with appropriate behavior to the trigger words implanted in those young minds by the despot's propagandists.

Self-government is in inverse ratio to numbers. The larger the constituency, the less the value of any particular vote. When he is merely one of millions, the individual elector feels himself to be impotent, a negligible quantity. The candidates he has voted into office are far away, at the top of the pyramid of power. Theoretically they are the servants of the people; but in fact it is the servants who give orders and the people, far off at the base of the great pyramid, who must obey. Increasing population and advancing technology have resulted in an increase in the number and complexity of organizations, an increase in the amount of power concentrated in the hands of officials and a corresponding decrease in the amount of control exercised by electors, coupled with a decrease in the public's regard for democratic procedures. Already weakened by the vast impersonal forces at work in the modern world, democratic institutions are now being undermined from within by the politicians and their propagandists.

Human beings act in a great variety of irrational ways, but all of them seem to be capable, if given a fair chance, of making a reasonable choice in the light of available evidence. Democratic institutions can be made to work only if all concerned do their best to impart knowledge and to encourage rationality. But today, in the world's most powerful democracy, the politicians and their propagandists prefer to make nonsense of democratic procedures by appealing almost exclusively to the ignorance and irrationality of the electors. "Both parties," we were told in 1956 by the editor of a leading business journal, "will merchandize their candidates and issues by the same methods that business has developed to sell goods. These include scientific selection of appeals and planned repetition.... Radio spot announcements and ads will repeat phrases with a planned intensity. Billboards will push slogans of proven power.... Candidates need, in addition to rich voices and good diction, to be able to look 'sincerely' at the TV camera."

The political merchandisers appeal only to the weaknesses of voters, never to their potential strength. They make no attempt to educate the masses into becoming fit for self-government; they are content merely to manipulate and exploit them. For this purpose all the resources of psychology and the social sciences are mobilized and set to work. Carefully selected samples of the electorate are given "interviews in depth." These interviews in depth reveal the unconscious fears and wishes most prevalent in a given society at the time of an election. Phrases and images aimed at allaying or, if necessary, enhancing these fears, at satisfying these wishes, at least symbolically, are then chosen by the experts, tried out on readers and audiences, changed or improved in the light of the information thus obtained. After which the political campaign is ready for the mass communicators. All that is now needed is money and a candidate who can be coached to look "sincere." Under the new dispensation, political principles and plans for specific action have come to lose most of their importance. The personality of the candidate and the way he is projected by the advertising experts are the things that really matter.

In one way or another, as vigorous he-man or kindly father, the candidate must be glamorous. He must also be an entertainer who never bores his audience. Inured to television and radio, that audience is accustomed to being distracted and does not like to be asked to concentrate or make a prolonged intellectual effort. All speeches by the entertainer-candidate must therefore be short and snappy. The great issues of the day must be dealt with in five minutes at the most—and preferably (since the audience will be eager to pass on to something a little livelier than inflation or the H-bomb) in sixty seconds flat. The nature of oratory is such that there has always been a tendency among politicians and clergymen to over-simplify complex issues. From a pulpit or a platform even the most conscientious of speakers finds it very difficult to tell the whole truth. The methods now being used to merchandise the political candidate as though he were a deodorant positively guarantee the electorate against ever hearing the truth about anything.

VII Brainwashing

In the two preceding chapters I have described the techniques of what may be called wholesale mind-manipulation, as practiced by the greatest demagogue and the most successful salesmen in recorded history. But no human problem can be solved by wholesale methods alone. The shotgun has its place, but so has the hypodermic syringe. In the chapters that follow I shall describe some of the more effective techniques for manipulating not crowds, not entire publics, but isolated individuals.

In the course of his epoch-making experiments on the conditioned reflex, Ivan Pavlov observed that, when subjected to prolonged physical or psychic stress, laboratory animals exhibit all the symptoms of a nervous breakdown. Refusing to cope any longer with the intolerable situation, their brains go on strike, so to speak, and either stop working altogether (the dog loses consciousness), or else resort to slow-downs and sabotage (the dog behaves unrealistically, or develops the kind of physical symptoms which, in a human being, we would call hysterical). Some animals are more resistant to stress than others. Dogs possessing what Pavlov called a "strong excitatory" constitution break down much more quickly than dogs of a merely "lively" (as opposed to a choleric or agitated) temperament. Similarly "weak inhibitory" dogs reach the end of their tether much sooner than do "calm imperturbable" dogs. But even the most stoical dog is unable to resist indefinitely. If the stress to which he is subjected is sufficiently intense or sufficiently prolonged, he will end by breaking down as abjectly and as completely as the weakest of his kind.

Pavlov's findings were confirmed in the most distressing manner, and on a very large scale, during the two World Wars. As the result of a single catastrophic experience, or of a succession of terrors less appalling but frequently repeated, soldiers develop a number of disabling psychophysical symptoms. Temporary unconsciousness, extreme agitation, lethargy, functional blindness or paralysis, completely unrealistic responses to the challenge of events, strange reversals of lifelong patterns of behavior—all the symptoms, which Pavlov observed in his dogs, reappeared among the victims of what in the First World War was called "shell shock," in the Second, "battle fatigue." Every man, like every dog, has his own individual limit of endurance. Most men reach their limit after about thirty days of more or less continuous stress under the conditions of modern combat. The more than averagely susceptible succumb in only fifteen days. The more than averagely tough can resist for forty-five or even fifty days. Strong or weak, in the long run all of them break down. All, that is to say, of those who are initially sane. For, ironically enough, the only people who can hold up indefinitely under the stress of modern war are psychotics. Individual insanity is immune to the consequences of collective insanity.

The fact that every individual has his breaking point has been known and, in a crude unscientific way, exploited from time immemorial. In some cases man's dreadful inhumanity to man has been inspired by the love of cruelty for its own horrible and fascinating sake. More often, however, pure sadism was tempered by utilitarianism, theology or reasons of state. Physical torture and other forms of stress were inflicted by lawyers in order to loosen the tongues of reluctant witnesses; by clergymen in order to punish the unorthodox and induce them to change their opinions; by the secret police to extract confessions from persons suspected of being hostile to the government. Under Hitler, torture, followed by mass extermination, was used on those biological heretics, the Jews. For a young Nazi, a tour of duty in the Extermination Camps was (in Himmler's words) "the best indoctrination on inferior beings and the subhuman races." Given the obsessional quality of the anti-Semitism which Hitler had picked up as a young man in the slums of Vienna, this revival of the methods employed by the Holy Office against heretics and witches was inevitable. But in the light of the findings of Pavlov and of the knowledge gained by psychiatrists in the treatment of war neuroses, it seems a hideous and grotesque anachronism. Stresses amply sufficient to cause a complete cerebral breakdown can be induced by methods which, though hatefully inhuman, fall short of physical torture.

Whatever may have happened in earlier years, it seems fairly certain that torture is not extensively used by the Communist police today. They draw their inspiration, not from the Inquisitor or the SS man, but from the physiologist and his methodically conditioned laboratory animals. For the dictator and his policemen, Pavlov's findings have important practical implications. If the central nervous system of dogs can be broken down, so can the central nervous system of political prisoners. It is simply a matter of applying the right amount of stress for the right length of time. At the end of the treatment, the prisoner will be in a state of neurosis or hysteria, and will be ready to confess whatever his captors want him to confess.

But confession is not enough. A hopeless neurotic is no use to anyone. What the intelligent and practical dictator needs is not a patient to be institutionalized, or a victim to be shot, but a convert who will work for the Cause. Turning once again to Pavlov, he learns that, on their way to the point of final breakdown, dogs become more than normally suggestible. New behavior patterns can easily be installed while the dog is at or near the limit of its cerebral endurance, and these new behavior patterns seem to be ineradicable. The animal in which they have been implanted cannot be deconditioned; that which it has learned under stress will remain an integral part of its make-up.

Psychological stresses can be produced in many ways. Dogs become disturbed when stimuli are unusually strong; when the interval between a stimulus and the customary response is unduly prolonged and the animal is left in a state of suspense; when the brain is confused by stimuli that run counter to what the dog has learned to expect; when stimuli make no sense within the victim's established frame of reference. Furthermore, it has been found that the deliberate induction of fear, rage or anxiety markedly heightens the dog's suggestibility. If these emotions are kept at a high pitch of intensity for a long enough time, the brain goes 'on strike.' When this happens, new behavior patterns may be installed with the greatest of ease.

Among the physical stresses that increase a dog's suggestibility are fatigue, wounds and every form of sickness.

For the would-be dictator these findings possess important practical implications. They prove, for example, that Hitler was quite right in maintaining that mass meetings at night were more effective than mass meetings in the daytime. During the day, he wrote, "man's will power revolts with highest energy against any attempt at being forced under another's will and another's opinion. In the evening, however, they succumb more easily to the dominating force of a stronger will."

Pavlov would have agreed with him; fatigue increases suggestibility. (That is why, among other reasons, the commercial sponsors of television programs prefer the evening hours and are ready to back their preference with hard cash.)

Illness is even more effective than fatigue as an intensifier of suggestibility. In the past, sickrooms were the scene of countless religious conversions. The scientifically trained dictator of the future will have all the hospitals in his dominions wired for sound and equipped with pillow speakers. Canned persuasion will be on the air twenty-four hours a day, and the more important patients will be visited by political soul-savers and mind-changers just as, in the past, their ancestors were visited by priests, nuns and pious laymen.

The fact that strong negative emotions tend to heighten suggestibility and so facilitate a change of heart had been observed and exploited long before the days of Pavlov. As Dr. William Sargant has pointed out in his enlightening book, *Battle for the Mind*, John Wesley's enormous success as a preacher was based upon an intuitive understanding of the central nervous system. He would open his sermon with a long and detailed description of the torments to which, unless they underwent conversion, his hearers would undoubtedly be condemned for all eternity. Then, when terror and an agonizing sense of guilt had brought his audience to the verge, or in some cases over the verge, of a complete cerebral breakdown, he would change his tone and promise salvation to those who believed and repented. By this kind of preaching, Wesley converted thousands of men, women and children. Intense, prolonged fear broke them down and produced a state of greatly intensified suggestibility. In this state they were able to accept the preacher's theological pronouncements without question. After which they were reintegrated by words of comfort, and emerged from their ordeal with new and generally better behavior patterns ineradicably implanted in their minds and nervous systems.

The effectiveness of political and religious propaganda depends upon the methods employed, not upon the doctrines taught. These doctrines may be true or false, wholesome or pernicious—it makes little or no difference. If the indoctrination is given in the right way at the proper stage of nervous exhaustion, it will work. Under favorable conditions, practically everybody can be converted to practically anything.

We possess detailed descriptions of the methods used by the Communist police for dealing with political prisoners. From the moment he is taken into custody, the victim is subjected systematically to many kinds of physical and psychological stress. He is badly fed, he is made extremely uncomfortable, he is not allowed to sleep for more than a few hours each night. And all the time he is kept in a state of suspense, uncertainty and acute apprehension. Day after day—or rather night after night, for these Pavlovian policemen understand the value of fatigue as an intensifier of suggestibility—he is questioned, often for many hours at a stretch, by interrogators who do their best to frighten, confuse and bewilder him. After a few weeks or months of such treatment, his brain goes on strike and he confesses whatever it is that his captors want him to confess. Then, if he is to be converted rather than shot, he is offered the comfort of hope. If he will but accept the true faith, he can yet be saved—not, of course, in the next life (for, officially, there is no next life), but in this.

Similar but rather less drastic methods were used during the Korean War on military prisoners. In their Chinese camps the young Western captives were systematically subjected to stress. Thus, for the most trivial breaches of the rules, offenders would be summoned to the commandant's office, there to be questioned, browbeaten and publicly humiliated. And the process would be repeated, again and again, at any hour of the day or night. This continuous harassment produced in its victims a sense of bewilderment and chronic anxiety. To intensify their sense of guilt, prisoners were made to write and rewrite, in ever more intimate detail, long autobiographical accounts of their shortcomings. And after having confessed their own sins, they were required to confess the sins of their companions. The aim was to create within the camp a nightmarish society, in which everybody was spying on, and informing against, everyone else. To these mental stresses were added the physical stresses of malnutrition, discomfort and illness. The increased suggestibility thus induced was skilfully exploited by the Chinese, who poured into these abnormally receptive minds large doses of pro-Communist and anti-capitalist literature. These Pavlovian techniques were remarkably successful. One out of every seven American prisoners was guilty, we are officially told, of grave collaboration with the Chinese authorities, one out of three of technical collaboration.

It must not be supposed that this kind of treatment is reserved by the Communists exclusively for their enemies. The young field workers, whose business it was, during the first years of the new regime, to act as Communist missionaries and organizers in China's innumerable towns and villages were made to take a course of indoctrination far more intense than that to which any prisoner of war was ever subjected. In his *China under Communism* R. L. Walker describes the methods by which the party leaders are able to fabricate out of ordinary men and women the thousands of selfless fanatics required for spreading the Communist gospel and for enforcing Communist policies. Under this system of training, the human raw material is shipped to special camps, where the trainees are completely isolated from their friends, families and the outside world in general. In these camps they are made to perform exhausting physical and mental work; they are never alone, always in groups; they are encouraged to spy on one another; they are required to write self-accusatory autobiographies; they live in chronic fear of the dreadful fate that may befall them on account of what has been said about them by informers or of what they themselves have confessed. In this state of heightened suggestibility they are given an intensive course in theoretical and applied Marxism—a course in which failure to pass examinations may mean anything from ignominious expulsion to a term in a forced labor camp or even liquidation. After about six months of this kind of thing, prolonged mental and physical stress produces the results which Pavlov's findings would lead one to expect. One after another, or in whole groups, the trainees break down. Neurotic and hysterical symptoms make their appearance. Some of the victims commit suicide, others (as many, we are told, as 20 per cent of the total) develop a severe mental illness. Those who survive the rigors of the conversion process emerge with new and ineradicable behavior patterns. All their ties with the past—friends, family, traditional decencies and pieties—have been severed. They are new men, recreated in the image of their new god and totally dedicated to his service.

Throughout the Communist world tens of thousands of these disciplined and devoted young men are being turned out every year from hundreds of conditioning centers. What the Jesuits did for the Roman Church of the Counter Reformation, these products of a more scientific and even harsher training are now doing, and will doubtless continue to do, for the Communist parties of Europe, Asia and Africa.

In politics Pavlov seems to have been an old-fashioned liberal. But, by a strange irony of fate, his researches and the theories he based upon them have called into existence a great army of fanatics dedicated heart and soul, reflex and nervous system, to the destruction of old-fashioned liberalism, wherever it can be found.

Brainwashing, as it is now practiced, is a hybrid technique, depending for its effectiveness partly on the systematic use of violence, partly on skilful psychological manipulation. It represents the tradition of *1984* on its way to becoming the tradition of *Brave New World*. Under a long-established and well-regulated dictatorship our current methods of semiviolent manipulation will seem, no doubt, absurdly crude. Conditioned from earliest infancy (and perhaps also biologically predestined), the average middle- or lower-caste individual will never require conversion or even a refresher course in the true faith. The members of the highest caste will have to be able to think new thoughts in response to new situations; consequently their training will be much less rigid than the training imposed upon those whose business is not to reason why, but merely to do and die with the minimum of fuss. These upper-caste individuals will be members, still, of a wild species—the trainers and guardians, themselves only slightly conditioned, of a breed of completely domesticated animals. Their wildness will make it possible for them to become heretical and rebellious. When this happens, they will have to be either liquidated, or brainwashed back into orthodoxy, or (as in *Brave New World*) exiled to some island, where they can give no further trouble, except of course to one another. But universal infant conditioning and the other techniques of manipulation and control are still a few generations away in the future. On the road to the Brave New World our rulers will have to rely on the transitional and provisional techniques of brainwashing.

VIII Chemical Persuasion

In the Brave New World of my fable there was no whisky, no tobacco, no illicit heroin, no bootlegged cocaine. People neither smoked, nor drank, nor sniffed, nor gave themselves injections. Whenever anyone felt depressed or below par, he would swallow a tablet or two of a chemical compound called soma. The original soma, from which I took the name of this hypothetical drug, was an unknown plant (possibly *Asclepias acida*) used by the ancient Aryan invaders of India in one of the most solemn of their religious rites. The intoxicating juice expressed from the stems of this plant was drunk by the priests and nobles in the course of an elaborate ceremony. In the Vedic hymns we are told that the drinkers of soma were blessed in many ways. Their bodies were strengthened, their hearts were filled with courage, joy and enthusiasm, their minds were enlightened and in an immediate experience of eternal life they received the assurance of their immortality. But the sacred juice had its drawbacks. Soma was a dangerous drug—so dangerous that even the great sky-god, Indra, was sometimes made ill by drinking it. Ordinary mortals might even die of an overdose. But the experience was so transcendently blissful and enlightening that soma drinking was regarded as a high privilege. For this privilege no price was too great.

The soma of *Brave New World* had none of the drawbacks of its Indian original. In small doses it brought a sense of bliss, in larger doses it made you see visions and, if you took three tablets, you would sink in a few minutes into refreshing sleep. And all at no physiological or mental cost. The Brave New Worlders could take holidays from their black moods, or from the familiar annoyances of everyday life, without sacrificing their health or permanently reducing their efficiency.

In the Brave New World the soma habit was not a private vice; it was a political institution, it was the very essence of the Life, Liberty and Pursuit of Happiness guaranteed by the Bill of Rights. But this most precious of the subjects' inalienable privileges was at the same time one of the most powerful instruments of rule in the dictator's armory. The systematic drugging of individuals for the benefit of the State (and incidentally, of course, for their own delight) was a main plank in the policy of the World Controllers. The daily soma ration was an insurance against personal maladjustment, social unrest and the spread of subversive ideas. Religion, Karl Marx declared, is the opium of the people. In the Brave New World this situation was reversed. Opium, or rather soma, was the people's religion. Like religion, the drug had power to console and compensate, it called up visions of another, better world, it offered hope, strengthened faith and promoted charity. Beer, a poet has written,

...   does   more   than   Milton   can
To justify God's ways to man.

And let us remember that, compared with soma, beer is a drug of the crudest and most unreliable kind. In this matter of justifying God's ways to man, soma is to alcohol as alcohol is to the theological arguments of Milton.

In 1931, when I was writing about the imaginary synthetic by means of which future generations would be made both happy and docile, the well-known American biochemist, Dr. Irvine Page, was preparing to leave Germany, where he had spent the three preceding years at the Kaiser Wilhelm Institute, working on the chemistry of the brain. "It is hard to understand," Dr. Page has written in a recent article, "why it took so long for scientists to get around to investigating the chemical reactions in their own brains. I speak," he adds, "from acute personal experience. When I came home in 1931 ... I could not get a job in this field (the field of brain chemistry) or stir a ripple of interest in it." Today, twenty-seven years later, the non-existent ripple of 1931 has become a tidal wave of biochemical and psychopharmacological research. The enzymes which regulate the workings of the brain are being studied. Within the body, hitherto unknown chemical substances such as adrenochrome and serotonin (of which Dr. Page was a co-discoverer) have been isolated and their far-reaching effects on our mental and physical functions are now being investigated. Meanwhile new drugs are being synthesized—drugs that reinforce or correct or interfere with the actions of the various chemicals, by means of which the nervous system performs its daily and hourly miracles as the controller of the body, the instrument and mediator of consciousness. From our present point of view, the most interesting fact about these new drugs is that they temporarily alter the chemistry of the brain and the associated state of the mind without doing any permanent damage to the organism as a whole. In this respect they are like soma—and profoundly unlike the mind-changing drugs of the past. For example, the classical tranquillizer is opium. But opium is a dangerous drug which, from neolithic times down to the present day, has been making addicts and ruining health. The same is true of the classical euphoric, alcohol—the drug which, in the words of the Psalmist, "maketh glad the heart of man." But unfortunately alcohol not only maketh glad the heart of man; it also, in excessive doses, causes illness and addiction, and has been a main source, for the last eight or ten thousand years, of crime, domestic unhappiness, moral degradation and avoidable accidents.

Among the classical stimulants, tea, coffee and maté are, thank goodness, almost completely harmless. They are also very weak stimulants. Unlike these "cups that cheer but not inebriate," cocaine is a very powerful and a very dangerous drug. Those who make use of it must pay for their ecstasies, their sense of unlimited physical and mental power, by spells of agonizing depression, by such horrible physical symptoms as the sensation of being infested by myriads of crawling insects and by paranoid delusions that may lead to crimes of violence. Another stimulant of more recent vintage is amphetamine, better known under its trade name of Benzedrine. Amphetamine works very effectively—but works, if abused, at the expense of mental and physical health. It has been reported that, in Japan, there are now about one million amphetamine addicts.

Of the classical vision-producers the best known are the peyote of Mexico and the southwestern United States and *Cannabis sativa*, consumed all over the world under such names as hashish, bhang, kif and marihuana. According to the best medical and anthropological evidence, peyote is far less harmful than the White Man's gin or whisky. It permits the Indians who use it in their religious rites to enter paradise, and to feel at one with the beloved community, without making them pay for the privilege by anything worse than the ordeal of having to chew on something with a revolting flavor and of feeling somewhat nauseated for an hour or two. *Cannabis sativa* is a less innocuous drug—though not nearly so harmful as the sensation-mongers would have us believe. The Medical Committee, appointed in 1944 by the Mayor of New York to investigate the problem of marihuana, came to the conclusion, after careful investigation, that *Cannabis sativa* is not a serious menace to society, or even to those who indulge in it. It is merely a nuisance.

From these classical mind-changes we pass to the latest products of psychopharmacological research. Most highly publicized of these are the three new tranquillizers, reserpine, chlorpromazine and meprobamate. Administered to certain classes of psychotics, the first two have proved to be remarkably effective, not in curing mental illnesses, but at least in temporarily abolishing their more distressing symptoms. Meprobamate (alias Miltown) produces similar effects in persons suffering from various forms of neurosis. None of these drugs is perfectly harmless; but their cost, in terms of physical health and mental efficiency, is extraordinarily low. In a world where nobody gets anything for nothing tranquillizers offer a great deal for very little. Miltown and chlorpromazine are not yet soma; but they come fairly near to being one of the aspects of that mythical drug. They provide temporary relief from nervous tension without, in the great majority of cases, inflicting permanent organic harm, and without causing more than a rather slight impairment, while the drug is working, of intellectual and physical efficiency. Except as narcotics, they are probably to be preferred to the barbiturates, which blunt the mind's cutting edge and, in large doses, cause a number of undesirable psychophysical symptoms and may result in a full-blown addiction.

In LSD-25 (lysergic acid diethylamide) the pharmacologists have recently created another aspect of soma—a perception-improver and vision-producer that is, physiologically speaking, almost costless. This extraordinary drug, which is effective in doses as small as fifty or even twenty-five millionths of a gram, has power (like peyote) to transport people into the other world. In the majority of cases, the other world to which LSD-25 gives access is heavenly; alternatively it may be purgatorial or even infernal. But, positive or negative, the lysergic acid experience is felt by almost everyone who undergoes it to be profoundly significant and enlightening. In any event, the fact that minds can be changed so radically at so little cost to the body is altogether astonishing.

Soma was not only a vision-producer and a tranquillizer; it was also (and no doubt impossibly) a stimulant of mind and body, a creator of active euphoria as well as of the negative happiness that follows the release from anxiety and tension.

The ideal stimulant—powerful but innocuous—still awaits discovery. Amphetamine, as we have seen, was far from satisfactory; it exacted too high a price for what it gave. A more promising candidate for the role of soma in its third aspect is Iproniazid, which is now being used to lift depressed patients out of their misery, to enliven the apathetic and in general to increase the amount of available psychic energy. Still more promising, according to a distinguished pharmacologist of my acquaintance, is a new compound, still in the testing stage, to be known as Deaner. Deaner is an ammo-alcohol and is thought to increase the production of acetyl-choline within the body, and thereby to increase the activity and effectiveness of the nervous system. The man who takes the new pill needs less sleep, feels more alert and cheerful, thinks faster and better—and all at next to no organic cost, at any rate in the short run. It sounds almost too good to be true.

We see then that, though soma does not yet exist (and will probably never exist), fairly good substitutes for the various aspects of soma have already been discovered. There are now physiologically cheap tranquillizers, physiologically cheap vision-producers and physiologically cheap stimulants.

That a dictator could, if he so desired, make use of these drugs for political purposes is obvious. He could ensure himself against political unrest by changing the chemistry of his subjects' brains and so making them content with their servile condition. He could use tranquillizers to calm the excited, stimulants to arouse enthusiasm in the indifferent, hallucants to distract the attention of the wretched from their miseries. But how, it may be asked, will the dictator get his subjects to take the pills that will make them think, feel and behave in the ways he finds desirable? In all probability it will be enough merely to make the pills available. Today alcohol and tobacco are available, and people spend considerably more on these very unsatisfactory euphorics, pseudo-stimulants and sedatives than they are ready to spend on the education of their children. Or consider the barbiturates and the tranquillizers. In the United States these drugs can be obtained only on a doctor's prescription. But the demand of the American public for something that will make life in an urban-industrial environment a little more tolerable is so great that doctors are now writing prescriptions for the various tranquillizers at the rate of forty-eight millions a year. Moreover, a majority of these prescriptions are refilled. A hundred doses of happiness are not enough: send to the drugstore for another bottle—and, when that is finished, for another.... There can be no doubt that, if tranquillizers could be bought as easily and cheaply as aspirin, they would be consumed, not by the billions, as they are at present, but by the scores and hundreds of billions. And a good, cheap stimulant would be almost as popular.

Under a dictatorship pharmacists would be instructed to change their tune with every change of circumstances. In times of national crisis it would be their business to push the sale of stimulants. Between crises, too much alertness and energy on the part of his subjects might prove embarrassing to the tyrant. At such times the masses would be urged to buy tranquillizers and vision-producers. Under the influence of these soothing syrups they could be relied upon to give their master no trouble.

As things now stand, the tranquillizers may prevent some people from giving enough trouble, not only to their rulers, but even to themselves. Too much tension is a disease; but so is too little. There are certain occasions when we ought to be tense, when an excess of tranquillity (and especially of tranquillity imposed from the outside, by a chemical) is entirely inappropriate.

At a recent symposium on meprobamate, in which I was a participant, an eminent biochemist playfully suggested that the United States government should make a free gift to the Soviet people of fifty billion doses of this most popular of the tranquillizers. The joke had a serious point to it. In a contest between two populations, one of which is being constantly stimulated by threats and promises, constantly directed by one-pointed propaganda, while the other is no less constantly being distracted by television and tranquillized by Miltown, which of the opponents is more likely to come out on top?

As well as tranquillizing, hallucinating and stimulating, the soma of my fable had the power of heightening suggestibility, and so could be used to reinforce the effects of governmental propaganda. Less effectively and at a higher physiological cost, several drugs already in the pharmacopoeia can be used for the same purpose. There is scopolamine, for example, the active principle of henbane and, in large doses, a powerful poison; there are pentothal and sodium amytal. Nicknamed for some odd reason "the truth serum," pentothal has been used by the police of various countries for the purpose of extracting confessions from (or perhaps suggesting confessions to) reluctant criminals. Pentothal and sodium amytal lower the barrier between the conscious and the subconscious mind and are of great value in the treatment of "battle fatigue" by the process known in England as "abreaction therapy," in America as "narcosynthesis." It is said that these drugs are sometimes employed by the Communists, when preparing important prisoners for their public appearance in court.

Meanwhile pharmacology, biochemistry and neurology are on the march, and we can be quite certain that, in the course of the next few years, new and better chemical methods for increasing suggestibility and lowering psychological resistance will be discovered. Like everything else, these discoveries may be used well or badly. They may help the psychiatrist in his battle against mental illness, or they may help the dictator in his battle against freedom. More probably (since science is divinely impartial) they will both enslave and make free, heal and at the same time destroy.

IX Subconscious Persuasion

In a footnote appended to the 1919 edition of his book, *The Interpretation of Dreams*, Sigmund Freud called attention to the work of Dr. Poetzl, an Austrian neurologist, who had recently published a paper describing his experiments with the tachistoscope. (The tachistoscope is an instrument that comes in two forms—a viewing box, into which the subject looks at an image that is exposed for a small fraction of a second; a magic lantern with a high-speed shutter, capable of projecting an image very briefly upon a screen.) In these experiments "Poetzl required the subjects to make a drawing of what they had consciously noted of a picture exposed to their view in a tachistoscope.... He then turned his attention to the dreams dreamed by the subjects during the following night and required them once more to make drawings of appropriate portions of these dreams. It was shown unmistakably that those details of the exposed picture which had *not* been noted by the subject provided material for the construction of the dream."

With various modifications and refinements Poetzl's experiments have been repeated several times, most recently by Dr. Charles Fisher, who has contributed three excellent papers on the subject of dreams and "preconscious perception" to the *Journal of the American Psychoanalytic Association*. Meanwhile the academic psychologists have not been idle. Confirming Poetzl's findings, their studies have shown that people actually see and hear a great deal more than they consciously know they see and hear, and that what they see and hear without knowing it is recorded by the subconscious mind and may affect their conscious thoughts, feelings and behavior.

Pure science does not remain pure indefinitely. Sooner or later it is apt to turn into applied science and finally into technology. Theory modulates into industrial practice, knowledge becomes power, formulas and laboratory experiments undergo a metamorphosis, and emerge as the H-bomb. In the present case, Poetzl's nice little piece of pure science, and all the other nice little pieces of pure science in the field of preconscious perception, retained their pristine purity for a surprisingly long time. Then, in the early autumn of 1957, exactly forty years after the publication of Poetzl's original paper, it was announced that their purity was a thing of the past; they had been applied, they had entered the realm of technology. The announcement made a considerable stir, and was talked and written about all over the civilized world. And no wonder; for the new technique of "subliminal projection," as it was called, was intimately associated with mass entertainment, and in the life of civilized human beings mass entertainment now plays a part comparable to that played in the Middle Ages by religion. Our epoch has been given many nicknames—the Age of Anxiety, the Atomic Age, the Space Age. It might, with equally good reason, be called the Age of Television Addiction, the Age of Soap Opera, the Age of the Disk Jockey. In such an age the announcement that Poetzl's pure science had been applied in the form of a technique of subliminal projection could not fail to arouse the most intense interest among the world's mass entertainees. For the new technique was aimed directly at them, and its purpose was to manipulate their minds without their being aware of what was being done to them. By means of specially designed tachistoscopes words or images were to be flashed for a millisecond or less upon the screens of television sets and motion picture theaters during (not before or after) the program. "Drink Coca-Cola" or "Light up a Camel" would be superimposed upon the lovers' embrace, the tears of the broken-hearted mother, and the optic nerves of the viewers would record these secret messages, their subconscious minds would respond to them and in due course they would consciously feel a craving for soda pop and tobacco. And meanwhile other secret messages would be whispered too softly, or squeaked too shrilly, for conscious hearing. Consciously the listener might be paying attention to some such phrase as "Darling, I love you"; but subliminally, beneath the threshold of awareness, his incredibly sensitive ears and his subconscious mind would be taking in the latest good news about deodorants and laxatives.

Does this kind of commercial propaganda really work? The evidence produced by the commercial firm that first unveiled a technique for subliminal projection was vague and, from a scientific point of view, very unsatisfactory. Repeated at regular intervals during the showing of a picture in a movie theater, the command to buy more popcorn was said to have resulted in a 50 per cent increase in popcorn sales during the intermission. But a single experiment proves very little. Moreover, this particular experiment was poorly set up. There were no controls and no attempt was made to allow for the many variables that undoubtedly affect the consumption of popcorn by a theater audience. And anyhow was this the most effective way of applying the knowledge accumulated over the years by the scientific investigators of subconscious perception? Was it intrinsically probable that, by merely flashing the name of a product and a command to buy it, you would be able to break down sales resistance and recruit new customers? The answer to both these questions is pretty obviously in the negative. But this does not mean, of course, that the findings of the neurologists and psychologists are without any practical importance. Skillfully applied, Poetzl's nice little piece of pure science might well become a powerful instrument for the manipulation of unsuspecting minds.

For a few suggestive hints let us now turn from the popcorn vendors to those who, with less noise but more imagination and better methods, have been experimenting in the same field. In Britain, where the process of manipulating minds below the level of consciousness is known as "strobonic injection," investigators have stressed the practical importance of creating the right psychological conditions for subconscious persuasion. A suggestion above the threshold of awareness is more likely to take effect when the recipient is in a light hypnotic trance, under the influence of certain drugs, or has been debilitated by illness, starvation, or any kind of physical or emotional stress. But what is true for suggestions above the threshold of consciousness is also true for suggestions beneath that threshold. In a word, the lower the level of a person's psychological resistance, the greater will be the effectiveness of strobonically injected suggestions. The scientific dictator of tomorrow will set up his whispering machines and subliminal projectors in schools and hospitals (children and the sick are highly suggestible), and in all public places where audiences can be given a preliminary softening up by suggestibility-increasing oratory or rituals.

From the conditions under which we may expect subliminal suggestion to be effective we now pass to the suggestions themselves. In what terms should the propagandist address himself to his victims' subconscious minds? Direct commands ("Buy popcorn" or "Vote for Jones") and unqualified statements ("Socialism stinks" or "X's toothpaste cures halitosis") are likely to take effect only upon those minds that are already partial to Jones and popcorn, already alive to the dangers of body odors and the public ownership of the means of production. But to strengthen existing faith is not enough; the propagandist, if he is worth his salt, must create new faith, must know how to bring the indifferent and the undecided over to his side, must be able to mollify and perhaps even convert the hostile. To subliminal assertion and command he knows that he must add subliminal persuasion.

Above the threshold of awareness, one of the most effective methods of non-rational persuasion is what may be called persuasion-by-association. The propagandist arbitrarily associates his chosen product, candidate or cause with some idea, some image of a person or thing which most people, in a given culture, unquestioningly regard as good. Thus, in a selling campaign female beauty may be arbitrarily associated with anything from a bulldozer to a diuretic; in a political campaign patriotism may be associated with any cause from *apartheid* to integration, and with any kind of person, from a Mahatma Gandhi to a Senator McCarthy. Years ago, in Central America, I observed an example of persuasion-by-association which filled me with an appalled admiration for the men who had devised it. In the mountains of Guatemala the only imported art works are the colored calendars distributed free of charge by the foreign companies whose products are sold to the Indians. The American calendars showed pictures of dogs, of landscapes, of young women in a state of partial nudity. But to the Indian dogs are merely utilitarian objects, landscapes are what he sees only too much of, every day of his life, and half-naked blondes are uninteresting, perhaps a little repulsive. American calendars were, in consequence, far less popular than German calendars; for the German advertisers had taken the trouble to find out what the Indians valued and were interested in. I remember in particular one masterpiece of commercial propaganda. It was a calendar put out by a manufacturer of aspirin. At the bottom of the picture one saw the familiar trademark on the familiar bottle of white tablets. Above it were no snow scenes or autumnal woods, no cocker spaniels or bosomy chorus girls. No—the wily Germans had associated their pain-relievers with a brightly colored and extremely lifelike picture of the Holy Trinity sitting on a cumulus cloud and surrounded by St. Joseph, the Virgin Mary, assorted saints and a large number of angels. The miraculous virtues of acetyl salicylic acid were thus guaranteed, in the Indians' simple and deeply religious minds, by God the Father and the entire heavenly host.

This kind of persuasion-by-association is something to which the techniques of subliminal projection seem to lend themselves particularly well. In a series of experiments carried out at New York University, under the auspices of the National Institute of Health, it was found that a person's feelings about some consciously seen image could be modified by associating it, on the subconscious level, with another image, or, better still, with value-bearing words. Thus, when associated, on the subconscious level, with the word "happy," a blank expressionless face would seem to the observer to smile, to look friendly, amiable, outgoing. When the same face was associated, also on the subconscious level, with the word "angry," it took on a forbidding expression, and seemed to the observer to have become hostile and disagreeable. (To a group of young women, it also came to seem very masculine—whereas when it was associated with "happy," they saw the face as belonging to a member of their own sex. Fathers and husbands, please take note.) For the commercial and political propagandist, these findings, it is obvious, are highly significant. If he can put his victims into a state of abnormally high suggestibility, if he can show them, while they are in that state, the thing, the person or, through a symbol, the cause he has to sell, and if, on the subconscious level, he can associate this thing, person or symbol with some value-bearing word or image, he may be able to modify their feelings and opinions without their having any idea of what he is doing. It should be possible, according to an enterprising commercial group in New Orleans, to enhance the entertainment value of films and television plays by using this technique. People like to feel strong emotions and therefore enjoy tragedies, thrillers, murder mysteries and tales of passion. The dramatization of a fight or an embrace produces strong emotions in the spectators. It might produce even stronger emotions if it were associated, on the subconscious level, with appropriate words or symbols. For example, in the film version of *A Farewell to Arms*, the death of the heroine in childbirth might be made even more distressing than it already is by subliminally flashing upon the screen, again and again, during the playing of the scene, such ominous words as "pain," "blood" and "death." Consciously, the words would not be seen; but their effect upon the subconscious mind might be very great and these effects might powerfully reinforce the emotions evoked, on the conscious level, by the acting and the dialogue. If, as seems pretty certain, subliminal projection can consistently intensify the emotions felt by moviegoers, the motion picture industry may yet be saved from bankruptcy—that is, if the producers of television plays don't get there first.

In the light of what has been said about persuasion-by-association and the enhancement of emotions by subliminal suggestion, let us try to imagine what the political meeting of tomorrow will be like. The candidate (if there is still a question of candidates), or the appointed representative of the ruling oligarchy, will make his speech for all to hear. Meanwhile the tachistoscopes, the whispering and squeaking machines, the projectors of images so dim that only the subconscious mind can respond to them, will be reinforcing what he says by systematically associating the man and his cause with positively charged words and hallowed images, and by strobonically injecting negatively charged words and odious symbols whenever he mentions the enemies of the State or the Party. In the United States brief flashes of Abraham Lincoln and the words "government by the people" will be projected upon the rostrum. In Russia the speaker will, of course, be associated with glimpses of Lenin, with the words "people's democracy," with the prophetic beard of Father Marx. Because all this is still safely in the future, we can afford to smile. Ten or twenty years from now, it will probably seem a good deal less amusing. For what is now merely science fiction will have become everyday political fact.

Poetzl was one of the portents which, when writing *Brave New World*, I somehow overlooked. There is no reference in my fable to subliminal projection. It is a mistake of omission which, if I were to rewrite the book today, I should most certainly correct.

X Hypnopaedia

In the late autumn of 1957 the Woodland Road Camp, a penal institution in Tulare County, California, became the scene of a curious and interesting experiment. Miniature loud-speakers were placed under the pillows of a group of prisoners who had volunteered to act as psychological guinea pigs. Each of these pillow speakers was hooked up to a phonograph in the Warden's office. Every hour throughout the night an inspirational whisper repeated a brief homily on "the principles of moral living." Waking at midnight, a prisoner might hear this still small voice extolling the cardinal virtues or murmuring, on behalf of his own Better Self, "I am filled with love and compassion for all, so help me God."

After reading about the Woodland Road Camp, I turned to the second chapter of *Brave New World*. In that chapter the Director of Hatcheries and Conditioning for Western Europe explains to a group of freshman conditioners and hatchers the workings of that state-controlled system of ethical education, known in the seventh century After Ford as hypnopaedia. The earliest attempts at sleep-teaching, the Director told his audience, had been misguided, and therefore unsuccessful. Educators had tried to give intellectual training to their slumbering pupils. But intellectual activity is incompatible with sleep. Hypnopaedia became successful only when it was used for *moral* training—in other words, for the conditioning of behavior through verbal suggestion at a time of lowered psychological resistance. "Wordless conditioning is crude and wholesale, cannot inculcate the more complex courses of behavior required by the State. For that there must be words, but words without reason" ... the kind of words that require no analysis for their comprehension, but can be swallowed whole by the sleeping brain. This is true hypnopaedia, "the greatest moralizing and socializing force of all time." In the Brave New World, no citizens belonging to the lower castes ever gave any trouble. Why? Because, from the moment he could speak and understand what was said to him, every lower-caste child was exposed to endlessly repeated suggestions, night after night, during the hours of drowsiness and sleep. These suggestions were "like drops of liquid sealing wax, drops that adhere, incrust, incorporate themselves with what they fall on, till finally the rock is all one scarlet blob. Till at last the child's mind is these suggestions and the sum of these suggestions is the child's mind. And not the child's mind only. The adult's mind too—all his life long. The mind that judges and desires and decides—made up of these suggestions. But these suggestions are *our* suggestions—suggestions from the State...."

To date, so far as I know, hypnopaedic suggestions have been given by no state more formidable than Tulare County, and the nature of Tulare's hypnopaedic suggestions to lawbreakers is unexceptionable. If only all of us, and not only the inmates of the Woodland Road Camp, could be effectively filled, during our sleep, with love and compassion for all! No, it is not the message conveyed by the inspirational whisper that one objects to; it is the principle of sleep-teaching by governmental agencies. Is hypnopaedia the sort of instrument that officials, delegated to exercise authority in a democratic society, ought to be allowed to use at their discretion? In the present instance they are using it only on volunteers and with the best intentions. But there is no guarantee that in other cases the intentions will be good or the indoctrination on a voluntary basis. Any law or social arrangement which makes it possible for officials to be led into temptation is bad. Any law or arrangement which preserves them from being tempted to abuse their delegated power for their own advantage, or for the benefit of the State or of some political, economic or ecclesiastical organization, is good. Hypnopaedia, if it is effective, would be a tremendously powerful instrument in the hands of anyone in a position to impose suggestions upon a captive audience. A democratic society is a society dedicated to the proposition that power is often abused and should therefore be entrusted to officials only in limited amounts and for limited periods of time. In such a society, the use of hypnopaedia by officials should be regulated by law—that is, of course, if hypnopaedia is genuinely an instrument of power. But is it in fact an instrument of power? Will it work now as well as I imagined it working in the seventh century A.F.? Let us examine the evidence.

In the *Psychological Bulletin* for July, 1955, Charles W. Simon and William H. Emmons have analyzed and evaluated the ten most important studies in the field. All these studies were concerned with memory. Does sleep-teaching help the pupil in his task of learning by rote? And to what extent is material whispered into the ear of a sleeping person remembered next morning when he wakes? Simon and Emmons answer as follows: "Ten sleep-learning studies were reviewed. Many of these have been cited uncritically by commercial firms or in popular magazines and news articles as evidence in support of the feasibility of learning during sleep. A critical analysis was made of their experimental design, statistics, methodology and criteria of sleep. All the studies had weaknesses in one or more of these areas. The studies do not make it unequivocally clear that learning during *sleep* actually takes place. But some learning appears to take place in a special kind of waking state wherein the subjects do not remember later on if they had been awake. This may be of great practical importance from the standpoint of economy in study time, but it cannot be construed as *sleep learning*.... The problem is partially confounded by an inadequate definition of sleep."

Meanwhile the fact remains that in the American Army during the Second World War (and even, experimentally, during the First) daytime instruction in the Morse Code and in foreign languages was supplemented by instruction during sleep—apparently with satisfactory results. Since the end of World War II several commercial firms in the United States and elsewhere have sold large numbers of pillow speakers and clock-controlled phonographs and tape recorders for the use of actors in a hurry to learn their parts, of politicians and preachers who want to give the illusion of being extemporaneously eloquent, of students preparing for examinations and, finally and most profitably, of the countless people who are dissatisfied with themselves as they are and would like to be suggested or autosuggested into becoming something else. Self-administered suggestion can easily be recorded on magnetic tape and listened to, over and over again, by day and during sleep. Suggestions from the outside may be bought in the form of records carrying a wide variety of helpful messages. There are on the market records for the release of tension and the induction of deep relaxation, records for promoting self-confidence (much used by salesmen), records for increasing one's charm and making one's personality more magnetic. Among the best sellers are records for the achievement of sexual harmony and records for those who wish to lose weight. ("I am cold to chocolate, insensible to the lure of potatoes, utterly unmoved by muffins.") There are records for improved health and even records for making more money. And the remarkable thing is that, according to the unsolicited testimonials sent in by grateful purchasers of these records, many people actually do make more money after listening to hypnopaedic suggestions to that effect, many obese ladies do lose weight and many couples on the verge of divorce achieve sexual harmony and live happily ever after.

In this context an article by Theodore X. Barber, "Sleep and Hypnosis," which appeared in *The Journal of Clinical and Experimental Hypnosis* for October, 1956, is most enlightening. Mr. Barber points out that there is a significant difference between light sleep and deep sleep. In deep sleep the electroencephalograph records no alpha waves; in light sleep alpha waves make their appearance. In this respect light sleep is closer to the waking and hypnotic states (in both of which alpha waves are present) than it is to deep sleep. A loud noise will cause a person in deep sleep to awaken. A less violent stimulus will not arouse him, but will cause the reappearance of alpha waves. Deep sleep has given place for the time being to light sleep.

A person in deep sleep is unsuggestible. But when subjects in light sleep are given suggestions, they will respond to them, Mr. Barber found, in the same way that they respond to suggestions when in the hypnotic trance.

Many of the earlier investigators of hypnotism made similar experiments. In his classical *History, Practice and Theory of Hypnotism*, first published in 1903, Milne Bramwell records that "many authorities claim to have changed natural sleep into hypnotic sleep. According to Wetterstrand, it is often very easy to put oneself *en rapport* with sleeping persons, especially children.... Wetterstrand thinks this method of inducing hypnosis of much practical value and claims to have often used it successfully." Bramwell cites many other experienced hypnotists (including such eminent authorities as Bernheim, Moll and Forel) to the same effect. Today an experimenter would not speak of "changing natural into hypnotic sleep." All he is prepared to say is that light sleep (as opposed to deep sleep without alpha waves) is a state in which many subjects will accept suggestions as readily as they do when under hypnosis. For example, after being told, when lightly asleep, that they will wake up in a little while, feeling extremely thirsty, many subjects will duly wake up with a dry throat and a craving for water. The cortex may be too inactive to think straight; but it is alert enough to respond to suggestions and to pass them on to the autonomic nervous system.

As we have already seen, the well-known Swedish physician and experimenter, Wetterstrand, was especially successful in the hypnotic treatment of sleeping children. In our own day Wetterstrand's methods are followed by a number of pediatricians, who instruct young mothers in the art of giving helpful suggestions to their children during the hours of light sleep. By this kind of hypnopaedia children can be cured of bed wetting and nail biting, can be prepared to go into surgery without apprehension, can be given confidence and reassurance when, for any reason, the circumstances of their life have become distressing. I myself have seen remarkable results achieved by the therapeutic sleep-teaching of small children. Comparable results could probably be achieved with many adults.

For a would-be dictator, the moral of all this is plain. Under proper conditions, hypnopaedia actually works— works, it would seem, about as well as hypnosis. Most of the things that can be done with and to a person in hypnotic trance can be done with and to a person in light sleep. Verbal suggestions can be passed through the somnolent cortex to the midbrain, the brain stem and the autonomic nervous system. If these suggestions are well conceived and frequently repeated, the bodily functions of the sleeper can be improved or interfered with, new patterns of feeling can be installed and old ones modified, posthypnotic commands can be given, slogans, formulas and trigger words deeply ingrained in the memory. Children are better hypnopaedic subjects than adults, and the would-be dictator will take full advantage of the fact. Children of nursery-school and kindergarten age will be treated to hypnopaedic suggestions during their afternoon nap. For older children and particularly the children of party members—the boys and girls who will grow up to be leaders, administrators and teachers—there will be boarding schools, in which an excellent day-time education will be supplemented by nightly sleep-teaching. In the case of adults, special attention will be paid to the sick. As Pavlov demonstrated many years ago, strong-minded and resistant dogs become completely suggestible after an operation or when suffering from some debilitating illness. Our dictator will therefore see that every hospital ward is wired for sound. An appendectomy, an accouchement, a bout of pneumonia or hepatitis, can be made the occasion for an intensive course in loyalty and the true faith, a refresher in the principles of the local ideology. Other captive audiences can be found in prisons, in labor camps, in military barracks, on ships at sea, on trains and airplanes in the night, in the dismal waiting rooms of bus terminals and railway stations. Even if the hypnopaedic suggestions given to these captive audiences were no more than 10 per cent effective, the results would still be impressive and, for a dictator, highly desirable.

From the heightened suggestibility associated with light sleep and hypnosis let us pass to the normal suggestibility of those who are awake—or at least who think they are awake. (In fact, as the Buddhists insist, most of us are half asleep all the time and go through life as somnambulists obeying somebody else's suggestions. Enlightenment is total awakeness. The word "Buddha" can be translated as "The Wake.")

Genetically, every human being is unique and in many ways unlike every other human being. The range of individual variation from the statistical norm is amazingly wide. And the statistical norm, let us remember, is useful only in actuarial calculations, not in real life. In real life there is no such person as the average man. There are only particular men, women and children, each with his or her in-born idiosyncrasies of mind and body, and all trying (or being compelled) to squeeze their biological diversities into the uniformity of some cultural mold.

Suggestibility is one of the qualities that vary significantly from individual to individual. Environmental factors certainly play their part in making one person more responsive to suggestion than another; but there are also, no less certainly, constitutional differences in the suggestibility of individuals. Extreme resistance to suggestion is rather rare. Fortunately so. For if everyone were as unsuggestible as some people are, social life would be impossible. Societies can function with a reasonable degree of efficiency because, in varying degrees, most people are fairly suggestible. Extreme suggestibility is probably about as rare as extreme unsuggestibility. And this also is fortunate. For if most people were as responsive to outside suggestions as the men and women at the extreme limits of suggestibility, free, rational choice would become, for the majority of the electorate, virtually impossible, and democratic institutions could not survive, or even come into existence.

A few years ago, at the Massachusetts General Hospital, a group of researchers carried out a most illuminating experiment on the pain-relieving effects of placebos. (A placebo is anything which the patient believes to be an active drug, but which in fact is pharmacologically inactive.) In this experiment the subjects were one hundred and sixty-two patients who had just come out of surgery and were all in considerable pain. Whenever a patient asked for medication to relieve pain, he or she was given an injection, either of morphine or of distilled water. All the patients received some injections of morphine and some of the placebo. About 30 per cent of the patients never obtained relief from the placebo. On the other hand 14 per cent obtained relief after *every* injection of distilled water. The remaining 55 per cent of the group were relieved by the placebo on some occasions, but not on others.

In what respects did the suggestible reactors differ from the unsuggestible non-reactors? Careful study and testing revealed that neither age nor sex was a significant factor. Men reacted to placebo as frequently as did women, and young people as often as old ones. Nor did intelligence, as measured by the standard tests, seem to be important. The average IQ of the two groups was about the same. It was above all in temperament, in the way they felt about themselves and other people that the members of the two groups were significantly different. The reactors were more co-operative than the non-reactors, less critical and suspicious. They gave the nurses no trouble and thought that the care they were receiving in the hospital was simply "wonderful." But though less unfriendly toward others than the non-reactors, the reactors were generally much more anxious about themselves. Under stress, this anxiety tended to translate itself into various psychosomatic symptoms, such as stomach upsets, diarrhea and headaches. In spite of or because of their anxiety, most of the reactors were more uninhibited in the display of emotion than were the non-reactors, and more voluble. They were also much more religious, much more active in the affairs of their church and much more preoccupied, on a subconscious level, with their pelvic and abdominal organs. It is interesting to compare these figures for reaction to placebos with the estimates made, in their own special field, by writers on hypnosis. About a fifth of the population, they tell us, can be hypnotized very easily. Another fifth cannot be hypnotized at all, or can be hypnotized only when drugs or fatigue have lowered psychological resistance. The remaining three-fifths can be hypnotized somewhat less easily than the first group, but considerably more easily than the second. A manufacturer of hypnopaedic records has told me that about 20 per cent of his customers are enthusiastic and report striking results in a very short time. At the other end of the spectrum of suggestibility there is an 8 per cent minority that regularly asks for its money back. Between these two extremes are the people who fail to get quick results, but are suggestible enough to be affected in the long run. If they listen perseveringly to the appropriate hypnopaedic instructions they will end by getting what they want—self-confidence or sexual harmony, less weight or more money.

The ideals of democracy and freedom confront the brute fact of human suggestibility. One-fifth of every electorate can be hypnotized almost in the twinkling of an eye, one-seventh can be relieved of pain by injections of water, one-quarter will respond promptly and enthusiastically to hypnopaedia. And to these all too co-operative minorities must be added the slow-starting majorities, whose less extreme suggestibility can be effectually exploited by anyone who knows his business and is prepared to take the necessary time and trouble.

Is individual freedom compatible with a high degree of individual suggestibility? Can democratic institutions survive the subversion from within of skilled mind-manipulators trained in the science and art of exploiting the suggestibility both of individuals and of crowds? To what extent can the inborn tendency to be too suggestible for one's own good or the good of a democratic society be neutralized by education? How far can the exploitation of inordinate suggestibility by businessmen and ecclesiastics, by politicians in and out of power, be controlled by law? Explicitly or implicitly, the first two questions have been discussed in earlier articles. In what follows I shall consider the problems of prevention and cure.

XI Education for Freedom

Education for freedom must begin by stating facts and enunciating values, and must go on to develop appropriate techniques for realizing the values and for combating those who, for whatever reason, choose to ignore the facts or deny the values.

In an earlier chapter I have discussed the Social Ethic, in terms of which the evils resulting from over-organization and over-population are justified and made to seem good. Is such a system of values consonant with what we know about human physique and temperament? The Social Ethic assumes that nurture is all-important in determining human behavior and that nature—the psychophysical equipment with which individuals are born—is a negligible factor. But is this true? Is it true that human beings are nothing but the products of their social environment? And if it is not true, what justification can there be for maintaining that the individual is less important than the group of which he is a member?

All the available evidence points to the conclusion that in the life of individuals and societies heredity is no less significant than culture. Every individual is biologically unique and unlike all other individuals. Freedom is therefore a great good, tolerance a great virtue and regimentation a great misfortune. For practical or theoretical reasons, dictators, organization men and certain scientists are anxious to reduce the maddening diversity of men's natures to some kind of manageable uniformity. In the first flush of his Behavioristic fervor, J. B. Watson roundly declared that he could find "no support for hereditary patterns of behavior, nor for special abilities (musical, art, etc.) which are supposed to run in families." And even today we find a distinguished psychologist, Professor B. F. Skinner of Harvard, insisting that, "as scientific explanation becomes more and more comprehensive, the contribution which may be claimed by the individual himself appears to approach zero. Man's vaunted creative powers, his achievements in art, science and morals, his capacity to choose and our right to hold him responsible for the consequences of his choice—none of these is conspicuous in the new scientific self-portrait." In a word, Shakespeare's plays were not written by Shakespeare, nor even by Bacon or the Earl of Oxford; they were written by Elizabethan England.

More than sixty years ago William James wrote an essay on "Great Men and Their Environment," in which he set out to defend the outstanding individual against the assaults of Herbert Spencer. Spencer had proclaimed that "Science" (that wonderfully convenient personification, of the opinions, at a given date, of Professors X, Y and Z) had completely abolished the Great Man. "The great man," he had written, "must be classed with all other phenomena in the society that gave him birth, as a product of its antecedents." The great man may be (or seem to be) "the proximate initiator of changes.... But if there is to be anything like a real explanation of these changes, it must be sought in that aggregate of conditions out of which both he and they have arisen." This is one of those empty profundities to which no operational meaning can possibly be attached. What our philosopher is saying is that we must know everything before we can fully understand anything. No doubt. But in fact we shall never know everything. We must therefore be content with partial understanding and proximate causes including the influence of great men. "If anything is humanly certain," writes William James, "it is that the great man's society, properly so called, does not make him before he can remake it. Physiological forces, with which the social, political, geographical and to a great extent anthropological conditions have just as much and just as little to do as the crater of Vesuvius has to do with the flickering of this gas by which I write, are what make him. Can it be that Mr. Spencer holds the convergence of sociological pressures to have so impinged upon Stratford-upon-Avon about the twenty-sixth of April, 1564, that a W. Shakespeare, with all his mental peculiarities, had to be born there? ... And does he mean to say that if the aforesaid W. Shakespeare had died of cholera infantum, another mother at Stratford-upon-Avon would need have engendered a duplicate copy of him, to restore the sociologic equilibrium?"

Professor Skinner is an experimental psychologist, and his treatise on "Science and Human Behavior" is solidly based upon facts. But unfortunately the facts belong to so limited a class that when at last he ventures upon a generalization, his conclusions are as sweepingly unrealistic as those of the Victorian theorizer. Inevitably so; for Professor Skinner's indifference to what James calls the "physiological forces" is almost as complete as Herbert Spencer's. The genetic factors determining human behavior are dismissed by him in less than a page. There is no reference in his book to the findings of constitutional medicine, nor any hint of that constitutional psychology, in terms of which (and in terms of which alone, so far as I can judge) it might be possible to write a complete and realistic biography of an individual in relation to the relevant facts of his existence—his body, his temperament, his intellectual endowments, his immediate environment from moment to moment, his time, place and culture. A science of human behavior is like a science of motion in the abstract—necessary, but, by itself, wholly inadequate to the facts. Consider a dragonfly, a rocket and a breaking wave. All three of them illustrate the same fundamental laws of motion; but they illustrate these laws in different ways, and the differences are at least as important as the identities. By itself, a study of motion can tell us almost nothing about that which, in any given instance, is being moved. Similarly a study of behavior can, by itself, tell us almost nothing about the individual mind-body that, in any particular instance, is exhibiting the behavior. But to us who are mind-bodies, a knowledge of mind-bodies is of paramount importance. Moreover, we know by observation and experience that the differences between individual mind-bodies are enormously great, and that some mind-bodies can and do profoundly affect their social environment. On this last point Mr. Bertrand Russell is in full agreement with William James—and with practically everyone, I would add, except the proponents of Spencerian or Behavioristic scientism. In Russell's view the causes of historical change are of three kinds—economic change, political theory and important individuals. "I do not believe," says Mr. Russell, "that any of these can be ignored, or wholly explained away as the effect of causes of another kind." Thus, if Bismarck and Lenin had died in infancy, our world would be very different from what, thanks in part to Bismarck and Lenin, it now is. "History is not yet a science, and can only be made to seem scientific by falsifications and omissions." In real life, life as it is lived from day to day, the individual can never be explained away. It is only in theory that his contributions appear to approach zero; in practice they are all-important. When a piece of work gets done in the world, who actually does it? Whose eyes and ears do the perceiving, whose cortex does the thinking, who has the feelings that motivate, the will that overcomes obstacles? Certainly not the social environment; for a group is not an organism, but only a blind unconscious organization. Everything that is done within a society is done by individuals. These individuals are, of course, profoundly influenced by the local culture, the taboos and moralities, the information and misinformation handed down from the past and preserved in a body of spoken traditions or written literature; but whatever each individual takes from society (or, to be more accurate, whatever he takes from other individuals associated in groups, or from the symbolic records compiled by other individuals, living or dead) will be used by him in his own unique way—with *his* special senses, *his* biochemical makeup, *his* physique and temperament, and nobody else's. No amount of scientific explanation, however comprehensive, can explain away these self-evident facts. And let us remember that Professor Skinner's scientific portrait of man as the product of the social environment is not the only scientific portrait. There are other, more realistic likenesses. Consider, for example, Professor Roger Williams' portrait. What he paints is not behavior in the abstract, but mind-bodies behaving—mind-bodies that are the products partly of the environment they share with other mind-bodies, partly of their own private heredity. In *The Human Frontier* and *Free but Unequal* Professor Williams has expatiated, with a wealth of detailed evidence, on those innate differences between individuals, for which Dr. Watson could find no support and whose importance, in Professor Skinner's eyes, approaches zero. Among animals, biological variability within a given species becomes more and more conspicuous as we move up the evolutionary scale. This biological variability is highest in man, and human beings display a greater degree of biochemical, structural and temperamental diversity than do the members of any other species. This is a plain observable fact. But what I have called the Will to Order, the desire to impose a comprehensible uniformity upon the bewildering manifoldness of things and events, has led many people to ignore this fact. They have minimized biological uniqueness and have concentrated all their attention upon the simpler and, in the present state of knowledge, more understandable environmental factors involved in human behavior. "As a result of this environmentally centered thinking and investigation," writes Professor Williams, "the doctrine of the essential uniformity of human infants has been widely accepted and is held by a great body of social psychologists, sociologists, social anthropologists, and many others, including historians, economists, educationalists, legal scholars and men in public life. This doctrine has been incorporated into the prevailing mode of thought of many who have had to do with shaping educational and governmental policies and is often accepted unquestioningly by those who do little critical thinking of their own."

An ethical system that is based upon a fairly realistic appraisal of the data of experience is likely to do more good than harm. But many ethical systems have been based upon an appraisal of experience, a view of the nature of things, that is hopelessly unrealistic. Such an ethic is likely to do more harm than good. Thus, until quite recent times, it was universally believed that bad weather, diseases of cattle and sexual impotence could be, and in many cases actually were, caused by the malevolent operations of magicians. To catch and kill magicians was therefore a duty—and this duty, moreover, had been divinely ordained in the second Book of Moses: "Thou shalt not suffer a witch to live." The systems of ethics and law that were based upon this erroneous view of the nature of things were the cause (during the centuries, when they were taken most seriously by men in authority) of the most appalling evils. The orgy of spying, lynching and judicial murder, which these wrong views about magic made logical and mandatory, was not matched until our own days, when the Communist ethic, based upon erroneous views about economics, and the Nazi ethic, based upon erroneous views about race, commanded and justified atrocities on an even greater scale. Consequences hardly less undesirable are likely to follow the general adoption of a Social Ethic, based upon the erroneous view that ours is a fully social species, that human infants are born uniform and that individuals are the product of conditioning by and within the collective environment. If these views were correct, if human beings were in fact the members of a truly social species, and if their individual differences were trifling and could be completely ironed out by appropriate conditioning, then, obviously, there would be no need for liberty and the State would be justified in persecuting the heretics who demanded it. For the individual termite, service to the termitary is perfect freedom. But human beings are not completely social; they are only moderately gregarious. Their societies are not organisms, like the hive or the anthill; they are organizations, in other words *ad hoc* machines for collective living. Moreover, the differences between individuals are so great that, in spite of the most intensive cultural ironing, an extreme endomorph (to use W. H. Sheldon's terminology) will retain his sociable viscerotonic characteristics, an extreme mesomorph will remain energetically somatotonic through thick and thin and an extreme ectomorph will always be cerebrotonic, introverted and over-sensitive. In the Brave New World of my fable socially desirable behavior was insured by a double process of genetic manipulation and postnatal conditioning. Babies were cultivated in bottles and a high degree of uniformity in the human product was assured by using ova from a limited number of mothers and by treating each ovum in such a way that it would split and split again, producing identical twins in batches of a hundred or more. In this way it was possible to produce standardized machine-minders for standardized machines. And the standardization of the machine-minders was perfected, after birth, by infant conditioning, hypnopaedia and chemically induced euphoria as a substitute for the satisfaction of feeling oneself free and creative. In the world we live in, as has been pointed out in earlier chapters, vast impersonal forces are making for the centralization of power and a regimented society. The genetic standardization of individuals is still impossible; but Big Government and Big Business already possess, or will very soon possess, all the techniques for mind-manipulation described in *Brave New World*, along with others of which I was too unimaginative to dream. Lacking the ability to impose genetic uniformity upon embryos, the rulers of tomorrow's over-populated and over-organized world will try to impose social and cultural uniformity upon adults and their children. To achieve this end, they will (unless prevented) make use of all the mind-manipulating techniques at their disposal and will not hesitate to reinforce these methods of non-rational persuasion by economic coercion and threats of physical violence. If this kind of tyranny is to be avoided, we must begin without delay to educate ourselves and our children for freedom and self-government.

Such an education for freedom should be, as I have said, an education first of all in facts and in values—the facts of individual diversity and genetic uniqueness and the values of freedom, tolerance and mutual charity which are the ethical corollaries of these facts. But unfortunately correct knowledge and sound principles are not enough. An unexciting truth may be eclipsed by a thrilling falsehood. A skilful appeal to passion is often too strong for the best of good resolutions. The effects of false and pernicious propaganda cannot be neutralized except by a thorough training in the art of analyzing its techniques and seeing through its sophistries. Language has made possible man's progress from animality to civilization. But language has also inspired that sustained folly and that systematic, that genuinely diabolic wickedness which are no less characteristic of human behavior than are the language-inspired virtues of systematic forethought and sustained angelic benevolence. Language permits its users to pay attention to things, persons and events, even when the things and persons are absent and the events are not taking place. Language gives definition to our memories and, by translating experiences into symbols, converts the immediacy of craving or abhorrence, of hatred or love, into fixed principles of feeling and conduct. In some way of which we are wholly unconscious, the reticular system of the brain selects from a countless host of stimuli those few experiences which are of practical importance to us. From these unconsciously selected experiences we more or less consciously select and abstract a smaller number, which we label with words from our vocabulary and then classify within a system at once metaphysical, scientific and ethical, made up of other words on a higher level of abstraction. In cases where the selecting and abstracting have been dictated by a system that is not too erroneous as a view of the nature of things, and where the verbal labels have been intelligently chosen and their symbolic nature clearly understood, our behavior is apt to be realistic and tolerably decent. But under the influence of badly chosen words, applied, without any understanding of their merely symbolic character, to experiences that have been selected and abstracted in the light of a system of erroneous ideas, we are apt to behave with a fiendishness and an organized stupidity, of which dumb animals (precisely because they are dumb and cannot speak) are blessedly incapable.

In their anti-rational propaganda the enemies of freedom systematically pervert the resources of language in order to wheedle or stampede their victims into thinking, feeling and acting as they, the mind-manipulators, want them to think, feel and act. An education for freedom (and for the love and intelligence which are at once the conditions and the results of freedom) must be, among other things, an education in the proper uses of language. For the last two or three generations philosophers have devoted a great deal of time and thought to the analysis of symbols and the meaning of meaning. How are the words and sentences which we speak related to the things, persons and events, with which we have to deal in our day-to-day living? To discuss this problem would take too long and lead us too far afield. Suffice it to say that all the intellectual materials for a sound education in the proper use of language—an education on every level from the kindergarten to the postgraduate school—are now available. Such an education in the art of distinguishing between the proper and the improper use of symbols could be inaugurated immediately. Indeed it might have been inaugurated at any time during the last thirty or forty years. And yet children are nowhere taught, in any systematic way, to distinguish true from false, or meaningful from meaningless, statements. Why is this so? Because their elders, even in the democratic countries, do not want them to be given this kind of education. In this context the brief, sad history of the Institute for Propaganda Analysis is highly significant. The Institute was founded in 1937, when Nazi propaganda was at its noisiest and most effective, by Mr. Filene, the New England philanthropist. Under its auspices analyses of non-rational propaganda were made and several texts for the instruction of high school and university students were prepared. Then came the war—a total war on all the fronts, the mental no less than the physical. With all the Allied governments engaging in "psychological warfare," an insistence upon the desirability of analyzing propaganda seemed a bit tactless. The Institute was closed in 1941. But even before the outbreak of hostilities, there were many persons to whom its activities seemed profoundly objectionable. Certain educators, for example, disapproved of the teaching of propaganda analysis on the grounds that it would make adolescents unduly cynical. Nor was it welcomed by the military authorities, who were afraid that recruits might start to analyze the utterances of drill sergeants. And then there were the clergymen and the advertisers. The clergymen were against propaganda analysis as tending to undermine belief and diminish churchgoing; the advertisers objected on the grounds that it might undermine brand loyalty and reduce sales.

These fears and dislikes were not unfounded. Too searching a scrutiny by too many of the common folk of what is said by their pastors and masters might prove to be profoundly subversive. In its present form, the social order depends for its continued existence on the acceptance, without too many embarrassing questions, of the propaganda put forth by those in authority and the propaganda hallowed by the local traditions. The problem, once more, is to find the happy mean. Individuals must be suggestible enough to be willing and able to make their society work, but not so suggestible as to fall helplessly under the spell of professional mind-manipulators. Similarly, they should be taught enough about propaganda analysis to preserve them from an uncritical belief in sheer nonsense, but not so much as to make them reject outright the not always rational outpourings of the well-meaning guardians of tradition. Probably the happy mean between gullibility and a total skepticism can never be discovered and maintained by analysis alone. This rather negative approach to the problem will have to be supplemented by something more positive—the enunciation of a set of generally acceptable values based upon a solid foundation of facts. The value, first of all, of individual freedom, based upon the facts of human diversity and genetic uniqueness; the value of charity and compassion, based upon the old familiar fact, lately rediscovered by modern psychiatry—the fact that, whatever their mental and physical diversity, love is as necessary to human beings as food and shelter; and finally the value of intelligence, without which love is impotent and freedom unattainable. This set of values will provide us with a criterion by which propaganda may be judged. The propaganda that is found to be both nonsensical and immoral may be rejected out of hand. That which is merely irrational, but compatible with love and freedom, and not on principle opposed to the exercise of intelligence, may be provisionally accepted for what it is worth.

XII What Can Be Done?

We be educated for freedom—much better educated for it than we are at present. But freedom, as I have tried to show, is threatened from many directions, and these threats are of many different kinds—demographic, social, political, psychological. Our disease has a multiplicity of co-operating causes and is not to be cured except by a multiplicity of co-operating remedies. In coping with any complex human situation, we must take account of all the relevant factors, not merely of a single factor. Nothing short of everything is ever really enough. Freedom is menaced, and education for freedom is urgently needed. But so are many other things—for example, social organization for freedom, birth control for freedom, legislation for freedom. Let us begin with the last of these items.

From the time of Magna Carta and even earlier, the makers of English law have been concerned to protect the physical freedom of the individual. A person who is being kept in prison on grounds of doubtful legality has the right, under the Common Law as clarified by the statute of 1679, to appeal to one of the higher courts of justice for a writ of *habeas corpus*. This writ is addressed by a judge of the high court to a sheriff or jailer, and commands him, within a specified period of time, to bring the person he is holding in custody to the court for an examination of his case—to bring, be it noted, not the person's written complaint, nor his legal representatives, but his *corpus*, his body, the too too solid flesh which has been made to sleep on boards, to smell the fetid prison air, to eat the revolting prison food. This concern with the basic condition of freedom—the absence of physical constraint—is unquestionably necessary, but is not all that is necessary. It is perfectly possible for a man to be out of prison, and yet not free—to be under no physical constraint and yet to be a psychological captive, compelled to think, feel and act as the representatives of the national State, or of some private interest within the nation, want him to think, feel and act. There will never be such a thing as a writ of *habeas mentem*; for no sheriff or jailer can bring an illegally imprisoned mind into court, and no person whose mind had been made captive by the methods outlined in earlier articles would be in a position to complain of his captivity. The nature of psychological compulsion is such that those who act under constraint remain under the impression that they are acting on their own initiative. The victim of mind-manipulation does not know that he is a victim. To him, the walls of his prison are invisible, and he believes himself to be free. That he is not free is apparent only to other people. His servitude is strictly objective.

No, I repeat, there can never be such a thing as a writ of *habeas mentem*. But there can be preventive legislation—an outlawing of the psychological slave trade, a statute for the protection of minds against the unscrupulous purveyors of poisonous propaganda, modeled on the statutes for the protection of bodies against the unscrupulous purveyors of adulterated food and dangerous drugs. For example, there could and, I think, there should be legislation limiting the right of public officials, civil or military, to subject the captive audiences under their command or in their custody to sleep-teaching. There could and, I think, there should be legislation prohibiting the use of subliminal projection in public places or on television screens. There could and, I think, there should be legislation to prevent political candidates not merely from spending more than a certain amount of money on their election campaigns, but also to prevent them from resorting to the kind of anti-rational propaganda that makes nonsense of the whole democratic process.

Such preventive legislation might do some good; but if the great impersonal forces now menacing freedom continue to gather momentum, they cannot do much good for very long. The best of constitutions and preventive laws will be powerless against the steadily increasing pressures of over-population and of the over-organization imposed by growing numbers and advancing technology. The constitutions will not be abrogated and the good laws will remain on the statute book; but these liberal forms will merely serve to mask and adorn a profoundly illiberal substance. Given unchecked over-population and over-organization, we may expect to see in the democratic countries a reversal of the process which transformed England into a democracy, while retaining all the outward forms of a monarchy. Under the relentless thrust of accelerating over-population and increasing over-organization, and by means of ever more effective methods of mind-manipulation, the democracies will change their nature; the quaint old forms—elections, parliaments, Supreme Courts and all the rest—will remain. The underlying substance will be a new kind of non-violent totalitarianism. All the traditional names, all the hallowed slogans will remain exactly what they were in the good old days. Democracy and freedom will be the theme of every broadcast and editorial—but democracy and freedom in a strictly Pickwickian sense. Meanwhile the ruling oligarchy and its highly trained elite of soldiers, policemen, thought-manufacturers and mind-manipulators will quietly run the show as they see fit.

How can we control the vast impersonal forces that now menace our hard-won freedoms? On the verbal level and in general terms, the question may be answered with the utmost ease. Consider the problem of over-population. Rapidly mounting human numbers are pressing ever more heavily on natural resources. What is to be done? Obviously we must, with all possible speed, reduce the birth rate to the point where it does not exceed the death rate. At the same time we must, with all possible speed, increase food production, we must institute and implement a world-wide policy for conserving our soils and our forests, we must develop practical substitutes, preferably less dangerous and less rapidly exhaustible than uranium, for our present fuels; and, while husbanding our dwindling resources of easily available minerals, we must work out new and not too costly methods for extracting these minerals from ever poorer and poorer ores—the poorest ore of all being sea water. But all this, needless to say, is almost infinitely easier said than done. The annual increase of numbers should be reduced. But how? We are given two choices—famine, pestilence and war on the one hand, birth control on the other. Most of us choose birth control—and immediately find ourselves confronted by a problem that is simultaneously a puzzle in physiology, pharmacology, sociology, psychology and even theology. "The Pill" has not yet been invented. When and if it is invented, how can it be distributed to the many hundreds of millions of potential mothers (or, if it is a pill that works upon the male, potential fathers) who will have to take it if the birth rate of the species is to be reduced? And, given existing social customs and the forces of cultural and psychological inertia, how can those who ought to take the pill, but don't want to, be persuaded to change their minds? And what about the objections on the part of the Roman Catholic Church, to any form of birth control except the so-called Rhythm Method—a method, incidentally, which has proved, hitherto, to be almost completely ineffective in reducing the birth rate of those industrially backward societies where such a reduction is most urgently necessary? And these questions about the future, hypothetical Pill must be asked, with as little prospect of eliciting satisfactory answers, about the chemical and mechanical methods of birth control already available.

When we pass from the problems of birth control to the problems of increasing the available food supply and conserving our natural resources, we find ourselves confronted by difficulties not perhaps quite so great, but still enormous. There is the problem, first of all, of education. How soon can the innumerable peasants and farmers, who are now responsible for raising most of the world's supply of food, be educated into improving their methods? And when and if they are educated, where will they find the capital to provide them with the machines, the fuel and lubricants, the electric power, the fertilizers and the improved strains of food plants and domestic animals, without which the best agricultural education is useless? Similarly, who is going to educate the human race in the principles and practice of conservation? And how are the hungry peasant-citizens of a country whose population and demands for food are rapidly rising to be prevented from "mining the soil"? And, if they can be prevented, who will pay for their support while the wounded and exhausted earth is being gradually nursed back, if that is still feasible, to health and restored fertility? Or consider the backward societies that are now trying to industrialize. If they succeed, who is to prevent them, in their desperate efforts to catch up and keep up, from squandering the planet's irreplaceable resources as stupidly and wantonly as was done, and is still being done, by their forerunners in the race? And when the day of reckoning comes where, in the poorer countries, will anyone find the scientific manpower and the huge amounts of capital that will be required to extract the indispensable minerals from ores in which their concentration is too low, under existing circumstances to make extraction technically feasible or economically justifiable? It may be that, in time, a practical answer to all these questions can be found. But in how much time? In any race between human numbers and natural resources, time is against us. By the end of the present century, there may, if we try very hard, be twice as much food on the world's markets as there is today. But there will also be about twice as many people, and several billions of these people will be living in partially industrialized countries and consuming ten times as much power, water, timber and irreplaceable minerals as they are consuming now. In a word, the food situation will be as bad as it is today, and the raw materials situation will be considerably worse.

To find a solution to the problem of over-organization is hardly less difficult than to find a solution to the problem of natural resources and increasing numbers. On the verbal level and in general terms the answer is perfectly simple. Thus, it is a political axiom that power follows property. But it is now a historical fact that the means of production are fast becoming the monopolistic property of Big Business and Big Government. Therefore, if you believe in democracy, make arrangements to distribute property as widely as possible.

Or take the right to vote. In principle, it is a great privilege. In practice, as recent history has repeatedly shown, the right to vote, by itself, is no guarantee of liberty. Therefore, if you wish to avoid dictatorship by referendum, break up modern society's merely functional collectives into self-governing, voluntarily co-operating groups, capable of functioning outside the bureaucratic systems of Big Business and Big Government.

Over-population and over-organization have produced the modern metropolis, in which a fully human life of multiple personal relationships has become almost impossible. Therefore, if you wish to avoid the spiritual impoverishment of individuals and whole societies, leave the metropolis and revive the small country community, or alternatively humanize the metropolis by creating within its network of mechanical organization the urban equivalents of small country communities, in which individuals can meet and co-operate as complete persons, not as the mere embodiments of specialized functions.

All this is obvious today and, indeed, was obvious fifty years ago. From Hilaire Belloc to Mr. Mortimer Adler, from the early apostles of co-operative credit unions to the land reformers of modern Italy and Japan, men of good will have for generations been advocating the decentralization of economic power and the widespread distribution of property. And how many ingenious schemes have been propounded for the dispersal of production, for a return to small-scale "village industry." And then there were Dubreuil's elaborate plans for giving a measure of autonomy and initiative to the various departments of a single large industrial organization. There were the Syndicalists, with their blueprints for a stateless society organized as a federation of productive groups under the auspices of the trade unions. In America, Arthur Morgan and Baker Brownell have set forth the theory and described the practice of a new kind of community living on the village and small-town level.

Professor Skinner of Harvard has set forth a psychologist's view of the problem in his *Walden Two*, a Utopian novel about a self-sustaining and autonomous community, so scientifically organized that nobody is ever led into anti-social temptation and, without resort to coercion or undesirable propaganda, everyone does what he or she ought to do, and everyone is happy and creative. In France, during and after the Second World War, Marcel Barbu and his followers set up a number of self-governing, non-hierarchical communities of production, which were also communities for mutual aid and fully human living. And meanwhile, in London, the Peckham Experiment has demonstrated that it is possible, by co-ordinating health services with the wider interests of the group, to create a true community even in a metropolis.

We see, then, that the disease of over-organization has been clearly recognized, that various comprehensive remedies have been prescribed and that experimental treatments of symptoms have been attempted here and there, often with considerable success. And yet, in spite of all this preaching and this exemplary practice, the disease grows steadily worse. We know that it is unsafe to allow power to be concentrated in the hands of a ruling oligarchy; nevertheless power is in fact being concentrated in fewer and fewer hands. We know that, for most people, life in a huge modern city is anonymous, atomic, less than fully human; nevertheless the huge cities grow steadily huger and the pattern of urban-industrial living remains unchanged. We know that, in a very large and complex society, democracy is almost meaningless except in relation to autonomous groups of manageable size; nevertheless more and more of every nation's affairs are managed by the bureaucrats of Big Government and Big Business. It is only too evident that, in practice, the problem of over-organization is almost as hard to solve as the problem of over-population. In both cases we know what ought to be done; but in neither case have we been able, as yet, to act effectively upon our knowledge.

At this point we find ourselves confronted by a very disquieting question: Do we really wish to act upon our knowledge? Does a majority of the population think it worth while to take a good deal of trouble, in order to halt and, if possible, reverse the current drift toward totalitarian control of everything? In the United States—and America is the prophetic image of the rest of the urban-industrial world as it will be a few years from now—recent public opinion polls have revealed that an actual majority of young people in their teens, the voters of tomorrow, have no faith in democratic institutions, see no objection to the censorship of unpopular ideas, do not believe that government of the people by the people is possible and would be perfectly content, if they can continue to live in the style to which the boom has accustomed them, to be ruled, from above, by an oligarchy of assorted experts. That so many of the well-fed young television-watchers in the world's most powerful democracy should be so completely indifferent to the idea of self-government, so blankly uninterested in freedom of thought and the right to dissent, is distressing, but not too surprising. "Free as a bird," we say, and envy the winged creatures for their power of unrestricted movement in all the three dimensions. But, alas, we forget the dodo. Any bird that has learned how to grub up a good living without being compelled to use its wings will soon renounce the privilege of flight and remain forever grounded. Something analogous is true of human beings. If the bread is supplied regularly and copiously three times a day, many of them will be perfectly content to live by bread alone—or at least by bread and circuses alone. "In the end," says the Grand Inquisitor in Dostoevsky's parable, "in the end they will lay their freedom at our feet and say to us, 'make us your slaves, but feed us.'" And when Alyosha Karamazov asks his brother, the teller of the story, if the Grand Inquisitor is speaking ironically, Ivan answers, "Not a bit of it! He claims it as a merit for himself and his Church that they have vanquished freedom and done so to make men happy." Yes, to make men happy; "for nothing," the Inquisitor insists, "has ever been more insupportable for a man or a human society than freedom." Nothing, except the absence of freedom; for when things go badly, and the rations are reduced, the grounded dodos will clamor again for their wings—only to renounce them, yet once more, when times grow better and the dodo-farmers become more lenient and generous. The young people who now think so poorly of democracy may grow up to become fighters for freedom. The cry of "Give me television and hamburgers, but don't bother me with the responsibilities of liberty," may give place, under altered circumstances, to the cry of "Give me liberty or give me death." If such a revolution takes place, it will be due in part to the operation of forces over which even the most powerful rulers have very little control, in part to the incompetence of those rulers, their inability to make effective use of the mind-manipulating instruments with which science and technology have supplied, and will go on supplying, the would-be tyrant. Considering how little they knew and how poorly they were equipped, the Grand Inquisitors of earlier times did remarkably well. But their successors, the well-informed, thoroughly scientific dictators of the future will undoubtedly be able to do a great deal better. The Grand Inquisitor reproaches Christ with having called upon men to be free and tells Him that "we have corrected Thy work and founded it upon miracle, mystery and authority." But miracle, mystery and authority are not enough to guarantee the indefinite survival of a dictatorship. In my fable of *Brave New World*, the dictators had added science to the list and thus were able to enforce their authority by manipulating the bodies of embryos, the reflexes of infants and the minds of children and adults. And, instead of merely talking about miracles and hinting symbolically at mysteries, they were able, by means of drugs, to give their subjects the direct experience of mysteries and miracles—to transform mere faith into ecstatic knowledge. The older dictators fell because they could never supply their subjects with enough bread, enough circuses, enough miracles and mysteries. Nor did they possess a really effective system of mind-manipulation. In the past free-thinkers and revolutionaries were often the products of the most piously orthodox education. This is not surprising. The methods employed by orthodox educators were and still are extremely inefficient. Under a scientific dictator education will really work—with the result that most men and women will grow up to love their servitude and will never dream of revolution. There seems to be no good reason why a thoroughly scientific dictatorship should ever be overthrown.

Meanwhile there is still some freedom left in the world. Many young people, it is true, do not seem to value freedom. But some of us still believe that, without freedom, human beings cannot become fully human and that freedom is therefore supremely valuable. Perhaps the forces that now menace freedom are too strong to be resisted for very long. It is still our duty to do whatever we can to resist them.

Printed in Poland
by Amazon Fulfillment
Poland Sp. z o.o., Wrocław

63972655R00101